Santa Takes A Wife

Betsy J. Bennett

Ahead of the Press Publishing

St. Louis, Missouri

Library of Congress Cataloguing-in-Publication Data

Santa Takes A Wife

By: Betsy J. Bennett

ISBN   KINDLE Mobi   978-1-950392-36-0   (ebook)

ISBN   PAPERBACK   978-1-950392-35-3

Ahead of The Press Publishing

St. Louis, Missouri

Santa Takes A Wife
Table of Contents

DEDICATION:

To Earl, Meredith and Francesca
Because family is all that matters.

CHAPTER 1

Last Year:

Foamy sweat glistened on the backs of the nine reindeer, although at the height they flew the temperature hovered a few degrees below freezing. Their heads hung low, and their pace now more frantic than joyous, indicated exhaustion. They could barely keep the altitude, and in the driver's seat, holding onto reins in hands that had long since grown numb, Santa knew there wasn't much more he was going to get out of them. Not this year.

The tug appeared again, that half-conscious awareness that the present should be delivered here, but it was so ephemeral he knew it wasn't worth checking out again. He'd been over this spot a dozen times. Then two dozen. There wasn't anything there.

The fear which he had been trying to ignore for the better part of forty-eight hours returned, sharpened, honed in on the acids churning in his stomach.

"No, guys," he told the reindeer, "we're going home."

Whatever it was, he wasn't going to find it. If it meant failure, than Nicholas St. Noel was well aware that the failure was his own, not anything that had to do with tradition, or with goodness and light, the things he should stand for, and was not altogether certain he believed in anymore.

Even exhausted, the reindeer responded to his command, yet when he tugged on the reins, Donner, the lead, dropped slightly, as if he would pull strength from some hidden fastness, some reserve he hadn't yet tapped, and circle around again.

"No," Nicholas insisted, touched by the creature's loyalty. "You have done everything you could." This time he gave a firmer order, home, that the reindeer latched onto.

"You're late," Marlett, the head-elf bellowed as the sleigh slid into the barn a few minutes later. "We were starting to worry."

"Rub them down well." Nicholas tossed reins to a waiting elf. He pulled his gloves off abruptly, angrily. "They worked extra hard this year." Because he was upset, he made an effort to speak softly to each of the nine, complimenting them, scratching their ear ridges, rubbing the soft fuzz of their antlers.

"You're late," Marlett said again, a short creature, with a normally soft voice. The bells on his booties jingled. Why, when that was generally such a happy sound, did it grate along Nicholas' nerves, and sound more like a death toll, than anything having to do with Christmas?

A dozen more elves appeared, as if by magic. They bounced with the gaiety of the season, and the final notes of the carols they had been singing lingered, as if reluctant to depart for another year. Harness bells sounded as straps were unbuckled, and the deer were released from their once-a-year assignment. They'd be well taken care of. Seeing to the needs of the reindeer was an honor among the Christmas elves. Nicholas wouldn't worry about the caribou.

"No, leave it." Nicholas slashed his fist sharply, as three elves arrived to take the sleigh and do whatever it was they did to it this time of year. In the background, toward the main house, Nicholas heard rebounding echoes of elf merriment continuing with increased enthusiasm, now that he had returned. Elves partied once the sleigh lifted off, the festivities continuing for several days after. They sang year-round, never more fervently than this specific week, keeping their Christmas carols ringing until their voices gave out. Then they would sleep in heaps under tables or against door jams for about a week, their snores as loud as their singing voices, and then return to their workbenches making presents for the next year. They put in long hours, deserved their merriment.

Marlett shuffled his feet in the clean straw. "Was there a problem?"

"A problem? What makes you say that?" Nicholas ground his teeth together, spoke sharper than he intended.

Although a creature who knew laughter every day of his life, over the past twenty centuries, Marlett had become sensitive to the moods of his Santas. "Come in the house, Nicholas. I've got hot chocolate waiting."

"I can't." The denial was drawn out, carried more than exhaustion.

"It's easy enough to do. You put one foot in front of the other, it's called walking." His eyes twinkled. Marlett was used to being obeyed. Every Santa Claus for two thousand years had complied.

Santa lifted his chin, looked past the straw and the merriment into a morning sky where the sun wouldn't rise for another three or four months. "I have to go back out."

"No, you don't. Don't be ridiculous. It's late, you need rest."

Nicholas removed his hat, then ran his hands through sweat-soaked hair. This one day a year it was longer than he normally wore it, and the beard had come in, full and bushy. "You don't understand. One present hasn't been delivered."

Marlett heard the cry in his voice, the desperation that spoke of pain. Delaying, the elf scratched facial hair that reached down below his belt. Elves took pride in many things, but none more than their beards. "I was wondering when that was going to happen."

"What do you mean?" He wasn't a man who could swear, but at times like this, it would certainly come in handy. "Is this your doing?" If he couldn't select appropriate words to fit the situation, at the moment he firmly felt himself capable of murder—even on elf hide considered immortal.

"Then your father didn't tell you?"

Nicholas snorted, sounding, oddly enough, like the reindeer which had just left. The previous Santa Claus had not been one for long heart-to-hearts with his son.

Marlett walked forward, placing his curled-toed booties carefully in the straw covered barn, the jingling sound of his bells now sounding jarring, invasive. "Nicholas, get the present. I know what it is. It's not the disaster you think it to be. I'll explain over cookies and hot chocolate."

Santa, and this Santa was young, just twenty-nine, released the top button of his suit and exhaled slowly, letting a long stream of breath escape. "The problems of the world cannot be solved over cookies and hot chocolate."

"This one can." It was Marlett's belief that most of them could. Weren't most problems caused by a lack of communication?

"Your father—" he started, but Nicholas cut him off.

"I am not my father. I can never be my father."

"No one's asking you to be, are they?" the elf asked.

Nicholas growled. He felt no need to tell this fantasy creature that was exactly what they were trying to do. He was supposed to be his father. Wasn't that the whole point? The fear which had held him in such thrall hadn't dissipated. It tightened his guts, made his muscles weak, his head spin.

"Tell me what it is, before I take another step."

Exhausted, bone-weary, Nicholas slumped against a barn wall, sinking slowly until he sat in the straw. His head dropped low on his broad shoulders. His hands shook.

"You're going to ruin that suit."

Nicholas curled a lip. Marlett decided now was not the time to discuss dry-cleaning bills. He climbed into the sleigh, pulling himself up, then disappearing momentarily. He reappeared almost instantly with the gift. The wrapped package was small, tiny almost, considering the size of many the gifts Santa delivered. Odd, he hadn't known it was there and he'd always known before.

"Here, open it," Marlett said, after he climbed out again.

"Are you telling me this is my gift?"

"Yes, and no," Marlett answered.

"Which is it? Yes or no?" Nicholas didn't have strength in his arms to reach out.

"Open the gift, then we'll talk." The reindeer had vanished into their stalls. In addition to the distant sounds of elf merriment, he could hear brushes against the soft hide, and the mashing of oats and hay. The reindeer had already recovered from their exertions. Part of that was experience. Part was good breeding. But most was magic: Santa Claus' magic.

Marlett tossed it gently, dropping the present unopened into his lap. Nicholas wasn't certain he could control the tremors in his hands enough to tear ribbon and paper. "I can't do it," he said. His eyes closed as a dozen conflicting emotions battled within him, disguised by the two most prominent: exhaustion and despair.

Marlett retrieved it, silently caressing the present, then with work-worn fingers, did the deed himself. It revealed a small jeweler's box, and inside a diamond ring, the stone small, probably on the order of a half caret, a fraction of the size of the last one he'd seen just about thirty years before. He handed the box over to Nicholas.

"I know what this is," Santa said, his voice rasping. Regardless of popular myth, it had been days since he'd had anything to eat or drink. He was generally too busy to stop and sample cookies left for Santa, although he certainly had sampled them, as a boy, when he trailed in his father's wake.

"Although my experience is limited, I can tell you this isn't the type of present Santa normally delivers."

Marlett laughed until the ceilings echoed with the sound. "Have you never heard how Santas take a wife?"

"If this is something my father should have taught me, I'm afraid he never quite got around to it." There was a rumble to his words, which bothered Nicholas, for he felt, he knew, that he should be jolly all the time. For all practical purposes he was genetically predisposed to eternal happiness. Then why this edginess? This feeling that there was a hole in his life and he would do anything, even slide down on his knees and beg, if he could find the way to fill it?

His father had been Santa Claus, like his paternal grandfather, and all the grandfathers way back into that first original Christmas when one of his relatives had witnessed something miraculous and heard angels singing about it. There had been more visitors to that stable than shepherds and one hapless drummer boy. Bathed in the light of a brilliant star, an innkeeper's son had visited, carrying a fabric-wrapped loaf of fresh bread, and stayed long enough to beg to atone for the crowded conditions of a city overrun.

But giving wasn't enough for this Nicholas. He knew he needed something desperately, something elves in his massive workshop could not devise, something flying reindeers could not deliver. Something, he very much suspected he should not crave at all.

Marlett stopped laughing and waddled over, settling down

beside him. He fiddled with his beard for several long minutes before he spoke. "Are you happy, Nicholas?"

Nicholas grabbed his traditional red hat with its fat white ball at the end and threw it as far as he could. "Shouldn't my happiness be intrinsic? Isn't it part of the job description?"

"Who taught you that nonsense?" Marlett huffed. Size was no indication of strength of will, and for a creature who should be jolly himself, he had a fine stabbing thrust with sarcasm.

"I'm bloody well miserable. Is that what you wanted to hear?" There was a relief, a massive loss of pressure just admitting it. Moisture pooled at the bottom of his eyes, threatened to spill. Viciously Nicholas swiped at it. Usually when he cried, and frankly he often did, they were silent tears of joy. He was a man who had only recognized unhappiness when watching the desperate needs of others, cried when somehow those needs were filled.

"Why can't I feel joy?" he wailed. In the next stall over Comet kicked his two rear hooves in a loud, resounding crash. Reindeer were sensitive to his thoughts, his moods. It was how he directed them one night a year.

"Is there no joy left in the world?"

"Calm down, Nicholas. The world is as fine. The problem is you."

His breath hitched and he felt a stab, somewhere center chest. "Don't you think I realize that?"

"We can hold this conversation in the house. Be warm. Drink hot chocolate."

"I don't want any damn hot chocolate." Somewhere, deep in the back of his mind, he wondered if that was the first time in the history of the Universe, that a Santa had swore. Although there were times when his father had exhibited quite a temper, Nicholas was predisposed to think yes, right then he had been the first to have broken some unwritten law. There was also a part of him, further down inside, that didn't give a good no-never-mind.

"All right. We'll hold this conversation here, but Callie will nag me for centuries if I get straw in my beard."

"I'm through trying to placate Callie," Nicholas growled.

Callie, the broody-hen ruler of the roost, and Marlett's wife since before miracles started appearing in Galilee.

"Centuries," Marlett said, shaking his head sadly. "Centuries."

Nicholas dropped his chin to his chest, clamped his eyes shut. He didn't have to see to know straw was even now climbing up Marlett's legs to find refuge in the beard. That beard seemed to have a propensity for attracting all kinds of unsavory invaders. Other elves, no matter what they were doing, managed to stay spotless. His head elf, however, always needed a good brushing.

"Nicholas, I know you ache. And I know why."

"I'm not good enough." This fear was his constant companion, one he carried with him not only one endless night a year, but everyday, spring, summer, fall, winter. He wasn't good enough. It gave him nightmares, for he knew the needs and the miracles his vocation allowed him to perform.

"Let me tell you what this present means. You are lonely. You need to choose a wife."

"A wife?" He choked the words out, wondering if he were having a heart attack. His throat felt like it had closed. No air reached into his brain.

"For heaven's sake, Nicholas, breathe." Marlett hopped up and down, stopping only long enough to thump Santa on the shoulder. "Breathe. You're turning all blue and red."

Nicholas gasped the air helping to erase those black splotches which had formed behind his eyes. "I need a wife? And you know this how?"

"Relax Nicholas. This isn't a death sentence. Take short, even breaths."

"Easy enough for you to say. You've got Callie."

"Well, it's time for you to choose your own wife."

"How do Santas choose a wife?" Nicholas had snapped back. However they did it, he always assumed it was done the way normal human beings did it, dating, dinners, movies, museums, long walks around the park sharing confidences, then long evenings in front of a blazing fire when the two got to know each other better in every way possible. Then a ring, a quick wedding ceremony, and introducing the new bride to his family: over a hundred miserable immortal elves.

"Well—" the final consonant was drawn out, one of those hedging noises that indicated a box had been opened and there was no way to close it now. The damage was done.

Nicholas lowered his eyebrows, set his teeth. Marlett understood the look. "Well," he continued, "there is a test." He rocked back and forth on his heels, looking rather pleased with himself. "You pass then you get to be Santa."

"I already am Santa." Every day for years he prayed that statement was true. If only Clement Moore could see him now.

"Yes," Marlett said, "and no."

"You rather like that phrase, don't you?" Nicholas spoke through clenched teeth. Elves, on the whole, had no duplicity. Still, it would be easy to take out his aggression on the long-bearded tormentor. It might even be worth the effort.

"You cannot really be Santa until you pass this test. You can lead the team every year, and drop off the presents, but until you pass, you're just passing time."

"My father was Santa."

Marlett rubbed his beard. He swore that he would never tell this Nicholas, and he had kept that promise. Nicholas' father had not been Santa, not in all the ways that really mattered. He had failed the test. It was the main reason the former Santa and this one never got along.

"You are meant to be Santa. Will you listen to me?"

"As if I've got anything better to do." But Nicholas did have better things to do: Hiding under the bed for one, denying his genetic predisposition to delivering presents, strangling elves with their own long beards. The list was practically endless.

Nicholas struggled to his feet, then followed Marlett out of the barn, across a frozen path lit by a multitude of brilliant stars, into the massive kitchen. They passed the party where gingerbread and punch reigned supreme, and where the laughter was joyous, and where all the Christmas carols spoke of a universal truth from centuries before involving silent nights and sheep lowing and angels trumpeting joyous announcements. No snowman songs tonight, no odes to glowing reindeer noses. There was a place for those songs at the North Pole, but not in December, and not on Christmas.

Marlett shoved an oversized mug of hot chocolate in his direction, put a platter with several dozen cookies in his reach. Nicholas scratched at his thick white beard. It always came in full early Christmas Eve morning, no matter that he preferred to be clean-shaven. He would hack the thing off the moment he could get strength to return to his hands.

Nicholas picked up a spoon, dug into the whipped cream. The food at the North Pole was without peer anywhere on the planet. Elf magic, no doubt.

Marlett waited until Nicholas consumed a dozen cookies, until there was nothing left in the mug but dregs. "The Santa test has been going on since the first Santa, the one who knew the Truth."

"Humph," Nicholas said, crunching, instead of another cookie, an apple. He had eaten enough cookies before Christmas to last him six or eight months.

"Once each lifetime Santa comes back from a ride with one undeliverable present and an opportunity to take the Test."

"The ring?"

Marlett continued. "That present is the gift which will make one person happy."

The apple was sweet, crunchy, but for a second time his throat tightened, and as he swallowed, he choked, had to cough a few minutes before he could speak clearly. "There should be no problem. Don't I have the ability to discern what present will make each person happy?"

"Yes, you do. You can find the secret desires of each and every human being on this planet. That is one of Santa's gifts. Every human, that is, except one."

"There is one person whose heart I cannot read with my magic?"

"Yes."

"And I am to find that person, and give him or her the

present?"

"Yes and no."

"Will you stop that?"

"Yes and—" Marlett looked sheepishly from under shaggy brows and started pulling straw out of his beard. "The person whose heart you cannot read is your own. You must find the singular gift which will make you happy. When you do that, you will know who to give this engagement ring to."

"Engagement ring?"

"You're getting married, Nicholas. Trust me on this. Callie will be excited. It's been a long time since she's had a Mrs. Claus to fuss over."

"I don't want to get married."

"I know that. But I also know when you pass the test, you will."

"You're saying marriage will make me happy?"

"Yes, it will. Every day for the rest of your life."

"That's all there is to the test? I pick a bride and happiness flows through me?"

"You pick the right bride."

"And I pass?"

"Yes."

"And this nameless ennui will vanish?"

"Yes, Nicholas. That's all there is to the test. After you get married, you will be Santa, and you will be happy."

"A bride?" he asked. Suddenly the idea didn't seem so awful. He was used to having wide-eyed children sit on his lap, but for the first time the idea of a woman in the same position held some appeal. Strength started returning to his hands. He knew this because his fingers tingled, as if they ached for the touch of smooth skin, the trembling responses of a woman pleasured.

"How will I know she's the right bride?"

Marlett chuckled silently. "That I can't tell you."

"I've entertained you?"

"Finding your life's mate is not easy Nicholas. Every single Santa has had trouble with this Test. Every one has no knowledge of who or what will make themselves happy. Not momentarily satisfied, not pleased for a week or so, but happy. Joyous."

Nicholas slumped his head into his palms. "Then I've lost." It had been years since he'd felt joyous.

"You can pass this test, Nicholas. I guarantee it. And when you do, you'll fill your nights and days with love."

"What do I do?" He was willing to take advice from anyone, even someone he often considered strangling.

"You look."

"Look. How easy you make it sound. I suppose I can do an internet search, WWMS: women willing to marry Santa. There should be a category in all those on-line services."

"Do not mock this."

"Marlett, how can I help but mock this?"

"It won't be easy, but you can do it. You won't find her here at the North Pole, so you must leave. You need to search the world. Find a place and be Santa. When you settle into your role, you will find her."

"No doubt she'll sit on my lap, tell me what she wants for Christmas."

"I will leave all the dating techniques up to you. As you know, elves…"

Marlett let the sentence fade, for which Nicholas considered himself grateful. From what he could tell, Christmas elves' dating rituals involved the woman pulling the beard of the first unattached male who caught her fancy. If there was more, and there had to be more, didn't there, Nicholas had never bothered to find out. Anything else definitely fit into TMI.

"You'll be fine."

"If my father did this than so can I." Nicholas headed up the stairs. Following the sun around the globe, it had been a long night.

"But your father failed the test," Marlett said to the empty kitchen. "That's why I'm counting on you to bring the joy back to Christmas."

CHAPTER 2

This year:

As Nicholas walked the predawn town, he dug his hands deeply in his pockets. His thoughts remained locked on a conversation he'd had a little over eleven months before. His breath curled out in front of him as if he walked in a fog, which was fine, for his memories were all muddled. He was a man who could remember every child's name on the entire planet, what they needed, what he could do to make them happy, but this distant conversation seemed more than a trifle fuzzy around the edges.

Nicholas continued along the narrow sidewalks. The wind was sharp, biting, found its way under his collar and down his back. He shivered instinctively. He didn't feel the cold. That too was one of his gifts. What would be the use of living and working in the North Pole if the cold burrowed deep into his bones and sent in a chill his father always said. This shiver then, had to be something else. Very likely it was dread.

He pulled a deep breath of the freezing air into his lungs and held it before he exhaled slowly, heating it within his body, letting even more of his inner warmth dissipate into the predawn light. He found the atmosphere rich with all the sensations described in the Christmas-song line, "In the air there's a feeling of Christmas." He recognized hope and promise and generosity coming from no specific source, but imbedded, inherent, in the buildings, the streets, and the homes surrounding him. Christmas was not dead, nor was it solely the media/consumer extravaganza he had feared. In places, it was as alive as it had been that first silent night.

Even with Santa working actively against Christmas, or rather, doing nothing to promote Christmas, the holiday was coming anyway. Nicholas adjusted the collar of his heavy coat while he continued slowly down the sidewalk of the old fashioned center-of-town. This town of Seven Sisters was a close-knit community locked in the middle of central Pennsylvania, a place where "progress" was slow to encroach. Here the last vestiges of Main Street America still thrived in the Five and Dimes, the beauty parlors, the Mom and Pop grocery. The churches were filled on Sundays, as were the PTA meetings and the city council hearings on the nights they met. People were friendly to strangers. They put the flag up, not just on the Fourth of July, but every day through the summer. They grew fat tomatoes which they plopped in Mason jars and their bounty included zucchini and marigolds and children with freckles. They didn't need to lock their doors. They had an unassailable faith in any number of things: the mercy rule in Little League, the strength of the American military, the dedication of the tooth fairy.

He stopped here because this is where the present last year had beckoned him to stop, the ring whose owner he still hadn't found. If worse came to worse and left him no other options, he would go door to door, until he found the woman he was seeking. He wondered if it would come to that, acting like some ridiculous Prince Charming in some Cinderella mockery: try the ring on. If it fits, you're mine.

"Go," Marlett had ordered him, so here he was. The fact that it had taken him eleven months to obey was no coincidence. He had paced and moped at the North Pole until Christmas started pressuring him, and to force him from the workshop, Marlett made up some ridiculous errand.

Nicholas knew this place, in his heart and his gut. He'd spent a few months here, when he was nothing but a child, when his father was Santa, when excitement had filled him and he couldn't wait until he was old enough to sneak in under cover of darkness and leave presents of hope. There had been a girl then, although she had been a child too. He wondered if she were still around. Rachael was her name. It could hardly be a coincidence that the one girl he remembered lived in the exact city where a diamond engagement ring wanted him to find a bride. Maybe there was hope for Santa Claus after all.

Nicholas turned on a bootheel, inhaling the cinnamon and glitter enhanced ambiance once again. Seasonal lights twinkled on every shop, from the brick craft and hobby store, to the gently-recycled clothing store. On the lamp posts from the far end of town where the first filling station was planted nearly seventy years before, to the other end of the long street, where the garden shoppe stood, red and green decorations sparkled. They swayed and twisted under the rising breeze, impervious to the north wind.

The towns he'd driven through had old fashioned names, Good Spring, Minersville, Red Rock, Beaver Brook, and had been founded by pioneers of no less sturdy values than the current residents, their proud decedents. The rivers had been discovered by the Indians: Susquehanna, Mehoopany and Lackawanna, rhythmic names which only intensified the natural beauty of the countryside, obvious even in the denuded winter branches of beech and maple. He'd stopped here hoping to find the peace he'd once discovered, even if he didn't expect to find a wife.

Nicholas still felt guilty. He should give, not take, please, not desire. He needed, he thought with self-deprecation, to get a good solid grip on himself before he started crying like a baby.

He hadn't walked half a block before his shoulders drooped and the old familiar fear seeped back, easily supplanting his wants and his confusion. The fact that he enjoyed Christmas, reveled in it, was only a symptom of his hypocrisy. He also feared it.

The house was there, where he had stayed all those years ago, another family just stirring now. Using his sensitivities, he counted three children and a mother still asleep, and a scruffy, unshaven father, waddling, closed-eyed toward the bathroom, having just turned off the alarm. Nicholas would not disturb them. There was no need, not until Christmas night, when there would be presents for the children, when he could sneak in and out with no one being the wiser. The house was close enough to downtown to walk. Nicholas remembered how he and his mother had dragged kitchen chairs out less than half a block to watch the Fourth of July parade. He remembered too that Christmas Eve when the sleigh had stopped, right about here, when his father appeared, offered to take him for a ride.

His once-a-year father.

Now he didn't even have that. Nicholas realized it wasn't his father he missed so much as someone else to accept this heredity position he didn't want. Still, until he got a son, he was Santa, for all it entailed.

Nicholas hadn't lived in that sturdy house long, only a few months, but the time was sharply etched in his memory as some of the happiest days he'd ever spent. He walked on, not to Rachael's house, for he wasn't about to tip his hand quite this soon, but to her grandmother's. He checked his watch, wondering if five minutes to seven in the morning was too early for a visit. Why not? He had pleasant memories of sitting at her kitchen table, drinking hot chocolate, spilling his guts to someone who would listen.

He bypassed the front door, and walked around to the back, and knocked.

Catherine Vacchioni looked up, surprised at the sound. In her world, there were two kinds of people: friends, who pounded on the back door then let themselves in, you-who-ing as they did, for the door was never locked, and front door people, usually selling vacuum cleaners or raffle tickets or UPS delivery people, dropping off packages. There was no category of back door people who knocked and didn't enter.

Rustling up old bones, she got to her feet and shuffled in fuzzy pink bedroom slippers to the door.

He was tall, towering six feet three of solid muscle, and handsome enough to warm even her ancient chilled blood. And there was more than a trace of familiarity about him, in his blue eyes and the sharp cleft of a dimple in his chin. His cheeks were reddened with cold, for all he was bundled up tight, so there was little else she could see of him. Nothing, the old woman thought, except the entreaty he wore so clearly she could read that he was in need, even if she also knew he would never ask for what he wanted.

"Mrs. Vacchioni, I'm certain you don't remember me—" he started.

It was the voice that did it, or rather the spunky grin, that came with the words. "Of course I do, young Nicholas St. Noel. Please come in before you freeze to death."

She opened the door wider, making room. He held his hands out. "I don't want to bother you."

"It's no bother, that I can guarantee you. I've got water on the stove, for hot chocolate."

How did she know? Of course. All those years ago he drank hot chocolate. It was his one tie to his father, for his mother couldn't stand the stuff. He stamped snow off his boots, then slowly entered the kitchen, as awkward and confused as he had been that first time he entered this room. But she had been a friend, a mentor, had listened, and he was certain, had loved the lost-waif boy he had been then, when he had not fit into his father's world, had no idea how to belong to his mother's.

"Tea, if you've got it." He would be perverse. Act like a grown up. How many grown men still drank hot chocolate?

"No problem, Nicholas. Now take your coat off, there's a rack there, and warm yourself by the fire."

She kept a coal fire burning in a huge, old fashioned oven, that radiated enough heat to cook a chicken at twenty paces, and for the first time in years, North Pole not withstanding, Nicholas felt like he'd finally come home.

"So, what brings you this way, and how long can you stay?"

So, he sat at her table, and drank her tea, munched her old-world sugar cookies, and shared what pieces of his life he felt comfortable offering. And when he said he hadn't found a hotel yet, she offered the middle bedroom, and wouldn't take no for an answer, hounding him, until he agreed to stay. Just until the twenty-third, she told him, when all the family would start descending. That would be perfect, he told her, for he had to leave then anyway.

And she smiled when he left, her secret smile, for although she recognized him as Nicholas St. Noel, she also knew him by his other name: Santa Claus. For when young Nicholas had been in school, his mother had spent hours at her table, talking, sharing the pain of the divorce, the problems of raising her son, the difficulties of living with the one true Santa Claus.

And Catherine, with her maternal instinct, knew what this Santa needed: a wife. And she had just the granddaughter for the job.

As she rocked back and forth in the maple chair which had comforted each of her nine children and her twenty-seven grandchildren and eight great-grandchildren, her heart thumped irregularly. The old pump didn't have many more beats left to it, so it was a good thing he showed up now. She'd be able to get the most important thing she needed to accomplish done.

Yup, this afternoon she'd do what she could to reintroduce Beth to Nicholas, patron saint of Christmas, then maybe she'd let her old, yet surprisingly full heart find rest.

It came as a surprise as he entered a store, that although it was only eight o'clock in the morning, the place was jammed.

Nicholas suspected he had entered a war zone. As he inched his way between the racks in the women's clothing department, then sidled past the jewelry counters, he noticed skirmish after skirmish of warriors, in this case mostly women, out for blood. The soft, gentle strains of Christmas carols were piped in through the overhead sound system, and were intended to have a calming effect he assumed, except it had exactly the opposite. The sound added to the fever, the power-lust control.

The Yule season images which graced Christmas cards, of rosy fires, understated yet professionally decorated trees, snow blanketing forest panoramas, was not the experience he witnessed now of battering-ram shopping carts, dominance contest tug of wars over small blister pack goods with odd sounding names and endurance races toward that most magical of all words "On sale."

Given his options, he would be far more comfortable turning tail and running for the nearest Buddhist monastery or any other place where they had never heard the phrase "Merry Christmas". Whatever present Marlett wanted him to find, he doubted very much it would be here, or if it were, he would likely pass it by blindly, simply because of the desperate carnage going on all around him. He had promised the long-bearded candy-cane sucker to find a gift, and find a gift he would, even if it meant wallowing through the trenches. Looking over his shoulder to get his bearings, Nicholas bumped into a woman wearing a red wool swing coat. She was familiar somehow, and he felt the need to kiss her, although he couldn't remember why. With a shrug of her shoulders indicative of a wordless "no harm done" and a quick turn up of her full lips, she disappeared.

For long seconds traces of her perfume remained, scents which had his blood boiling and his palms starting to grow moist. Cinnamon, he thought, ginger, spicy bar soap and…white school paste? Whatever the combination, it seemed to do the trick, starting his pulse throbbing. He hadn't caught a glance of her figure, the Red Riding Hood cloak had certainly prevented that, nor had he caught a glimpse of her hair color, for quite sensibly, she wore a green knit beret style cap.

Then the scent faded, and his heartbeat regulated so Nicholas aimed straight for the back of the store where the toy isles were wedged between hardware and electronics. Because he had no shopping cart and he wasn't distracted by randomly abandoned displays of steering wheel locking devices or herbs that grew on planters shaped like goats, he was making more progress than some, but still not moving fast enough to ease his growing frustration. Normally a patient man, sanity seemed to have abandoned him this morning. He wanted that toy and he wanted it now.

It was two weeks before Christmas, and already the twinkling lights, the holly edged tablecloths and the Happy Holiday embroidered towels were half-off. Apparently the shoppers and the store owners had heard that Santa wasn't real enthusiastic with the idea of making the trip this year and were doing everything in their power to make up for the lack. The thought should have given him more comfort than it did.

To make matters worse, it was only eight o'clock in the morning and the store had been open for two full hours. For all the Christmas shopping he'd done in the past, this was his first exposure to extended Christmas hours. Nicholas had had the misguided impression that he could get in and out of the store before anyone else in this town was even awake, yet here he was facing a crowd larger than the Times Square assembly on New Year's Eve and all of them, apparently, headed in the same direction he was.

"Attention shoppers," the loud speaker blared, "until ten o'clock this morning every item in our toy department is twenty percent off. Thank you for shopping—"

Nicholas didn't hear the rest. He was too busy fighting for his life against the women armed with Mastercards, long shopping lists he had no doubt they'd already checked twice, and lethal shopping carts who were out for blood.

He humphed, an explosion of breath, which was the best he could manage. "What was Marlett thinking of, when he asked me to get this one, specific microscope?"

He swerved around a harried-looking woman holding a runny-nosed two-year-old who was completely blocking the isle while she looked at some diabolical device that made potato curls, whatever they were, and got a dirty look for his efforts. What had happened to all the good will and cheer he had noticed the day before? The child was puff-eyed, tired, hungry and bored, a dangerous combination. Nicholas paused for a second, and called on the magic he had at his disposal. With his whispered prayer, the child calmed down, content to wait within the security of his mother's arms.

His senses tingled. A fresh surge of insight from his hereditary profession flared in full bloom. There, on the top shelf, past the Barbies and the Tonka toys, half hidden by Leggos, resided the dusty microscope. The one and only specific microscope that Marlett said he needed. Miserable elf. Serve him right if this were the end to Christmas.

Nicholas inched forward, almost there. He raised his hand, reached out, and was less than an inch away from his target when it was swiped away at the last second by some renegade shopper.

"Hey, Lady, I saw it first."

Right. Some Santa he was. He sounded like his manners hadn't altered since his kindergarten days. Gimmie. I'm bigger than you are. Is that what Christmas shopping had degenerated to, if even Santa couldn't control himself with the need for acquisition?

She, the woman with the microscope, flashed him a quick, no-nonsense, *possessive* smile. "Sorry."

An opening appeared in the aisle, and she pushed her shopping cart through, heading for the check-out lines, her red swing coat flaring behind her.

Without thinking, he hopped, skipped and jumped until he managed to wedge himself in front of her. "No, you don't understand, I need that microscope."

She raised her eyebrows and smiled like the before-Christmas Grinch, showing a good deal of teeth. "Good luck finding one." Then, to make matters worse, she added that seasonal rejoinder that had Nicholas curling his fingers preparatory to strangling her. "Merry Christmas!"

Little red riding hood. He'd hope the wolf would eat her. She attempted to go around him, but the transient opening had vanished, filled to over-capacity by shoppers desperate to have a full stash under their trees before the week was out. "Excuse me." Her smile this time was just a shade less sincere.

"Perhaps you didn't understand," Nicholas said, holding onto his temper only through a strongly imposed will. "I need that microscope."

She wasn't very tall, and she couldn't weigh much, but she gripped the box with the same possessive nature he had witnessed in a mother grizzly protecting a cub. "I doubt there's a national shortage of them. Bobbins, down the street had some advertised. You could go to Scranton. You could go to Pittsburgh." If she said he could ask Santa, he was going to be the first bearded-present-bringer in the history of the institution to face homicide charges.

He exhaled slowly. He held his hands out. Decided to look pitiful, to beg. "I haven't got time to go to Pittsburgh. And I need that one." When this was all over, he was going to shred every curly-toed elf bootie he could find and he was going to amputate Marlett's pointy ears. Try wrapping _that_ in tissue paper.

He reached for his wallet, understood for the first time the finer nuances of bribery. "I'll make it worth your while."

She stabbed a slender finger in his direction as she locked her jaw, spoke through clenched teeth which would likely have the wolf running for the sunset. "It's people like you who give Christmas a bad name."

If she only knew.

"Lady—"

The woman shrugged, decided, Nicholas could tell, that in addition to being the Christmas season, it was also the football season. She pushed, met an immovable force, his body, the contact between them electrifying enough that she stepped back immediately. She raised her eyelids, and he met the most sparkling green irises he'd ever seen.

"Would you mind? I'm meeting someone."

Shocked by his unexpected reaction, Nicholas intentionally made his comment sound lewd. "I'm sure you are."

Color flashed into her cheekbones, as well as high anger. Unless he kidnapped her, then dumped her in some back alley, he realized the potential of gaining possession of the microscope decreasing rapidly. "Listen, I'm sorry I was rude. I'll gladly buy you another microscope, but I need that specific one."

Her head tilted and she waited, as if he had yet to deliver the punchline of a long, involved joke. "Something to do with the serial number, no doubt."

There, she could be reasonable. "Yes. Exactly." Nicholas wondered how his father would have handled this situation. He could just imagine that jolly Santa leaving a flood of dead bodies in his wake as he rescued the items Marlett required. Why wasn't there a Santa handbook, a job description, amnesty for homicide committed in the best interests of a child?

A cart moved. Without waiting for him to explain further, she darted past him, landed in a ten-items-or-less line which had just opened up. With a shrug which lacked any kind of sympathy, she set the boxed microscope set on the conveyer belt and pulled out her charge card.

He followed her, got a second broadside whiff of her perfume, had to clear his head to remember what it was exactly he wanted from her. He cleared his throat, wondered why his heart was racing. They hadn't, after all, run that far. "At least let me tell you who that microscope is supposed to go to."

"I beg your pardon?"

"The microscope," Nicholas said, feeling desperate, "you're going to give it to the wrong person."

She was younger than he thought, and there, just for a second, she had that radiance he'd noticed over the years in all true believers. She signed a receipt, pulled her purse up over her shoulder, then grasped the bag tightly. Her look vanished, replaced by a no-nonsense one that said, quite plainly, without words, "I know my rights, and Mister, you're about to be talking with an officer of the law in the next few minutes."

"Listen, I'm sure we're both reasonable people—" Actually, he very much doubted that was true. *He* wasn't feeling the least bit reasonable, and judging by the expression on her face, the way she raised one eyebrow and placed her hands firmly on her slender hips, reasonableness wasn't a high priority with her either. Still, he was Santa Claus, and he did have some powers at his command. "I want to tell you who the microscope should go to."

She kept her features purposely blank, but he could see the gears turning, knew, without a doubt, that if she acted on whatever she was thinking she'd be off his "good" list forever.

"Oh, isn't that too bad. But, don't you think, since I've bought and paid for it, that I should be the judge of where it goes?"

With a swish from her red mid-calf wool coat, she escaped out the automatic door, and vanished into the early morning darkness, leaving Nicholas with a revised priority list, headed by learning every swear word in a minimum of thirty-seven languages, and a new resolve to torture one specific Christmas elf.

He was just contemplating returning to the store to see if he could find another microscope, when a Help Wanted Sign caught his eye. He stopped, backtracking through recent memories while Marlett's words echoed in his brain: *You need to pass the Test, Nicholas. Find a place, anywhere, and be Santa. I promise you if you do, you'll locate the one person who will make you happy.*

He could feel the ring in his pocket, knew, as he had known over the previous eleven months since Marlett had spoken to him, that he had no idea at all how to make himself joyous. He could bring others laughter, but had no clue how to do it for himself.

Before he could think, before it could deny the impulse, he nodded. Maybe being Santa in a department store would be a good idea.

He must have spoken out loud, for a voice behind him interrupted his musings. "You, sugar? You want to be Santa?"

Nicholas turned slowly and gave an appraising glance to the woman who had answered his query. She wore high heels and nylon, and a come hither glance that was echoed in every delightful curve of her body. She wore earrings that glowed red, had a small Christmas tree broach at the collar of her dress, both concessions to the season. Her dress, however, had nothing to do with what was going on all around them. It was more suitable to private entertaining. His hands grew damp. Without drawing on any Santa insight, Nicholas knew it would take very little to get her out of it.

She looked him over with a matching assessing glance, then walked two long fingers up the buttons on his shirt. "We usually hire retired people. Aren't you a little young to be playing Santa?"

And then, in that moment, he knew her. Rachael, the woman he'd come to see. Well, well, well. Maybe he could satisfy Marlett, and do something about his other problem at the same time. This, indeed, had potential.

"I'm Rachael Jardino," she said, adding a last name which was different from the one she'd had nineteen years before. Her smile was slow, predatory. Were she a big game hunter and he an elk, he'd be wise to start heading for the brush. Instead, Nicholas felt the very real need to allow himself to get caught in her sights.

"I'm the assistant store manager. Maybe we should go into my office, where we can discuss the terms and conditions of the job." Her voice was sultry, and the promises she expressed had very little to do with taking toy requests from children or filling out W2 forms.

"I'd be glad to follow you," he answered, slick with innuendo. She placed hot, damp palms on his washboard abs. "Oh, we'll probably have to see about some padding, but I think, Sugar, that you'll do just fine."

CHAPTER 3

The line snaked a good twenty feet through the Winter Wonderland of mechanized elves painting, wrapping, pounding, and hopefully thrilling the wide-eyed true-believers who waited. It was a scene of Christmas enchantment, the North Pole workshop, complete with long-tongued stuffed puppies entangled in glittered paper, and any number of packages, undoubtedly hiding treasures. Beth Anderson had seen it last year and the year before, and a dozen years before that. The scene of Christmas merriment no longer pleased her. Beth didn't want newer, bigger, or better, but a few inexpensive changes would give the decorations a more festive, fresher look. Just changing positions of a few of the mechanical dolls would do wonders.

Christmas songs spewed from the speakers, but all around Beth heard the cash registers sing the song of the season, the one more musical than Jingle Bells, at least to the mall managers and shop clerks. Expectations soared. In an unprecedented stroke of good fortune—for store owners—it had snowed that morning, nothing significant, less than an inch and that melting quickly on the gray Pennsylvania thoroughfares, but enough to reinforce the encroaching deadline. Christmas was coming. Whether anyone was ready for it or not, Christmas was coming.

"We're almost there," Beth said as the line moved another two feet forward. A group of three lively children moved off Santa's lap, holding their wrap-around paper hats which were designed to look like reindeer antlers. The small candy canes store-Santas used to give out were apparently no longer politically correct.

"We're almost there," her young nephew echoed, his eyes glistening with the seasonal expectation of miracles.

"Excuse me," a pixie-like young woman, wearing a short, short skirt, a jingle-belled hat and curly toed booties, said as she stepped between Beth and the family ahead of them. "Santa needs to go out and feed his reindeer. He'll be back in about ten minutes."

Beth exhaled a sigh of exasperation. "Ok, Jamie, let's just go home."

He tugged on her coat, entreaty visible in his wide brown eyes. When Beth shook her head slowly, almost imperceptibly, he turned his look to the young woman. "Please," he asked the Santa's helper. "Please, can't we see Santa? I'll be quick."

The pixie's sympathy was apparent as she looked to Beth who tousled his sandy blond hair and shook her head. "Jamie, I'm tired. We've still got some shopping to do. You've already seen Santa this year, and there will be a Santa at my party."

"No, today, please."

"That's ok," Rachael said, appearing from nowhere, tapping the employee on the shoulder in a curt dismissal. "They're family. Let them see Santa."

The pixie silently moved the sign from in front of Beth to behind her. The four-year-old belonging to that family let out an ear-piercing wail.

"Come to see Santa, have you?" Rachael asked, looking down her nose. In heels, she was a good five inches taller than Beth.

"Jamie wanted to see him." Beth tried desperately to keep her emotions in check. She'd been having this particular argument with her cousin since they were both younger than Jamie was now.

Rachael folded her arms across her breasts, a power position of smug conceit. "And aren't *you* going to sit on his lap, tell good ol' Santa that you're a true believer? When you do, I'd sure like a picture. Just tell the clerk it's on the house."

Beth had the very real impulse to cover Jamie's ears as they continued this conversation, not so much so that the boy wouldn't be exposed to the does he/doesn't he exist argument, but so that she would have something to do with her hands so she wouldn't pull Rachael's hair out in great clumps. There was only one person in the entire world who could make her angry, discounting of course, the fellow this morning with the microscope, and she was standing right in front of her.

"Santa knows that I believe in him."

The line moved forward. A matched set of four carbon-copy stair-step children moved onto Santa's lap, and his jolly Ho, ho, ho rang around the center courtyard of the store. Something inside Beth's chest jumped in acknowledgement. Santa, she whispered silently. Santa.

"Oh, and don't be too late getting home," Rachael said over her shoulder as she headed through the crowded toy section toward her office. "I've got a delicious surprise waiting for you there."

"Surprise," Beth said grinding her back teeth, "probably snakes in my underwear drawer."

Jamie tugged on her sleeve until she looked down at him again, her gaze softening. "We're almost there," he whispered.

"We're almost there," she repeated, her good humor restored.

In young hands betraying a nervousness she rarely noticed in the third grader, Jamie toyed with the paper reindeer antlers. He hadn't joined her singing, and he wore that pale, not-feeling-well expression she saw on him too frequently.

"How did your talk with Santa go? You were with him a long time."

He shrugged, looked down at nothing in particular, the movement highlighting the hollow gauntness of his eyes.

"What did you tell Santa you wanted?" If it were within her power, whatever it was, Beth would move heaven and earth to make the child happy.

"I didn't ask for anything. Not for myself anyway."

She had no trouble believing that. Precious, angelic Jamie Steelgrave only wanted to make others happy. It was rare when he requested anything for himself. "But you spoke for such a long time." Long enough that the next work shift started and the new Santa appeared before the one Jamie spoke with had finished with him.

For a long minute the silence grew between aunt and child, then Jamie spoke again. "Have you ever asked anyone a question you already know the answer to, just to see how they respond?"

"Jamie, I teach school. Of course I do." She took her eyes from the road as her car crept through the sluggish traffic. "That's not what you meant, is it?"

"I wasn't testing him, trying to see if he were the one and only Santa, nothing like that, but I'd already made my mind up about something, and I wondered if it were the right thought, if he felt the same way."

"Jamie?" Concern rang straight from her heart.

"No, it was all right, Aunt Beth. It really was. He said what I needed to hear."

She tilted her head, mulling over his words and the implications. "And sometimes that's easier coming from a stranger?" she guessed.

"Yeah."

Beth reached out, laid her hand gently on his knee for just a second before returning it to the steering wheel. "So what did you talk about?"

"Before I tell you, why don't you tell me what's in the bag you bought this morning."

Conniving devil. How she loved him. "No deal. Besides, I do buy presents for people other than you," she teased. "It's ugly purple socks for your mother."

For just a transient second, his eyes twinkled. "You wouldn't dare."

"You're right. But that package isn't necessarily for you."

"Ha!" he said with eight-year-old insight. "Just one clue."

"No clues. You're too good at guessing."

"Then it is for me."

"Why do you say that?"

"You were worried this morning, you're calmer now, you wouldn't let me hold the bag, and you know I never get enough presents..."

"You're going to get coal, if you keep that up," she said, but the bantering lightened her spirits. She loved the give and take teasing with the boy. It gave them both so much happiness. "Now, tell me what you asked Santa for."

He didn't hesitate, and he didn't sugar-coat it. "I asked him what I could do now to make my parents less sad when I die."

She had thought she would be prepared for anything he might

say, but she was wrong. The tires slid on wet pavement, and Beth almost lost control of the car. "Jamie! I don't want you thinking about that, and I don't want you discussing it with—"

"Santa Claus?" His pixie look only highlighted how young he was.

She tweaked his nose. "Yes. Even with Santa Claus."

Traffic moved forward. The car put on a burst of speed. Beth blinked rapidly, keeping emotions under rigid control. "What did he say?"

The silence grew, long and drawn out, a boy not delaying so much as he was struggling to remember the exact words, to hold onto the wisdom he had gained. Beth didn't rush him. Part of the closeness of their relationship was that they could talk about anything comfortably. She let him think while she drove, no longer seeing beauty of the roller coaster countryside, only the pain and sorrow that she tried to keep deeply buried behind her smile.

This time it was Jamie who reached out, touched her knee, with comfort, understanding, with a youthful inevitability. Death was never something Jamie feared, except how it impacted the others he knew.

"He said a lot of different things. That I was right to be concerned, that grieving is a natural process and is healthy, that if my mom and dad are sad that it's only because they loved me."

Beth moved the fan switch another notch to the right. The windshield was fogging. It was becoming impossible for her to see.

"And that's what you decided?" she asked.

"Yeah. And he said not to dwell on it. That if my life was to be short, that I should try even harder than other people to make sure that I lived every minute that I could."

Her bottom lip quivered. "Jamie, I—"

He raised his chin a notch, and life sparkled again in his spunky grin. "That means that we get to go sledding on Christmas break, doesn't it?"

She lowered her eyebrows. "If Santa told you that, I will personally pluck his eyebrows out, lash by lash."

"No, he didn't," Jamie insisted with his strong show of

loyalty that he'd always had defending Santa. "But I didn't get to go last year."

Last winter there had been surgeries and long, extended hospital stays. "I want to go."

"We'll see," Beth said, stopping her car into a narrow parking space for the last errand of the evening. Jamie smiled. With Aunt Beth, "We'll see," always meant yes.

***

"Gram? Gram, I'm here."

Beth slipped out of her wet shoes and left them on the rubber mat beside the door. She hung her coat on a hook to drip. The morning's snow had metamorphosed into an oily rain, and there was no sense putting her coat in the closet until it dried. Always practical. Always sane. It was enough to make her want to scream.

Stocking-footed, she backstepped. A large, undecorated Scotch pine stood in the ancient Christmas tree stand just to the left of the coal shovel. "Gram," she muttered under her breath, "I told you I would get to it."

Her eyes misted, and instead of pleasure a perfect tree usually brought her, there was just the beginning trace of anger. Since she had first gotten her driver's license, it had been her job to select the tree. And this year, more than any other, she needed to maintain tradition. She needed to do one thing, then another, then yet another in time honored habit, in an effort, no matter how futile, to bring back that spark which was so sadly lacking. Now she didn't even have this.

The family—those who were coming—weren't expected to start descending for another three or four days. She wondered which one of billions had arrived early to help with the preparations. She should be grateful, instead Beth swallowed hard and had to physically restrain herself from running into her room and having a good solid cry.

There were three bedrooms on this level. The front bedroom where her grandmother slept, the center bedroom reserved for visiting family and except for holidays rarely used, and the third was Beth's. In her room she gave her heavy canvas briefcase a long, hard look, wondering now if she would have time to get to the work she had stuffed within. She had hoped after dinner she would find some time to catch up on her grading, although considering the condition of the living room, she found that unlikely. The tree, and whoever had set it up, would undoubtedly demand priority.

Then for courage, and because it was as much a habit as breathing, she checked her Santa collection. She'd been collecting Santas since she was ten years old, and year round the group of them never failed to cheer her. She found her favorite, her first. Beth picked it up, fingered it tenderly. Memories swirled around her, of Santa and magic, and a time long ago. Sad memories, but no less pleasant because of that.

As she set the small wood-carved figurine aside, something tickled her memory, an insight involving the Santa who Jamie had spoken with. He reminded her of the real Santa, the one she had met under twinkling lights and Christmas illusions long ago. Santa. But it wasn't possible. It was time she grew up.

Before she headed downstairs, Beth snuck her head into the middle bedroom. An empty suitcase rested open upon the double bed. Whoever had come had already unpacked. Beth couldn't imagine her mother setting up the Christmas tree and the room showed none of the crush-of-traveling-family that was always in evidence when her relatives arrived. A man's electric shaving razor on the dresser caught her attention. There was no unattached man in the family and she could determine nothing of a feminine nature within the room. A guest? That was possible, however her grandmother had stopped inviting impromptu friends years before when her health seriously started to deteriorate.

Embarrassed to pry, and feeling she'd find her answers in the kitchen, Beth left the middle bedroom and stopped to admire the tree for another second, anything to revive her sagging Christmas spirit.

"Are you sure that's *all* you want for Christmas?"

Beth startled. She hadn't heard him sneaking up behind her. "Excuse me?"

He wasn't a relative, and she didn't recognize him. In this a small town, everyone knew everyone elses' business, and all things considered she was related, directly or by marriage, to more than half the people in the county. Beyond that, she had taught elementary school, helped on the PTA and the woman's auxiliary in her church. If she didn't know him, she undoubtedly knew *of* him.

He set down two boxes she recognized as containing ornaments and gave her a wink in which she was certain his eyes twinkled.

"You were whistling '*All I Want for Christmas is my two front teeth.*'"

"Good Lord, it's you again," she screamed. The maniac from the store this morning. "If you followed me here, hoping to get that microscope, I have to warn you that I'm willing to call the police, for this could be considered harassment."

"This has nothing to do with the microscope," he said. "I'm here as a guest of your grandmother's. Besides, we were talking about your two front teeth."

"I absolutely, positively think you're a maniac. I'm going to have a talk with my grandmother right this minute. How dare she invite strangers into this home!"

"It's her home. I imagine she can do what she wants."

"We'll see about that."

He gave her an appreciative glance, the kind usually followed by a wolf-whistle. "Don't you think we should introduce ourselves, before you call the police, that is?"

"I don't believe that's necessary. I will call you an intruder, and that's a good enough description for the police."

He enveloped her fingers in his warm, masculine grasp, and tremors of heightened awareness surged through her body. This was not a handshake, it was a prelude, but to what she had absolutely no idea. For some reason she couldn't define, she wanted to sit on his lap, tell him what she wanted for Christmas, things she'd never wanted before, black nightgowns, satin sheets, intimate privacy. She really was losing her mind.

He smiled easily, a friendly, open smile which she knew held no hidden agenda. She judged him approaching thirty, for his face looked comfortable, well lived in, but young enough that time hadn't etched any character lines yet. His shoulders were broad, his body well proportioned, but while a muscular man usually frightened her, in some inexplicable way she was set at ease immediately. His was the strength of character instead of strength of body, a fine distinction most men of her acquaintance didn't recognize. He was a man at peace with himself as well as those around him.

"I know you," Beth gasped, breathless. "You're Santa Claus!"

CHAPTER 4

Santa Claus.

How could she know, when he'd questioned for so long himself? But there was no doubt. Beth knew it intrinsically. After a shaft of caught-again fear, Nicholas' heart swelled, filled with pride and a soaring kind of happiness. The doubts he'd felt, the confusion, the terror of not belonging vanished in the split instant of her certainty. While he pulled in a deep breath, his heart thumped, loud enough that he had no knew she could feel it.

"Yes, Beth, I'm Santa Claus." His voice resonated with power.

Looking at her, seeing the potpourri mixture of faith and amazement, he wanted to put on the costume, call the reindeer, fulfill the traditional calling. He wanted to be Santa Claus. Not the once-a-year Claus that he had been for two years now, not the blinders on, nothing-but-Christmas Santa his father had been, but a fully developed, loving Santa Claus. With Beth he could become the Santa Currier and Ives would draw beside a fireplace, the jolly old elf Clement Moore would tear open the shutters and throw up the sash to see, the man Francis P. Church had written about in a 1897 New York Sun editorial, "*Yes, Virginia, there is a Santa Claus. He exists as certainly as love and generosity and devotion exist.*"

This was what he had been born for, this purpose, this sense of self-awareness.

"Santa Claus." Beth whispered, wondering why his eyes had gone all funny, and the look on his face had changed to something bordering on mystical ecstasy. It didn't make sense to her and she was about to step back, put some distance between him and herself. "At the store."

"The store?" Nicholas asked blankly.

"O'Reilley's. You were there today. Spoke with my nephew."

Nicholas shook his head, belatedly coming to his senses. Shock registered somewhere deep inside and there was an uncomfortable feeling of having a balloon of expectation pop deep in his gut. "The boy with the heart condition."

She had no idea what she had done to him, the distance he had fallen in the last fifteen seconds. Beth continued blindly. "I want to thank you. What-ever you said to him was apparently the right thing. We don't tip-toe around Jamie, sugar coating the truth. Not many strangers are perceptive enough to be honest with children."

His head dipped a little to the side as he listened, and the fuzziness she'd noted in his pupils and around his irises returned, making him look dreamy, or perhaps other-worldly.

"But I am Santa Claus, Beth." They were words he needed to say, but had never had the courage before.

Her anger flashed to boiling, even though she knew the root cause of it: this was a battle she had been fighting her entire life. Her nostrils flared. She set her hands on her hips and thrust her chin forward. Beth met his taunt with one of her own.

"I'm not a doctor, but I play one on tv," she growled.

"I beg your pardon?"

"There's an aspirin commercial or something for hemorrhoids or whatever. It's a line the actor says. I'm not a doctor, but I play one on tv. It's a reminder not to be confused with a role you've been hired to play."

Although still fighting his own shock, Nicholas had the peace of mind to grin. "What is the point you're trying to make?"

High color rode on her cheeks and she showed teeth. "I'm trying to make? You're doing this deliberately, to get my dander up, aren't you?"

"Doing what?"

"Teasing me. Mocking my belief in Santa. Tell me, who sent you? What are you doing here?"

"I'm Santa, Beth." Oddly enough, the stronger her rising doubt, the firmer his own conviction. He spoke slowly, distinctly, as if he were sitting on that traditional throne, trying to convince a toddler with a quivering lower lip. "I'm not here to deceive you, or to tease you or to mock you. Faith like yours is rare, Beth. I would never do anything to destroy it."

"Who sent you?"

"I'm a friend of the family—"

"Who sent you?"

He let several long seconds pass, knew he would rather cut out his own heart at that moment than speak. This too was part of his traditional power, his magic. Santa Claus knew clearly what would hurt as much as he knew which presents would bring laughter.

"Rachael." The word came out reluctantly and it was as if her worst nightmare had been given form.

Beth tightened her eyes as she growled. "That explains it then. We both know how Rachael fells about Santa."

"She believed once." This morning, slipping into his costume, Nicholas realized it was his hope that she could learn to believe again. That they could learn together.

Beth had kept her eyes locked on his, now she pivoted, studied the naked tree, not seeing the perfection of the branches, instead seeing into the past. "She never believed. If she said she did, it was only so she could claim more presents than I did. Oh, yes. Every December First, on the dot, as a child Rachael turned into this paragon of virtue, but December 26th she was back to being the same old snotty kid she always was, and let me assure you, she hasn't improved much as an adult."

He had to clench his fingers deep into cardboard to avoid putting his arms around her in an embrace that he would intend only to comfort. "I don't want to talk about Rachael."

"No, I don't suppose you do."

The box felt heavy, and Nicholas realized he still held it. He bent slowly, settling it down as if it held poorly wrapped Llardo figurines instead of hand-made Christmas decorations created from egg cartons, paper doilies, glue and glitter. His mind twirled, spun, mixing up time and place. Santa Claus—not himself—and Beth, nineteen years younger at a bus stop with a black eye, and Rachael, today at the store whispering seductively into his ear, "Santa, should I tell you what I want for Christmas?" And he knew, without reading her mind, that it started with a dollar sign, and had a minimum of five digits to the left of the decimal point. Regardless of cost, Nicholas doubted it was the kind of present Marlett created in his laboratory.

"So, you're a friend of Rachael's," Beth said. The words themselves were taunting and just a little bit nasty.

He had to avoid this topic at least until the inner turmoil in his brain settled. Time for a little misdirection.

"Your grandmother caught me up on the latest family gossip and she has told me everything there is to know about you."

Beth tightened her eyes and looked at him with a growing suspicion. "My grandmother? How does she fit into this?" Rachael, generally, wasn't clever enough to involve other people in her schemes. When she had a goal in mind, she went after it on her own.

In her anger she was beautiful, absolutely, completely stunning. She had radiated a drab exhaustion while she waited in line that afternoon, making it easy for him to overlook her, concentrate on the boy. Now her eyes sparkled, adding a depth of green that spoke of life. He could see that she spent most of her time smiling. Her lips were full, red, pursed now. If she wore makeup it was long gone, but her own vitality made lipstick and mascara superfluous. Odd that he hadn't noticed this perfection while she whistled. She was small, but it was her face he studied, not her body. Her chin was thrust out, taunting. Firm and defiant, she was a woman made of fire. Standing there, facing him in her wrath, Beth was the most sensual woman he had ever seen.

She glowed with passion. And she believed. She might fight him for a few hours, or days, but she believed.

Nicholas folded his arms against his broad chest and nodded his head slowly with masculine possessiveness. It was one of those unexpected Eureka events, the kind of serendipity that involved finding exactly what he needed when he had been looking for something else entirely. Steam curled around her gnarled teeth, and there was still a high probability that she'd scratch his eyes out. Still, he thought, she was lovely. For the moment he was exactly and precisely where he wanted to be—facing this lioness, but then, he wasn't exactly unarmed, was he?

"I'm staying here for a few days until Christmas. I had a lovely talk with your grandmother."

She stabbed a sharp, pointed finger at his chest, in a gesture which was unexpectedly familiar. "You leave my grandmother out of whatever plots you're cooking up."

He chuckled, and she wondered afresh if he were mocking her. "That's going to be hard to do, since I'll be sleeping in the middle bedroom. Until Christmas."

"What's the matter, Santa Claus," she snapped. "Too far to commute to the North Pole?"

Heavens but she was gorgeous when she snarled. He wouldn't change a single freckle about her, not her ears, which were a shade too large, nor her nose which was a fraction too small. More than anyone he'd ever been introduced to, she met, and exceeded, his definition of perfection. She glittered, she sparkled, and for reasons he couldn't go into at the moment, she made his blood run hot. He had thought he wanted a temporary woman like Rachael, a woman he could share a night or two before he left with no regrets, not one who tripped his pulse. Not one who would be impossible to forget.

Nicholas rubbed a clean shaven jaw. He had exercised his razor almost an hour before, destroying the heavy, thick beard which was so traditionally Santa, which had grown instantly as he set his arms into the sleeves of the red furred costume before he took to the throne. Now, with hormones gurgling, he might have to shave again, or at the very least take a long, cold shower. As Santa he frequently felt androgynous, sexless, using his compassion and caring for others, ignoring his own sexuality in order to more fully fit into a mold set into place by relatives who knew far better than he the role he had to play. Never had he felt this completely male, nor this out of control.

Fresh possibilities arranged themselves in his suddenly coherent mind. Possibilities which didn't involve Rachael, or anything which Marlett would approve of.

She tapped her foot, waiting. He liked her impatience. He adored the fire she exhibited, the danger. For all the fireplace chimneys he'd crawled down, Nicholas thought how pleasant it would be, just this once, to be burned.

He looked her over slowly, from sensible, low-heeled shoes

to brunette curls. "It would be no trouble to show you just how fast I could take us to the North Pole."

He hadn't meant it that way, but he could see by the tightening of her jaw and the dilating of her pupils, Beth took his statement not so much as a direct threat, but a lewd one. She set a steel rod in her spine. "I'm sure on your Santa sleigh, there's only room for you and Rachael."

It had never occurred to him before that he could tease about sexual interest—and Santa—in the same breath. What he told Marlett was true: whenever he thought about a woman, Santa was the last thing on his mind.

He rubbed his chin, spoke slowly, adding a drawl. "Ahh, but you know Beth, it's a big sled. There's always room for—how should I put this—goodies?"   Her hand drew back and the impulse to slap him adsorbed momentum. "You raging lunatic. I want you out of this house this instant."

"And what would your grandmother say?"

"Grandmother?"

He wanted to laugh at her confusion. He wanted to crow with his own good fortune. He knew that she loved Santa, and still he wanted to alter the nuances of that love, to something a bit more intense.

"That was what we were talking about. She invited me to stay for a few days. I couldn't disappoint her and move out, could I?" He let a beat go by, then another, before he lowered his voice, and allowed a range of possibilities surround them. "Especially since she told me all about you."

"Oh?" From his silk-sheets look, Beth wondered just what tidbits her grandmother had divulged. Trying to deny the potent magnetism of his charm—and his brass sensuality—she rubbed her palm where the awareness of his touch still tingled. If she had any sense at all, she would slap that grating smirk off his face. That would put paid to the dazzling awareness of his touch as well as offering a measure of satisfaction. Just who, exactly, did he think he was?

"Your grandmother is a special woman and she enjoys

talking about her family, although I will confess, I pumped her shamelessly for information about you once she told me how pretty you were."

Her eyes clouded again, and the look of defiance she had earlier turned to one of scorn. "Pretty. Right."

"Pretty," he echoed, "Right." The emphasis he settled on the words was decidedly different from what she had used. Nicholas had struggled, which came as something of a shock to him. One of the advantages to his vocation was that he always had at his command the ability to say the right thing, except today, like a schoolboy, he felt awkward and tongue tied. He knew exactly how much was riding on this first encounter. "I apologize. I did not anticipate the woman you'd become when I met you years ago."

From the scowl settling between her eyebrows he knew she didn't believe him, but what he had told her was the truth. He did see her as lovely. While he had been mesmerized by a blossoming Rachael when he had been here before, he hadn't given any consideration at all to Beth. At ten Beth had that awkward, unfinished look children often get, too thin, too short, with large teeth her face hadn't had the time to grow around. She'd had dirt under her fingernails, scabs on her knees and innocence in her eyes. The innocence was still there, but it was wrapped tightly around a healthy skepticism. She didn't trust him. At the time, Rachael had been a tease and his hormones had been active enough that he had noticed, even if both of them had been far too young at the time for him to have acted upon, or even understood, his desires.

Beth's eyebrows had lowered with stark determination and if she had a red cape, any self-respecting bull would have turned tail and run. "Have we met before?"

"Yes." Hidden under her exhaustion, Beth had that spark of life within her that spoke of an appreciation of living. Not quite an aura, he didn't read auras, but even without using his magic Nicholas could interpret nature and hers was giving, nurturing, exciting. Beyond that, buried deeply, was a bright, thick swatch of sensuality she had denied herself but which was vital and strong nevertheless. Already the thought of releasing her passion had him breathing deeper in his chest.

Her hair was rich, thick reddish brown. It glistened like tinsel with a vitality the most expensive shampoos in the world couldn't create. She wore it clipped short and permed, and the curls shaped themselves around her face with flattering overtones. Even after the rain and the cold humidity which was even worse, every coil was in place. Like her third-graders, it probably didn't dare misbehave.

She was small. He often delivered Christmas packages bigger than she was. Her statue was one of the things which endeared her to him. Her clothing was prim. She wore a white cotton blouse he could only see the neck-buttoned collar from, a red and green wool plaid skirt, and a kelly green cardigan that highlighted the green from her eyes. She had a pin above her left breast, one of those small fuzzy Santa Clauses with a string hanging down. Pull the string and its eyes would light up, or it would Ho, ho ho. He thought it was the only jewelry she wore, but he realized he was mistaken. Imbedded in her ears were more Santa Clauses, these about an inch long, dangly things done in rather ugly parody.

She noticed where his eyes went, felt self-conscious, rubbed an earring, almost in affection. "A present from one of my students last year. I couldn't resist."

"I see." Santa Clauses. He was beginning to feel right at home, but then, he knew from the instant he met her grandmother that settling in wasn't going to be a problem.

Already from watching her less then ten minutes, during which time she stood almost rigidly still, he knew when she moved she would do so with the grace, and with the exuberance of a woman one-fourth her age. Nicholas could well imagine her on the playground jumping rope and playing hopscotch with each child in her class. He had no doubt that every single student in her charge fell instantly in love with her. He was already more than half-way there himself.

Unlike Rachael, Beth was not classically beautiful in a Hollywood sense, but clean and wholesome. She could give honor to the cover of a country magazine, or to any Christmas ad featuring a La-Z Boy, a roaring fire, a box of Hallmark cards. His heart continued to crash against the walls of his chest and he rather hoped she couldn't hear it.

"You really are very lovely."

Nicholas became even more intoxicated with her as he watched a hint of color creep up to tinge her high cheekbones. He had wanted a woman capable of blushing, had doubted he would find one.

"Thank you for the compliment, but I assure you that's not necessary, Mr.—" then she added with far less sarcasm than Rachael would have used, "I don't suppose I should call you Santa."

"I'm sorry. I actually do answer to Santa, but I'm Nicholas St. Noel. It's honestly a pleasure to meet you again."

He waited for the name to ring a bell. It didn't. She raised a honey blond eyebrow which had not darkened to the brown of her hair.

Nicholas rocked back on his heels, his hands firmly locked behind his back before he did something way too precipitous like caressed her cheek before she gave him permission. "We met briefly nineteen years ago."

"Oh." Not quite an acknowledgement. Beth felt an increasingly desperate need to change the subject and she had no idea why, except perhaps that they were getting too personal too quickly.

Strength of presence. If she had to describe him in a single phrase it would be that. Oddly enough another song from her third graders rang through her mind, *Here comes Santa Claus*. Beth shook her head to clear the image.

"Were you the one who set up the tree?" she asked, breaking her gaze and facing the perfectly proportioned evergreen filling a very large section of the living room.

"Yes. I'm sorry if I stepped on your toes. I know it was your pleasure to select the tree."

She shivered, felt as if she looked at a photograph of herself smiling, yet couldn't remember what had made her so happy. Her *pleasure*. For how long now had she seen it as nothing more than another chore? How long had it been since selecting the tree had been fun? She looked to see if he were teasing her, instead met only sincerity. How could she bite into him when he was so clearly apologetic?

Beth reached out, almost touched him, pulled her hand back when she remembered vividly the shock of passionate awareness she'd experienced during their handshake. She wasn't quite ready to test her hastily derived hypothesis that it was nothing more than imagination.

"No, really, I appreciate all the effort you've gone to. It's one less thing that I have to worry about." It surprised her that she meant it.

"After supper we'll have time to decorate it."

She didn't bother to ask if in defining the pronoun he meant himself—and Rachael. He was far too distracting, far too charismatic for her peace of mind. She kept her eyes glued to the tree simply so she wouldn't be caught with her mouth hanging open. With trembling fingers she reached out, caressed the needles, soft, fragrant, vibrantly alive.

"You must have an eye. It's the most perfect tree I've ever seen."

He shrugged his shoulders, negating the effect of her compliment even while inside a warm glow surfaced. Her voice was melodic. He hoped she liked to sing. "It's something of an acquired talent. I've had a lot of practice. And Beth, I hope you don't mind that I'm staying."

"Of course I don't mind, as long as you don't expect to be waited on hand and foot."

"Forgive me for breaking off this conversation, but at the risk of sounding rude, I've got to get moving."

"Moving?"

"Cookies," he said, and with what almost looked like a courtly half-bow in her direction, he took off at a lope for the stairs down to the kitchen.

"Cookies," Beth mumbled toward his retreating back. "I always run when I need a cookie too." Of course if he'd waited for her comment she would have muttered some priceless maternal advice, along the lines that it would ruin his supper. It was the same thing she would have told any third grader at this hour of the day.

The house smelled good. It took her a minute to recognize the mouth-watering aroma beyond that of fresh pine pitch was the old-world gingerbread cookies, a Christmas tradition the world over, and an absolute requirement in the Vacchioni home. Baking was another of the projects she had scheduled for the evening. One of thousands of chores that she had to accomplish before the hoards of starving relatives descended upon them, expecting everything exactly the same, no matter what else pressured her.

By the time Beth reached the kitchen, she caught Nicholas reaching into a steaming oven, pulling out a tray of bloated gingerbread figures: bells, trees, reindeer, stars. Three broad wire racks held the cooling results of previous batches.

She stopped dead-still in her stocking feet. "You made cookies?" Her voice sharpened, the last syllable an octave higher than normal. If it sounded like an accusation, that's exactly what she intended. It was her duty since she was old enough to be trusted near the coal burning stove, to make the Christmas cookies. Selecting the Christmas tree was bad enough. This territorial invasion approached a capital offense.

He grinned, looked boyish and totally unrepentant. "There's no need to worry. Your grandmother oversaw the entire process. I haven't changed a thing. Would you care to try one?"

Beth pivoted on her heel to face her ninety-two year old relative. She seemed like an easier target than the rock solid man standing in front of her.

"Grandma, what have you done?"

From her perch on a worn rocker at the far side of the stove, Catherine Vacchioni showed a yellow-toothed grin and emerald green eyes which had seen too much suffering but which sparkled anyway. She waved a gnarled hand in Beth's general direction. "Sit down. Relax. There's nothing going on here to get your dander up."

Elizabeth prickled. "I sincerely doubt that. All I'm asking for is a straight answer. Who is he, and why is he making my cookies?"

"Your cookies? I thought they were Santa's cookies."

Catherine giggled, and standing by the oven, Nicholas gave into a deep belly laugh. Instead of forming into fists, Beth's fingers tightened into claws as if she was about to rip that miserable smirk right off his face.

"Something funny?"

"It's sort of an insider's joke."

He must laugh a lot. Without knowing why, Beth was certain all the character lines on his face were the direct result of laughter. Her fingers softened. She'd leave his face the way it was—for the moment.

With deft strokes of a spatula, the newest contingent of cookies joined their forbearers on the cooling rack. She watched his hands, firm and sure and experienced. She started to drool and could only hope it was a direct result of her love for gingerbread and not a serious indication of something else, like insanity.

Nicholas handed the last cookie from the pan, still steaming hot to Beth's grandmother. Catherine accepted it, burning her fingers as she did so. Another tradition. The last cookie from every batch went to her grandmother, a sort of official quality control. She bit into it aggressively, like cookies should be eaten.

"Yup. This batch meets the standards," she said. Catherine Vacchioni winked at Nicholas, and drat his scurvy hide, the miserable bum winked back at her. Another private, family tradition. How did he know? And why should it hurt so much that he did?

"I'm sure they're not as good as yours," Nicholas said, turning toward Beth, which had the unfortunate result of making her feel like raw cookie dough, full of sugar, molasses and butter but completely without shape.

Catherine rocked a little faster. "Nonsense. These are every bit as good. Why don't you try one for yourself?"

"Grandma, you know I don't like to eat cookies without icing."

"Well, maybe it's time you did."

Again, Beth tried to get a handle on her emotions, and found them all twisted. Anger, annoyance, something that felt very much like she should check her Christmas stocking to see if Santa had filled it early this year, but beyond that, she felt a singing sense that something wonderful was happening all around her. She wondered if she were witnessing a miracle—which because she doubted was true, only served to make her madder still.

"Now that you've finished your cookie, Gram, why don't you tell me exactly what is going on here?"

"It's really nothing to get all riled up about, girl. Nicholas is an old friend."

Beth looked over toward the oilcloth covered kitchen table where Nicholas was busily rolling out more cookie dough. He was humming something very familiar. Darn if it didn't sound like '*I saw Mommy kissing Santa Claus.*'"

"A friend?" Sure. She supposed Jack the Ripper had friends. Even the before-Grinch had that loyal dog Max. It was odd. She'd never known anyone that Rachael liked who had friends.

"While I'm staying Beth, I'm going to help out. I only work a few hours a day at the store." He met her gaze and it was hot as the emanations from the coal burning stove. "Especially at this time of year I find I need to keep busy."

Catherine licked her fingers, the last of the treat disappearing. Beth decided she should feel grateful. Her grandmother ate so little that anytime she swallowed anything it was a cause for celebration, even if it were Christmas cookies some interloper made in *her* kitchen.

"You've been trying to do too much."

Elizabeth grabbed the straight back of a white enameled kitchen chair before she fell. "How about if we just back up a step or two. Why don't you tell me exactly why you think we need this—" Was fiend too strong a word? How about invader? "—gentleman to help us?"

She might have been imagining it, but it looked to her as if Nicholas' shoulders shook. With laughter. He started humming '*Nuttin' for Christmas.*' She'd heard poinsettias were poisonous. Beth felt like the time had come to shove some where it would do him the most good.

"There's enough work to do here. You have been so busy that

nothing has been done."

"You've been sick." It was both an accusation and an excuse.

"Christmas is too important to let slide," the old woman insisted. "That tree should have been up two weeks ago." Where Catherine walked with a cane and could no longer hold her knitting needles because of arthritis, her voice was still strong enough to bring four generations in from sledding.

Elizabeth's fingers tightened on the chair while her teeth clenched. "I said I would get to it."

"But you hadn't." No apology, no contrition. Elizabeth was about ready to add her grandmother's name to the growing list of people she planned to strangle.

"I have other priorities such as taking care of you. I was going to spend the entire evening—"

Her grandmother had fallen, broken her hip, then while recovering had caught a case of pneumonia. While the pneumonia had been mild, it couldn't be ignored. Her strength was only now returning, and her lungs had been clear for months.

"And you still can. The tree needs decorating. Do you think that can be done in fifteen stolen minutes? Even with the cookies baked, they still need icing. With your fastidiousness, it will take hours. I know how you pipe the icing for every bow-tie, every hair-ribbon, not to mention the candy trinkets you use to decorate each cookie. There are presents to wrap. I may not be able to reach your hiding places, but I know where they are, and that not a one of them is wrapped. You don't have to do it all alone."

"I've been doing it by myself for years." She sounded like a shrew and she never sounded like a shrew. For years she had been lauded as the one teacher who never lost her temper, who could make the hellions of third grade behave and never raise her voice. Many of the presents had been bought months ago, and she frequently started wrapping as early as August, so that in the final days before Christmas, all she had to worry about was the food, the general house cleaning and the pageant. But in August her grandmother had been in the hospital, and in September she'd been back again. With school, and the other standard crises, a niece with a premature baby, another with a small house fire, and the call from her church for fund raisers, there honestly hadn't been a moment's free time.

Catherine rocked slowly. "When Mr. St. Noel isn't Santa Claus, he is a handyman."

"A handyman?" He didn't look like a handyman. He looked like—Santa after eighteen months on a Health Rider. Grudgingly she admitted he did look like a handyman. Whatever they looked like. The other was simply too uncomfortable to think about.

Embarrassment flooded her at her awareness of his masculinity. She lowered her eyes, made another tactical mistake. His jeans were well worn, faded and creased, and drew her interest, albeit unwillingly, to his firm butt. To avoid what could easily turn into a blush, she left his very attractive nether region and turned her attention to his feet, a safe enough area generally. He wore thick soled hiking boots, again, well worn and comfortable looking. Somewhere she had read ankles were sexy, and she had no idea why that little bit of trivia was suddenly thrust into the forefront of her consciousness. He was now humming 'Santa Claus is coming to town,' and she suspected he was doing it deliberately, keeping her off balance, confused.

In addition—for what it was worth—her palm still tingled from his handshake. And if she were honest with herself, more than that particular part of her anatomy hummed.

"Mr. St. Noel," Beth said to his back as he slipped another blackened cookie sheet in the oven, "whatever my grandmother told you, we don't need a handyman."

"Beth, I taught you better manners than that. And we do need him. There are a thousand things around here that he can do."

He locked his fathomless gray eyes with hers with an invasive intensity she'd never been susceptible to before. And then, when he was certain she wouldn't look away, he deliberately, sensuously—maliciously—licked his lips. "Your grandmother's right, Beth. There are many things I can do around here." His voice was smooth, deep, caressing. Really, if her grandmother felt that strongly about hiring a handyman, why couldn't she chose one with a lisp and hair growing from his ears?

She felt warm, and cold. Beth rubbed her arms through the scratchy material of her sweater where goosebumps were raising in glorious profusion. Her heart started beating just a little faster and her breath was coming in quick little pants. She felt as if she were a Christmas present that he had been coveting for a long, long time, and now that he found her he was going to take his time in unwrapping her, until they were both screaming with—

Madness.

She smiled falsely, then blanketed herself in nonchalance.

"Mr. St. Noel, would you excuse us for a minute?"

"No problem. I have more boxes of Christmas decorations to bring down from the attic. In eleven minutes though, the next batch of cookies are going to be ready to come out of the oven."

If he were giving her a reprieve, it wasn't going to be a very long one. "Fine. I'll take care of it."

He disappeared up the stairs with silent tread and some of the nutmeg feeling disappeared with him. At least she could breathe easier.

"Grandma, are you out of your mind?"

Although the old woman's body had betrayed her, becoming bent over the years, her mind was still sharp. "No. The work needs to be done."

"I don't deny that. But how are you going to pay him? Out of your social security? You're barely making ends meet as it is. And my money doesn't go that far." Her paycheck, and her hefty Christmas club went to presents to all the grandchildren and great grandchildren in her grandmother's name. Anything left over went into anonymous gifts to out of work neighbors and the local toy drive put on by her church. Christmas was a way of life she planned for all year long.

"There's no need to get your dander up, Marzipan," her grandmother said, using her favorite nickname for Beth. "He's staying for room and board and only until Christmas Eve day. After that he's got another commitment. I could hardly turn him down, could I?"

"Grandma, you don't understand. I have to do it myself."

The old woman rocked a little bit more firmly. "I know what's bothering you. Mr. St. Noel is exactly what you need."

"All right, there's only two things I demand to know. What's bothering me, and what *exactly* do you think I need?"

Catherine chuckled. "What's wrong with you is that you're lonely. You need a man in your life, and Mr. St. Noel is a perfect candidate."

CHAPTER 5

Before Beth could answer her grandmother, she stopped, the words of denial she had been about to deliver never finding form. Instead, she felt electricity, or for want of a better word, anticipation, and maybe, beyond all those other confused emotions, suspense. Suspense, like when she had shopped for days for just the right present and found it, wrapped it beautifully, and when the recipient was about to open it, decided that perhaps it was all wrong, that she had made, with the best of intentions, an absolutely classic mistake.

And then, as if she had called him, Nicholas appeared, a large box perched on his left shoulder, a smaller one tucked securely under his right arm. She felt her cheeks heat, hoped he hadn't overheard her grandmother's plans for him, hoped that earlier she hadn't made a fool of herself. She wasn't used to men. Not that she didn't date, because she did, and she enjoyed that other gender, which was so far removed from her own that she frequently considered men a different species. But she wasn't used to men-men, which Nicholas was. For all his politeness, for all his identifying with her own long-held beliefs, there was something primitive about him, something decidedly masculine.

He fit in her kitchen with its ancient coal burning stove, but she suspected he would just as easily fit in at a campfire a century past, or maybe as many as two thousand years before. She shook her head to break the image. There was nothing primitive about him.

Nothing that she couldn't deal with. Except that it would be easier if he wasn't two feet away from her, if she taught his children and knew his wife from church. Then she could dismiss him as no threat. She understood how a woman could be afraid of a man, but this fear she felt, if it were fear, had more to do with him invading her comfort zone, and the pain he would cause her would only come from his leaving.

You need a man, and Mr. St. Noel is the perfect candidate. There had to be some flaw she had overlooked in starry-eyed wonder, blinded while she studied the Christmas tree, or when he pulled cookies from the oven. If there were a flaw, it wasn't readily apparent. The fabric of his sleeves bunched, highlighting sharply defined muscles and the material stretched across his back almost as if it were an invitation, like the back of an envelope: to open, tear here.

After all these years, she thought "visions of sugar plums" meant candy. It was rather a shock to discover that in her own case, it did not. My, my. Where had this sweet tooth come from?

Beth averted her head, silently cursing herself for a coward. There was nothing wrong with feasting on what the man was dishing up, was there? Nicholas invaded the kitchen, too large, too vibrant to be ignored. She didn't know him, except that somehow Rachael had laid claim to him, and Beth had intimate knowledge of what that entailed. Should she became interested in a man Rachael marked as her own, she would only suffer pain and embarrassment, for she would be the loser.

Her grandmother said something to Nicholas, and he laughed, and responded, but the conversation did not register in Beth's consciousness. The dangling Santas at her ears rustled softly against the sensitive skin of her neck, and although she'd worn them all day, this was the first time she was aware of them. Her nerve endings felt sensitive, alert, alive, a new feeling, one that was vaguely uncomfortable even as it was pleasurable. Beth was ready to pull the string on her Santa pin, watch his eyes glisten, but expected that would be overkill. Nicholas' eyes sparkled with such an incredible degree of electricity anything battery operated would pale.

Beth ached to touch him, and he was close enough that she could. Because she wanted to, because, all things considered she wasn't a coward now, nor had she ever been, she reached her hand out. She had been defending Santa Claus her entire life, and from that, she had realized that she was strong enough to fight for what she believed in, had the courage to defend her convictions, whatever they were. And she had already suffered humiliation at Rachael's hands. One more time wouldn't matter.

He sidled closer. One side of his mouth quirked up in a ready smile, and she knew she'd acted foolishly, that he was very aware she'd placed him on the dinner menu under dessert. The smile hadn't been one of scorn, or one of conquest. And it hadn't been brotherly.

"Excuse me for interrupting." His voice was hot like the burning embers in the coal stove, heating her gurgling hormones to a simmering pitch. The tones wrapped around Beth, dissolving her anger with her grandmother, and her own confusion, replacing it was an unfamiliar emotion. Longing.

Under his gaze, she felt beautiful, was surprised how powerful it made her feel. Like everything else, the definition for that word seemed to have been significantly altered as well. He saw her beauty, deep, inner, harmonious beauty, and that too was like a gift he had given her.

She sought a different feeling to cling to. Not that frustration would be much better, and desperation was out of her league. No, the emotion she sought and greedily grasped onto, was annoyance.

In exaggerated pantomime, as much for her own benefit as for his or her grandmother's, Beth dropped her hands to her hips and stared at him—this time with malicious intent. For good measure she gnashed her teeth. She remembered quite distinctly that Christmas was her providence, and hers alone, especially this year when she needed its rejuvenating magic.

Dimples deepened in both his cheeks and again, as irrational as it seemed, she was certain his eyes twinkled. Like Fourth of July sparklers or blinking Christmas lights, except these emitted intimate and incredibly personal tentacles which zeroed in on her heart. Beth wasn't sure if he were taunting her and she should run—or offering an open invitation—and she should run.

Had she noticed the dimples before? Had his cheeks always been that rosy? It wasn't that warm in the kitchen. He couldn't be flushed, not to the same degree she was.

The world did an extremely surprising thing then. It grew smaller. The kitchen vanished, as did her grandmother and every bit of Pennsylvania, leaving only Nicholas and Beth, standing together, closer than she remembered being to any other man.

She was mesmerized or drugged, but it didn't matter. Beth lifted her hand, finding strength in her trembling arms to actually touch him. It was the boldest thing she'd ever done. But it was not the sensuously dimpled cheeks she was after. No, her aim was only slightly lower.

She touched his lips. Happiness instantly flooded her, and she almost rocked back in shock, almost had to step away, break the contact, but she held firm when she realized it wasn't static electricity per se, but Christmas spirit, a hundred thousand times stronger than anything she'd ever had occasion to call hers. She sensed generosity and compassion and an impression of tradition, but beyond it all, love, unstinting, unselfish, completely exhilarating love.

"I want you to understand," he said, and she was relatively certain he hadn't spoken aloud. Again, her fingertips tingled, as did her heart and the skin on her arms. It felt like she breathed in glitter, and that it made her sparkle from the inside.

"I—um—" she struggled for words. For a heartbeat she looked away, but he was too mesmerizing, and her own desires were too persuasive. *I want you* she almost said. If he read her mind he would know it.

He raised an eyebrow, granting her permission to speak. A hundred images flowed through her mind, a thousand. "You feel like Christmas," she thought. The type of Christmas she always had when the relatives had gone home, when the presents were unwrapped, when there was silence and colored lights and deep-rooted satisfaction. Not the hustle-bustle, holly-jolly panic of Christmas, nor even a child's Christmas, with its magical wonder, but something deeper, more eternal, more solid. He felt like Christmas, and he felt like the piece of *her* Christmas, which had been missing far too long, but which now found, made her complete.

"I am Christmas, or at least a small part of it."

Beth felt adrift, yet could not doubt him. His statement had been a confession or perhaps a testimony. His face was clean-shaven, his hair dark, his lived-in work clothes nothing out of the ordinary, but just for the moment all that changed. His beard grew, his hair lightened, turned white, his outfit—costume? was red, with plush deep enough to bury her fingers. Juxtapositioned over this transient image were other faces, bathed in the eternities, one layered over another, all with the same dedication, the same vocation.

Feeling like a coward or a voyeur, she closed her eyes. She'd never known dizziness could be such a breathtaking sensation. She had tried on a friend's glasses once, the lenses stronger than anything she had ever been exposed to before. That had made her dizzy, had changed the way she looked at things, had made her appreciate the subtle nuances of sight. She was looking through his eyes now, seeing things as he saw them.

"Heaven save me from bad clichés," she muttered, still swaying to visions not her own.

"Beth," he whispered, around her and through her, and deep, deep within her, "just accept."

"I'm afraid," Beth stammered in confusion. Of what she wasn't sure. It certainly wasn't the fear of monsters, or even the more corporal fear that a loved one would be hurt. The sensation was rooted in facing the petty weaknesses she had hidden away, deceit and ignorance and worse, an unexplored wantonness. This man read her soul. Her barriers tumbled before him. There was more than one way to be naked.

"You shouldn't be." His glance softened. The pewter of his eyes adsorbed color, deepened to navy, bottomless and intoxicating. She almost expected condemnation, found instead acceptance, the trace of something she wanted to believe could turn into love. He hadn't made a sound. She knew this because she rested the pads of three of the fingers of her left hand on his lips, and they hadn't discovered any type of movement at all. Still, nothing was reliable. It could be that he spoke, and her fingers lied, when she had always been able to count on their sensitivity before. She rocked babies to sleep with these hands, wiped a fever soaked brow, salted a stew, plucked a fat tomato. Like her eyes, either she couldn't trust them, or her fingers had transversed normality, to a heightened sensitivity.

"How?" she asked, even as a couple more of those investigative questions rattled her brain, what, why, when, where, who.

"This is for us, Beth," he said, and he looked rather pleased with himself, downright smug. Then he shifted, inched back far enough that he broke contact with her flesh, and the world which had been put on hold, was back again, as real and insidious as ever.

She swayed, dizzy, rubbed the taut skin at her temples until she felt the Santa Clauses tingling at her ears, until reality had her grounded once more in non-fiction.

Racks of cookies loitered on the counters, the heavy scent of old-world gingerbread permeated the air. The floor, the air, her cheeks, were warm from heat adsorbed from the coal burning stove. Her grandmother rocked, holding a Christmas card, acting as if nothing unusual, nothing catastrophic had occurred.

Somewhere, way off in the distance she could hear church bells. The possibility arose that she had been dreaming, or that she had done something unpardonable like have a fit of some kind, but her grandmother wasn't alarmed, and Nicholas was back to being Nicholas, with a box on his shoulder and one under his arm, with that delightfully appealing shirt still highlighting muscles she could only anticipate.

"What's all this?" The words were soft, whispered. The arousal slipped back, leaving memories of an encounter so personal it could easily be considered sensual. It was then she realized how much safer it was dealing with third-graders, with family, with tradition which required no courage at all.

He tilted his head toward the boxes, grinned in amusement as if she certainly should know what the familiar cases held. "Christmas lights."

"I can see that. What are they doing here?"

He chuckled, a sound that found its way directly into her heart. Again, she thought he looked familiar, like the Christmas imp who haunted her nights whenever she dreamed of love.

"Your grandmother is graciously allowing me to put these lights up on the roof."

Beth arched one finely plucked eyebrow. "Oh?" The problem was, it made it sound as if Catherine Vacchioni was doing him the favor, instead of the reverse. Beth stole a look at her grandmother, stunned by the changes she noted. Catherine looked ten years younger, livelier, more vital. The woman who had been turning old before her eyes had vanished, leaving a person with a will to live. The wrinkles in her face had softened, and she sat straighter, as if her shoulders didn't pain her, as if the chronic throbbing in her back had eased.

Catherine put a bony arthritic hand out, touching her granddaughter with chilled fingers. Even her skin, which had grown dry and nearly translucent, was pinker, more youthful. "Beth, relax. He's here to help."

Beth turned slowly back toward Nicholas. Her question was in her eyes and her heart.

"I want you to know, whatever you're thinking, that I'm not here to destroy the sacred nature of your Christmas. I really am here to help."

Flustered, Beth mashed a cookie cutter into chilled, rolled dough as she created dozens of cookies. "I've always been able to keep Christmas without any help."

"I know that. In the whole world there probably aren't five people alive who celebrate Christmas with the same selfless dedication that you do. But Beth, regardless about what you've learned about giving, all the great miracles of the season come from sharing. I'd honestly like to share a trace of my Christmas spirit with you, and I'm in desperate need to have you share a little bit of your spirit with me."

He didn't laugh. That would have been too overt, too frivolous for his words that had a tone of prayer about them. She wanted to hug him with warmth and affection and familiarity, and then she wanted to kiss him until that shadow which looked like sadness etched deep within his brow disappeared forever. The intimacy they had shared—or whatever it was—gave her the right.

Since she had been ten years old, nineteen years ago, she had thought love had to be bought and Christmas meant giving, but maybe he had a valid point. Maybe the secret that she had long forgotten involved sharing.

Then with an impish grin which completely broke the mood, he added, "I also came to check up on the cookies."

She stepped back, emotionally more than physically and clutched the heavy white kitchen timer. Less than a minute to go. She would grasp any distraction with desperation and relief. She scooped the formed cookies onto a heavy cookie sheet blackened after decades of use. "I'm in charge now. You don't have to worry."

He inched closer in a move that wasn't invasive so much as it was passionate. His breath tickled her ear and she had never felt quite so responsive to a man's presence.

"I wasn't worried."

She licked her lips, caught her breath, tried to think of something to say in response that didn't sound completely inane. He smelled of pine and ginger and promises, innately, as if these weren't things he had picked up that morning at a tree lot or discovered huddled over a coal burning stove, but which were a part of him since before time began.

And the last one. What did a promise smell like? Sweet and sassy like peppermint. Fragrant and earthy like cinnamon. Warm and familiar like hot chocolate. And in this case, musky and sensual like a man.

The look he gave her when he made eye contact was appreciably different from his earlier ones. It wasn't quite so innocent. And if she thought of a babe when she looked at him, it wasn't the Christ child whose birthday they celebrated this season, but an infant all her own, a piece of her taken and made flesh.

Before she thought he might ask to fill her stockings. Now she was sure he was wondering how to help her out of them. With the way her heart was fluttering, Beth was almost ready to ask.

An ancient, shapeless apron covering her school clothes, a hot pad grasped tightly in her fingers, she opened the oven door, rescued gingerbread cookies on the first ding from the timer. With her free hand, she shoved another tray into the oven's gaping maw. She looked down, surprised. These, by some odd coincidence, were all Santas. Beth had cut them. What could she possibly have been thinking?

"The house will be filled with relatives by the weekend. Someone will get the lights up." Beth cringed at the unfamiliar sharpness in her voice. If anyone needed Scrooge's three unearthly visitors, she did. In the oven, the Santa's would be puffing, baking, their aroma more enticing than the previous batches. She was losing her mind.

Nicholas shifted the boxes with ease. "Your relatives come to celebrate the holiday with family. They should relax with nothing more strenuous then shaking presents in order to guess what secrets they hide. I'll see to the lights."

The rocking chair creaked, below a black and white cat turned figure eights. "It should have been done three weeks ago."

"Gram, you know—"

"That wasn't a condemnation of you, girl, only a reminder that Mr. St. Noel is willing to help. I say we allow him to do his job."

He had felt like Christmas. Yet she was a rational woman. She used her imagination only for encouraging the exceptional creativity nearly all third graders possessed. She would not be taken in, taken over, by repressed emotions.

"You have nothing to worry about, Ms. Anderson. I'm actually very good at my job."

Where in the blazes was that twinkle coming from?

With the flat spatula she liberated cookies from the tray, settling them one at a time on the cooling racks. Reindeer, a church with steeple, stars and bells and sleighs. He hadn't cut a single Santa. She had more than made up for his oversight.

When she looked up, Nicholas had his box hooked on one

hip and was stealing an uniced cookie with an unrepentant gleam, daring her to protest.

Her hackles raised. Her finger pointed. Her mouth opened. She would give Nicholas St. Noel a tongue lashing he'd never forget. "I'm saving those cookies."

He raised a migratory eyebrow.

"I know I only caught you eating one, but I know to the man how many cookies this recipe makes and there are quite a few missing. It's not so much the family I'm worried about, but I leave cookies for Santa, and I'm sure he'll be disappointed if they're all gone."

A hearty roar of laughter interrupted her tirade. "Actually, that's not as much of a problem as you think it is, but if it worries you, I am more than willing to make up another batch."

Her grandmother, too, chuckled. "Beth, leave the man to his work. There are plenty of cookies—for Santa and everyone else."

"Gram—"

Nicholas spoke over his laughter. "Now, if you will excuse me, I have work that I want to get finished before supper."

Hands rested on hips in that superior, snide attitude that she had never once used on her students. "I assure you that it will take longer than that to get those lights up."

Muscles flexed, as did what she read as self-confidence—or flaunting ego. "Oh, I don't think so. I'm somewhat of an expert. I'll get the job done."

"It will be dark in an hour."

"Yes, but it's stopped raining, and they need to be settled in before the snow tonight." Then, taking his box, and licking his fingers, Nicholas disappeared.

"Snow? Tonight? Ha!" Beth felt herself finding comfort in the oddest things, even perversity. "Who in the world does he think he is, Father Christmas?"

"With a name like that, I imagine he does." Catherine took another bite of her hot gingerbread cookie, eating it slowly, as if considering all the repercussions of her actions. "Marzipan, what's got you so upset? I've known you your entire life and I've never seen you bristle like this."

Beth moved to her grandmother's side, touched her frail shoulders, with the bird-like brittle bones. "Oh, Gram, it's everything. I don't know—"

Catherine patted Beth's hand. "You will, child. Believe me, you will."

Beth squatted down beside the old woman, in a position which she had been perfecting over twenty years and which was totally familiar.

"Then you don't remember. I would have thought you would. He was such an important part of your life."

"Nicholas? I don't—" but then memory flashed around her, taking her back through the years. There weren't many children at the bus stop, it was a rural route and the busses made long trips twice a day, but ten year old Beth stood shivering. "I suppose you wrote your letter to Santa Claus," Michael said, a tormentor two grades ahead of her.

Beth saw nothing to be ashamed about in the question. Writing her letter held almost as much excitement for her as did opening presents Christmas morning. "Of course I did."

"Baby, Baby," he taunted sing-song.

"There is no Santa Claus." Rachael had been there, thirteen and already filling out a sweater. Her voice higher, more biting than the others. She figured, perhaps rightly, that Santa only "watched" when adults were around.

Beth had heard this before, of course, but there always had been an adult in the vicinity telling her that it was okay to believe. This time she was on her own.

She stood tall and strong and defiant, a true believer, in spite of overwhelming evidence to the contrary. "Yes, there is. He reads every letter, he delivers the presents." Then she found her face being rubbed into the greasy black snow, and for two weeks she carried a black eye. Still she knew that her faith was being questioned, a faith as primal as anything taught in Sunday school. Even in pain, she wouldn't back down. "Santa is as real as you or I."

Then as if he were an answer to a prayer she hadn't uttered,

Nicholas appeared, defended her honor, picked up her scattered school books, then told her that there was a Santa Claus. After that they became fast friends, the ten year old girl, the boy who had to be at least fifteen. He'd meet her at the bus stop, walk her home. He had built a snowman with her once, helped her decide on Christmas gifts over long walks in winter twilight. And she remembered why she had blocked the memory. She saw him one final time, in a dream, although then she swore she was awake, that it was reality and not her subconscious desires brought to life. No, simply because she had a crush developed in pure innocence, that didn't make him Santa Claus.

Beth rubbed her eyes, slipping back from her memory. "I do remember." She would apologize for the things she said, the things she thought. And she would go upstairs, rifle through her Santa collection, find her favorite, the one she was certain Santa had given her, even if at the time he had been a boy of fifteen.

***

Marlett paced back and forth muttering under his breath. His wife Callie watched indulgently while she organized decades of Christmas ideas from more than four different Santas. Seeing no hypocrisy in the thought, she honestly believed each one was her favorite. She handed a box, overflowing with half-finished projects to her husband. "Carry that out to the workshop, will you? I'll deal with it later."

"Workshop? Are you daft woman? Nicholas will need these things."

The smile that crossed her lips was one of woman's knowledge, the kind Marlett suspected he'd never be able to decipher. "Yes, he will. But I doubt he'll be needing them in the master bedroom for the next little while."

Marlett accepted the box, set it down about six feet from where it had rested and continued his pacing. Callie, like all Christmas elves, had never learned to swear, but there were times when she could certainly appreciate the need.

The dust on the headboard was probably three years thick,

deep enough to plant potatoes, some former Mrs. Claus would have mentioned, although she couldn't remember for sure which one. "This room hasn't been cleaned since before the last Santa died," she said, arching her back, trying to straighten out a kink.

"We've had too much to do to clean, and we still are too far behind for this folderol. Work is backing up. Come to the workshop."

Callie resumed dusting. This current Santa was like all the others—he wouldn't notice dust if he had to shovel it, and it was just about thick enough that he needed to.

"After I clean. If you're not going to help, could you settle somewhere? That carpet is only slightly younger than you are, and I would rather not have to replace it this close to Christmas."

Bells, sewn into booties, jingled. "Carpet? The world is coming to an end and you're worried about carpet?"

She continued polishing the large cherrywood wardrobe with lemon oil, her slightly out of focus reflection shining back at her. "The world isn't coming to an end. And if you'd think like a woman instead of a man, you'd know why I'm worried about the house."

"Christmas is at the end of the week. Nicholas is rebelling. Who do you think is going to drive the sleigh? Me?"

"You could, if it came down to that. But don't worry, Santa will be here. He always is."

Marlett grabbed a handful of beard and tugged. He didn't grimace, even when a dozen crinkly strands separated from his chin. "Yes, but we've never had a Santa like this one. Have you considered what the next few years will be like if he takes after his mother?"

"I always liked Lorraine. Still, how could she—how could anyone—not like Christmas?" Frustration merged with confusion, giving her polishing arm extra strength. "Nicholas won't recognize this place when he returns."

Marlett humphed. He'd been hanging around the reindeer so long he'd begun to sound like them. "What do you mean, if I'd think like a woman?"

"He'll be bringing back a bride, won't he? She'll need this place clean. We've been so blasted busy with Christmas that the cobwebs in the barn are thick enough to use as packing material."

Marlett humphed, thought, considered, humphed again. "He's bringing back a bride?"

Callie laughed. "Isn't that why he left?"

"He left because he was frustrated—"

"Of course he's frustrated. You'd be too, if you had to sleep in that gigantic old bed by yourself. Now don't you have some preparations to oversee?"

"Preparations? Yes, I have preparations. That's why I need you in the workshop. If Nicholas doesn't come back—"

"Scrubbing the reindeer barn," Callie said. "And when you finish that, you might try rounding up some helpers to mop the floor in the workroom."

"The floor in the workroom? I can't even find the floor in the workroom. I only know that it's under some snippets of ribbon and bits of wrapping paper—"

"And sawdust and mismatched wagon wheels and heavens only knows what else. It's about time the floor was mopped."

"Four days from Christmas?"

Callie nodded. "Do you think you'll have any more time four days after Christmas?" Before he could answer, she continued. "There had better be more than a few elves mopping or they'll answer to me."

"I'm the head elf around here—" he said, but even while the words flowed from his mouth with such profound superiority, he knew by the not so subtle tap to her foot, just what exactly he could do with his head-elf title.

Humbled, chastised, he lowered his eyes. "If you need me, I'll be in the barn. After that, I'll oversee the cleaning of the workroom."

"Good. And Marlett—"

"Yes?"

"There's no need to make a present for her. Nicholas will do that. He doesn't realize it yet, but he's got the gift."

CHAPTER 6

"Oh, good, I haven't missed dinner." Rachael slipped in the back door, made herself at home while opposite her, Beth put the platter of sliced roast on the table. "You usually eat so ungodly early."

Beth bit her tongue as she bit back caustic comments and set another place at the table. There was enough food. Over the years she had gotten used to cooking for unexpected relatives. Not that it mattered much. Rachael, keeping her figure, wasn't likely to eat more than a bite or two.

"Where's Nicholas?" her tone was honey sweet. Nicholas had been conspicuous by his absence for the past hour.

"I suppose I'm going to have to call him." Beth removed her apron, subtly pleased for this additional excuse to get her dander up.

With bones that creaked as loud as the rocking chair moaned, Catherine stood slowly. "Try out the front door. I'm sure that's where I heard him last."

"What?"

"Don't give me that look, Marzipan. I may be getting old, but there is nothing wrong with my hearing."

"Oh, all right." Beth climbed the stairs, certain she was wasting her time until she noted the glow of Christmas lights through the sheer curtains which fronted the living room windows. Beth opened the front door and stepped onto the porch where she stood speechless. Not only was her three story Victorian was festooned with Christmas lights, Nicholas was climbing down the ladder with a job-well-done smirk.

"You did all this?"

"Of course. I told you I would."

"It usually takes an entire weekend. Santa and all his elves couldn't do this in two hours."

He chuckled again, holding the door open for her to reenter the warmth of the house. "Actually, Santa could probably handle it all by himself."

"But how did you manage?"

"I have some experience climbing around rooftops."

"Have you worked in construction?" Beth asked.

"Only in building miracles."

He left her to wash his hands before she could decipher his meaning and she was certain she heard him whistle *'It's beginning to look a lot like Christmas'* with a joy and a vitality which hadn't been present before.

"So where have you been, Nicholas, since we saw you last?" Rachael asked as she freshened her lipstick. She had toyed with the food on her plate, eating only a bite here, a swallow there, while Beth and Nicholas had feasted heartily.

If he had been surprised to see Rachael, he hadn't made any comment. "Up north."

"Maine? Vermont?" Catherine prodded, with a look in her sharp eyes not at Nicholas, but at Beth. Beth had been far too quiet the past half hour, and Rachael had manipulated the conversation for far too long.

"No, further than that."

"Canada?"

He shrugged his shoulders, wiped his mouth with a napkin that someone had embroidered with a small counted cross stitch Santa in one corner. "There abouts."

"So what are you doing in Pennsylvania?"

"Trying to find a home for a present."

"I beg your pardon?" Beth asked.

"I meant, looking up old friends." The look, specifically, was meant for her. Rachael noticed, leaned closer. She had changed her clothing. This dress showed not quite as much thigh, but plenty of cleavage.

"Do you have any family around here?"

"Beth," Rachael said interrupting, "it's obvious Nicholas isn't going to tell you, so I will."

"Tell me what?"

"Do you know Hello Noel?" Rachael mentioned a trendy store found in almost every mall across the country. Hello Noel sold imported linens and drapes, curios and knickknacks, antiques and potpourris, and hidden in the back of every store, where it could be almost overlooked, was a Christmas section, stocked year round with holiday memorabilia. A shopper could find modern lights and ornaments, but the stores were famous for antique decorations, some priced high enough to rival the cost of a small car, but all breathtakingly beautiful. It was Beth's favorite store, even if there was never anything there she could afford. She liked to slide through the crowded aisles, especially in July when Christmas seemed so far away, and cherish the traces of Christmas displayed beside Lladro and Hummel figurines.

"What about Hello Noel?"

"Nicholas' mother is the sole owner. You remember, don't you, when they were here nineteen years ago, that she was planning on opening an antique store? Well, it took off."

"Is that true?"

"Yeah. Mom travels. Visiting her stores keeps her happy. Beth, the dinner was delicious. You are an excellent cook." Elves, on the whole, didn't cook beef, although, now that he thought about it, he had no idea at all what they did cook.

Rachael leaned over, draped a possessive arm around his shoulders. Beth, uncharitably, thought it would take a bathroom plunger to get her unstuck.

With far more finesse than she would have expected, Nicholas extricated himself from Rachael's headlock, then stood, stacking plates. Rachael moved in for the assault. "Oh, Nickie, no. Don't do that. Beth's used to cleaning up. Let her do it. You can take me shopping."

From powers developed from his hereditary profession, Nicholas knew exactly what kind of present she had in mind and he wasn't interested. "I've got a lot to do tonight. I planned to help decorate the tree."

"That wouldn't be as fun as shopping with me."

"I like decorating trees. It's one of my favorite Christmas activities."   "But Nickie, I could show you things."

That thought made him shiver. He had never been particularly fond of one night stands, although he'd had his share of them over the past few years. He brought his dishes to the sink. With his back to the three women, Nicholas tightened his eyes and thought for a minute. A second later the telephone rang.

Beth picked it up, listened for a moment before she handed the receiver to Rachael.

"I shouldn't have done that," Nicholas said, as he continued clearing the table.

"Done what?" Beth asked, while Rachael slammed the phone down then muttered words an elf would never use.

"There's been a leak in the sprinkler system," Rachael said. "It dripped all over the Christmas menagerie. Things have had to be moved. Everything is a disaster."

"Oh?" Nicholas asked, not so much unconcerned as not surprised.

Rachael pouted prettily. "You want to go with me and survey the damage? We could stop later, get a drink, so the whole evening won't be wasted."

"No. I'm going to help here."

"You're welcome to help when you get finished at the store," Beth offered to her cousin charitably.

Rachael growled but said nothing, although her look needed little interpretation. It said, *I'll be back and it won't be to help. Keep your hands off him. He's mine.* With that, Rachael buttoned her leather coat and vanished out the back door.

"What did you mean, you shouldn't have done that? Did you sabotage her sprinkling system?"

Nicholas shrugged, started filling the sink. "It really might be an improvement," Beth said. "Those decorations really would look much better if she'd just move them around a little bit." She was imaging things. He wouldn't have sabotaged the sprinkler system. He couldn't have. Yet...

Nicholas opened the refrigerator and wedged the milk and a jar of mustard pickle in. She was getting too close to an off-limits area. Time for a little misdirection. "Just who exactly is going to eat all this food? Your grandmother doesn't eat more than a few bites and I can't see you eating all this."

"The rest of the family will. Believe me, it will all be gone before long and this refrigerator will have to be refilled several times before they all leave."

"How many are there to your family?"

Beth shrugged, strangely in no hurry to leave the table or to take her customary place at the sink. "At last count, a billion."

"Fairly high number of relatives."

"And those are just the ones who are directly related to Gram."

He was back at the table, lemon-scented dish soap bubbles clinging to his wrists. Catherine moved to a rocking chair closer to the fire, uprooting a black and white cat.

"At Thanksgiving, this place is unbelievable. At Christmas it's even worse. We have to serve in three separate sittings."

"Have all the rest moved away?"

"Most of them, yes."

"Are your parents still alive?" he asked.

"My mom is. She lives upstate New York."

While he washed, Beth could not sit idly by. She dug out the old mixer from the bottom cabinet, it weighed nearly as much as she did, and started measuring powdered sugar, vanilla, cream, butter, food coloring. The icings took form under her capable hands. By the time Nicholas was finishing up the roasting pan, and wiping down the tables and the cookie sheets, she was stuffing the bag ready to pipe icing.

She turned to face him, her eyes wide with innocent questioning. "Why is Christmas always crazy?"

"Why are you asking me?" Unexpectedly, Beth thought she heard the undercurrent of annoyance.

"No particular reason," she lied, hiding her desperation to know. Although her hands shook, icing oozed with an artist's deft strokes. Bow ties. Buttons. Boots. He played Santa Claus. He felt like Christmas. Something inside of her recognized an answering reflection in him. "You're available, aren't you?"

Available. Nicholas rolled his eyes. If she only knew.

She could hear time passing, the ticking of the grandmother

clock on the mantle or the inexorable beating of her own heart. He shifted and she doubted he'd answer if she didn't prod him one more time.

"Nicholas, why is Christmas always so crazy?"

He groaned, low, yet on another level, fought with sexuality. Lions, she knew, growled when they mated.

"I've given it a lot of thought. It's, um, one of the great mysteries of the universe I guess. My mother hates Christmas."

Beth smiled slowly, sadly, lowered her chin as if she wore a heavy blanket of shame. "So does mine."

"There's no one easy answer to your question. What makes Christmas crazy for you, is not necessarily what makes Christmas crazy for me." He shrugged, tried to remember lessons his father taught him about giving and dedication and devotion. Sad though, especially considering who his father was, that Nicholas could only remember these quiet talks on beaches somewhere, or in remote hotels or grocery stores where they had stolen a few minutes to talk while waiting for a shop clerk to ring up bananas and Hostess Cup cakes. For Santa Claus, Christmas was particularly crazy.

"For most people Christmas is an excuse to do good. Whether or not it's true, most people think of themselves as selfish the entire year, so this one season, this one day, they try to make up for the oversight. It's sort of an atonement for not having the time to make homemade cookies the rest of the year, an apology for being sharp in the mornings or for missing all those baseball games."

She startled, felt tears bubble at the corner of her eyes. She didn't keep a diary, so how could he have her so clearly pegged? How naked was she in front of him? Rachael didn't know. Her grandmother wouldn't have told, even if she suspected. She was raw, and if the blood was close to the surface now, it was only so she could bleed.

One fat tear dropped, slatted. Beth tightened her lids. "You think people need an excuse to do good?"

He looked toward a fat puffed gingerbread Santa. She had piped red and white icing, highlighting a bulky suit with buttons, a rotund figure, a laughing, innocent mentality, but it was only caricature, and had no basis in reality.

"Many people need an excuse."

Beth considered, analyzed, fretted over her own motivations. "Then it's all based on guilt."

Behind her, Nicholas wrapped warm, supportive palms on her shoulders. She shuddered with an unexpected chill, then leaned against his warmth. "No, I didn't mean to imply that, but I think a great deal of holiday-hyperactivity is. Of course, as with any answer, it's far too simplistic to call it solely guilt." He doubted his father dealt much with guilt, but then, there was always the relationship between him and his mother. Perhaps there had been guilt there. What about his grandfather? The other Santa Clauses? The legend itself. That wasn't guilt, it was altruism—the sacrifice of one, so that others could survive. Wasn't it?

"I think it's no coincidence Christmas happens at the end of the year. We realize we're older, that the kids are changing, that the family, by whatever definition is current, is in continual flux, and that in another week we've got to start a new calendar."

"Gather ye rosebuds while ye may."

"Laugh, but it makes sense, doesn't it?"

"What about love? Where does that fit in?"

Nicholas shook his head, wished he could stop her tears with magic or insight or a package brightly wrapped. "I don't know. As a child I thought that with love anything was possible and while I don't exactly disbelieve that, I know love by itself is not a static emotion. Too many other feelings play a role. Many parents have this almost primal need not to become their parents, and then at Christmas, the rules change, and that's exactly what they want. They need things to be the same, the anticipation, the pleasure, and especially the memories."

Beth found herself teetering as if she'd had too much to drink, or far too much to think about. He would ask her then about her secret, her shame, and she would tell him, and then he wouldn't be able to love her for she was unlovable. He would go back to Rachael, and find whatever it was he needed there, and she would be alone again, left with nothing but an unfailing belief in Santa Claus, and an impossible mission to make the world all right all by herself.

Her scars would never heal. She was a fool to think they could. And then she came back to her senses, found she was in his arms, and it was warm and comforting, and on another level, frightening simply because it was so warm and unexpected. The silence felt, as silence often did, as if it had been around too long and had grown old.

"Shhh," he whispered against her hair which smelled of peaches. "Nothing's happening here."

Beth doubted that was true. She was curled around a man, a man she didn't know, who was as familiar to her as the boy she had once befriended.

The phone rang before she had the time to do anything foolish and they broke the embrace. She left the kitchen to answer the heavy black phone with a rotary dial, a relic from another era.

"Beth, dear, I'm afraid I have some rather bad news."

Her mother's voice brought an immediate ache to the pit of her stomach. She rubbed her eyes, thought of guilt, of craziness, of abandonment. "What?"

"I'm afraid I won't be able to make it to your pageant after all. I'm rather bogged down here."

She would have been far more able to handle this conversation if she hadn't just bared her soul to Nicholas. "You said this year for sure. Mom, Jamie's going to be in the pageant. If you won't come for me, at least come for him."

"You know I would if I could."

"Ok, sure." Disappointment rattled her bones.

"Beth?" Nicholas stood in the doorway from the kitchen, clearly apologetic, as if he didn't want to intrude. She looked down, realized she still held the phone receiver in her hands, that it was beeping, repeating that "If you wish to make a call, please hang up..." monologue. She set the phone down, blinked, smiled, blinked.

"Can I help you?"

She shook her head slowly, sadly, the universal, no-I'm-alright-I-can-handle-this gesture, too bruised to speak. She was an adult. It shouldn't hurt. She should be over this, and for most of the year she was. By New Year's she was fine. By Valentine's Day she had forgotten all about it. Not once during the summer, during the fall term at school, did a stray thought cross her mind, that her mother didn't love her, that there was nothing she could do, no matter how hard she tried to pull her life back together and make the family she wanted.

"Please, I just need to be alone. I'll be in to finish the cookies in a minute."

"No, I don't think you should." Before she could protest, before she could develop a hard shell and a smile that he wouldn't be able to see through, Nicholas wrapped his arms around her and gently, softly cuddled her. Beth accepted the embrace as if she were ten, as no one but her Grandmother had ever cuddled her, unless she counted Jamie and a score of other children whose lives had touched hers over the years.

"I'm not going to cry." And she wouldn't have, if he hadn't been so sympathetic. He held her, only a few minutes, but long enough for the healing to start, and she dampened his shirt with tears that she had been storing for nearly two decades.

He waited until her breathing regulated, until he felt her gaining control. Nicholas was glad he had sent Rachael away, for if she had been here, Beth would have coped, as she had always coped, decorating her cookies and refortifying the walls she had built around her and he never would have known what was broken deep inside of her.

"Do you want to talk about it?"

"No."

And with her head still pressed gently against his chest, Nicholas closed his eyes, concentrated, called on the intuition which he had at his command.

"Beth, I'm willing to listen."

"I'm sorry, first Jamie dumps all that I'm-dying agony on you, and Rachael barrels in here like her pants are on fire, and now me, falling apart. Are you sure you wouldn't rather go upstairs and find a good book to read?"

"Beth, I could feel your pain from the kitchen, and it

wouldn't be any less intense if I were a mile away. I really would like to help or baring that, at least listen."

They stood in the formal dining room, a large room off the kitchen which was only used for state occasions, Christmas, Easter, the blessing of another great-grandchild. A trace of light escaped from the staircase from upstairs and a little bit more entered from the crack where the kitchen door stood ajar, but basically they were entwined in darkness.

"I always was able to tell my problems to you," she said, knowing it a cliché but feeling better already. As younger versions of themselves, they had talked for hours, comforting discussions of poetry and the placement of the stars and which gift her grandmother would prefer.

"Yes. We were always able to share." He hadn't been quite so open with her. "That Christmas," he prompted. "You were here, and the rest of your family was still in New York."

She should have known that he would dig to the root of the problem immediately. That he would remember, even then, that something hadn't been right. Still, it was a surprise that the words she had hidden for so long came so easily.

"My parents were having problems with their marriage. They separated almost immediately after Christmas and although the divorce didn't come through for some time, I think the marriage was over then."

Released from his hold, she sat on a high-backed chair, shoulders slumped, fingers knotted together between her knees, feeling his nearness as if he still held her. "They...um...sent me down here to be with Gram."

Not her two brothers, he knew. Not her two sisters. Only her. At the time it had been an adventure. She had been a "big girl" and the treat hadn't been extended to the others. She had loved her family, but had cherished the quality time with her grandmother, with the relatives who lived locally.

"I had the best Christmas of my life. There was you, of course, even if you did spend most of your time with Rachael, but I got to help with the stove, with wrapping the presents, with preparing dinner. Everybody came for Christmas, but in many respects, I had been given my present early, time with my grandma. Then, right after the holidays, everything changed. Dad moved out. Mom said I was too much of a handful. She left me here." The baby, Ronald, had been eighteen months, Susan, only five. "As the middle child I wasn't considered old enough to be left alone, nor young enough to need watching over. Mom kept the rest of the kids and left me here."

"I'm sure she didn't mean to abandon you. She wanted you to be happy. The younger children would have been too much for your grandmother to handle, and she needed the older ones to help with the housework."

"But I was able to do the housework. I helped."

"I'm sure you did."

"I remember it all so clearly. Christmas day I told Mom I had seen Santa Claus, and she yelled, told me to stop acting like a baby. She made it sound as if I lied."

So, that one finite moment had as much of an effect on her life as it had on his. "Beth, I'm sorry—" It was his own clumsiness which had caused the problems in her family. He was responsible. This sin was on his soul.

"No, Nicholas, there's no need for you to apologize for my mother. I'm sure you're right. I'm sure she thought she was doing the best she could. The divorce was traumatic. She couldn't handle all of us. Getting rid of me probably made sense to her. It's not as if she tossed me out on the streets, not as if I didn't love it here with my grandma."

"She never 'got rid' of you. She only made choices—"

"Oh, yes she did. And she still can't face me after nineteen years. No matter what I do, she has no time for me. She's never been proud of me. Not once. Not when I got my degree, not when I see to it that the family gets Christmas."

"Beth, why Christmas?"

Tears fell fresh over a quivering smile which made her look so vulnerable, so whipped. "Sometimes I wonder if deep inside somewhere I keep thinking if I do it all right, the baking and the presents and the decorations that she'll ask me to come home."

"Your home is here."

"I know. It was a figure of speech. I want her to say, Beth, you've done all right, or Beth, I knew I could count on you, or even, heaven forbid, how many times I've dreamed this one, Beth, I wish I'd never let you go. I need you so much—"

Gently Nicholas raised her to her feet and he held her again, although this time it took longer for the tears to pass, because in her confession, she had left herself shattered. "And that's why I do it all by myself. I have to, don't you see?"

A little girl's ache, trapped in a woman's body for nineteen years. And he had been instrumental in creating the vortex which had swept her so low.

"Beth—"

"No, Nicholas. See, I'm better all ready. We've got to get back or those cookies will never be finished." She walked for the door, but she didn't open it, when it only would have taken a push. "Nicholas?"

"Yes?"

"You did something back there, didn't you?"

He thought she meant the past, the time when he had been a boy, masquerading as a child's fantasy, an interloper in a job that shouldn't exist to begin with. It was not a confession he could make. Not now. Not when the embarrassment was fresh and his wounds reopened. By the tree he had told her he was Santa, and an hour ago he had told her he was Christmas, but those testimonies mocked him now, made him ashamed.

"Something to make me talk. Something you did."

"Is that possible?" he hedged, feeling relieved.

"No, I guess not. Still..."

"Are you two all right in there?" Catherine called.

"Yes, Grandma," Nicholas called, using a relationship he had no claim to.

"Enjoy yourselves," she said.

Nicholas laughed, and although it was far too dark to see if Beth blushed, he heard her moan. "We intend to," he called to the old woman, "as soon as we get our clothing all organized."

Beth swatted in his general direction, pleased, and somehow not healed exactly, but cleansed. "You've just ruined my reputation."

"No." In the dark, she thought she saw him wiggle his eyebrows. "I've enhanced it." As Nicholas pushed the door open, he looked as if he had been granting royal favor. And because of his smug self-conceit, Beth laughed and the pain which had been building around her mother's betrayal vanished, and left her mood light.

She hummed while she worked on her cookies, and realized something that surprised her. While she loved Christmas and enjoyed all the massive preparations that went into each and every long standing tradition, she had also come to resent it. Now, with Nicholas, or maybe it was simply that she wasn't alone, she could relax, enjoy, savor. Her song was less forced. Her Christmas spirit was returning.

Nicholas dug through the spices until he found the decorations she would need, the three different kinds of colored sugar sprinkles, the silver balls, the cinnamon dots. While Beth iced, Nicholas decorated, turning the cookies into masterpieces. One could almost say he had a 'gift.'

Beth set the icing tube down and fluffed the bangs which had fallen over her eyes. "I've never had that job go quite so quickly before."

"We've only finished half." His smile took life on only one side, but was all the more endearing because of it.

"We can do the rest tomorrow."

"Good idea. Are you ready to trim the tree?"

She looked at her watch. "I don't know. It's late. Maybe we should wait." But she hadn't been sleeping. And she wouldn't be able to sleep until the tree was decorated.

"It's important to me, Beth."

It was to her, too. "All right." She set the piping bag on the counter by the sink and followed him up the stairs all the while wondering if he had done something to make her tell the secrets she had guarded for years.

CHAPTER 7

Nicholas settled his hands on his hips and the noise which escaped his lips sounded surprisingly like a growl. From her position on the couch, a distance of less than three feet, Beth considered her options then broke out in peals of laughter. She covered her mouth with hands in a delayed effort not to wake her grandmother, but that only served to make her giggle all the harder.

Denim stretched taut as he shifted, rising to his full height, dragging a strand of Christmas lights which couldn't have been in worse shape had a troop of Weebelos used them as practice for their knot-tying merit badges.

"It's not that funny."

She wiped her eyes, her giggles drifting into a sense of Christmas contentment. "I'm sure you're right. It's not, but I think this clearly falls under the category of 'If you could only see yourself—'"

"It's a matter of pride," he said, renewing his growl. But he didn't look at the tangled wire, instead he locked his glance with hers, his pewter irises darkened in the shadowy room light, looking both gray and mesmerizing. "I am an expert."

Beth lowered her gaze, sating a hunger far beyond her own ability to control, watching the perfect symmetry of his body. From crawling around on the roof, the knees of his jeans were stained, the material thinner than she was certain it had been when she met him beside the Christmas tree. Worse, he had caught his hip on something sharp, a nail perhaps, which had torn a small triangular shaped opening through the material, leaving a tantalizing image of the firmly muscled flesh of his upper thigh. Her heart flipped, turned, fought something that was a magnitude or two stronger than butterflies.

"An expert?" She swallowed, wondered why her lips felt so dry and her palms so moist. "In knots?"

"In Christmas. Are you sure—"

She suspected he was going to ask about the merit badge, but from the resulting stammer, Beth gauged the statement to be a romantic form of ineptitude.

"I told you it was likely to be quite a challenge."

A challenge. Like becoming attracted to a man Rachael had already set her sights on. Beth wiggled her feet which were curled up underneath her. On one level she was concentrating on the papers she was correcting, on every other, she was extremely cognizant of Nicholas, up to and including his breathing. The more frustrated he grew, the stronger her pleasure.

Haloed in seventy-five watt brightness to help her decipher young scrawlings, Beth had all the light she needed, but Nicholas had lit candles around the living room, for atmosphere, she decided, and the flickering light provided him with a ruddy complexion which was forcing the math test to take second place.

"I am willing to help." For dramatic purposes only, she prepared to set her schoolwork aside. They'd been over this ground before and it wasn't likely he had changed his mind.

"No, I can manage this by myself."

In addition to the growl he started mumbling words, which were not snatches from '*Joy to the World*,' the song he had been singing only minutes before. Thus far he'd tried everything just short of brute force.

Beth decided it had to be one of those guy things, the hunt and conquer mentality which said no mere string of electrical wire was going to come off victorious in a battle of wits with him. She had two brothers who felt the same way when faced with such daunting prospects of changing the oil or opening a bag of pretzels.

"What's this? More evidence?" His look darkened and a homicide detective wouldn't have treated a smoking gun any differently.

In hands lined with experience, Nicholas cupped a small, familiar object. With a startled cry, Beth jumped to retrieve the pacifier. Their hands met, touched briefly. As if the contact opened a conduit to his deepest thoughts, she felt she could read his private images. A baby suckling, yet it wasn't a pacifier, nor a bottle's nipple. Her breasts felt full, heavy, the tips hard and straining.

And, whether or not she had actually read his mind, she felt instinctively that he had insight into hers—and the wanton desires that burned hotter than candle flame. She babbled, uselessly, as if her words would cool her fevered flesh. "So that's where it went. I wish I'd known that last year. It's Sarah Catherine's, one of the littler members of the family, and it was her favorite. I think she cried for three weeks when it turned up missing."

He looked, somehow, vindicated and the pressure which had been building up between them, which had nothing to do with what they were talking about, eased slightly. "You see? I told you these lights were maleficent."

"Yes, of course," Beth agreed with a false chuckle, both relieved and disappointed. "We should have seen that sooner."

She stretched back on the couch and left him to his trial, occasionally smirking, continually fascinated with the byplay of testosterone and wire. Her grandmother had gone off to bed almost an hour before, and Christmas—whatever it was which made it a living, vibrant entity and not a multi-media event—had slipped all around her and lodged, firmly and completely in her heart. Whoever he was, this handyman and part-time Santa her grandmother had invited into their home, she was very grateful to him for that.

"The lights that went up on the roof were perfectly preserved," Nicholas said, making it an accusation. "There had to be fifteen or twenty strands and not one snarl."

Beth double checked her answer key to be certain eight times five was actually forty. Her brain had stopped functioning sometime before. "That makes sense."

Nicholas rocked back on his heels and held her with his gaze. A private glance, one, she thought ended with a question mark. Heat rose to her cheeks. In the glow his—what other word was there for it—intimacy? her brain turned to stuffing.

"What are we talking about?"

He chuckled, a resonant ho, ho, ho, which did not so much break the mood as enliven it. "Christmas lights. You were about to tell me why the fact that they're snarled makes sense, and in return I'll tell you if I'm going to let you live or torture you to death."

In a moment, considering body responses, hers and his, she was about to request the torture. Beth swallowed, blinked, shook her head. She'd always found the safest course, and it was safer, much safer, to answer the question he'd vocalized and not the one his body language posed.

"The men take down the outside lights, in a sort of male bonding ritual. The children take down the inside lights. You see, there's always left over candy canes, brownies, other treats only the most intrepid and aggressive of the kids can find."

Beth had to get up and move before she did something totally unconscionable, like melt. As a ploy or an escape, the movement was wasted. Nicholas, with his grace and his strength slid up behind her, touching her with nothing but the sweet warmth of his breath and the promise of tenderness.

"Someday I'd like to be the one who discovers all your hidden treats."

She waved her hands in exasperation. "Brownies. We're talking about brownies."

His voice was seductive. Sinful. "I know what we're talking about Beth. You do too."

Beth shut her eyes, dreaming. She could rock back an inch, maybe less, feel the strength of his body. She could, if a strong line of self-preservation hadn't been bred into her. "Someone has to do it."

"Do what?" he asked, answering her whisper, which might have only sounded in her head.

"I hate taking down the tree. Of all the activities having to do with Christmas, the ones I hate the most involve packing the ornaments away, admitting that the season is over. Next year always seems so far away."

He rubbed a clean shaven chin, gnawed the inside of his cheek. "You'd have Christmas every day of the year?"

Her breath caught. "Yes."

"Are you sure this doesn't have anything to do with guilt? With your mother?"

Eyes met eyes. Funny, why when it was the wire which was

knotted did her stomach felt so confused? "No, beyond everything else, I like Christmas. What it is. What it could be, how it makes me feel."

He shifted, rocking from foot to foot, making the tiny hairs on her arms reach out, striving for his touch.

"And is there some reason the children deliberately secure all the light clips to other strands?"

She lowered her lashes, inhaled slowly, exhaled on a sigh. "Fun?" This time she was the one to drop the question mark. Beth shut her eyes for just one second, allowed the tensions accumulated over the months to drain from her, slowly. There were a thousand things she had to do, responsibilities which crowded her, but for the moment, she couldn't remember one.

She raised her lips, preparatory for a kiss, but he had other plans. "Beth, giving shouldn't involve pain. It should be based on love." His words touched her in a hollow ache she had kept empty for nearly two decades. With his arms wrapped around her, with his strength and his belief, she wanted to fill the void with hope and compassion. She raised her chin. Her lips parted. She could feel him, sense him, moving closer.

When the doorbell rang, she jerked back, wide-eyed and stunned—not from the interruption, but from what might have happened if it hadn't.

Nicholas stepped back, giving her space, but also non-verbally telling her that their conversation wasn't finished, that he would discover all her secrets. The thought no longer terrified her.

Beth flicked on the porch light, opened the heavy outer panel, gasped as she watched fat white flakes drift down in flagrant non-concern. The snow picked up the colors from the Christmas lights on her house, and those glimmering on her neighbors' homes. A pristine scene, one covering old scars of the gray nondescript winter day with a fresh coating of red and green renewal. She looked out, and bent, meeting the child at eye-level. "Jamie, what are you doing here this late?"

Beth ushered the small bundle into the living room, unbuttoned the snow parka from her nephew, removed hat, scarf, mittens, sweater, until she had unburied the waif.

She squatted beside him, tweaked his button nose between index and middle finger, a light, familiar teasing which curled the edges of his lips toward his tousled hair. "Jamie, you silly elf, what were you trying to do, catch cold?"

Color settled on his cheeks, the red, blustery hue of exposure, but his hands were warm, and there was no hint of fever to his forehead. He looked brighter than normal, as if an image stolen out of time, a movie special effect. No, that wasn't it, not exactly. It was more as if he were surrounded by angels and although she couldn't see them, they lent him their light and he basked in their reflected glory.

She led him to the couch, sat beside him, holding his frail, trembling hands. Nicholas had disappeared, returned almost immediately with milk and a small bowl of applesauce which he had heated in the microwave and sprinkled with cinnamon. How he knew, she didn't dare guess, but although the boy was underweight, they weren't allowed to give him much sugar, and the applesauce she had canned herself and had nothing but the natural sweeteners inherent in the fruit.

He accepted the bowl gravely, allowed Nicholas to set the milk glass down on the end table. "Some'in's funny at home."

"Funny?" Beth asked, trying to modulate her voice while her heart strangled her throat. Part of the sparkle, the unusual brightness to his eyes, was moisture. "What do you mean?"

"Mom and dad, together, talking. Mom's crying."

She stood, was half-way to her coat. "I'll go over there."

The boy pulled her back with only a word. "No. They're working it out. That's what they told me, they're working it out. But I had to see you, Aunt Beth. Just for a minute. Then I'm going right straight to bed."

"Your folks know you're here?"

"Yup. They said it would be all right, for a minute."

"What couldn't wait on such a cold night?" Nicholas' voice, low and raspy and so very seductive, was filled with genuine concern for the boy. Jamie tilted his head, and looked at him long

and hard as if he recognized him and couldn't place him. After Beth
made the introductions, the quizzical expression on the child's face
didn't ease, but he accepted Nicholas as he might accept Clark Kent,
all the while knowing the truth.

"Would you tell me the story, Aunt Beth? About the first
time you saw Santa Claus?"

It was not what she expected, but considering the various
topics that his parents might be discussing, it was a far easier
question than she could have anticipated. "Jamie, you know that
story by heart."

"I'd really like to hear it again."

Beth reached over, pulled him onto her lap. He went
willingly. She was a hugger. She craved touch, especially a child's
love. He snuggled down against her, nestling against her breasts.
"The story of how I met Santa, huh?"

"Yup."

"And nothing else will do?"

"Nope. Nothing. Not the Grinch or the Polar Express or even
the Night Before Christmas. I want the true story."

From the corner of her eyes, she witnessed movement, and
watched Nicholas, who looked as if he were planning an escape. His
hands were buried deep within his pockets and he looked away,
strangely enough, embarrassed. "I'll go...um...check the downstairs."

Beth turned her head slightly, familiar with the sensation of
disbelief. "Be my guest, but you're welcome to stay."

"It sounds like a private matter, between you and Jamie."

Jamie piped up. "You need to hear the story too. I think you
could learn something from it."

"Because I play Santa at a store?"

Jamie's expression of supreme disbelief was almost Nicholas'
undoing. He expected the boy to blurt out his version of childish
wisdom, "No, silly, because you're Santa Claus and it was you she
saw," but instead he said something far more devastating. "No,
because it's the truth, and whenever you learn truth, really learn it
and not just been exposed to it, you've captured a little bit of life you
can keep forever and no one can take away from you. It's like a gift

making you more than you were, more than you thought you could be."

Beth, apologetic, turned to Nicholas. "It's what I tell the kids when I'm trying to teach them multiplication. It doesn't necessarily apply to Santa Claus."

"Yet Santa Claus is the truth," Jamie insisted.

Nicholas waited, his heart lodged in his throat. He wondered what she would say, wondered what his father would have said in the same situation, and knew, beyond a doubt, that had the boy been asking him, he would have denied it. There is no Santa, only a myth that makes some people feel good. Only an excuse that isn't really necessary.

"Yes, Jamie," Beth said, conviction ringing through her words, "Santa Claus does exist. I've seen him. Nearly the entire town knows it, as do all my relatives, and some of them live as far away as California." She grinned, felt elfin. "As a matter of fact I worried that I wouldn't get hired for my teaching job because the principal of the school knows the story too, but I convinced her it would be to her benefit to have a teacher who met the one and only Santa Claus. Who knows when having friends in important places can be of help?"

Jamie laughed, young, carefree. "We're even going to invite Santa to the pageant some year. It's the best in the world. Everyone says so."

"The pageant huh? I just might have to stick around long enough to see that myself." With that thought, running away no longer seemed as important. "Are you sure I won't be interrupting any private family moments if I listen?"

"Please, Nicholas, stay. You might as well here the whole truth, even if—"

"If?" Nicholas questioned by raising an eyebrow, and staring at her with that piercing yet gentle gaze of his.

"Her mamma, my Aunt Marta doesn't believe it," Jamie said in all innocence. "She thinks Aunt Beth made the whole thing up. And my Aunt Rachael--"

"We'll discuss your Aunt Rachael some other time," Beth

said. Nicholas winked at Beth. He would, undoubtedly, get the other version of the story from Rachael.

The young boy wouldn't be put off. "But we know it's true, don't we, Aunt Beth?"

She tousled his hair, finger-combing the pale blond locks with a gentle, maternal caress. "Yes. We do."

The child nibbled applesauce. Trying very hard to still the turmoil in his soul, Nicholas freed another strand of lights, wishing it were that easy to untangle his own emotions. Beth leaned further back against the couch and a slight, enigmatic smile settled on her lips. "I wasn't much older than you," she started, but then her voice grew far away, and her eyes went fuzzy, and she was transported back in time, as she often was, when she told this story. Back, to when she was ten years old and she met the real Santa Claus.

It wasn't noise that woke her, for she was fairly certain that there hadn't been any sound, not that jingle of sleigh bells which she'd been expecting to hear since she was three years old, nor the moaning and groaning as a rather rotund man tried to squeeze down a chimney pipe, nor even the jolly yet muted sound of ho, ho, hoing, the traditional Santa laughter. Not reindeer stamping in the cold, not an eagerly anticipated interloper munching gingerbread cookies, not the tinkle as a Christmas ornament was displaced accidentally while a large present was shoved under the tree.

Silence actually. Perhaps it had been the ethereal silence which had woken her, but to this day she suspected the reason couldn't be quite that conveniently explained. Beth believed what woke her was her conviction that Santa really existed, her faith stronger than any denial. Because she believed, she saw. The trouble with that argument was, she still believed, and had not seen him since.

And really, what else had she asked for that Christmas? Candy? Dolls? Tinker Toys? No, only Santa himself. In childish writing, cursive, because it made her feel so grown-up, she had written him three weeks before, at the start of the Christmas season, when Thanksgiving left-overs still made daily appearances at the dinner table and the tree was freshly decorated and the anticipation was building to a peak. *Please, Santa, what I want this year won't cost you anything. Not a penny. You can give my gift, if you were going to give me a gift at all this year, to someone else, because what I really want, what I really, really want, is to see you. I know you're real. That you're alive, not made up, and not my Uncle Jake dressed in a costume wearing funny whiskers. I would like to see you.*

And so as her eyelids raised and she sat up against her pillow on the twin bed, Beth knew with the absolute certainty that he was here. Really, positively and honestly here.

There really is a Santa Claus, she whispered to herself. There really is a Santa Claus. At this point checking would be confirmation, not conviction. She already knew he was there, with a child's simple faith, certainly, but she was convinced.

She crawled from the bed, not bothering to turn on the light, not thinking to wake Susan, who could have stood as a witness when push came to shove. No, this miracle was hers alone.

She didn't notice at first how young he was, that he was a child, scarcely older than herself, not with his face hidden with the bushy beard, with the costume which hid far more than it revealed. He continued working for a moment, emptying presents from a huge sack, humming contentedly, when he turned and noticed her.

She stepped forward, bare feet on worn carpet, the exact same carpet she stood on now, into the reflected light which came from no discernible source. "Hello, Santa. Merry Christmas." Her voice was young, high pitched, warbled.

He smiled, or rather his body lit up with exuberance. "Merry Christmas, Beth."

Her mouth dropped open, and she understood for the first time the words of the Christmas carol that went "With wondering awe." That was exactly how she felt.

"You know my name."

"I know every child's name."

"What was he doing, Aunt Beth," Jamie prodded as her voice drifted off to the present.

"He was leaving gifts. What do you think Santa was doing?"

"For you?"

"For me, for Rachael, for your mom and the others in my family. They didn't believe in Santa though."

"I think if they didn't believe, that they shouldn't get anything."

Nicholas sighed. "Ah, the test of faith, the Naughty or Nice Provisional. I think Santa should leave gifts to whoever he wants to, regardless of whether or not they believe—however I think those who have been really bad shouldn't get any candy canes."

"Don't be silly," Jamie giggled, "we're not talking about candy canes."

She didn't dare look over at Nicholas. "You're right. We're not talking about candy canes."

Jamie slipped off her lap, waddled toward the third bedroom, disappeared for only a minute, before he was back, holding an old stack of yellowed envelopes tied with red ribbon. "And this is the ribbon from the package Santa gave you."

"Yes. That is the ribbon." She slipped it over the envelopes, removed the piece of shredding fabric, held it lightly against her lips as if she'd kiss it, but her lips didn't move and her eyes looked sad.

"And then he left?"

"Yes." She had wanted him to say something profound. Even at ten she had needed the secret between them to be broader, larger than life. "Don't tell anyone you saw me," or "Never deny the true faith," or even "Only the pure of heart can see me."

"What he really said was "Go to bed. There'll be a present for you in the morning." And like the fool I was, I went to bed. I didn't see him slide up the chimney, I didn't feed the reindeer or even offer him cookies. Can you believe what a dolt I was?"

"I bet he put a spell on you. Made you sleep."

"I'm sure that was it," and beside the Christmas tree, holding lights that glowed with a steady confirmation, Nicholas chuckled, yet there was only a fraction of the embarrassment he expected. The rest felt strangely like love.

"And when you woke up, there were ten thousand presents

under the tree. How did you know which present was from him?"

"I just did."

"What was in the package Santa gave you?"

"Oh, Jamie, certainly you know the story by now."

"I do, but Mr. St. Noel doesn't."

"It wasn't just one present like I thought it was, instead it was a lot of little presents, all put together. There was writing paper. And stickers and notebook paper and on top of it all, a candy cane, a special one from Santa himself." And there was another present. A small hand carved Santa Claus which didn't look like the boy she had seen.

"And you don't have anything left, except for this bit of ribbon." She still had the Claus, but she wouldn't tell Jamie that.

"That's right. I wish I did. I knew how important it was, and still I used up every bit of that writing paper."

"Tell him what you did."

"I started a play school. I'm sure that's when I decided I wanted to be a teacher. We didn't have any school for the next nine or ten days and I got a bunch of my cousins together, some of them older than me if you can believe it, and a bunch of the neighborhood kids and I was the teacher. I gave them lessons, and stickers for rewards."

"You still give stickers for rewards."

"Yes, I do, don't I. I suppose I have Santa to thank for that. I wrote thank you letters with the fancy writing paper, to my aunts and my grandmother for the gifts they had given me. And I wrote a long letter to Santa thanking him for letting me see him. I think a lot of people think nothing of asking Santa for gifts but they never write to thank him when they get what they want. I learned later that my mother destroyed my letter. She yelled at me for a long time about wasting my time writing to fairy tales. That might have been another reason why I started the preschool. I wanted to prove to my mother that I was good for something. I kept the kids quiet that whole winter break, and they learned some things too. But I always grieved that Santa didn't get my letter. I wrote him another one the next year but I always figured it was far too late then, that he would think I was thanking him only so I could be sure he'd give me more presents again that year."

"You should have written him another letter that same year."

"I know. I don't know why I didn't think of it then, but my mother had destroyed the one letter I wrote, and it was as if she'd destroyed my only chance for communicating with him that Christmas. It doesn't make sense now, but it did then, or at least it did to a ten year old."

She let out a slow breath, realizing how tangled her Christmas beliefs had become over the years. If only they could be freed as easily as Nicholas working with light strands. "Come on, Jamie. Let me bundle you back up, then I'll drive you home."

"Beth?" Nicholas stood, almost blocking her path. She backed up a trace, startled, wondered if she should be frightened.

"Yes?"

"Let me take him."

"No, really, it's no bother. The car is just outside." If she could get it to start. But even then, it wouldn't be warm, not in this lifetime anyway.

"You stay here and finish your papers. I'll carry him home. He'll be warmer in my arms than he would be in that dinosaur of a car of yours, and I'll be back in under ten minutes."

"If you're sure it's no bother?"

"No bother. I need to do it." Need. There was that word again. *I need a woman.* I need time. And now, I need this.

He thought she would call him on it, question him, and he wasn't sure he had any answers to give her that wouldn't give too much away, especially things he wasn't sure about any longer. Pieces of truth. What was it Jamie had said? They make you stronger? He wasn't feeling very strong at the moment, but confused, and perhaps ashamed. How could Beth believe? How could he not?

"All right. Sure. Thanks. And you're right. It would be faster to walk him than to take the car."

She put Jamie's sweater back on, his scarf, his coat, his hat and his mittens, bundling him up until there was nothing left to see except his nose, and she planted a kiss there, to keep that one exposed part of his body from freezing.

Nicholas slid on his coat, opened the door and slipped outside, his boots sinking into the fresh layer of wet snow. With an unexpected spurt of boyish laughter, Jamie dropped his head back, opened his mouth, feasted on the drifting flakes as if they were the forbidden candy canes. It was not a heavy, blinding snow, but a silent one, a Christmas snow. Nicholas pulled the boy up into his hip, waited while Jamie settled his arms around his neck.

He had been warmed by Beth's story, pleased with how she remembered it, which was significantly different than how he recalled the event—his one great moment of shame—when the child, as children often do, asked that one, probing question that had him rocking back on his heels.

"Do you believe in Santa Claus, Mr. St. Noel?"

CHAPTER 8

"You don't pull any punches, do you?"

Jamie nodded his head sagely, a sixty pound, eight year old guru. "It's important. If you're going to be here, helping, I have to know if you believe in Santa."

Nicholas swallowed hard, had to cough to clear his throat before he could speak. With the veil between life and death for this boy so thin, he could only offer honesty, even if it were painful. "Sometimes I do. Sometimes I think Santa is the most important part of my life. Other times I don't know."

"You don't know? How could you not know?"

"I wish it were simple. It's not. It's one of those complex grown-up things. I want to believe in Santa. I do."

The bone-thin arms around Nicholas' neck tightened a tiny fraction, in understanding, in comradeship, as if this too, were a cross Jamie had had to bear. "But too many grown-ups have told you that there is no Santa. Right?"

Too many grown-ups, or perhaps only one. Himself.

"Well, you don't have to worry anymore. There really is a Santa. You've heard my Aunt Beth. She saw him. You believe her, don't you?"

It had to be the snow. With a free hand, he wiped the moisture congealing at the corner of one of his eyes. "Yes. I believe in your Aunt Beth."

"She saw the real Santa."

"If you say so."

"I do say so. And I want you to repeat it. Aunt Beth saw the real Santa, not one of those shopping center Santas or bell ringing Santas. The real one. I'm smart. I know the difference between real and pretend."

"I'm sure you do."

"Now you've got to say the words."

"I don't know if I can." The boy's weight was negligible, but suddenly the burden seemed far too heavy. Only another block to go.

Heaven's above, would he ever get there?

"It's easy," Jamie insisted. "All you have to do is say the words. Once you say them, it's easier to believe them. But you have to say them first. Out loud. Like you mean it."

"And hope to die," Nicholas said, but it wasn't sarcastic. He was in dead earnest.

"And hope to die," Jamie said solemnly, far too solemnly for a boy his age.

"There really is a Santa Claus," Nicholas said, "And Beth saw him." His voice ran with conviction, but then he laughed and wondered what Marlett would say if he could see him now.

"That's right," Jamie said. "That's right."

And suddenly the boy's house was right in front of him, and the burden seemed much lighter.

"Now, have you written your letter to Santa?" Nicholas asked, remembering the child who hadn't asked anything for himself while he sat on Santa's lap.

He could feel the head shake against his ear. "I don't write letters. I always tell my Christmas wish to Santa at Aunt Beth's party."

"Maybe you'd better tell me now, so it can be waiting in the bag and you can have it early."

"I never wish for those kinds of things, the things you buy, that are easy."

"You only want the hard stuff."

"Yeah."

"I see." The kid had been corrupted by his aunt, that was for certain. Nicholas climbed the steps, set the boy down on the porch. "Ok, then, you'd better scamp inside." And Jamie disappeared to his family, where his parents were talking and his mother was crying, where he was dying by bits every day. No, he wouldn't want easy things.

But then, neither did Nicholas himself.

Beth came huffing up, shuffling in the wet snow trail that Nicholas had left, her coat half-buttoned, her scarf hanging long. "I thought I'd see if Susan and Jim need any help."

Nicholas nodded and stepped aside. "You can come in if you wish," she said. "I sure they won't mind—"

"No," he said, brushing snow from her hair, "this is a family matter. I'd only be intruding."

"Are you going back to the tree?"

"That is something I thought we could work on together," he said. "And it's a beautiful night. I thought I would take a walk, try to clear my head a little. Take all the time you need."

Beth let herself in, and removed her coat with the familiarity of someone who's well used to another's home. Susan stepped into the living room from the hall, holding Jamie's outer clothing in her hand. "Thanks for bringing the little skunk back."

"No problem."

Susan leaned against the hall wall. Her eyes closed and she pulled in a deep breath of air, as if the wall, and grit were the only things holding her together. She was a young woman who in many respects looked exactly like her sister, except that Jamie's prolonged sickness had taken a toll on her. She looked older than her twenty-seven years, and her eyes, even in family get-togethers when there was only joy, were often sad. Rail thin, and pale looking, Beth noticed the red rimming her eyes, and knew that Jamie had told the truth. His mother had been crying.

Susan forced a smile to her lips, in a look that Beth was familiar with, "a yes, I'm coping" statement, while her body was saying exactly the opposite. "There," she said, moving with her innate grace toward the hall closet where she hung up Jamie's coat, "he just wanted to see you."

"I glad I was there to help."

"Do you have a moment to stop for a cup of tea? I've already got the pot brewed." Theirs was a family that celebrated all the major happy events—as well as mourned all the tragedies—over a pot of tea.

For a split second, Beth wanted to say no. She had left something unfinished in her own living room, a kiss, and a man who more than intrigued her. She wasn't exactly sure that she hadn't run out into the night simply because she couldn't wait to see Nicholas again, that she needed to be with him, even if the only way she could do it was with her little nephew acting chaperone. The house closed in on her when Nicholas shut the heavy door. She grew restless and couldn't concentrate on grading her math tests. She had tried to tell herself there was no relationship, that she was reading too much into their conversation, and his saucy flirting, but by the same token, she couldn't passively wait for him. She had to go.

And with the thought that she wanted Nicholas, came the fresh stab of guilt. Her sister obviously needed her. Like she had always done, Beth would serve her family first, would put all her needs aside, until theirs were taken care of.

"Sure." She took her own coat off, rubbed her hands together for warmth. Her decision to come had been hasty, done without planning simple winter paraphernalia like gloves. Since the lights had gone up on the house, the temperature had dropped, but more than that, she had to touch the snow, to know, by more than one sense, that it was real. It was as if Nicholas himself had brought it, that it was an extension of him. Nicholas. She hadn't known him five hours, and already he was changing her perception of things, forcing her to reevaluate her own role within her family.

Susan opened her mouth, started to speak, shook her head, then said something which Beth decided was completely different from what she had originally intended. "Jim went for a drive. I expect him back any minute."

From the worn, haggard look on her younger sister's face, Beth doubted there would be good news. "Sit," Beth ordered. "I'll get the tea."

Beth busied herself in the kitchen, a place she was almost as familiar with as her own. Cups, saucers, freshly baked oatmeal cookies.

She had just returned to the dining room, to set the pot on the table when Susan blurted out, "Beth, I'm pregnant."

Beth stood in shocked silence for the space of a heartbeat while the full implications of the statement registered, then deliberately, so she wouldn't drop the teapot, set it aside as she hugged her younger sister warmly.

More than a little stunned, Beth stepped back, looked away when she realized she didn't have the courage to meet her sister's gaze. Jamie's heart condition was heredity. There was a good chance that this unborn baby would pick up the defective gene and the hole in the ventricle that invariably proved fatal.

The living room was scrupulously neat, even if every single piece of furniture had been donated by family members when they first moved in. Theirs was a humble home, the small living room brightened by a small tree, scraggly, already starting to drop needles, but the love was sincere, and their hearts were in the right place. Susan and James didn't need presents to celebrate Christmas, only each other, which would make the eventual loss of their son that much harder to bear.

"I'm so very happy for you." They hugged again, this time both their eyes were moist with emotion.

"Thank you for understanding." Susan touched her still flat stomach. "This wasn't exactly something we planned."

"Jamie doesn't know."

Susan nodded, her face sad but resolved. "We're trying to keep this secret for a few more days, get the holiday out of the way at least."

"Do you want me to tell Gram?"

"No. Jim and I will, after I tell Jamie and mother."

Beth hugged her again, then ordered Susan to take care of herself. She did not let her shoulders slump, her hands shake until she was outside on the porch, heading for home. One more thing piling up. One more potential disaster.

She tried to be happy for her sister and brother-in-law. They loved children. They deserved the large family they wanted. And this was Christmas, the season of miracles. She would pray that they would find one, when she finished, she would tack on the fifty thousand other things she needed help with.

Exhaustion clogged her arteries, tore strength from her muscles and her spine. So many problems...

"Where is Santa when I need him?" she whispered to the

night sky.

***

It didn't take him long to make the return trip, or it wouldn't have, if he hadn't gone around the block twice, trying to clear his head. Nineteen years before, Beth had caught him. It was the first house he'd entered all by himself. He didn't quite have the courage to do it alone again until his father was dead and shock carried him through closed doors. And it didn't matter that his father had given him her letter to Santa, the one that said she only wanted to see him. He was clumsy. He intended only to give her a gift, yet he had proved himself incompetent.

Nicholas remembered the night as if it were yesterday, a cliché certainly, but then the most profound experiences are usually degraded to clichés sooner or later, simply so they can be survived. Like most teenagers at that age, he'd been suffering under an oppressive identity crisis.

What good is Christmas anyway?

Thirteen year old Nicholas sat at the kitchen table and pondered his mother's words. Hot chocolate sat congealing to his right, forgotten, equally ignored were the gifts from the neighbors, the friendly Pennsylvania folks who had adopted them almost as family. These good, hard working people, suffering under an uncertain economy, their coal worthless, their factories closed, their jobs non-existent, had opened their arms and sheltered them. On the dining room table, plates of butter cookies glittering with red and green sugar, homemade chocolates, a fruitcake wrapped in cheesecloth, soaked in rum, potent and powerful and as traditional as anything his father stood for. And his mother's argument still haunting him, taking from him the one piece of stability in his life.

"What good is Christmas anyway?" his mother asked. She had come in, stripped off her mud-soaked shoes, slumped into a couch worn down by more than a decade of use. The rental house was nothing fancy, one of a hundred like it that they had stayed in across the country, across the globe. His mother could afford better, never quite bothered to, as if she were drawn to the downtrodden, to those struggling lower-class workers who would never quite reach the better life they dreamed of.

Nicholas, ignoring opened schoolbooks and the necessity of homework, had thought it a rhetorical question. He knew her, or at least knew the way her mind operated on this one subject, knew it wasn't worth arguing. Then he heard sleigh bells, the snort of a reindeer, and the glossy glide of polished runners on snow, dragging to a stop.

"There's your father. I suppose we should ask him. He's the expert on Christmas." From the sneer in her voice, he knew the word expert was hardly a compliment. It came as no surprise. What did was that he couldn't remember what he had told that little girl just that morning. Couldn't, for the life of him come up with an explanation for his mother about the benefits of Christmas. But for Beth he had.

"Nickie, my boy, are you ready to go with me?" Santa, larger than life, more potent than Superman, more endearing. Except that it was his father. Nicholas knew Santa put his socks on one at a time like everyone else, that he snored when he slept, that he often became frustrated, that he had no life, except one night a year, and that for most people, that was too few.

"Before you take the boy, answer one question for me. What good is Christmas?"

Nicholas senior laughed, full, honest. "I'd think after all these years of putting up with me, you'd know the answer to that one."

"No, I really want to know. I ran out of toothpaste of all things, decided I couldn't survive for two days without it so I decided to brave the drug store. Not the mall, mind you, the drug store. And all those maniacs were there, buying their perfumes and their smoked salmon and their overpriced chocolates shaped like bells, shoving each other out of line as if the world was coming to an end, without even bothering to wonder why they were buying smoked salmon in a drug store in the first place. Then, toothpaste in hand, I get toppled by some overweight maniac with bulging packages barreling out of a liquor store, into a pot hole overflowing with a good eight inches of slush."   "Dad," Nicholas cleared his throat, wished he didn't sound like such a child. "Dad, I don't think I'm going this time." He had most certainly planned on going. He always went. He loved the thrill, the almost illicit pleasure of sneaking into houses when everyone was asleep, anticipating joy, relief, a renewal of faith. Except that it was in his nature to give gifts, and Nicholas decided at the spur of the moment that if he stayed, he might, possibly, be giving his mother a gift, not so much of his companionship for the day, but his acceptance of her position.

A jolly, boisterous ho, ho, ho rang out, rattling the lamp hanging over the dining room table, causing the tinsel on the small tree to sway back and forth. "What? You've got something better to do, than to go with Santa?"

"Dad, I think I just need some space. Maybe next year."

Santa pulled out a mismatched chair that rocked on four uneven legs. "We've got a few minutes, let's talk." In true Santa form, he pulled the cheesecloth from the fruitcake, and Lorraine was there beside him, handing him a knife, a dessert plate.

"You'll ruin that suit," his mother said, pulling up a third chair.

"Fruitcake doesn't stain," Santa answered, mouth full.

"You can have your Christmas," she said. "Just don't ask me to share it." And in January and February and March he would take time he could little afford to be with them, visiting Yellowstone or Disneyland or skiing or white water rafting, any of a thousand activities without a strand of mistletoe in sight. And again in the summer, another week stolen from his responsibilities. Weeks spent on beaches slicked with SPF35, where he told other oil-slicked vacationers he was a consultant, that he went into remote locations and hot-wired all kinds of miracles. They nodded their heads in understanding, expecting he did something with computers or telecommications, or an MBA. Santa Claus in swimming trunks, who would have believed it? Not even his own wife.

She wasn't a Bah Humbug Scrooge. She only sought more than tinsel, more than garland. Except for this one night when he came to pick up his son, Nicholas the father didn't see his wife at all during the month of December. It was a rough compromise.

He finished the fruitcake slice, started in on the fudge. "Listen," Lorraine said. "I'll let Nicholas go with you if he can answer the question. What good is Christmas?"

"I don't want to go anyway," sparked teenage rebellion. Telling the kids in high school he moonlighted for Santa Claus over the Christmas break would be a real treat.

Santa stood. "All right. You don't have to go, but I've got this letter for you. It's addressed to me, but it's yours." He handed the opened envelope to Nicholas. "I've got to run now. If you change your mind, you know how to contact me. I'll come get you no matter where I am."

"I can't. Not this time."

And while his mother had gone out to the movies, some action-packed, car-chase bloody slasher movie, Nicholas read the letter, and tried to come up with an answer for his mother. *I believe in you Santa. In all that's good and kind and giving.*

An hour later Nicholas stood outside Beth's house, shivering in the Christmas cold, stamping his feet, knowing if he could do this one thing and do it right he would have an answer for his mother and one for himself. It wasn't long before the sleigh pulled up and his father waved, full of sparkle and cheer and magic.

"Um, how's it going?"

The big man put his arm around his son's shoulders, pulled him closer. "Better, now that you're here."

"I thought you'd show up eventually," Nicholas muttered, head down, as if ashamed he had anticipated Santa Claus.

"Are you coming in?"

"Yes." Through some facet of magic Nicholas couldn't manage on his own, his clothing changed and he wore the traditional red suit. "What's this?" he fingered the unfamiliar growth at his face. When he'd gone in on previous years, he'd been unencumbered by an uncomfortable facial hair.

"What does it look like? Santa needs a beard. It's part of the image."

"Dad, can I do this one myself?" It was a bold request, taking more courage than he thought he had. And it was one of those questions that just pop out, the kind that if he'd thought about it, he never would have considered.

"Of course. I've been wondering when you were going to ask. I'll stay here, reload the packages." His father's eyes, his voice, held pride.

"Dad, thanks."

He slipped in through the door, chimneys being far too much bother, and 'through' the door was the operational phrase, as opposed to through the *opened* door. He was feeling rather full of himself. And then she caught him. And when she went back to bed, he ran from the house, from his father, like Cinderella at the stroke of midnight his clothing changing back to what he'd worn before, the beard vanished, the red suit gone, in his eyes, disgraced.
***

"I was about ready to call out the National Guard," Beth said, looking up from her papers.

"I had some thinking to do." Nicholas clicked the door shut behind him, leaned against it, his head against the thick wood, his hands hanging limply at his side.

"I know." Like Susan, like Nicholas, Beth had leaned against the door, needing its support to hold herself up.

The house was quiet. The night settled hard around them, but it was a silent-night, the time for sharing confidences and intimacies. "Did you find your faith?" she asked, sitting up, watching him with a feeling she didn't recognize. It was almost maternal, the need to comfort him, to hold him close, to merge her strength with his so that together they could be far stronger than either one alone.

Nicholas shut his eyes, rubbed his face with his fingers, weariness and exhaustion in every pore of his soul. "I wish I could take Jamie, capture the faith inside him so that I could take it out, one drop at a time, whenever I needed the courage to go another step. I wish adults could learn more from children."

She made no comment, profoundly moved in a manner that only sharpened her awareness of him.

"Where does it go?" Nicholas asked her, holding his head up

now, stabbing her with a gaze so intense she felt it straight into her heart. Around her, candles flickered, sending out fresh shards of aroma. She thought she saw the tree sway, moving to an unfelt, unnoticed breeze.

Beth raised to her feet, moved closer to him, needing proximity of intimacy, even if what passed between them was something profoundly different than the sexual awareness she had experienced earlier in the evening. "What?" She shook her head, held her hands out. "Where does what go?"

"The faith that children have. Where does it go? Why is it never there when we need it?"

"It doesn't matter, does it?" Unaware of what she was doing, she touched the lip of his zipper, slid it down, separated the two halves of his coat. Then as if it were the most natural haven in the world, she eased against his chest, her head fitting snugly under his chin, her arms wrapping around his back, adsorbing the warmth of the coat, the life from the man.

He wrapped his arms around her back, feeling the slenderness of her waist, experiencing the sense of completeness he'd never once experienced on a sleigh. She breathed deeply, no longer smelling scotch pine or bayberry or gingerbread, but only man, full of questions and pain and desperation, but with of goodness born of promise.

Nicholas kissed Beth, gently, on the crown of her head. Overflowing with innocence and intelligence and the faith that Jamie had no monopoly on, his body stirred to life, an awkward, inappropriate time, but if nothing else, an honest time. When he told Marlett he needed a woman, he wasn't referring to a superficial encounter that was intimate only by definition. He needed a woman to match him, in all things, as this woman in his arms matched him. This then was what Jamie interrupted with his unexpected arrival, except holding Beth was already stronger, more vital than it had been, just the hour before.

His body ached. Blood rushed. His loins hardened. Pain never felt so good. He couldn't do anything, not even shift weight from one foot to another for that would give away his condition and undoubtedly make it worse. She couldn't hold him so trustingly and know of his rising response. He bit the inside of his lip and held still, except for the chuckle, which bubbled up from somewhere around his funny bone.

"Do you keep mistletoe in the house during the holiday?"

His words by themselves were caress enough but they startled her with their implication so that her eyes flashed opened and she shifted on her toes, raising her chin from its secure nest against his heart to face him.

Mistletoe. He wanted mistletoe. Her body tingled. Fingers. Toes. Breasts. She was breathing far too fast, and felt the uncontrollable need to match his laughter—even if she knew, beyond a shadow of a doubt, that what they were talking about wasn't funny.

"Yes, there's always some around."

Nicholas moved then, pushing her back, for he was already pressed tight against the door. He strained his neck, scanned the ceiling with the intensity of a shopper with a long list of presents ten minutes before the store closed on Christmas Eve. His breath was clearly as loud as hers and his voice sounded strangled. "Where is it?"

"I haven't bought any yet."

A shiver ran through him. "Trust me when I tell you it will be the first thing I get to in the morning."

But as if he knew he had been holding her prisoner, Nicholas bounced away, returned to the tangle and managed to separate a rather nasty clump of intertwined Christmas lights and gain all of two feet of liberated bulbs from a snarl which had to involve at least three or four different strings, judging by the number of ends he'd managed to unearth.

Beth knelt beside him, opened a box, starting uncurling newspaper from decorations. The urgency cooled. Not the anticipation. That still boiled fresh and ferocious, but he could think about Christmas now, instead of sliding between her legs, her heels locked over his spine, his hips rocking.

"We don't have to finish this tonight," she said, apparently reading the heightened color to his cheeks.

"If we don't—" he struggled for an explanation that wasn't descriptive. "If we don't, I won't sleep." She wouldn't either. He'd make sure of that. He would take his time loving her, long into the wee hours of the morning. Beth had to work tomorrow, and she'd have a hard time teaching when she was in no condition to even stand.

"The tree—" he muttered.

"The tree," she echoed.

Nicholas plugged in the string of lights. Beth was ready for him with a grocery bag filled with replacement bulbs. His face absorbed color. The room was no longer familiar, but magical. With electricity, with enchantment, they had both been transported, and it was too special to even acknowledge.

They worked together until the lights and the decorations were up, her voice merging spontaneously with his in 'Deck the Halls,' and other perennial favorites. The grandmother clock chimed the hour, then another, then another. They didn't hear, over the sounds of the music, their own breathing, their frantic desperation not to say anything, do anything, which would take this further, faster, than they were ready for. This night was worth savoring.

Finally, the last box emptied, the tree all but sagging under the combined weight of decorations, he paused, hands to his hips, admiring his handiwork and the sense of satisfaction which had been missing from his life for far too long. "In all the years I've been decorating trees, I don't think I've ever had this much fun."

"It is a beautiful tree," Beth agreed, slipping a small stuffed Santa ornament onto a branch, which she had held onto, for a reason she didn't understand, wanting, needing it to be the last ornament to go up. She fluffed his beard, grown gray from age.

Nicholas smiled. It wasn't the tree he had been thinking about at all, but rather the company and the tradition which surrounded them. He had hung store bought decorations, but they were by far in the minority. With equal reverence, Nicholas and Beth hung crocheted stars, lace angels made with clothespins and doilies, drums created from aluminum foil covered thread spools, and all manner of things improvised from former egg cartons, Styrofoam cups or half-pint milk cartons, the kind handed out with every school lunch.

From the very first box he opened, he knew there would be absolutely nothing artificial about this tree, and by the time they were finished he was satisfied that it was, without a doubt, the most beautiful expression of Christmas cheer he'd ever seen. Color coordinated, professionally styled trees had their place, but for his tastes, homemade made Christmas.

"Tinsel?" he asked. A tree wasn't a Christmas tree without tinsel. It was one of those unwritten laws.

She finger-combed a strand of hair which had dipped to her forehead. "Tomorrow, thank goodness."

"Getting tired?"

She arched stiff muscles and wiggled toes which hadn't seen much circulation in the past few hours. "Heavens yes, but that's not the reason. "Tomorrow, you'll see."

He was willing to wait, maybe, but not long. Another minute maybe. Or twenty seconds. He pulled her against him, until they both collapsed against the couch, her back against his chest, his arms wrapped quite properly against her stomach. "Have you ever been in love, Beth?" Nicholas asked, out of the blue, intoxicated with the scent of her shampoo, still fresh, even after the long day.

She leaned back against him, comforting, secure, home. "I don't know. Maybe. Sure. Nothing ever came of it." She was too tired, and her emotions were too close to the surface to follow this line of questioning any further.   "Oh, it's late."

"What time is it?" Then without asking her permission, Nicholas touched her wrist, turned it so that he could check her dial.

"It's already tomorrow."

Her watch was one of those novelty things, a fat Santa Claus whose uneven arms pointed out the hours and the minutes. "I think I'm ready to turn in. It's been a long night." He pulled her to her feet, suddenly felt chilled without her warmth against his length.

"Good night then," Beth said, rubbing her arms, hugging herself, as if she too were cold.

"You coming?"

She didn't look at him, instead she studied their handiwork and the smile on her face was wistful. "In a little while. I want to look at the tree for a few minutes."

Her head tilted at a dreamy attitude, her hands neatly folded over her belly and she rocked, silently, to music which had stopped playing several hours before.

"I'll stay—" he started, but then muttered "Good night," again and shut the door of the middle bedroom behind him. He would leave her her privacy, her introspection, her dreams, for if she agreed to become his wife, this would be the last year she'd have to dream alone.

Beth blew out the candles and inhaled deeply of the scent of burned wax merging with fresh pine pitch. She shut her eyes, happy, content, more than a tiny bit aroused. Nicholas, she thought, Nicholas.

Her body swayed, tentative dance steps of released vitality, mixed equal parts with Christmas and fantasy. She had no idea what love should feel like, but except that her body tingled with new, unfamiliar feelings.

The lights on the tree were steady, bright and clear. A few years past Beth had experimented the with small, plastic, flashing kind in an effort to modernize their holiday, but she had given those lights to a married cousin just starting out and had gladly returned to tradition. The star on top was simple, lovely, and filled her with sentimental longing. Even with her eyes shut she could see it.

Each year she made a Christmas wish. It started when she was a child and the tradition continued through her adult years. Although she no longer wrote letters to Santa Claus, and her Christmas wish was silent and infinitely private it was not a tradition she would easily relinquish.

Nicholas. But no. Not yet. And not for herself. She would save her wish for something important.

Beth leaned against the door jam to her room to get a better perspective. Christmas trees had personalities. Although she would never admit this little quirk to anyone, Beth strongly felt that she could portend the coming year with a high degree of accuracy based on nothing more than the overall physical configuration of the family Christmas tree.

Spindly trees with widely spaced branches indicated a lack of Christmas spirit which would trickle down to all areas of life during the coming year. Short, bushy trees indicated prosperity, but no personal growth. Any tree flocked in pink or yellow or blue she knew for a certainty was the sign of a sick mind.

In her more rational moments, Beth was willing to accept that there was room for a good deal of error in her Christmas tree tarot card theory, in part based on the judgment of the person who picked it out and prevailing weather conditions. For example, any tree picked off an open lot during a late December rain storm was less likely to be chosen for aesthetic beauty, and more likely grabbed because it was the first tree which came in reach. Any tree picked out by a gaggle of children was bound to have some significant flaw, but on the whole, Beth had come to recognize that tall, bare trees indicated a lean year ahead, no new friends, little laughter, but plenty of room for growth; trees with dry, brittle needles which wouldn't pull up any water indicated something serious would be lacking: health, money, jobs, happiness.

Worse than any of the others, a very noticeable bare spot on a Christmas tree, especially one which was visible no matter how deeply imbedded in a corner the tree was, indicated there would be a significant personal loss in the coming year. She was silently grateful that this tree was perfect. The needles were soft, responsive, the sides equally full. No bare spots. Good. She would live with the illusion, perpetrated by the perfection of the tree, that this coming year would be her best yet.

She turned, walked on silent feet two steps into her bedroom, before turning around, facing the tree again. "Goodnight, Santa," Beth whispered.

In his bedroom, Nicholas cupped his hands between pillow and head. "Good night, Beth."

CHAPTER 9

Callie stopped in her tracks, the bells on her booties jingling indecisively. She inched another step forward, then looked over her shoulder, half convinced she'd walked into a brand new building, which was fairly impossible, since the last time a new structure had been built at the North Pole, Columbus hadn't quite gotten around to learning to sail.

With her mouth open, she turned in a complete circle, studying the structure from ceiling to floor, from every angle in between. Then, not quite believing what her eyes registered, she squatted down, touched the plank floor, let her work-worn fingers caress the smooth, glossy texture of the fresh polish. Callie slowly straightened, moved to the closest workbench, where presents were stacked neatly wrapped, but beyond that, all the clutter had been removed, and the wood surface had been polished to a high sheen. Marlett hopped from foot to foot, betraying his nervousness, and the other elves huddled around him, waiting wide-eyed.

Callie nodded slowly scarcely believing her senses. The tools of their craft lay in ordered rows, knife and scissor edges sharpened, paint brushes cleaned, and all manner of small repairs made. Wood stood stacked beside the fireplaces, in orderly contained cords, and everywhere the disorder and confusion she had lived with for so long had disappeared.

"Would you look at this," she said gloriously, her face finally echoing her pleasure. "There are miracles at Christmas."

With her words, the elves exhaled the breath they had been holding, then they jumped, celebrating, as they did when the sleigh came back and all the presents had been delivered. Over the centuries, they had learned the worth of a job well done.

Callie put her hands on her hips, silencing them with only her glare. "I suppose I'd better see what the barn looks like."

Marlett danced forward, taking her hand. The barn glistened. The reindeer had always been well taken care of, but the little used recesses of the rafters had been ignored far too long and the corners, where used tack and broken pieces of odds and ends had collected had been taller than she was for longer than she could remember. The trash was removed. Everything had a fresh, clean scent.

"Nicholas will be pleased," she said, doubting he would even notice. Santa Clauses on the whole only paid attention to what went into their sleigh, not what went on all around it. "Still, this might be just the thing to get him excited about Christmas again."

Marlett rubbed his hands together, and tiny motes of straw chaff flew up into the air. A reindeer beside him, Donner, snorted, then sneezed. "You know, beyond Nicholas, it will help the workers. Now that they have room to work, now that everything is in its place, I know our efficiency is going to double, perhaps triple. As it better, this close to Christmas."

Callie offered a low whistle of appreciation. "My, my, she'll be impressed, she will. A few more touches, and this place will be perfect."

Marlett growled, the timeless response of the over-worked husband, then he stopped long enough to pull a piece of straw from his beard. "What are you doing here? I thought you said you were modernizing the kitchen. The last I heard there was talk of removing walls."

Female elves didn't grow beards, but that didn't mean they didn't rub their chin as if appreciating one. "Decided to wait on that. The misses can make any changes she requires. Of course, I'll be around to tell her what I think."

"Of course," Marlett answered dryly. He held the beard out, inspecting it minutely. It would never be the same. Never. A dozen washings and he'd still be pulling twigs from it.

"Besides," she fumbled in the cavernous pocket of her apron, until she pulled out a well creased, yellowing sheet of notebook paper. "I found this in Nicholas' room. It's a letter to the old Santa. I don't know what it was doing in there, but I'm going to shove it back where it belongs."

Marlett grabbed it, scanned it quickly, with all his generations of experience in reading Santa-letters. "Then you'd better leave it be. That's her."

"Her? Santa's wife?" Callie recovered the letter from her husband's possession.

Marlett nodded sagely. "The one Nicholas's interested in. I've seen him holding that letter off and on since he was just a tyke. You better put it back."

Callie wasn't an eavesdropper. She respected privacy, especially the current Santa's privacy, but she was used to reading Santa letters.

"Now you put that back," Marlett growled, making a lunge for the letter.   Callie knew her husband, timed her move to the second so that she was out of his way and his hand was empty, his body off balance enough that he plopped flat on his face on the reindeer bedding which thankfully, had been changed just that morning.

"Now look what you've done," he said, despair ringing in his voice. More straw in his beard.

The writing was childish, but then Callie was used to that. Any letter that wasn't childish was undoubtedly written by a parent on behalf of a child too young to hold a pen. The ink had faded a bit, and the folds were so worn that the letter wouldn't hold together much longer. It was crinkled as if it had been carried in a pocket for years.

"Let's see what our little bride wanted." Callie lowered her head, started reading. *I believe in you, Santa. I know you exist.*

"There's almost a dozen other letters from her back in the mailroom," Marlett added.

Callie smiled, touched the yellowed paper thoughtfully. All premonitions of disaster faded from her mind. She should have known this Santa would find a woman who believed in him. Maybe that was the problem with the last Mrs. Claus. She married Santa, but Callie doubted that she ever believed in him.

Bells pealed, a familiar carol. Part of the magic of the place, which involved flying reindeer and sleds which carried any amount of presents, was that the current Santa could communicate with the elves whenever he needed from the beginning of the tradition of Santa.

"That'll be our boy now," she said. They had all been "our boy."

It wasn't exactly a telephone, but that was what Lorraine St. Noel had started calling it, and the name somehow had stuck.

Marlett picked himself up from the fodder, made no attempt to brush straw from his clothing as he made a dash for the phone.

"Heavens, Nicholas, do you have any idea how close to Christmas it is?"

"Yes, Marlett, I know."

He sounded different. Marlett couldn't quite decipher what the difference was, until he realized he sounded more alive, more vital. They'd become rather used to this Santa running at half speed.

Marlett was about to yell, give an order, when Callie shook her head, made patting-down motions with her hands. The old elf softened his voice. "I'm concerned. Are you coming back?"

"Not until I discover Christmas."

The grizzly old head elf stared around the spotless barn, to the freshly groomed reindeer, to the sleigh with its new coat of paint. It would all be a wasted effort if there were no Santa around to appreciate it.

"Are you any closer to finding what you seek?"

Marlett could hear Nicholas rubbing his face, knew from the soft rustling sound his sharp ears picked up that Nicholas' beard had come in full and heavy. Then he was acting as Santa, even if at the moment he couldn't admit that's who he was.

"No. I'm nowhere near finding the answer." He paused, but Marlett didn't interrupt, let the silence grow, while Callie hopped on one foot, desperate to know what was going on. "I'm warm for the first time in years," he said. I'm warm, blending love over a coal burning stove, or putting up tree lights or sleeping on flannel sheets. Warm, for when he was with Beth and her family, he was too firmly ensconced to feel the cold of loneliness.

"I've found things that make me happy," he said at long last, the earlier exuberance of his voice dissipated, and the slow, measured tones back. "I've always been able to find things, people, that make me laugh, but I don't think that's what you mean, is it?"

A rhetorical question, but Marlett answered anyway. "No, what you need is something far deeper than that. The pleasure from most Christmas presents is transitory at best. A week, a couple of months, and the gift is forgotten for something newer, brighter, more intense, but every now and then, there's a gift with lasting consequences, one that is dragged from childhood to adulthood, one that with memories alone shapes the future."

"Yes," Nicholas answered. As Santa, he knew how often he supplied that gift, how often parents did, in knowing their children, and their need to shape the future with joy.

Marlett looked to his wife, remembering how he had grumbled when he worked, yet how satisfied he had felt as he watched her pleasure over the back-breaking work he had just completed. He looked around the empty reindeer barn, empty because there was no Santa there to bring it life.

"Do you know what the difference is, between an average Christmas present and one that changes a life forever?"

Luck? Early planning? Poverty? "Love," Nicholas finally answered.

"Love is only part of it. And knowledge between the giver and the receiver is only part of it." Marlett hesitated, wondered if he were giving too much away. Wondering if he had come to these conclusions himself only this minute.

"And the rest?" Nicholas asked. His voice trembled as if he couldn't face whatever answer Marlett was about to supply. It was a familiar sound.

"Sacrifice."

"Sacrifice?"

"I could give you the platitudes, Nicholas, the 'nothing comes easily' clichés, but answer me, is there ever anything easy that is worthwhile?"

Easy. Nicholas leaned against the kitchen wall, dropped his head back as he gazed at nothing in particular and let his thoughts wander. Easy. Watching Beth smile. Buying mistletoe to have an excuse to kiss her. Easy, the laughter they shared over eggnog and knotted tree lights....or easy, a young child with a defective heart and a wish that his death not hurt his parents.

Shock ran through Nicholas as a fresh thought arose. They weren't talking about easy. They were talking about sacrifice. If he decided he was Santa, that the one thing in the world that would make him happy was supplying toys and the magic of belief to children, then he would have to give her up, this vibrant woman who made his blood hum. To be Santa, he would have to cease being Nicholas St. Noel.

For a second, he felt his knees buckle, was glad the wall was there, offering him support. "I don't think I can face the sacrifice." Because he didn't think he could face himself, the petty greed with which he contained his own pleasures. As a child, sacrifice hadn't been on the agenda. He'd been given almost everything he wanted, except time with his father, the commitment of his parents to each other. He was used to giving, but then, for Santa, that was a world away from sacrificing.

Sacrificing. Like his parents had, living apart, fighting conflicting values. The North Pole was a harsh mistress. There wasn't anything left, not time or money, for growing a family in warmth.

"I don't think I'm meant to be Santa."

"Then you should have stayed here, Nicholas. Maybe you're looking for the wrong woman. Come back."

"I can't, Marlett, not yet." Sacrifice, that ugly word, taunted him. Still, he grew brave, had to, to defend his own chosen lifestyle. "I don't think Christmas can be defined by what goes on at the North Pole—or the shopping malls for that matter," he added before Marlett could interrupt. "And there has to be more to it that sacrifice. How could I be happy if someone sacrifices for me, and how can my own sacrifice make me happy? That is what we're talking about here, isn't it? Happiness?"

"Have you found her?"

"The woman, yes. If she'll have me. But that wasn't the true problem. I think I can convince her to love me. I know I'll have no difficulty falling in love with her. I'm already there. One smile and she had captured my heart. She likes singing, Marlett."

"Be nice to have another woman in the house. And a woman singing, well you know that always makes our jobs go faster. So, what's the problem?"

The was a pause on the line, long enough that Marlett held the receiver from his ear and wondered if they'd been disconnected. "Marlett, How can I ask her to accept Santa Claus?"

"What are you talking about, Nicholas? You're not making any sense."

"I might not ask her to share this life. I might want more for myself, for my wife, for my children."

"You can't mean that."

"She's happy here. She's got family and a job and a niche so strongly built that if I moved her, I might change her and I love her exactly the way she is."

"But she'll understand."

"Do you remember what we were talking about the last night I was there?"

Now it was Marlett's turn to let the silence on the line grow dusty. Marlett shivered. There might be more wrong with this day than fodder in his beard. He had no experience with subtly, only with honesty. The last day he was there, they had discussed the possibilities that Nicholas was not Santa Claus, that he would deny the hereditary position.

"Are you coming back?"

"I don't know if I can. I'll tell you why. I've done what you asked, I've gotten a job as a store Santa, and I've been listening to the children, and to the parents, and to the store keepers. I think Santa Claus does the world a disservice. We don't help everyone. We can't even help all those with real need. All we've been offering is false promises. Every time a special treat isn't under a tree, we've failed. Most kids don't need *more*, Marlett, and what they do need, they can get from their parents or their physicians, or from their family preachers."

"We offer hope."

Nicholas was quick to deny it. "We only offer illusion. Write a letter to Santa and win the lottery. Christmas doesn't need us. It's strong enough by itself, on so many different levels."

"Santa has nothing to do with Christmas, Nicholas." The ancient elf waited for a response, but for a long time heard only silence. He decided to continue. "Nicholas, it isn't Santa that brings Christmas, and it never has been. People bring Christmas. People are supposed to."

"I don't understand."

"Well, you believe that if you have enough faith that a mountain can be moved?"

"Yes." He'd always believed that, had seen it more times than he could count. Problems, mountains moved.

"And how is it done?"

"Miracles," Nicholas responded. "Miracles pure and simple."

"Yes," Marlett said, "but not so simple. When a mountain is moved, 99.9 percent of the time it's because a group of people got together to move it, shovel by shovel. They hold fund raisers, or blood drives or clean up neighborhoods together, holding paint brushes and pushing wheel barrows. Miracles, Nicholas, are done by hand."

"Then what do we do?"

"Sometimes, with a well-chosen gift, we provide the shovel. Sometimes, by example, we move the first clump of dirt, to prove that it can be moved. But mostly, Nicholas, what Santa does is keep people young at heart. Do you know why that's important, Nicholas?"

Silence again, and then a reluctant, long drawn out, "No."

"Because it is only the young who believe in miracles. It is only the young at heart who are willing to believe the mountain can be moved in the first place. If we make a child happy, even if it's with a toy, we've made more than a child happy. The parents are happy. The grandparents are happy and sometimes even the neighbors. It eases some of the stress, these very tiny miracles we bring, so that they are willing to straighten their back, pick up the shovel, tackle some other problem that's been bothering them for years or for decades or for generations. They feel good, so they write a check to their favorite charity, or they invite a lonely neighbor in for dinner, or they go to a nursing home, bringing not so much treats as their very presence. Oddly enough, more miracles occur from a person's presence," and here he spelled it, "then from a person's presents. Nicholas, am I getting through to you?"

Silence again, this time longer that before, more uncomfortable. "Marlett, if I don't come back, what will happen to Christmas?"

And before Marlett could format his answer, there was no one on the end of the line to speak with.

***

"You're up early." At not quite four o'clock, Nicholas was surprised at finding Beth's grandmother seated at the kitchen table. She must have gotten up while he was out shoveling the snow from the sidewalks, trying to work off some of his frustrations. The fire was already stoked, the kitchen toasty. It was a morning stolen from time. Marlett would have felt at home here crushed between the heavy cast iron pots, the dish towels and the knickknacks and the memories.

It was a kitchen of old things, Mason jars and oilcloth, but more than that it was a haven of stability. Beth had been rocked in that chair, and how many other countless others. Thousands of potatoes had been peeled at the sink. Hundreds of skinned knees had been kissed. Lives had been lived in quiet perfection. Nicholas loved it.

Catherine wore a cotton print dress, a red sweater and old fashioned stockings, the thick, opaque kind knotted above the knees. Her thin white hair was coiled primly in a bun at the back of her neck, covered with a hair mesh as finely woven as spider silk. Her face was deeply etched with character lines, not the mark of shame television commercials for moisturizers would have him believe, but a sign of endurance and beauty. She was a strong woman, whose strength had never been measured in her back or her shoulders, although she had known years of back-breaking work.

One of the gifts from his mother that Nicholas had accepted early in his life was an appreciation of the value of people: their courage, their pains, their very uniqueness. She taught him to find radiance in children, those wrapped in lace, those raised in squalor. She showed him the beauty of adulthood, bodies at their prime, in the full bloom of well-proportioned human symmetry, but most of all she convinced him of the elegance of old age. The magnificence of bowed backs, gnarled fingers, sad yet undefeated eyes. No matter where he went, as Santa Claus or as Nicholas St. Noel he cherished the dignity of survivors.

Catherine smiled, showing yellowed teeth, still her own. The lines in her face deepened, as descriptive as any photographic album of her happiness, far more enduring than any pain she'd suffered.

"Old bones," she said. "They don't quite allow me the sleep I need. Besides, I've been getting up this early all my life. It's a hard habit to break. There's coffee on the stove if you want some."

Nicholas cleared his throat, wondered if there were something about this home that made him maudlin. "Actually, I'd like some hot chocolate."

"I'm not certain there is any. The last time we had the family over I think the grandchildren polished off what I had left."

"No problem. I bought my own." He walked into her pantry, a large, stone-walled cellar situated off the main kitchen which had been there, unchanged, for over a hundred years. It was cold, the heat from the stove didn't reach that far, and the one light bulb, hanging down from a wire, with a single pull string to light it, was dim. The shelves were bloated with rows of bounty: peaches, pears, tomatoes, spaghetti sauce, and probably fifteen different kinds of pickles and relishes. Beth's work, although it took little imagination to realize how many years Catherine Vacchioni had done her own canning.

Nicholas found a large mug, he was very impressed with large mugs, and spooned generous spoonfuls of his secret recipe chocolate into it. Then he found a second large mug and prepared it the same way.

"Would you like some?" he asked, rejoining the old woman at the kitchen table.

She shook her head, her smile deepening the etchings on her

face. "I'm afraid I've of all the things I've lost over the years, the one that annoys me the most is my sweet tooth. Besides, the doctors have me on such a regimented diet, I don't think I better."

Nicholas filled his cup from the kettle kept on simmer on the stove at all times, then eased his feet under the table. He sighed, but then he must have given some other sign, a softening glance, or a self-satisfied grin for the old woman spoke, reading his mind.

"She's a very special woman."

"Beth? Yes, indeed she is."

Beth's grandmother stabbed him with direct, piercing eyes. "I don't want her hurt."

He chuckled, a ho, ho, ho, less forced than any he could remember in a long time. "I'm rather well known for spreading good cheer."

"All the same, you have that look in your eyes. I don't want her hurt."

He set his cup down on the table, and looked into her eyes for answers. Sacrifice, he thought. In light of Marlett's comments, maybe it was not only his own sacrifice the miserable elf was alluding to, but Beth's as well, in that he would hurt her, by any number of reasons, but mostly from his part-time commitment to a life she could never be part of.

"Should I leave now?" Leave now and it would break his heart, but it might be for the best.

She stared at him, taking his measure. In her prime, he'd bet Catherine Vacchoni could stare down a sunset. "Look in her room sometime today when she's not there and answer that one for yourself. All she's had all these years is doing for other people. She needs someone to look after her."

Warmth filled him. He found the idea of looking after Beth very enticing. "I'll try my best."

Nicholas took a deep drink of chocolate, contentment settling in his bones. Beth's touch was evident in every inch of the home. If he married her, he wouldn't change a thing, except to be there, as he had been the night before, to wash her dishes, and to dry her tears.

"Why were you here, those few months long ago?"

He stirred the chocolate, letting the whirlpool bring back nearly forgotten memories. "Funny, I was just thinking about that myself. My mother wasn't much into Christmas. It made living with my father somewhat of a challenge. They compromised. She and I traveled the world, settling for a few days or months at a time and Dad would join us whenever he could. It gave me a rather broad education."

"And a restlessness you haven't grown out of."

"That, and an unusual point of view." His mother's one major contribution to his education was that she taught him there was more to life than Christmas. His father's lesson slanted in the opposite direction.

"Your mother dead?"

"Oh, heavens no. She still wanders the globe. I look her up every Christmas, don't see her much more than that."

"I'd like to meet her again."

"I'm sure she'd enjoy that. My father loved her very much although they had very different personalities. I think they both would have been happier if there had been a way he would have given up his profession to be with her all the time, but it wasn't a decision he could make. Sparks flew whenever they were together, but in passion, never in anger. My mother couldn't compete with my father's dominant personality while she was home. They thought once I was born she'd settle down. It didn't quite work that way. I still to this day don't understand what fueled their love."

"I suspect you will, soon."

Stiff backed, Catherine made her way to the stove, replenished her coffee, stirred the oatmeal simmering on the back burner. "And don't think I don't know who you are young man."

He chuckled. That morning he had refilled her coal bucket, had emptied the ashes from her stove. That morning he had spoken with an elf, on an instrument which had been around centuries longer than a telephone, and had denied exactly who he was.

"I'm nothing but a simple handyman, experienced with any number of chores, eager to help out for a few days until Christmas."

"I expect you're willing to help out with Christmas, but I

don't for one second believe there's anything simple about you."

Nicholas reached across the table, placed his large, warm hand over her frail, chill one. "No, that's where you're wrong. My needs are few. A cup of chocolate, a blazing fire, friends, Christmas..."

"A woman?"

"If she'll have me."

"And nine flying reindeer."

He retrieved his hand, shrugged his shoulders in nonchalance. "I think you're talking about fantasy."

"And I think because you're here that I'm not. I saw you once when you were working, a long, long time ago although I suspect that was probably your father or your grandfather. I suppose you're going to tell me it was some clumsy accident, or a child's overactive imagination?"

"You saw Santa? The real Santa?"

"Why? Did you think you were the first who ever got caught accidentally?"

Nicholas sparkled, letting a degree of his Santa persona shine through. There was no disguising it around Beth, but he hoped he'd be more successful around the others of her family. "Believe it or not, it never occurred to me that people had seen him."

"Well, Beth is a true believer. Has been all her life."

He struggled for a response, this woman who believed, when he did not. And her belief hadn't been easy to maintain. Because she had proof that Santa existed, she suffered nineteen years of torment, the criticisms which were as intense as ever, judging by comments Rachael made. Still, wasn't her faith in Santa the single, main thing which drew him to her?

"I know. There are not many people with her faith."

"And she needs—"

Movement from the dining room startled Nicholas and he looked up to see Beth standing in the door well, her arms folded under her breasts, showing a pair of raised, disbelieving eyebrows. "It seems I've walked in on this line before. What do I need, Grandma?"

Nicholas rotated his hips slowly along the smooth surface of the painted chair, breathing in her beauty. She hadn't been there long, and she hadn't over-heard her grandmother's conclusions. Beth wasn't a woman who listened at keyholes. He would tell her himself, if she didn't discover his identity on her own.

"Lord a mercy, girl, you startled me. What are you doing up so early?"

"I've got work to catch up with at school. Now you'd better tell me what family secrets you've been telling Mr. St. Noel. What exactly do you think I need?" If it were that man business, she had brought up the afternoon before, heads would roll.

"Breakfast," Nicholas said, rising quickly to his feet. "Start with this." He poured boiling water into the second mug he had prepared. "It's medicinal. It will help you get through the entire morning."

"I'm sure it will," she said, accepting the hot chocolate with grace. He forced her into a kitchen chair and before she could protest, he set a steaming bowl of oatmeal in front of her. The milk and sugar bowl were already on the table.

"Eat." He decided to make it a command. Everyone in her large extended family expected her to wait hand and foot on them. While he could, he would make sure that he didn't.

Nicholas ladled himself a bowl of oatmeal, then rooted around the cabinet where she had stored the cookie decorations until he found a small bottle of round cinnamon candies. He added a handful to his cereal, then stirred. The candies left red trails of dissolving sugar in the wake of his spoon.

"For breakfast?" Beth asked, tweaking an eyebrow which must get a lot of exercise.

"Oatmeal needs something to spice it up. Care to try some?"

"Sure, why not?"

He made sure when he passed the candy across, that his fingers touched hers, that he felt the caress he had been craving all night, and that it had lost none of its power with the passing of their first day together. The shock of awareness swirled through him, vital and full-formed. Her eyes widened, and she quickly pulled her fingers back, not denying, so much as not accepting what had happened so spontaneously between them. She poured the candies into her steaming oatmeal, tasted it, wondered why something she had been eating every day of her life now tasted so wonderfully fresh and sweet.

They ate in companionable silence for all of three minutes, sharing looks, and intimate fantasies, before Catherine disturbed the quiet, a Cheshire cat grin dominating her features. "What's that in your pocket, Nicholas?"

His look of devilment intensified. "Mistletoe."

The breath knocked from Beth's lungs. "Oh? For Rachael?"

He'd strangle her. He really would. How could Beth think he could ever spare a thought for Rachael after he'd met her? "Do you think Rachael needs mistletoe?"

Beth swallowed before she choked. "Ahh, no."

"Then I guess it must be for you." With slow deliberateness, Nicholas reached into his pocket, feeling a wash of masculine satisfaction as her mouth parted, and a betraying flash of color pinked her cheeks. Four o'clock in the morning and this lady wasn't quite as disinterested as she seemed. He removed the small piece of greenery from his pocket, set it down on the tablecloth directly in front of her. He marked his time, waiting until she looked up at him, but not long enough for Beth to have completely recovered her composure. "I think we could find a place to hang this, don't you?"

He wanted to laugh. He wanted to pull her to him right then and there and kiss her senseless, with or without the prompting of a mistletoe bough. His body tightened, hardened, and that pleasure/pain was back again, more intense than ever.

Beth picked up her chocolate mug, set it down, locked her fingers together, all the time, never removing her wide-eyed glance from his. "I suppose since it is tradition..."

"Tradition be hanged, Beth." Because tradition stated he'd have to kiss anyone parked under the mistletoe, and at the moment he was feeling relatively selfish about sharing his kisses with just any member of the family. "This is for you, Beth. Your first present of the season. And it's for me. It will be something we'll share."

"Why?" She sputtered, clamping her hands over her lips. Apparently that wasn't what she meant to say. And Nicholas, who had been trained to make people happy, had never realized how much fun there was in making someone just a tiny bit unnerved.

I want you naked in my big four poster bed, my lips caressing your breasts, my heart captured by yours. But he really had just met her the day before, and her grandmother was listening, and they both needed at least twenty-four more hours to get used to this upheaval in their lives so Santa backed off a bit. "I think Christmas isn't complete without mistletoe," Nicholas said, but *that* look was back and they both realized he wasn't specifically talking about tradition.

Ignoring the flash of heat she felt creeping up her cheeks, Beth checked her watch. "Goodness, will you look at the time. I need to get to school. There are a lot of things I have to do."

Nicholas picked up her cereal bowl and mug on the way to the sink. "I'd like to go with you."

"That's not necessary," Beth struggled into her parka and draped a homemade knit scarf around her neck. Nicholas could see she was trying very hard to avoid looking at that tiny sprig of green growth, and equally avid that she escape him.

As a man who appreciated beautiful women, he had never realized before how much beauty had nothing to do with physical appearance. "I'd like to be with you. What I have to do around here shouldn't take all day and my stint as Santa isn't until later. It will give me something to do." He wasn't sure why he was pressuring her so, except that he wasn't willing to say good-bye to her yet, even if their separation would only last a few hours.

"I don't really think—"

His fingers sprang up, settled themselves against her lips, silencing her. With their contact, the magic blossomed again, turning his want into an ache. "You'd be doing me a favor, actually. I can help you with your tasks, then, I'd like to borrow your car to do some running around. I'll be back to pick you up when you're finished."

He waited for her nod, before he dropped his hands, freeing her. Without the mistletoe on his person, or hanging somewhere above her, Beth felt safe.

She gave him a sugar and spice grin. "I don't think you quite realize what you're getting yourself into."

Nicholas grabbed his coat. "Maybe not, but I am willing to help." There was tenderness in his words, and oddly enough, apology.

"Well, if you wouldn't mind, I could sure use you."

"Christmas songs sure have the right of it," Nicholas said a few minutes later as they walked to the car. In the glow from the house lights, and seen against the blackness of the pre-dawn night, the crystallized snow glittered. "It does look like a winter wonderland."

While he unlocked the doors and struggled to get the defroster blowing on the windshield, he waited for her response. Snow, after all, was snow, but anticipation, like rose colored glasses, colored perceptions until they bore little resemblance to reality.

Beth surprised him. She stood silently, making no move to grab the car door handle for a second, then she spread her arms out wide, as if she could single-handedly encompass the entire vista surrounding her. As if she were giving the starlit, snow blanketed neighborhood a single, heart-felt hug. Then she laughed, pure and honest and sincere.

"Yes," she said, nodding, finally finding her way into the car, still grinning with third-grade enthusiasm, that usually the students—not the teachers—caught. "In the air there's a feeling of Christmas. Isn't it marvelous?"

The car started grudgingly and they drove slowly. The salt-crews would be out soon, and by afternoon, most of the snow would be history but that morning the roads were almost slick enough to have been laid down by a Zamboni for Olympic figure skating try-outs. The radio offered nothing but static. Nicholas, still tingly after her spontaneous joy, would have been happier if he could have ignored her while listening to the national news, the farm report, or even some version of the Top 40 count-down. With her cheeks reddened by the cold, and her eyes sparkling, she was almost as appealing as she had been last night by the tree, but her holiday anticipation grated on raw nerves. After his conversation with

Marlett, he didn't want to feel Christmas. He wanted to ignore it.

"So, I thought your grandmother told me that you had none of the Christmas decorations up." He let his voice sound gruff.

The mug he had used for his hot chocolate had a red and white candy cane handle but the basis of it was a wide-eyed, open-mouthed Santa, complete with curled beard, traditional red suit. That one he could handle, could almost expect.

Beth scrunched down in the seat, looking smaller, younger than she was, and the grin that she had discovered before she hopped in the car, was still completely and firmly in place. "I went digging through the decorations a few weeks back looking for props for my pageant and brought some stuff down. I was beginning to think it was all we were going to have of Christmas this year, but then again, if I had my way, we'd never take the tree down."

He let the last image pass. It was easy enough to say that a week before Christmas. Like the snow, the New Year would see an entirely new perspective on decorations.

"And the shower curtain? Is that your doing?" He'd been sharpening his back molars on this one quite a while, but hadn't wanted her grandmother, with her insight, to hear his comments.

Beth laughed, full bodied and amused. "I'll admit it surprises me a bit every time I discover it hiding in the decorations. I tried to keep it up all year, after all, it is functional, and it doesn't make much sense owning two shower curtains, does it?"

"But the Committee for Santa's Decency forced you to take it down?" he asked hopefully.

"No. Actually, I like it more when it's up only a few weeks. It's more special that way. More meaningful."

Meaningful. Nicholas groaned out loud. He hadn't noticed it when he'd used the facilities before bed and this morning it had caught him quite literally with his pants down, although perhaps he should have expected it. Leave it to Beth not to have the standard opaque vinyl shower curtains common in most homes. In the main floor bathroom, where anyone walking in could notice it, was a clear plastic curtain decorated with—of all things—a showering Santa covered with only strategically placed bubbles. Santa showering.

Yes, he was supposed to be a role model for children, and yes, hygiene was important, but really, a line had to be drawn somewhere.

"Oh, don't worry. I'll take it down about mid January, then be all the more surprised next year."

"I see." It was worse than he thought. He'd have to have a good, long talk with her. There was a reason for the bulky red suit that wasn't limited to Arctic cold. It was modesty. Given his druthers he undressed in the dark. He wore pajamas to bed. It was bad enough showering in a room without a lock on the door without having to face an image of himself, or heaven forbid his father, stark naked except for a handful of bubbles. *That* Santa had been jolly. This Santa had a classic case of red cheeks.

"I've got connections at the North Pole. I'll make sure you get another curtain." Maybe one with Marlett wearing only bubbles, serve the miserable elf right for all his machinations, but then, that sight would bring nightmares. Better to find something neutral. "If you want a decorative Christmas shower curtain, I'll find one with a tree scene."

"I like the one I have." She crossed her arms.

"I don't." He ground his teeth.

"Too bad." She stuck her tongue out.

"I'll see it suffers an unfortunate accident." He perfected a sneer.

She tightened her eyes a tiny bit, looked at him with a devil-may-care glance. "I'll buy them in bulk, and give them free with every Christmas present I deliver for the rest of my life."

"In that case, you'll not live long enough to deliver another Christmas present." His nose wrinkled and he executed a perfectly smug smile.

She sat up tall in the seat. "I'll commission an entire line of provocative Santas. Put them on greeting cards, have Santas in the Victoria's Secret catalog modeling everything from—".

"That's enough," Nicholas interrupted. "I get the picture. I'm not going to fight you over this when you know perfectly well I'm right. That shower curtain is a menace."

"You're right?" Just how many octaves could she raise her voice? He might never hear out of his right ear again. "I know you're right?" Then, unexpectedly, she burst into peals of laughter, until she had to hold her sides. "For your information, everyone else who's seen the shower curtain likes it."

He blushed. Other people had seen it? Just how many lewd men did she have over taking showers in the morning? The damage might be far worse than he thought. How in the world was Santa ever going to repair his image now?

"The shower curtain stays."

He wanted to argue, put up a fuss so big NBC news would cover it until he decided this wasn't exactly a topic he wanted covered on the evening news. One shower curtain, what would it hurt? Obviously the repercussions to taking it down would be far worse than leaving it alone. Besides, he didn't have to shower again while he was here, did he? Or, he could close his eyes. Pretend the person wrapped in bubbles was her.

Images formed quickly, with no effort on his part. He shook his head, lowered the window an inch. No. That wouldn't work either.

Nicholas grinned to himself, a sly, smug grin of self-awareness. Who would have thought that he would be attracted to a stubborn woman? There were enough stubborn creatures in his life with Marlett and the rest of those miserable elves.

He downshifted, feeling the car start to fishtail as he turned into the school driveway. Still, Nicholas was determined to get the last word in. "The shower curtain comes down." Why couldn't it have been Andy Rooney wearing nothing more than bubbles?

"If that's the way you feel about it, you'd better stay out of my bedroom. I've got this rather adorable Santa pattern on my sheets, and they're wearing—"

Mercifully he groaned out loud and missed the rest of her statement.

CHAPTER 10

There wasn't another car in the parking lot when they pulled into the elementary school, although the plow had been through leaving only the slick, ice coated asphalt. The school was a one story brick affair, sprawling in a T pattern, down three long halls. In the pre-dawn light it looked forlorn, ancient, abandoned. From where he stood as he exited the car which was still wheezing from its cold-morning trip, he couldn't see the swing sets and the slides, the gentle sloped hill where generations of small feet had run up, rolled down. The cold windows reflected nothing back but the spider-web pattern of frost. On many of them taped construction paper hung, but he couldn't make out designs or decorations, felt, perhaps, the paper was only there to keep out the sporadic appearances of the sun, making the inside even more oppressive. More lifeless.

Beth, undaunted, hummed Christmas songs so joyously, that he couldn't determine exactly which one. It could have been all of them together. Whatever monstrous behemoth they were about to enter, it wasn't effecting her. She walked carefully, but quickly toward the door, her stride firm, her chin high. She already had her key out. She practically reeked anticipation. He was about to tell her that he'd changed his mind, that he wasn't going to help, that he was going to return to bed, pull the covers well over his ears and sleep until he discovered the warmth he craved, and which he had found that morning in her kitchen. He had things to do. Places to go. Shower curtains to shred.

Nicholas felt the first tinges of depression. He halted in his tracks half way between the car and the sidewalk as he debated the merits of going on. Ahead of him, Beth turned, the main door unlocked, held open a scant three inches. She raised a brow, a "are you coming?" look that she didn't need to vocalize. Perhaps she knew the quandary he faced, the empty, oppressive nature of the building itself. Perhaps she was giving him the opportunity to turn tail and run.

Then she smiled and her eyes lit, and in the overhead light, which had to have all of twenty-five watt dimness, she shone and he knew right then that he would follow her anywhere. Nicholas raced to catch up with her, held the door so they could pass through side by side.

He followed quietly as she whisked through the silent corridors, his senses on high alert. He was sensitive to feelings, and residual emotions hung thick around him, filled with laughter and challenge and education. Impressions of caring and dedication echoed silently from the rooms and throbbed from each handmade Christmas decoration attached to the corridor walls. He saw creativity at its most basic, a vital necessity for growing healthy students. He had been afraid that all schools had become dumping grounds, institutions that kept kids off the street for seven hours of custodial care. He was very pleased to find himself wrong.

"What can I do?" He removed his coat in a silent and spotless workroom where she stopped long enough to turn on a flood of overhead lights. In cubbyholes tall stacks of construction paper in rainbow colors waited. Copy machines, paper cutters, pieces of technology he could only guess at, loitered on the counters. There was a plethora of scents he recognized, chalk dust, rubber cement, magic marker ink. It helped him recall stolen moments of his own childhood education. He ran his fingers along the spotless counters, further heightening his impressions, afterimages of what had passed here. Maps of the United States from no less than five different time periods as the boarders increased westward, a hundred different worksheets with math problems, lessons involving predicate verbs— whatever they were.

Nicholas hooked a hip on the counter. Now that he was certain of the validity of the school, he could revert back to his favorite pastime, concentrating on her. Beth looked better bathed only in tree lights, softer, gentler, more feminine which was a good thing. Christmas tree bulbs were considered "natural lighting" at the North Pole.

She pulled out a rubber backed woodblock, about five inches long, half that in width. He grinned as he studied the object. He should have guessed. More Santas.

"Do you know how to use this die-cut machine?" Her hand rested on a small piece of technology which looked like a small hand-operated printing press.

"No, but I suppose it can't be too difficult."

Her erratic eyebrow raised again and her voice sharpened. "Why, because I can do it?"

"No, because whatever you want done has to do with Christmas, and I'm an expert at anything to do with Christmas."

She was about to argue. When it came to this particular holiday, *she* was the expert, then decided it wasn't worth the effort. "I want die cut Santas."

"Sounds painful," he said. He didn't shudder, which he intended, instead he undulated, hips particularly, and a brilliant flush of color rose to Beth's cheeks as she understood the full implications of his actions.

"Listen," she demanded through clenched teeth. "What exactly is going on here?"

Nicholas wasn't sure himself. He really had intended on helping, not unleashing a previously inactive libido. He moved closer, raised his arms, settled them against her shoulders, intending to pull her closer, rest her body against his, the way they had at the door the night before. Maybe touching her would ease the ache.

Beth moved with jerky deliberation, setting a distance between them more with her don't-touch attitude than the negligible space. "Pay attention."

His grin intensified and his pulse sped up another fifteen beats a minute. The woman wasn't unaffected. She had been a spitfire at ten with her black eye and her skinned knees and her defense of Santa Claus. He was glad the fire within her hadn't been quenched, but more than that, he wanted it to burn him, to consume them together. While Nicholas deliberately unfastened the first button of his flannel work shirt, and then the second, Beth demonstrated how to cut the paper then feed it into the machine, coming out with a perfect Santa, about four inches tall, a hole right in the middle where the round belly went.

"Do you think you can do it?"

Here? he almost asked. In an elementary school? Oh, yes, sweetheart. He could do it.

Anger flashed. Her eyes were larger, greener, more expressive than they had been the afternoon before while she had waited so patiently for her nephew to see Santa Claus. Nicholas couldn't help but tease. "What goes there?" he asked indicating the hollow stomach. Gingerbread cookies would have been his first guess, even if at the moment he was fighting other appetites.

Beth hadn't gotten much sleep before and exhaustion was catching up with her, especially since the sensual, tormenting thoughts of him should have vanished with the full light of day. She slapped a palm hard against the counter, still didn't look at him, at the trace of inviting chest hair peaking through the V of his shirt, at that little grin that offered pleasures she only dreamt about. "I haven't got time to put up with your clever little insinuations. Either you help, or you leave now, go back to Rachael."

Rachael was the farthest thing from his mind. Nicholas stepped back, abashed. He really had pushed her too hard, too fast. "It was an honest question." His innate sense of symmetry indicated something lacking.

Some of the fire went out of her eyes, as she accepted what he meant as an apology, as she accepted her own limitations. He couldn't have meant what she thought he did. She was overreacting again. Beth breathed deeply, counted to ten, composed her inner turmoil. When she finally had the courage to look at him, she was the professional, sexless Beth she felt comfortable with. The one who taught third-graders. "I planned to stick pictures of the kids there. Now, do you want to help?"

His answer was soft, more than a little compassionate. "Yes, Beth, I do."

She nodded crisply. "When you've got them all cut out, I'll find the school pictures, then I'll show you how to run the laminating machine. After that, we'll tie a piece of ribbon in the hats, and wa-la, the kids have a present for their parents."

"Sure. No problem. How many do you need?"

Her lips thinned, straightened into one flat line. "One

hundred-twenty-five should about do it."

"125? You can't possibly have that many kids in your class."

Hands behind her back, she looked like a cat caught with canary feathers on her lips. "Well, I did promise the other third grade teachers that I had the time."

His immediate response was anger. "With your grandmother so ill? You still think you can do it all?"

"The other teachers are just as busy as I am, and they help me out when I need it."

It didn't take a drop of his intuition to realize that minute per minute she'd never come out ahead. It was her nature to provide for others. In this they were equally matched.

"Well, it's a good thing I showed up. And what will you be doing while I'm cutting out half a billion Santa Clauses?"

"Follow me."

She disappeared through the media center, past low book cases filled with a wide assortment of reading material, not bothering to turn around to see if he could keep her long legged pace. He caught up with her in a dim corner where a rack held a dozen three foot wide rolls of paper in various rainbow hues. Beth pulled long streamers of paper. "The big Christmas production is tomorrow night. I have to color all the background scenery."

"If I get through in time, I'll help you."

She cut off a sheet with a deft tweak of her wrist and shoved it at him before she reached out and pulled more. "We'll see who gets through. We'll both probably have to come back after dinner tonight."

If he had diffused the tension surrounding them, he hadn't completely forgotten it. "I've got plans for after dinner tonight, and they don't involve spending time at school."

"Take that back to the workroom," she ordered, "and get busy. I'll be there in a minute."

Beth disappeared, but was back immediately with her arms full of colorful artist chalk, rulers, additional craft supplies, many similar to Marlett's stash. She spread the paper out on the floor, taping it together so that she had enough to use as a tablecloth for a football field. She was slender and petite, and at the moment, on her hands and knees coloring, she didn't look much different from the children who would soon be filling her classroom. He found Beth a beguiling contradiction of youth and innocence and fire and sensuality. Her hands were competent, moving chalk effortlessly across the paper with bold strokes. He could only imagine, painfully, what it would be like if she turned her talents to him.

Lecherous old Santa. Marlett would laugh. His mother, however, would undoubtedly cheer. He worked quickly, glad that the exercise freed his mind. What did he want in a woman? Watching Beth, Nicholas was no longer sure. Not a woman who would walk out on him, like his parent's relationship, yet not a dependent creature who couldn't think beyond the kind of treasures possible with a gold MasterCard. Maybe a complex woman. Like Beth.

Nicholas, making die cut Santas, spoke over his shoulder. "What exactly are you building?"

"The North Pole."

He stroked a clean-shaven chin and tilted his head, hoping to improve his perspective. While he had been working her outline was starting to take form. "I wouldn't have recognized it."

Beth looked up from her coloring, her eyes uncertain, as if debating if he were making fun of her. Whatever trust she needed to completely accept him, she hadn't found it yet. She had a smear of yellow chalk dust across her cheek and it was all he could do not to touch it, caress her.

She rose to her knees, with a defiance she had honed in the nineteen years since he met her, when at ten, she had defended his father's honor, and unknowingly, his own. "So, you're some bigshot expert on the North Pole?"

"Yes." This was the second time now he had admitted his vocation to her when in the past it had been painful even acknowledging it to Marlett. She hadn't believed his first heartfelt confession, "Beth, I'm Santa Claus," by the undecorated tree the day before, but that hadn't mattered. What had been significant was that he had said it, meant it on an unconscious level, had accepted it in himself, when he had denied it at the North Pole, where it should have been easier. A big shot expert on Christmas. Not, I can't be my father. A distinct difference.

It was a very good feeling. He flicked the handle. Another half dozen die cut Santas were added to his pile. While he worked, Nicholas would stop occasionally, offer a bit of advice about decorations which, on the whole, Beth ignored.

"You'd best keep working. I need them all finished by tomorrow."

"Well, I'm ready for the pictures now." He'd made 135. She'd use the extras for decorating the principal's office. She just didn't know it yet.

"You couldn't possibly have them all finished."

"I told you, I work fast at anything having to do with Christmas." Beth was just about to give him her best third-grade lecture on how to count when she noticed a stack of perfectly trimmed Santa Clauses. And better than all that, there wasn't six inches of trash littered all over the floor. Whatever mess he had made, he had apparently cleaned up while he worked.

"I'll get the pictures."

After Beth disappeared to the third grade rooms, he studied her interpretation of Santa's Workshop. "Isn't she going to be surprised," he muttered to himself.

"Surprised?" Beth asked, sneaking up behind him. "About what?"

Again, time for a confession he wasn't certain he was ready for. "Santa's workshop," Nicholas answered when he realized he couldn't dissimulate this question. "It really is quite plain inside, utilitarian. No candy canes on the walls, no holly around the calendars, no mistletoe above the door frames."

"Ha!" she said, handing him the pictures. "I've been to North Pole, New York, and they told me that the one and only official Santa Claus decorated their Santa's Workshop, and this is exactly what it looks like."

His laughter rang around the walls. "Well, it certainly is good to know we've got such an expert in our midst." He meant his statement as a compliment, not a criticism, and in growing closer to

Beth, Nicholas found an added, unexpected bonus, like one last, hidden Christmas present, scrunched in the toe of a stocking. He was finding it very easy to accept her version of Santa Claus, when he'd never been able to accept his own.

Nicholas started pealing backing off pictures, sticking smiling faces of front-toothless third graders onto replicas of a very fat traditionally dressed Santa.

"I'll warm up the laminating machine." Beth disappeared again, a bundle of energy. It was not any easier for him to breathe with her gone than it had been while he stood only two feet from her. Her scent was of shampoo and wholesomeness, but it was her essence which stuck him hard in the chest.

He hummed while he worked and the time passed quickly. He took the mile length of clear plastic laminate and started slicing, separating the Santas.

"I don't know how to thank you. I never could have gotten a fraction of this work done without you." Her gratitude warmed him as he helped her carry her chalk painted workshop outside into the freezing December morning where she sprayed the entire workshop poster with some kind of toxic smelling fixative.

Red-cheeked, hooded children were drifting in from all directions. He wondered if she'd be surprised if he told her he knew all their names, their parents, their grandparents back several generations. He loved children but so much of his time they were asleep when he visited.

"We still have a few minutes before the bell rings. Would you like to see my classroom?"

Oddly enough, it was an offer he cherished as much as being invited into her bedroom. "There's nothing I'd like better." He bundled up the ornaments he'd finished into five piles, one for each of the third grade classes, and the leftovers for the main office and dogged her steps, as devoted as any of her students. The room was large, bright, cheerful, and like the woman herself, it took his breath away.

Beth set the rolled Santa's workshop into an already overcrowded corner, beside a small Christmas tree, an artificial fireplace. She bent down, shoved a plug into a socket and the 'fire' fluttered with electrical intensity.

"Santa Claus himself would feel comfortable here." And this time, for the first time, when he said Santa Claus, he didn't mean his father or any of the previous Clauses whose boots were starting to fit.

"I suppose my grandmother told you how much I like him."

Yet he didn't understand how a woman who could make others happy at Christmas all by herself, would also need the legend to give legitimacy to her actions.

"It seems I can recall her mentioning a thing or two about it," he said with a chuckle. He roamed idly, touching worn encyclopedias and crayons less than an inch long. With each item, new visions flooded him, subliminal images trapped, waiting only for someone with his sensitivity to pick them up.

"I can feel the love here. It's in everything in this room." She gave more than time when she taught and he knew, down to the last child, how many lives she had touched for the better, for eternity.

Pain rolled through him, real and sharp. He tightened his eyes and the muscles across his shoulders bunched. His fingers formed into frustrated, I-am-doing-the-wrong-thing fists. He had no right to take her from her life where everything she did made the world a better place. Her empathy was strong. Beth moved closer, puzzled. "I've done something to upset you."

"No, never think that."

She didn't understand. Beth moved back toward the desk, her hands occupied. She wasn't a woman who fidgeted. "My grandmother. You won't hurt my grandmother."

"No. You have my word." And his heart. She had held that since the first moment he caught sight of her. It would be hell to walk away, but it might be worse if he stayed.

He had to get out, breathe air with snow in it, and realign his priorities. But the classroom held him with its small desks and red and green garland festooned from corner to corner. Through it all, everywhere he looked, Santa Clauses. Hundreds of Santa Clauses. Most were done with ingenious third-grade creativity, but more than a few exhibited her touch, had captured her spirit. His feet were leaden, his legs felt paralyzed. Stacks of mimeographed handouts, still redolent of duplicating fluid stopped him. Rudolph. Bears with bows. Santas.

"It's hard to keep their attention this time of year," Beth said, maintaining her distance, still uncertain about what had happened. "After math we have art. After reading we have art. When they come in from recess..."

"You have art." He laughed again, feigned, but cognizant that every single one of the little people who spent time here loved her.

They loved him too. Third grade was the height of the true believers, but what Elizabeth Anderson offered them was real. These twenty-five children needed reality in their lives. Maybe more than they needed him, a benign figment of fantasy, they needed a caring adult who would lead them through increasingly complex reading and arithmetic and learning the facts of the Gettysburg Address.

And maybe, as long as he was on that tangent, they didn't need him at all. Maybe the legend had become strong enough that it could carry on, without his input at all.

"I've upset you."

"Beth, no." The first bell rang. Doors opened. The gold rush had begun. Twenty-five kids stood by hooks and cubby holes, storing boots and jackets, mittens and brown paper bags hiding bologna sandwiches. He watched them, pleased with their vitality, with the fact that they were healthy, physically, mentally, emotionally. "You've got to work. I've got to go."

The intercom sputtered. Beth listened, heard her own name. "Stay for a few minutes, will you? I've got to run to the office." She didn't give him time to refuse.

Her children sat crosslegged on a mat, wiggling, and giggling, but on the whole, ready to settle down. Attendance? Show and tell? He had no way of knowing. Still, it wasn't as if she were throwing him to the lions. Children he could handle, except that he never had, without a beard, without a red suit. Without a bag filled with goodies and what-can-you-get-me questions.

Feeling quixotic, Nicholas settled himself in the chair in the center, adsorbed the adoration of their smiling faces. Blond hair, black hair, red and brown. Her students came in all colors. But they were children and love filled his heart. "Ms. Anderson got called to the office. I suppose you know what that means?" He wiggled his eye brows, looked stern.

"Sure. She's in big trouble now," one live wire provided the answer he was looking for, while the others erupted in giggles at the thought of their teacher in trouble.

"She left me in charge. I thought we'd start with the beatings."

They howled with laughter. These were not kids who were repressed in any manner.

"No? How about math? We could practice some long division."

"Nooooo!"

"Then I suppose you want a story."

They reacted predictably with cheers.

"A new story, one you haven't heard before?"

Their approval rocked the walls.

Nicholas groped around trying to come up with something which would hold their attention. "Do you want to hear how the elves came to be trapped at the North Pole?" he asked.

The agreement was unanimous.

"This is a true story, and it's one based on love."

A couple of the boys made faces. One particularly rowdy specimen of juvenile masculinity did not bother with the mat, instead he was doing somersaults near the far wall.

"You guys know Santa right?" Cheers answered him and heels pounded on the floor and arms waved. This time of year all children knew Santa. The yelling quieted, the eyes grew wide, the mouths open. Expectation and anticipation grew. The spirit of Christmas spirit throbbed all around him.

"For the first couple of Christmas' Santa pretty much handled everything by himself. I don't mean to imply he was alone. He had a wife and she worked as hard as he did, even if when you see the pictures of her, he's working and she's knitting by some hearth with a blanket on her lap."

Beth slipped in quietly, her business at the principal's office taken care of already. She folded her arms, leaned against the door jam, and watched this very confusing man weave his coat of fantasy.

"Anyway, it wasn't long before Mr. and Mrs. Claus realized they couldn't do it all by themselves. The reindeer needed looking after, and always there were too many children needing presents. Now they had a son, and they trained him to work, but still, they were smart enough to know that Santa needed help if there were going to be presents enough to make the trip worthwhile. He needed elves. That would solve a lot of his problems. Now this was a long time ago. A long, long time ago, when elves still pretty much wandered free, hiding from big people and generally getting themselves in all kinds of trouble, but they were dying out, and Santa knew if he didn't bring them to the North Pole they'd all fade away, and he'd still be stuck with all this work and no one to do it.

"Not many big people could find elves, but Santa knew where they lived and he went to their mess, by the way, it's no coincidence that a group of elves is called a mess, much the same way a group of lions is called a pride, and I'd tell you about that story, but then we'd never get to the part about how they got tricked, and how they got captured."

He caught Beth's eye. He had no idea how long she was standing there, but she raised her hand, palm out, in a please continue motion, and he couldn't refuse her. If her face had been bathed only in amused tolerance, he might have thought differently, but she looked as enthralled as any of the children.

"Anyway, this Santa Claus went to the head elf, Marlett, and asked him to come and help. Marlett refused. They had a pretty good thing going for themselves, stealing watermelons and picking berries, nesting down in dairy barns or under evergreens whenever they strayed away from home. Don't let anyone tell you differently, elves are basically lazy and when this Santa Claus, his name was Nicholas, did I tell you that? All the Santa Clauses are named Nicholas. It's a rather stupid habit, but Mrs. Santa Clauses usually bow to their husbands wishes on this one matter and name their children Nicholas, although there are many perfectly good names to be had, names like Anthony. Don't you think?" He posed the question of a carrot topped ragamuffin seated closest to his boots. The boy beamed. Anthony was an ok name with him, especially since his mother told him it was the greatest name of all, which is why she gave it to him.

"Are we ever going to get to the trap?" asked a boy who had been doing cartwheels, yet who had been as enraptured as the rest.

Beth's grin grew more spontaneous. Nicholas gave her one of his potent, Santa-knows-who's-been-nice winks, that nearly bowled her over like nine-pins.   "The trap. Heaven forbid! We'd better get on with the story before Ms. Anderson gets back in here and makes you guys do multiplication." Groans were universal, as were sparkling eyes.

"Where were we? Oh, yes. Lazy elves. They weren't about to give up the good life to commit themselves to a life of slavery working for any Santa Claus. Oh, they believed in Christmas but naps suited them fine. And singing under the stars and dancing. Elves are great dancers. To this day they dance whenever anyone isn't watching. So they wouldn't go with this Nicholas. Marlett, as a matter of fact, laughed. Then Santa got smart. He invited them to a Christmas party. All the food they could eat for free, and elves can eat a lot of food, did I tell you that? Well it's true. And he said there would be dancing. Now, where this mess was, food wasn't exactly plentiful. They were lazy elves and they'd raided every barn and granary for miles, dug up every edible root, plucked clean every berry. And the tail end of December isn't a real easy time to find a lot of food anyway, and the farmers were on to them, buying big dogs to protect what little food the elves hadn't managed to steal yet. So, a party with all the food they could eat sounded like a good deal to them. You, Caroline, would you go to a party when there was all the food you could eat?"

Caroline, a dark skinned child nodded enthusiastically.

"When are we going to get to the trap?" asked the cartwheeler.

"Vinnie, we're already at the trap," he said with feigned

exasperation. "Nicholas had baited his trap with Christmas cookies, the same way you'd bait a hook with a worm, or put a carrot out if you wanted to capture a bunny. And the elves followed him to the North Pole, where poor Mrs. Claus had been baking for weeks. Pies and cookies and sweet rolls and any kind of delicacy you could imagine. Those elves just about dropped dead when they saw all that food. "To celebrate Christmas," the Santa told them. And so they ate. And they ate some more, and they ate until they fell over into their ice cream bowls too stuffed to eat any more. Now comes the capture. How do you think he captured them, William?"

"It's Bill."

"Oh? I was certain you signed your letter to Santa Claus William. I'm sorry, I won't make that same mistake again. So, how did he capture them?"

"Cages?"

"Nope. Not cages, and you could guess from now until, well, Valentine's Day at least, and you wouldn't get it. He used scissors and honey. It was a very ingenious capture, but then, it was a particularly smart Santa. Now, Marlett kept yelling, "Party over! Let's get out of here!" 'cause he sensed something wrong, but Mrs. Claus kept bringing out more gingerbread and Nicholas kept filling up the punch bowl, and the elves kept gorging themselves and dancing until they all fell asleep. Then Nicholas...."

Silently, from the back of the room, Beth marveled at his mastery in telling this story. She marveled at something else. She knew, watching him enthrall these kids of hers, that what she felt for him was more than simple attraction. The word twirled around in her mind, confusing, but clear, far clearer than she would have expected. Was it possible to love a man she had only known one day? Or more specifically, was it possible that she had fallen in love when she was ten years old, and harbored that love secretly, like her love for Santa Claus, until now?

The thoughts confused Beth. It couldn't be love. It had to be attraction or desire, or even a transferred allegiance to Christmas. Except that this emotion tugging strings in her chest and her mind and her loins felt whole. And with those other things, attraction and desire and Christmas, Beth had always felt there was something vital missing. Something. Or someone.

Thirty five pairs of hands clapped, forcing Beth from her reminiscing. "...and that's how the Santa found elves to help him," Nicholas was saying to the appreciative audience. Beth shook her head, disorganized, yet the school clock indicated that only a few minutes had passed.

"Back to your desks now," she told the students, who scattered quickly. "It's almost time for the Pledge of Allegiance."

"Are you all right?" Nicholas asked.

She didn't think so. Love was many things, but never anything as simplistic as "all right."

"Sure," she answered as she walked him toward the back door. "But I missed the ending. You'll have to fill me in, sometime. I'd never heard it before."

"See, kids," Nicholas said with a conspiratorial wink toward her, "you guys thought Ms. Anderson knew everything there was to know about Christmas, yet she'd never heard the tale of how the elves got trapped."

Twenty-five kids howled with laughter. "Now, you be good for Ms. Anderson, and remember, you never know when Santa's going to be watching."

She wanted to say something, some secret code of confession, something only he could understand to mark this milestone, when she had fallen in love for the first time, and Beth would have, except the door opened before Nicholas had a chance to slip through it, and Rachael, dressed in leather, with boots to her thighs, entered.

She smiled with a thousand watt brightness and wrapped her arms around his neck. "Nickie, Grandma told me you'd be here."

Beth was too controlled to sneer. Instead she watched Rachael, her make-up applied so artfully she could grace the cover of *Cosmo* at a moment's notice, with her possessive hold, molding against him, when the scurvy bum didn't even bother to pry himself away. Nicholas didn't say anything, but his answering glance, Beth thought was far too warm.

"I've authorized some changes at the store. I thought you'd like to see them, before I sat you back on the throne."

Throne? Who died and made him king? Until she realized Rachael meant Santa's throne. Santa, who now Beth was thinking, was the worst traitor since...well since ever.

"I'd love to see what you've done," Nicholas answered, honey sweet tones, and a grin as possessive as any miser with a dime.

The opening address from the principal arrived over the loud speaker, introducing the student whose turn it was at the Pledge. Automatically Beth put her hands over her heart. Her broken, shattered, useless heart.

"I'll tell you about the elves later," Nicholas told her as he vanished out the playground door, into the snow, into Rachael's arms.

"Great." Yeah, really great. She gets the true story of the Christmas elves and Rachael gets a partner for gymnastics on silk sheets. Fair trade, Beth groused, watching Rachael swagger against him, rubbing hip against hip. After I pluck her hair out and pull her fingernails and break her legs.

When she got home, Beth decided she would check to see if parasitic mistletoe was poisonous. If it were, she'd certainly find a use for it.

And no matter what, she'd survive. For the heaven she thought she'd found had another name. Hell.

CHAPTER 11

Beth flew out of the school, her coat unbuttoned, the wool scarf she wore flaring out behind her. She was half-way into the parking lot before she stopped in her tracks. Her car wasn't where she normally parked it.

She was too upset, too harried, too exhausted to do anything but choose some rather select four-letter words, not that some of them weren't considerably longer. Grinding her teeth she plotted the demise of every single Christmas elf she would come across—even if she never learned how they got trapped.

The day had been long. Anticipating the holiday vacation, high on candy canes and Christmas baking, her normally attentive, intelligent kids acted like monsters fed after dark. They had done everything but swing from the chandeliers, and she wouldn't have put it past any of them to do that, had they been able to round up a chandelier.

But the absolute, positive worst blotch on a day that was ink-stained since five that morning was that every single minute she had a chance to take a breather, her miserable, traitorous body thought of Nicholas. Nicholas and the way he looked at her which made her feel warm and cherished. Nicholas and the way he touched her that brightened up her life with more wattage than the spotlights on the national Christmas tree. Nicholas who made her feel like a woman.

After the 4:10 bell and the school had emptied out, Beth forced herself to keep busy. She hung up her workshop in the auditorium, made adjustments to the other decorations, and worked on or finished some seventy-odd projects that were piling up all around her. Not that it helped. She hadn't realized this, but it was entirely possible to think of Nicholas, feel entirely wanton, and hang one hundred and twenty-five construction paper Santas in the hallway between the main school door and the auditorium. As a matter of fact, each time she touched another Santa, it only brought his image into sharper focus.

Standing in the deserted parking lot, Beth took stock of her current situation. Throwing a tantrum seemed to be her most viable option, for although she had a building key, and thus access to a phone, the outer door had locked behind her, and it was far too dark to dig through her purse to locate the key.

The winter night had fallen significantly sometime in the last half hour, and snow which had been slushy when she rushed out of the building was already starting to freeze into rather significant ruts. Apparently the temperature was dropping faster than her spirits, if such a thing were possible. She had a party to prepare for, even if she had to—perish the thought—buy the necessary brownies at a store on the way home. If she could get home, which didn't seem likely since her car had vanished.

If someone had stolen the miserable junk heap, she supposed that would be a blessing, but why did it have to happen tonight of all nights?

So who did she call first, the police the report a missing car or the holiday suicide hotline? But no, the decision was taken from her hands. Her car appeared, slowly creeping up the driveway toward her, which should have, but didn't, make her feel better. Whoever had stolen the car decided it wasn't worth ripping off.

Nicholas leaned over, opened the passenger door. "I'm sorry I'm late. I had breadsticks in the oven that I couldn't leave, and then this heap of junk stalled at every major intersection, and—" then he looked at her, and whatever complaints he was about to air dropped off into oblivion, and he grinned, intimately, potent enough to make Beth forget that the second before she had been on the verge of freezing to death.

"Get in. I know you've had a bad day, but we've got to hurry. The kids have already started to arrive."

Which meant it was exactly as she suspected: a total disaster. The day had just gotten worse.

Beth slammed the car door from the inside and it locked with a solid thunk. The heater didn't seem to be working, and the windshield was doing its best to reach one hundred percent opacity. Nicholas shifted into drive and was heading toward home before she even got her seat belt secured.

"Did you have a pleasant day with Rachael?" Petty jealousy didn't sit well with her, and almost immediately she regretted her barb.

"Yes. The Christmas decorations look much better. She has them positioned differently. The kids love it."

Kids? The school day hadn't been that long. He and Rachael couldn't possibly have... "Oh, kids. At the store."

Nicholas raised an eyebrow, looked at her as if she'd grown another eye. "You look like you had a miserable day."

"I did." Sitting beside him wasn't making things any easier. Still, even if it were petty and belittling, she had to know. "About Rachael—"

"Beth, I didn't even see her for more than a few minutes. I spent the morning as Santa and the afternoon in the kitchen. Now, are you satisfied?"

No. Not until Rachael gained fifty pounds and developed dermatitis. His sincerity, and her own whimsy tickled a funny bone. With her laughter, she felt better. Less jealous, less bitter, more...in love. Better. "Yes," she answered.

"Beth, if it makes you feel any better, she doesn't know about the mistletoe."

It made her feel a thousand times better.

"Now put your head back and relax. You've got ten minutes of peace before I drop you back into the thick of things."

It was an offer too good to refuse. With her eyes shut and her breathing starting to regulate, Beth wondered if he were indeed magic, for the tension drained out of her in waves. "I'd forgotten you had the car. I was about to put out an APB."

"I hadn't expected you'd be so late."

That he hadn't responded to her statement didn't surprise her quite as much as the fine print between his words. She hadn't called to tell him when she was leaving, and yet he obviously hadn't been cooling his heels in the parking lot for the past two hours.

Love, was it ever easy, or was it like believing in Santa, something far more suited to children? And like her belief in Santa, her love was not something she could turn off. It had taken residency deep within her chest, and wasn't about to be evicted by half-truths and past resentments. Even if she had to treat it circumspectly and never let him know, love was here to stay.

"Oh, I almost forgot." He reached behind him to the back seat and pulled out a foil wrapped package, about a foot long, half that in diameter. "Eat this. It's not much, but I doubt you'll have time for much else once I throw you into the fray."

Absently, too exhausted to show much curiosity, she unwrapped it, finding three plump cheese-sprinkled breadsticks, still toasty warm from the oven. It explained the earthy, yeasty smell from the car which she had been half-tempted to attribute to lust.

Beth bit into the first heavenly light breadstick. It was precisely and exactly what her body had been craving. Then, with one hand still on the wheel, he reached back, and returned with a thermos. "Drink. It's the best I could do."

It was, oddly enough, milk, the perfect compliment to the bread. When Nicholas pulled onto her street, Beth found herself licking her fingers, the impromptu meal finished. And so, apparently, was her temporary reprieve. Panic seized her.

"Not here. We've got to get to the store."

"No," he answered calmly. "I've got everything under control."

"Nicholas, you don't understand. We've got to rush. There's a hundred thousand things that we have to do in the next half-hour."

Nicholas reached out, touched her arm, already taking liberty he promised himself he wouldn't. "Relax. Everything is ready."

"You don't understand." Her breath came out in great gasps, fogging up the windshield. "All my students, almost every kid in the family and more than half the neighbors are coming. Nothing is done."

It had quite literally slipped her mind. Ordinarily her party took place on a Saturday afternoon, and earlier in the month, but this year, between other parties, dance lessons, karate instruction, sickness, school and fifty other interruptions, the only time the majority of the kids could make it was tonight.

Beth ran out of the car before he brought the engine to a

complete stop, and vanished down the stairs to the kitchen, throwing her briefcase and all winter paraphernalia onto the bed without putting them away.

"Grandma!"

Her grandmother sat, as customary, in her rocker. In her arms, cradled and sound asleep, one of the younger family members, two month old Jason William. Five other children, relatives all, sat in varying degrees of repose around the coal burning stove and now that she had time to think about it, there were many, many more nieces, nephews and students upstairs by the tree. She had passed them without really seeing them in her flurry to leap headfirst into the preparations.

From upstairs she heard the record player kick out '*O Come, All Ye Faithful*,' and children's laughter wafted down, stronger even than the familiar carol. It didn't matter at all that someone up there had started festivities. This whole thing had the makings of a catastrophe of the highest order.

As she had when she realized her car was missing, Beth stopped and took stock of the situation in a calm, rational manner, starting with a rather sustained scream, and from there, thrusting her hands into her curls so she could pull out all her hair in great, painful clumps.

The kitchen looked to be what could only be described as detritus from a Force 10 earthquake. Every pot, every pan, every serving bowl, mixing bowl, cereal bowl and cat food bowl was filthy, piled haphazardly, some in stacks ready to come crashing down at any second. The counters were covered in flour or crumbs or onion wrappings. A baby slept soundly in her grandmother's arms, and a black and white cat placidly licked a front paw, but they were the only two who hadn't realized yet that all hell had broken loose.

There was no way she could cancel the festivities or postpone it for the ten or so hours it would take to put this kitchen back to rights. This party was a time out for the parents to catch up on some last minute shopping, to surreptitiously wrap presents or to just fall into a heap on the living room couch and plan new strategies for the coming season. No, there had to be a party, and this was what she had to work with.

Beth threw her hands up in the air. "Grandma, what happened here?"

But it was Nicholas, not Catherine, who answered. "Christmas. It happens this time every year."

His chuckle by itself was enough to make her want to wrap her hands around his throat and strangle the life out of him. She turned to face him, her anger finally finding a target. "Christmas? Do you mean to tell me that in the name of Christmas, you trashed my kitchen on the day I've got fifty thousand kids coming here to see Santa Claus?"

Neither her tirade, nor the fact that somehow she had picked up a rather large carving knife and pointed it at him, seemed to have any effect on Nicholas. He was, drat his miserable soul, "ho, ho, ho-ing," as if this were, really and truly, a natural disaster staged solely for her benefit.

"Yes," he answered simply.

If there was more to his explanation, Beth didn't give him the opportunity to say it. "I don't have time to clean up."

Realizing she still held the knife, Beth dropped it, watching in horror as a stack of dishes teetered and almost fell.

"You don't have to clean up."

"I don't? I suppose some Christmas elf is going to appear and magically wash the dishes."

Catherine chuckled, and Nicholas with his twinkle firmly entranced in his eyes muttered, "Something like that."

"No, really, what's going on?"

From upstairs Beth heard the doorbell chimes, and it occurred to her the sound had been rather continuous since she flew down the stairs. Her party was happening whether she was ready for it or not.

Nicholas, minus his coat and gloves, was already busy rolling up the sleeves of his plaid chambray shirt. "Relax. Count to ten, then go up and supervise your party."

"I'm about ready to scream." Except she had already tried that and it hadn't worked. The kitchen still looked like she should fill out paperwork for federal disaster relief.

Setting aside the bottle of lemon scented dish soap he had just squirted into a basin, he gently pulled her into his arms and thumped her, quite comfortingly, on the back. His voice was lowered, private, soothing.

"Beth, people will still love you if everything's not perfect, but that is beside the point. It may not look it but everything is under control. Your grandmother told me what needed to be done and I did it. And don't worry about the mess. I made it, I'll clean it up." He held her out from his chest, not quite the length of his arms. "Are you okay?"

"I don't believe this." Where had the anger gone? She only knew that no one ever had treated her with such sensitivity.

Without releasing Beth from his embrace, Nicholas turned off the kitchen taps. He cupped her face in his hands, kissed the worry-lines on her forehead. Already she was starting to feel familiar, a part of him. The moment might have lengthened, except around them the children who had been nestling on the linoleum scampered up, toward the stairs, toward the party with very loud screams, that could only be described as war-whoops. Whatever Beth's grandmother had promised them had certainly caught their interest.

Except for Catherine, still rocking the baby, on one long-tailed cat practicing yoga contortions to lick its own tail, they were alone.

"Beth, I told you I would help you."

Tears pooled in the corners of her eyes. She was as close to collapse as any woman he'd ever seen. "I was going to get to it."

"I know you were." The words were wrapped in kindness.

"You should have let me."

He kissed her forehead again, one gentle brushing not enough for either of them. Nicholas fought down a primal urge there really wasn't time to explore. Every time he held her, every time he thought of her, his hormones explored the possibility of taking their relationship further.

"It's my job, my responsibility." Beth hadn't caught on to the private war Nicholas was waging with his own body. Thank goodness.

"How? The kids are already here. I didn't mean to take over. I only meant to help. Now go, enjoy yourself and make this party one of those memorable experiences they'll still remember years from now. I'll be up to help you when I can. I've got everything under control."

She shrugged from his touch and surveyed the kitchen, realizing belatedly that it wasn't all disaster. A double batch of chili simmered in the stew pot and two batches of homemade breadsticks cooled on racks which the night before had held gingerbread cookies.

"Your grandmother said they would eat chili only if they had breadsticks," Nicholas murmured softly.

"And these?" Her hands shook. She was still willing to lynch him for jurisdictional—and hygiene—problems, but little by little she discovered order in the chaos.

Beth pointed to about three dozen foil wrapped squares which overflowed a yellow popcorn bowl. Each was tied like a package with red curling ribbon, and held a long loop, perfect for being draped on a Christmas tree.

"Brownies. Isn't that what you told me you needed?"

Beside that bowl was Christmas candy sealed in colored plastic wrap. Also for the tree. She would have done it exactly the same way herself, had she had the time.

With an unconscious movement Beth swiped at her eyes. "This isn't enough brownies. I'll have to make a more."

"No, there's a good six batches in the freezer, wrapped, ready for ribbon whenever you need them."

She did that too.

On the kitchen table, another surprise. "And the pecan logs?"

"I didn't know about that, but your Aunt Ruth was here most of the afternoon and told me precisely what she was expecting for Christmas."

The ludicrousness of the situation and the fact that he was clearly understating what had happened had her fighting giggles.

"Yes, she would."

Nicholas shoved the bowl of brownies into her hands as he picked up the one of wrapped candy and a large shopping bag of private recipe candy canes, sent with love from Marlett. "Now get yourself upstairs and enjoy your party. I'll help you carry these, then finish cleaning up down here. Yell when you're ready for the chili and I'll have it dished out, ready to go."

Beth stopped, stunned. "Nicholas, I—I'm sorry for the things I accused you of—"

"No problem. I had fun today. I like cooking, and I love Christmas."

"Santa—"

He was taken aback, for the tiniest second, thinking she had seen through his shallow disguise.

"Yes?"

"I'm expecting Santa Claus."

"You are?"

"What's gotten into you? For the kids. My friend Leonard."

Nicholas saw no need to tell her that her friend Leonard Pskowick had a solid case of the shingles. "When you're ready, Santa will be here." And hopefully for the rest of her life she'd have Santa. Or a reasonable facsimile.

"Nicholas, I want—"

"Beth, we will talk later. You've got to supervise seventy kids decorating our tree."

Our tree, she thought, climbing up the stairs. Our tree. If she had fallen in love, she realized, it hadn't happened with a silly story about elves, but in the comfort in the candlelit darkness decorating "our tree."

***

"What's the matter Beth, you seem a little distracted."

Distracted? Distraught was closer to the truth. Beth wrinkled her forehead as she surveyed the chaos which surrounded them. "It's just that Santa is late. Leonard should have been here a good twenty minutes ago."

As an excuse it was valid. Her party was deteriorating around her, and would be qualified as a disaster if Santa didn't put in an appearance soon. But as the truth, it only scratched the surface.

The old woman nodded sagely. "Fight for him, Beth. If he's what you want, you've got to fight for him."

"Leonard?" The man was sixty-two if he was a day, a hardened, roughened Pennsylvania mountainman.

"No, not Leonard, child. Nicholas."

She cuffed Vinnie on the neck as he was about to toss a missile formed from the aluminum paper used to wrap the brownies. The boy dropped his weapon, looked innocent, disappeared quickly. "Nicholas is with Rachael. He doesn't need me."

"I wouldn't be quite so sure about that."

"Well, what am I going to do?" She bent down, swiped at ice cream melting on the carpet.

"You could start by telling him that you love him."

"Grandma, I meant about Santa Claus. He's late."

The kids, which included almost one hundred percent of her class except for Mary Rose Jaworski who had pink eye and was forced to stay home, although she did send her younger sister in her place, were starting to bounce off the walls. These Pennsylvania bred kids with their cast iron stomachs had devoured all the chili and breadsticks as well as the cake and ice cream Nicholas had served for desert. They were more than half-way through their Santa lollipops--except for the kids who bit, they were finished—and had already started on the packaged brownies decorating the tree. The tinsel was up, as was the noise level. Everything else, including her tolerance for pain, was down.

"Ho! Ho! Ho! Merry Christmas."

Finally. Beth breathed a sigh of relief. Santa had come and not a minute too soon. Vinnie might live to see Christmas Eve after all.

But, something was distinctly wrong. Instead of entering in through the front door, Santa was coming up from the downstairs. Not that it mattered. There was screaming even the hearing impaired could hear as far away as New Jersey. Third graders weren't the only true believers. Every kid who was related to Beth knew that to get anything at all for Christmas he or she had to profess an undying belief not only in the real reason for Christmas, but in Jolly old St. Nick himself.

With screams and war-whoops, the man coming up the stairs was mobbed. A flash of panic seized Beth. By shape alone she knew it wasn't Leonard. This guy was a good six inches taller. The potential for disaster was high. One of the things that made her Santa party so special was that Santa always knew the children by name, always mentioned something rather specific, "Well, Joey, did you finally finish paying off that window you broke throwing acorns at the Johnson house? That's great. Then I guess I'll be able to keep you on my Good list."

Fighting through bodies with considerably less ease than she figured Moses had parting the Red Sea, Santa made his way to the heavy rocker which pre-dated even her. The traditional Santa seat.

It was then she caught that familiar twinkle in his eye and Beth knew with a surety who the stand-in Santa was. Nicholas.

With a look of exasperation at her grandmother, Beth darted through the swarm, hoping to prevent disaster.

"Peggy Jo, why don't you go first?" Beth said, highlighting the name. Please, she muttered to herself, let him pick up my clues.

"There's no need for that," Santa said with a chuckle. "I'm going to start right here with Sara Catherine." The baby, not quite eighteen months, smiled, completely at ease with the strange man in the red suit and long, flowing beard. "I especially wanted to thank you, Sara Catherine, for that fabulous letter you and your brothers wrote me."

The baby laughed again, and Beth knew the party was saved.

"So who's the new Santa?" Susan asked as she arrived over an hour later to pick up Jamie and four neighbors.

"A friend of Rachael's."

"Oh?" Susan asked, sensing more to the story.

"And an old friend of mine. Isn't he wonderful?" Unbelievable probably came closer to the truth.

"That's right. Jamie mentioned him. He really is good."

"He is at that." At the moment Beth figured her faith in Santa had peaked. Ruth and her grandmother must have tutored him for hours that morning, although she clearly overlooked the fallacy in that conclusion—they couldn't have known all the juicy tidbits about the students from her class.

Beth grabbed Jamie as he climbed off Nicholas' lap. The child felt frail. He'd been losing weight and the flush on his cheeks spoke of fever.

"Hi, Jamie, how did you like the party?" Susan had kept him out of school that day, fighting an infection, but after twelve hours in bed, he said he couldn't miss Santa. Susan, acting on doctor's advice that they treat him as a normal kid, had allowed Jamie to come.

"It was the best ever," the eight year old said. "I told you before, he has to be the real Santa, not one of his helpers."

"Oh, you're sure, are you?" Susan asked tousling his hair.

"Positive."

"You know," Beth said, watching as Nicholas pulled Vinnie Scalano up onto his lap, "I do believe you're right."

Beth didn't expel a sigh of relief until Vinnie climbed down. "That's the last of them," she whispered, feeling just a tiny bit complacent, just a moment too soon.

"Not quite," Nicholas said using a low, throaty voice, deeper, more intimate than he'd used on any of the children. "There is still one person who hasn't sat on old Santa's lap."

Realization dawned slowly as Beth looked around the now almost deserted living room. "Everyone's gone—" except that he was looking at her, and quick as a rattler's strike, Nicholas grabbed her wrist, started pulling her toward him.

"Don't fight this," he said with a smile wide enough to stuff an entire fruitcake into.

"No, absolutely not. No."

"Come on, Aunt Beth. You know you fight this every year."

She gave Jamie a don't-you-start-on-me look which cost her several inches. The few straggling relatives joined in the chorus. "Go for it, Aunt Beth."

"And to give you privacy," Susan said, thrusting all the

remaining children, including Vinnie, toward the door, "we're leaving."

With a look filled with desperation Beth silently begged her not to go. Susan's only response, a hearty laugh cut off as the heavy door shut behind her.

"It's tradition, isn't it, for Miss Anderson to sit on Santa's lap at the conclusion of the party?" Nicholas wrapped his arms around her. There was no way she was getting free.

Beth growled, decided to cede gracefully while she plotted what she would do to her grandmother for providing this priceless bit of embarrassment.

"Are you going to tell Santa what you want?"

The words were seductive and wrapped themselves around her with promises she had no intention of investigating. She struggled again, found it counter-productive for it only rubbed her sensitive body against far too much of his.

"I want you to go back to Rachael and stop bothering me."

"I don't think you do. Besides, Rachael is gone. Tonight there's just the two of us."

"Santa, really!" Beth let shock run through her words as he reached out, cupped her chin, moved his head close to hers. "Aren't you supposed to give me a candy cane, tell me to behave myself?"

His breath was sweet. The wiry mustache tickled her lips. "Candy canes are for the children, Beth and believe me, you're behaving exactly the way I want you to."

His hold changed in subtle yet significant ways. His fingers crept under the hair at the nape of her neck. Shivers merged with the new, yet inexplicably familiar feelings within her body. This was Santa. He should be safe. She shouldn't be yearning, aching, throbbing.

"You want to know what I want? I want you to stop this instant." One final, token protest which he recognized as well as she did. She didn't want him to stop, and she didn't want to think about Rachael. What had been building up between them had to be dealt with.

His eyes undressed her. His laugh started low in his chest,

seductive, enveloping, primal. "I know what you want this Christmas, Beth. I've always known. It really hasn't changed over the past ten years, although this is the first time I've been able to do anything about it." His words couldn't have been more intimate had they been spoken in the dark over a shared pillow.

"What do I want?" She wasn't being bold or brazen, nor was she being coy. Beth had some fairly indistinct ideas which were more feelings and yearnings than anything she'd been able to put into words. She wanted to hear his analysis, to see if he could decipher the motivations for the Christmas wishes she'd never wished for, all the years that she'd privately asked Santa for gifts for others.

Love. Love. Love. Was that her heart or his? The whisper was silent. Neither one of them had spoken, yet again she had the idea that words between them were unnecessary.

"How about if Santa tells you what he wants? One kiss, Beth. Just one little kiss."

Nicholas had every intention of leaving that evening. His bag was packed, he'd repaired all the damage done in the kitchen, all the dishes scrubbed, even the floor had a wet mopping, and he'd almost convinced himself that he'd gotten all he came for, or at least all he was going to take, and there she was, in his arms after whispering to Susan that he was the one and only Santa Claus.

The woman had no idea what she did to him. His body ached in places that Santa's body didn't normally ache, and it was all her fault. And it was growing geometrically worse every time she wiggled her tight little bottom against his loins.

He had only meant this to be a spontaneous hug, a friendly hug, a thankful hug, but the minute her body pressed against his, all his Santa-honed good intentions fled up the chimney.

Sparks. Firecrackers. The Hallelujah Chorus. Around him and through him the magic of Christmas bubbled beneath a new, sharper awareness. Beth. Crazy, sexy Beth.

Not that she was dressed anything like a vamp. The woman couldn't have looked more like a teddy bear had she tried. She wore an oversized white sweat shirt, with what he was coming to recognize as typical Beth aplomb, a liquid-embroidery Santa grinning across her chest. She wore pants, because, she told him that morning on the way to school, she had to do a lot of climbing and directing preparing the kids for the Christmas pageant. Her earrings were again Santas, these considerably less avant-garde than the ones from the day before. Beth and her love of Santa. Beth in his arms at long last.

Nicholas tightened the embrace. He kept his fingers intertwined behind her back, more than half afraid that he was moving too quickly. He wanted to tell her he loved her for there could be no denying that. Even when he had been planning on leaving her, the state of his heart had not been in question.

He wanted to tell her everything, confess what his family had been doing for the past two thousand years. He wanted to take her home and put his gigantic old bed to good use.

The fight flew out of her, and with what he hoped wasn't resignation but desire, she leaned her head against his shoulder. "I like the costume," she said.

"Thank you, it's my favorite." Not the one he wore for Christmas, but one which saw a lot of use nonetheless. Rachael hadn't liked it, but that no longer mattered. Rachael had brought him to Beth, for which she would be amply rewarded in her stocking this year. And Rachael now understood from his firm good-bye that there was no future for them. Regardless as to whether or not he would act upon it, his heart belonged to Beth.

She laughed and rubbed her nose against his, which unfortunately had the unintended result of also rubbing the tips of her breasts against his chest. He drew in a slow, shaky breath, had to deliberately stifle a groan. A heavy, thick costume. Layers of padding. And he felt the firm tips from her breasts against his chest as if they had both been naked. His body reacted predictably, feeding his own passion.

Beth tweaked the fluffy gray hair covering his chin. She laughed, liking the feel of it, enjoying the tactile sensation and the freedom. She'd never quite been liberated enough to touch Leonard's beard or any of the other fake Santas' she'd come across over the years.

It wasn't soft like the hair on his head, but thicker, scratchier. It was simply delightful. "And I need to apologize for all the beard pullers." The worst of the lot had been Vinnie Scalano who hadn't quit until he had a handful of hair. Nicholas was certain he'd have a permanent scan on his chin. "It's something of a tradition around here." So much of a tradition that Leonard, her missing Santa Claus, started growing his beard during deer hunting season and didn't shave it off until the swelling in his face went down, often days later.

The woman was raising all kinds of havoc with his body and she was apologizing? "Everyone who plays Santa gets used to it fairly quickly."

She tweaked harder, curious, but beyond that very much liking the feel of his hair between her fingers. "I don't know what you use to keep that thing on but it's really working."

"Ouch! Stop that." With a growl, he removed her hand. "I have to put up with that from the kids, but I draw the line at you."

"So it's natural?"

"Yup."

"From this afternoon, after you served the chili and cake?"

Nicholas scowled and his neck disappeared into his chest. "Why do you think it took me so long to come up the stairs? I could have been up a good half-hour sooner if I wanted to be seen in a wimpy beard."

"Oh, right."

"Really. The beard goes with the job, but on the whole I prefer to be clean-shaven."

"Beth, oh, excuse me. I didn't know."

Beth broke from the hug, stood quickly, her face colored red enough to put poor old Rudolph's nose to shame.

"Grandma, I didn't hear you. Mr. St. Noel and I were—"

"I could see what you were. Don't let it bother you. I'm going to bed. These tired old bones have had enough excitement for one day."

"You can't go now. We've got to put the manger up tonight."

Nicholas rolled his eyes. He didn't know where Beth found the energy. He was ready to drop and she was all set to start another project.

"It will have to wait until tomorrow. I don't suppose you realize how late it is, do you?"

"Eight?" Beth asked hopefully.

"It's after ten. Every single parent was late picking up kids."

That was the truth. They each had a different excuse, all which involved running all over town looking for the perfect present, or putting together a bike so it wouldn't have to be done Christmas eve, to trouble securing a racquetball court. It was a busy time of year. They had all taken advantage.

"As long as the manger is up before Christmas, it don't much matter to me. We'll do it after supper tomorrow."

Beth kissed her grandmother's paper thin cheek. "Please? I won't be able to sleep knowing it's still in the box."

"Nicholas, you talk her out of this."

His body still tingled, still felt hot. If the old woman went to bed now, he'd find some way to capture Beth into his arms again and they were moving far too fast. He wanted more than a quick tumble, things like trust and forever and promises, things that he wouldn't get if he betrayed her now with unbridled lust.

He had figured out, through touch and inspiration, exactly what was in the box. "It's important that the true meaning of Christmas doesn't get overshadowed with parties and presents."

"Open the box, girl," Catherine said with dry resignation. "It's time we unearthed the manger for another year."

Beth lifted the lid off, looked down through the crumpled tissue paper and the years of memories. She reached in and pulled the first piece out, a shepherd.

"May I?"

"Of course." With pride and reverence, she handed it to Nicholas.

"It's absolutely gorgeous."

"It's our treasure. Through all the years when my mother and her sisters were growing up and money was tight, from my childhood when I knew the budget couldn't cover everything I wanted, we always had this, and it was always enough."

The carved shepherd Nicholas held in his hands was both very simple and unbelievably complex. The figure wore a loose tunic and his feet were in sandals. On his shoulders, as traditionally recognized, rested a lamb with fleece thick enough to sheer. His face radiated awe and awareness through wide-opened eyes, a reverently tilted head.

Nicholas recognized the love that had been etched into this ornament. Reluctantly he handed the piece back to Beth knowing there were additional treasures, pieces of beauty that would still the restlessness of his spirit and return his conviction. Beth placed the shepherd gently on the coffee table.

In the Santa rocking chair, Catherine swung back and forth, silently. Beth's eyes were bright as she spoke. "Every Christmas from the first year of their marriage until the year he died, my grandfather carved a piece of the nativity set for my grandmother."

"Yes," Catherine added, her voice quivering. "I was so thrilled when he gave me the first piece, the Virgin mother."

Beth reached into the box, pulled out a second nativity piece. The Wise Man stood almost seven inches high, carved from a flawless piece of blond oak. The attention to detail was so perfect, Nicholas could almost swear he could see it breathe.

"It was the first present I opened that year and he gave it to me when we were alone and had finished decorating the tree. I don't know when Joseph found the time for he was working long hours. When he came home there were always so many things to do here, but I'll never forget what he said to me, "You are virtuous as the Babe's mother."

By this time, Beth had uncovered the Virgin, and Joseph Vacchioni's eye had been true, for Mary's features were based, through love, on Catherine.

"The next year he gave me Joseph, and after that the angel. The next three years he gave me the wise men, one at a time and after that he gave me the cow and the donkey together, then three camels. He said carving the animals was easier than the people. Over the next years I received two shepherds, and finally two sheep. I was desperate, every year thinking he would give me the Christ child, but he never did. For ten years I had a growing manger scene and no baby. I would beg him, year after year, to give me the infant, but he'd just laugh, saying don't you have enough babies of your own? I had seven children by then, and another one growing inside, and still no Christ child for my mantle.

"Then he was killed, three weeks before Christmas in a mining accident and my heart was gone. We didn't find the final piece until we were preparing the body for burial. It was there, in his Sunday suit coat."

She held the tiny, intricately carved child to her breast. "I think he knew his time was short, and he wanted to leave me something of himself."

"You must have loved him very much."

"I still do. All these years he's been gone and that hasn't changed."

With a hand gnarled with age, Catherine reached over and placed the tiny, intricately carved infant into Nicholas' palm. It was then he realized he still wore his Santa suit, the costume he had hid behind for almost three years. Santa Claus and the Christ Child, many people thought they were incompatible, the lesser overshadowing the power of the greater. Yet here in this simple living room he remembered the promise he made at his father's deathbed, to spread cheer in honor of the God who had been born an infant. What greater token could he offer?

"It's a beautiful set."

"It's more than that. It's my heart."

Catherine stood, setting the chair to rocking behind her as she swayed on knees which had seen too much work, too many years. "Now, I hope you two will forgive me, but I'm an old lady and I need my rest. Stay up, finish decorating the tree. From what I can see you've got at least another hour of work ahead of you to get all the tinsel on straight."

"Yes, Gram." Beth kissed her grandmother's onionskin cheek. Nicholas watched, feeling both an outsider and an intimate member of the family. It occurred to him that for all the times he'd been here delivering presents and promises, he had never noticed the nativity set. He'd always been too busy. Perhaps that was why his Christmas spirit had wavered. It's not that there was no beauty in the homes he visited, but that he'd stopped taking the time to notice.

Perhaps love had opened his eyes to many things.

CHAPTER 12

The tree was nearly perfect, which was the best she could hope for. There would always be tinsel clumped or bare spots, even if they worked year round. It was the nature of the beast. Still, concentrating on the decorations and not on her, Nicholas moved a strand, straightening it until the ends were even and it caught light, reflecting sparkles of red and blue.

Beth arched her back as she tried to work the kinks out. With her head and her shoulders back, her small pert breasts pushed forward in an invitation Nicholas wasn't quite certain she was offering. It didn't matter. He could no more avoid touching her at that second than he could give up Christmas.

"Here, let me."

Before she could respond, he inched aside her fingers, replacing them with his own. Within seconds of his massage, she started to purr. His own reaction was quite a bit more visceral.

Her scent was intoxicating, filling his mind and his senses, leaving him tingling. He felt drunk, as far out of control as he'd ever been. Beyond the tenseness of her shoulders, beyond the electricity they generated together there was softness, as well as a deep vulnerability that she would hide and he would protect.

"Once Christmas is over, I'll relax."

Now where had he heard *that* line before?

She had been right. Nicholas had suspected not a single thing could be added to that tree without the entire thing toppling down, but it did look better with three dozen peppermint candy canes, with what few brownies and plastic wrapped candy ornaments survived to decorate.

But he could find fault with her words. Nicholas doubted that once the holidays passed she'd relax. Teaching was a very demanding profession and her family took every bit of strength her classroom missed. They expected Beth to wait on them, especially Ruth, who didn't mind explaining what needed to be done, but who couldn't consider helping. This Christmas party for example, had been left completely to Beth, not one of the parents offering to help.

And him. Was Nicholas any different? Should Beth accept his proposal, there would be no rest for her. Only more work, a life of giving that for all her efforts his mother hadn't been able to manage.

Beth moved back, out of his reach, startled as if she'd finally realized how personal his ministrations had become. Heaven forbid, he was Santa Claus. Or at least he *looked* like Santa Claus. With the tousled, finger combed white hair, with the beard and the suit and the belly. Santa Claus, a children's image and what she had in mind wasn't childish at all.

"What's your earliest childhood memory?" Beth asked as she oozed from the couch and settled herself cross-legged on the carpet.

It was too much to suspect that she'd just go to bed, put an end to this madness for another day. Stalling, Nicholas picked up a plate he'd left on top of the television. He moistened his index finger, then proceeded to pick up all the crumbs he'd missed from the chocolate cake. His temporary move to Pennsylvania hadn't affected his appetite. Beth had snuck down to the kitchen a few minutes before, bringing up bowls of cheddar topped chili and the last of the chocolate cake he'd baked for the party. They had shared their midnight feast in silence that went well beyond companionable.

He became acutely conscious of the costume he wore, and the fact that right now might not be the best time to give her the truth. He didn't want to have to fight the legend. Not tonight—even if he dressed the part.

"I don't remember last week. When you get to be my age, all the major organs go, especially the brain." Of course, at the moment, other parts of his body were showing a high degree of enthusiasm not quite in keeping with insipid senility.

"Confess," she ordered in her stern, third-grade voice which couldn't have a Colorado quakie shivering in fear. Then she made her threat: "Or I'll tickle you."

How, in the name of all that was legend, did she learn that he was ticklish? It was times like this that he realized his grandfather made a serious mistake when he took time out that one Christmas

Eve to chat with Clement Moore. But then, there was nothing in that poem about him being ticklish, only that hateful statement about his stomach, "that shook when he laughed like a bowl full of jelly." Really. Enough is enough.

"I'm not ticklish." He pouted. He prepared to defend himself. If he needed to spawn an entire new series of rumors about Santa he would do it, up to becoming known as the slasher Claus. He would not let her tickle his extremely sensitive body.

The twinkle in her eye and the quirk to her lips completely belied that the tone of her voice spoke pure malice. "Should we just test that theory out?"

He'd bet not one single kid in the entire elementary school got away with throwing out their green beans when Miss Anderson pulled lunchroom duty. The woman was a tyrant. She deserved to be brought down a peg or two. Even with coal out of the running as a stocking stuffer, he wasn't completely out of options. There was always mistletoe.

She curled her fingers. She moved to her knees, attack position. Nicholas felt vulnerable as he never had before when he realized she could hit nearly any place on his body.

Beth checked a Santa watch, both hands over his head, swaying to the right. After one o'clock. His shoulders ached just thinking about maintaining that position. "You have five minutes."

The executioner had spoken. Nicholas leaned against the couch, hooking one ankle over another, highly polished black boots reflecting Christmas glow. "It's going to take me back a lot of years. A lot of years."

Beth swatted at him with an effort that moved more air than skin cells. "Yes, I can see how old and decrepit you are."

"Hey, the body's in excellent shape considering the mileage." He wiggled eyebrows, trying to prove a point. Proving her own point, she snuck a finger behind his knee. Nicholas exploded in giggles, quite unbecoming.

"I didn't realize I lived differently than other kids at first. Of course no one does. Every child thinks his upbringing is normal, whatever that means. Not that there were a lot of other children around. We lived in what you would call a rather remote area."

Beth shifted, making herself more comfortable, leaning against his legs. It was becoming increasingly difficult to remember what exactly he was trying to do here.

"My mother couldn't stand it. Not that she didn't love my father, not that she didn't believe, but it was just something she couldn't deal with. She needed people and restaurants. I remember once she was annoyed at something and she shouted, 'Doesn't anyone celebrate Easter around here?' It had never occurred to me. My life was Christmas. I must have been three or four, but it was rather profound. She went on, 'How about Valentine's Day? How about Thanksgiving?' So my father let her take me traveling. I know he was against it. Because he loved her, he wanted her to share his life, but he knew she was unhappy, and he did the best he could. We traveled around for years, spending the holidays in different parts of the world where my father would always look us up.

"I wasn't sure what I wanted. It was a confusing time for me. I could easily see my mother's point of view, there is more to life than Christmas, but my father was a very dynamic man, and once a year anyway the excitement centered around him. Mom and I lived out of suitcases. I never knew where her wanderlust came from, but at least some of it had a basis in guilt, after all, she knew who he was when she married him, and she knew it's never easy living with a legend.

"We ended up here, somehow, the car ran out of gas or there was a snow storm or she liked the sunset. My mother's reasons for settling were rarely logical. I was unhappy. I didn't like always being the new kid, and whenever I opened my mouth, I invariably put my foot in it. Like you, I had more than my fair share of black eyes defending Santa Claus to a world where basically no one wanted to believe anymore.

"Anyway, with one thing or another, by the time I was thirteen, I decided I didn't want to believe in Santa anymore. I didn't believe in the Easter bunny or the tooth fairy, did I? I decided my mother was right. I didn't have to follow in my father's footsteps. I could be a doctor or a lawyer or sell insurance. I was willing to—as my mother put it—to get out of the rut.

"So here I was with this new resolve to ignore the family vocation when I went out walking one morning and found you being tormented at the bus stop. It was like a cannon going off, so profound was the shock. Trying to make my mother love me, I had been denying Christmas, but I'd been born to celebrate Christmas and denying my role was against my nature. You put my life back into perspective. When I disappeared you must have thought I dropped off the face of the earth but I went home to my father, helped him, and while I was doing that, I learned what I was meant to do."

"And what was that?" she asked, her voice quiet.

"To give presents."

"Why?"

He shrugged, decided it might be safer for all concerned if he didn't follow his inclinations. "At first I gave gifts because my father did and it made me happy to follow his lead, and perversely, because my mother was against it and like most teenagers I had to flaunt her authority. Now there is a different reason for every present I leave under a Christmas tree."

"Tell me."

"Beth, I don't know. There's too many to think about."

"Nicholas, I want to know. It's important to me."

"You must know, Beth. You do it yourself."

"Please, just tell me."

The words came easily and he wondered if some of Marlett's instructions, some of his father's example hadn't rubbed off on him more than he suspected. "I do it to spread remembrance of the birth, bring happiness to others, ease suffering, reward good works, keep the faith alive, fight back against the darkness, create memories of hope or unity, and sometimes, simply, because I'm told to."

"Someone gives you orders?"

"Very, very rarely. Mostly I, and those who work with me, work on our own."

She smiled slowly, an action based on contemplation more than pleasure, a deep seeded smile, pulled from her values and not from her hormones. "I think you're a good man, Mr. Nicholas St. Noel."

He met her gaze, and again, inexplicably, his pulse climbed. "You wouldn't say that if you knew what I was thinking."

Her eyes were wide with innocence. "Why, what are you thinking?"

Nicholas held his hand out, and so lightly that she wasn't certain she even felt it, he traced the delicate structure of her chin. "I haven't changed my mind, you know. I meant what I said when Ole Santa had you on his lap. I would like to kiss you."

Her heart thudded once, deep within her chest, a passionate awareness that almost knocked all the oxygen from her lungs and all the sanity from her mind. It had been there, this awareness, since she first met him, standing by the naked Christmas tree. It had simmered as he baked the Christmas cookies and they bantered over pot roast and steamed veggies. It been heightened as she watched him handling the delicate, homemade ornaments, hanging them on the tree with respect and honor. And, it had intensified as tears flooded her eyes when they had recalled the history of her Grandmother's crèche. She had wanted this kiss an awfully long time.

Beth smiled, shy and uncertain, and knew more than desire. Happiness blossomed within her, although she couldn't quite discern the source. She hadn't known him that long for Nicholas to be completely responsible for this urgency she felt, but then, she very much doubted that it had its roots in loneliness or deprivation either. It was too strong, too right, to be anything she would ignore.

The house was silent. No traffic sloshed through the melting snow, no dog howled at whatever sliver of moon poked through the clouds. They were alone, a primal feeling, a beginning of time aura. They were wrapped in an intimacy of their own making.

"May I kiss you?"

Was it possible that he had taken her silence as refusal?

Beth reached out, cupping his chin, her hands trembling as his had trembled. "I would like that very much." Her breathing quickened, and the pupils of her eyes, which had grown small in the dim light, looked brighter, more intense. She didn't quite meet his gaze squarely, but she didn't look away. He saw that much as a concession on her part, a victory for his.

Her lips parted slightly, not a grin, not a frown, but maybe an invitation. The confusion he had seen so often in her, the is-this-the-right-thing-to-do look which she wore almost every time he touched her vanished, slowly heading toward an acceptance, of what he wanted, of what she did herself. He rubbed his index finger against her lips, lightly, barely a caress. The corners of her lips tweaked upward, then she let her tongue dart out, and moistened her lips, not quite accidentally touching his roving finger as well. It was the most seductive movement Nicholas had ever experienced.

He brought his other hand up, cupped her jawline, trapped her as he inched himself closer. "May I kiss you?"

There was no other light to the room but that from the Christmas tree, and she could see reflected in his pupils the red, green, blue and gold from the bulbs. "There is no need to be afraid," he said. It was perhaps, the first and only time he would lie to her.

"I'm not," Beth answered honestly, although her pulse raced and she had a very real feeling that she should bolt and hide somewhere, preferably under the bed.

With a slow, erotic scissor motion he caressed her ear, sending tingles to every throbbing cell within her body. She moaned, and her hips, responding to his stimulus rocked gently in the time honored pull-of-tide motion of lovers.

He whispered things, endearments more than words, expressions she'd never heard before, or read about in a book. His tones transcended language, spoke directly to her heart. Love responded, growing more complete. She'd always had a heart. Now, with Nicholas pressed against her, holding her, caressing her, she knew why.

With the knowledge that she had cut off one of her senses when she needed to experience this vibrant assault without limitations, Beth opened her eyes. She was thrilled to watch him, eager to experience all of the initiation he had to offer her.

"Mmmmm," she said, because she could think of no words which would adequately describe the sensation, not even the poetry he had been reciting. She had forgotten that he wore the beard and for a moment she didn't recognize him, not as Nicholas anyway. His eyes were dark, incredibly deep. His mouth was open. Inviting.

Beth filled her lungs slowly, breathing through her nose, hypersensitive to the expansion of her lungs, the intense way he watched her. The room smelled of fresh cut pine, of the brownies he had baked earlier, chili and chocolate and vanilla, and it smelled sharply of old, familiar tradition, but of Nicholas, she could pick up no intrinsic scent at all. Even this close to him, she only smelled Christmas, not man at all.

Then, almost before she was ready, he leaned over and brought his lips in contact with hers. The coil loosened and exploded, but it was easy to see that what she felt was only a minute fraction of the passion he could release within her. What she felt more than anything, was an awaking, as if today, this night, she had come out of a hundred year sleep.

"I think," she said when he released her and her voice worked again, "that was quite a bit more than I'm used to."

Nicholas rubbed his nose against hers, a playful action and an erotic one. "Elizabeth, Beth, do you know what you do to me?"

He took her hand, and she expected he would put it somewhere vulgar and ruin this exquisite tenderness they had developed between themselves, but instead he brought her fingers to his mouth where he kissed each of her knuckles individually. Then he kissed her palm and she could feel the tip of his tongue and it made her hold her legs tightly together for the passion he brought to her was so real she could not deny it.

"Where have you been all my life?" she asked, knowing it was a line, and expecting that he would laugh and accuse her of having no originality at all. She had certainly given him the opening.

"I have been waiting for Christmas." He hadn't thought, really, that this type of love was possible. Over the years, watching his father, Nicholas suspected all Santa's pleasures were involved with giving to others, not with what he could share with a willing woman.

"Then has Christmas come?" With her fingernail she made

patterns in the nap of his Santa suit, confusing designs which all looked like intertwined hearts.

He shook his head sadly, in resignation. "Maybe it never will again."

"I don't understand."

"I know you don't. I have so little time, and there is so much I need to explain."

"You're not telling me anything." She felt a growing desperation. With a flat palm she erased the patterns.

"I will, but it isn't easy. One step at a time."

"And tonight's step was the kiss?" she asked with scorn ringing through her voice. She raised her head, put distance between her breasts and his chest.

"Yes." His eyes lowered but he did not glance away. She moved back further, giving him an opening he took. Nicholas lifted himself up, got to his feet, until he stood towering over her.

Beth looked up the long, long distance and felt like road kill. "And did your experiment work to your satisfaction?"

He stroked the full white beard that had come with his Santa suit, an absent, intrinsic movement.

"Yes. Yes, and then some. Good night, Beth. If I stay here with you much longer I'll say things, *do* things, that I'm likely to regret. I promised I wouldn't rush you."

"And how to you expect me to sleep when you've taunted me with this—"

"—Desire?"

Holding onto the couch she pulled herself up, wanting to face him more as an equal. Her shoulders were back. Her knees were locked. There were flames in her eyes. "Is that what it is?"

"That, sweet Beth, and so much more." And with that he left her.

Nicholas couldn't get the soft, sassy image of Beth from his mind. His hands and lips still tingled from her unforgettable kiss although, hopefully after she left for school, he would be able to exert some degree of control over grinding pressure that thinking about her generally brought.

The woman had eighty-seven Santa Clauses in her room. Eighty-seven. That had to be some kind of record. Whereas some people collected silver thimbles or decorative salt and pepper shakers, Beth collected Santa Clauses.

Not all of them were children's toys. Many of them were good quality, expensive items, not one with a speck of dust, which, for his peace of mind would have made Nicholas feel better. Had they been dusty, had she been ignoring her collection, then he wouldn't have had as much cause to feel guilty. For he himself was seriously thinking about giving the whole mess up. He didn't really want to be Santa Claus. Well, not full time anyway. He wanted to settle down in some small town, preferably Pennsylvania, marry a career woman, maybe one who taught third grade, and raise up a generation of Santa believers himself. He wouldn't mind being Santa for her Christmas party. He liked that, especially all the benefits it provided, including the chance to get one fiery school teacher to sit on his lap and tell him what she wanted for Christmas. He wouldn't even mind keeping his temporary job at Rachael's store as their spokesperson for the North Pole, in order to keep his hand in. That much he could handle. It was the thought of this day and night job as Santa that he needed a break from. He couldn't ask that kind of sacrifice of any woman, especially not Beth.

Even if she did have eighty-seven Santas in her room.

The next morning, his thoughts were no more settled. Nicholas wondered what he was going to do as he took scissors, and clipped the miserable beard close to his chin. He'd slept in it last night, almost as if he were getting used to the hairy monstrosity. Santa should change with the generations, as indicated by the wide variety of costumes he'd noticed on her collection. Maybe this decade's Claus would be clean-shaven.

He pulled beard, chipped again. Not that he wanted anything to do with Santa.

Marlett, of course, couldn't understand why he shaved after his ride. Beards were a source of pride with elves, so much so that he even caught one or two of the females trying to grow one.

Oh, you are in a mood this morning, he told his disheveled appearance in the mirror. He looked like something half-finished. Half Santa, half Nicholas St. Noel. Bad enough he picked on himself, but the elves had never done anything to earn his animosity. They were loyal, true, hard working.

It that were the case, then why wasn't one of them Santa?

Except that he knew the answer to that one. Santa served the people, therefore Santa had to be one of the people. With heightened sensitivity and traces of magic, but he still had to be human. He had to fall in love, marry, father children, grow old. Die. All to help him understand the pain and the struggles of those he left presents for. It renewed the magic. And kept the legend strong.

Another handful of beard left his face, leaving the image staring back at him with a heavy three-day stubble. He flicked the switch on the electric razor. Traces of Santa vanished. He was becoming Nicholas yet again. Once he got his face shaved, he only had to deal with the shower curtain. The eighty-seven Santas he included in his count were only the ones in her room.

Showered, feeling better, more himself, Nicholas tied a towel around his waist, opened the bathroom door, almost ran smack dab right into Beth.

"Oh," she said startled. Her eyes dropped, to his chest. To the towel which was the only thing between him and total embarrassment.

The bathroom behind him steamed, none of it had anything to do with the water temperature he'd bathed in. "I didn't think you'd be up this early." It hadn't taken him that long to shave. It had to be just past six o'clock in the morning.

"Nerves," she said. Then to prove it, she bit a knuckle, looked younger than she had when at ten she'd surprised him under a Christmas tree.

"Another early day at school?"

"No, actually no. The pageant is today. There's not much more I can do. I mean if the kids don't know their lines by now, it's a little late, don't you think?"

Think? No, whatever she was talking about, he wasn't thinking at all. She wore a simple, furry bathrobe, which covered her like a shroud between neck and toes, but her feet were bare and her ankles were slender and he was about to lose his mind with wanting her, especially if she didn't have to be to school for another few hours. Without much difficulty, Nicholas could devise some way to pass the time.

Together they would create some magic. After all, that was what Santa did best.

Actually, the bathrobe itself wasn't the problem, so much as the fact that it bulged open just about the area of her breasts, not enough that he could see anything, enough that he ached. It was sweet, exquisite torture. He knew some women, and the men they enticed, needed perfume, nightgowns of sheer lace and satin, with holes cut in strategic locations, yet Elizabeth Anderson couldn't have been sexier had she been naked.

Her face was bare of makeup, not that she wore much in her teacher persona, but it shone with vibrancy and health and innocence. The freckles he remembered were still there, lightened, almost transparent, but enough to add to her farm-girl charm.

"You need the bathroom." Now what titillating conversation this was, Nicholas moaned. Where was his magic when he needed it? There wasn't much holding that robe closed, only one loosely looped belt, the kind any stray breeze could dislodge. He'd never been lecherous before, except that he found himself hoping for wind.

"No, I...um...heard you up, in the shower. I wanted to catch you, thank you for all you did to make my party so special."

"No problem." He still trembled from that kiss.

"I don't know how you did it. You knew all their names, everything they'd been up to. Did my grandmother tell you? Did you figure it out during that ten minutes I left you with my class?"

Not even the trace of cleavage was visible. Why then was she so outright sexy? She didn't smell of bottled enticements, only of sleep and there was another direction he dared not let his mind travel.

"I like children," he told her. "I hope to have one or two of my own some day." Santas, on the whole, spent more of their time with other people's children. Not that he had been neglected by his father, ignored perhaps, but never neglected. Still there were times when he thought there should have been something in Santa's magic bag for him. It had all gone to deserving children. All the Christmas gifts he'd gotten his mother had found on her travels, or Marlett had provided.

Still, at the moment, he didn't want to unwrap any packages, only hook his index finger under that belt and be through with the frustrating thing for good. He had no idea what Beth wore as pajamas, but he'd had some experience unwrapping gifts. He'd make short work of that as well.

"Children," she muttered, shaking her head, then changed the topic as if this was one she didn't feel comfortable tackling herself. "Anyway, I know the kids had a good time."

"That's what Santa is there for."

"Not just Santa. Everything. The dinner. The brownies. The putting up with my ranting and raving."

Putting up. If she only knew what was up, but then, he only wore a towel. There wasn't too much possibly of hiding the condition much longer, especially as he moved closer, rubbed the lower half of his body so very casually against hers. Sweet heavens it was torture.

She had the length of the living room to back up. She didn't. Instead she dropped a new bottle of shampoo which she had been strangling for the past three minutes. "Nicholas, I—"

She moved closer. Heaven erupted around her, like tidal waves and tornados. There was nothing subtle about its arrival.

"I, um, should get ready." There was no retreat in her words, no teasing artifice. Instead he sensed her pain with every ounce of his being. She was scared. Undoubtedly some maniac had chopped her up for hamburger and left her as carrion, but it easily could have been him. She'd fallen hard for Santa that one night, even if she had been ten years old. Maybe she'd been looking for a man to match up, knowing she'd never find it with a mortal. Hell, he was a creep, but knowing that didn't stop his next actions, instead it gave him impetus.

He tilted his head, lowered his lips to her slightly parted, slightly stunned ones. The kiss was more potent than any kiss at six in the morning should be, especially when he couldn't follow through on the actions. He'd only meant to touch her gently, tenderly, show her kindness, ease some of the pressures building up all around him, instead his own hungers overpowered him. The kiss, although not invasive, was not gentle.

"Nicholas." Beth had no idea how it happened, but her hands were around his back, touching the slightly damp skin of his lower spine, rubbing her hips against his towel. Oh glory. What she felt, what he did to her felt so fine.

She moaned. She seemed to be doing that a lot lately, but there was no way she could stop it. He matched her, in sound, in intensity, in the kiss which she had taken possession of. Beth held him tighter.

Her bedroom door wasn't eight feet away. At the rate the kiss was exploding around them, they probably weren't going to make it that far.

She wasn't used to naked men, for no matter what the dictionary definition, a man wearing nothing but a damp terry cloth towel hooked over his lean hips was distinctly naked. For mental stability, she hadn't given the towel more than a cursory inspection. She'd been startled by his chest hair. Not overwhelming, hairy or monstrous, but curled with residual traces of moisture from his shower, only slightly darker than the hair on his head. She had wanted to reach out, touch him, just to ascertain that he was real, not some figment of her dream-starved imagination.

His potency was so desperately, so quintessentially male, his kiss feeding a hunger she didn't recognize in herself. A need blossomed within that the woman she thought she was wouldn't deign to express.

"There's a party here, Christmas morning. You will stay, won't you? Meet all my relatives?" Beth wasn't sure what she was asking, knew though that she needed an answer before this insanity went any further.

He bit his bottom lip, looked so very apologetic. "Beth, please. You know I can't."

"They would like to know you. The things you've done. The way you make my grandmother smile."

"I've got to go. I can't be here on Christmas."

He hadn't been holding her, for when she released her locked fingers from behind his back, she almost toppled. She moved back, weight on her own feet, finding power in her own humiliation.

"Beth, let me explain." It was time he told her. Santa Claus had again usurped his chance for happiness, a cycle bound to repeat over and over. For regardless what he told Marlett, he doubted he could give it up completely.

"I don't want your excuses. I think I understand."

"No, I'm certain that you don't." He was all ready to get down on his knees and start a confession when the doorbell rang. Nicholas looked at Beth, she looked at him. Their thoughts were identical, each believed the other had manufactured the sound simply to prevent this conversation from going any further. It didn't make much sense, but then, love was rarely logical.

"Are you expecting anyone?"

"Nicholas, it's six o'clock in the morning."

Closer to six-thirty. That had been some kiss.

To prove that their imaginations hadn't created the doorbell peel, a hand knocked on the door.

"Stay," he told her. "I'll get it."

Nicholas opened the door, almost closed it just as quickly, instead he found himself opening outer screen door. "Mom, what are you doing here?"

From the background, about a million miles away, he heard, "Mom?" in echo. Beth's voice.

"May I come in, Nicholas?"

"Would you consider coming back in two or three hours?"

She needed few words. One look, or rather, one eclectic stab, had him stepping aside, opening the door wider. "Of course. Please come in. I'm just a guest here. I'm sure my hostesses don't mind unexpected company three hours before the sun rises."

"Thank you." Lorraine St. Noel had the grace of a queen, someone so confidently expected that she'd be welcomed anywhere. He ushered her past the door, shut it, when he turned around, the two women were taking each other's measure. He introduced them quickly. Beth stuttered as she shook hands and Nicholas noted absently that she had refastened that belt which had somehow, accidentally, dropped to the floor during their kiss.

"Mom, what are you doing here, at this hour?"

"I'm really too busy for this, Nicholas. I've got too much to do, but Marlett called me."

"Marlett?" Beth asked. "The elf?"

"Yes, Marlett the elf. Do you know anyone else by that name?"

Nicholas dropped hands to his hips. "This is preposterous. What did he want?"

"He was desperate. Said you weren't coming back."

"Back?" Beth asked. She still hadn't quite recovered from the kiss, from his betrayal that he would leave her. "Christmas Eve?"

"Then she knows?" Lorraine asked.

Nicholas shook his head only slightly. She would have, if this interruption had come a good six minutes later.

"Excuse me," Beth said, stooping to pick up the bottle of shampoo. "I've got to shower, get to work."

"Has she caught you wearing red?" Lorraine asked as Beth disappeared.

He had no time to answer, for the bathroom door swung open. Beth stood there, holding a handful of clipped facial hair, her mouth agape. "Nicholas, what have you done?"

Facing his mother in nothing but a towel, glancing at the woman who had been only moments away from being his lover, he was more than slightly disorientated. It took him a second to recognize what she held. "Trimmed my beard. I like to be clean-shaven. I told you that last night." He wasn't a slob. All the hair had gone in the waste basket and the sink had sparkled.

"You ruined the beard. It was the most beautiful beard I've ever seen."

"It itched."

"Nicholas, it was just a prop. A wig. You didn't have to shred it into tiny pieces." She shrugged, looked at him as if he'd grown horns instead of hair, and vanished back into the bathroom, the door shutting firmly behind her.

"Ahh, so she's seen you in red, and doesn't believe."

He shrugged, remembered who he was talking to. "No, she believes. She just hasn't convinced herself yet."

"It is rather a mouthful to swallow." Lorraine's comment was wry.

He directed his mother downstairs, and disappeared long enough to put some clothes on. When he returned, she had the coffee brewing, had freshened the coals in the stove. Nicholas poured her coffee, made hot chocolate for himself.

Nicholas folded his hands, twirling thumbs. "Marlett's that worried?"

"Catatonic."

"I'm sorry he had to bother you."

"No problem really. I was in the area. There was an estate sale."

"Find any bargains?"

"A few."

"Any I can use?"

"No. That was a nasty habit of your father's and I won't let you adopt it. Now, are you really going to quit?"

He shrugged, sipped hot chocolate. "I don't know. Don't you think I'm a little old for believing in Santa Claus?"

"Don't you dare throw my own words back at me, Nicholas St. Noel. You know what you were born for."

"Spreading cheer. But I can't spread any if I haven't got any myself. Hell, Mom, if I could just sit down, have a good heart-to-heart with the Easter Bunny, find out how he does it—"

"Don't swear, Nicholas. And there is no Easter Bunny and you know it."

"No tooth fairy. No Cupid. Why am I the only fictitious—"

"You didn't look like you needed Cupid when I came in."

"I'll not apologize for that. Beth and I—"

"You'll have to tell her."

"How? Obviously whatever words Dad used on you didn't have much of an impact and I refuse to live without her. Marlett's right. I would rather have Beth than Santa Claus. I need some time alone with Beth, or barring that, I need some time for myself."

"Oh, Nicholas, I never meant to teach you selfishness. I only wanted you to see, to experience everything before he locked you away in that icy fortress of his. You have to know the pain of the people you serve…their needs, their simple pleasures. I wanted to unlock your sensitivities."

"I want her, Mom, all the time. I couldn't live if she left, taking my child away from me. Marlett is going to have to find someone else."

"No, you're going to have to find—" but she was interrupted as Beth's grandmother waddled slowly into the kitchen.

Again, Nicholas preformed the introductions, made the old woman her scant breakfast, fixed a place for Beth, who couldn't be much longer.

"I am so glad to meet you again," Catherine said. Beth ambled down a few minutes later, pulled herself up in front of her oatmeal, chewed, swallowed, felt so very grumpy.

"So, how did you meet your husband, Mrs. St. Noel?" Catherine asked. For some reason Beth couldn't devise, the old woman looked like she swallowed some miserable canary. The smirk of her face couldn't have been sweeter if it had been made of royal icing. Opposite her, Nicholas looked as if he sat on Mexican jumping beans. Both of them obviously knew something she didn't, although judging by reactions, it was two totally different things.

Lorraine was about to protest, then wondered if Nicholas knew the story. If he didn't, perhaps it was time he did.

"I'm an antique buyer. Now I've got some shops all across the country but mostly back then I traveled, looking in attics and garages for bargains. Nicholas and I met, oh a couple of times. It seems we were always interested in the same things. It wasn't necessarily a coincidence. When a good estate sale comes up, everyone in the business goes. I often run into the same people and think nothing of it. Nicholas, my son's father's name was Nicholas as well, knocked me off my feet. I didn't have time for an affair, or for a relationship, but we'd go out to dinner, dance into dawn, make each other frustrated. He was much older than I was, old enough to be my father. He'd been too busy with his career, when he decided it was time for a wife and child. These were always secondary to him, I found out. He much preferred his work. Anyway, during one such auction he arrived late and I successfully bid on something he decided he couldn't live without. Funny, I don't even remember what it was now, something of profound personal value for someone he was trying to please, but whether it was a silver tea service, a Scottish Claymore or a dry sink and ewer, I can't for the life of me recall. Perversely, I wouldn't let him have it, even when he offered me double, then triple what I paid for it. I can be stubborn when I want."

Nicholas knew that for a fact, and judging by the I-believe-that look, Beth had no trouble accepting it either.

"Anyway, that Christmas Eve he appeared, dressed in full regalia as Santa Claus, decided one last time to get what he wanted. I laughed, lost my head, told him he could have the object for free if he'd marry me, and our son was born twelve months to the night."

Nicholas sank lower in his chair. So he hadn't wanted her, only some dilapidated wash basin he could deliver as Santa Claus, but that didn't explain the real love that he knew existed within his parent's marriage.

Beth stood, brought her empty oatmeal bowl to the sink. "I've got to be going."

"Do you need help?"

"No, really, everything is done. I'm going to pace back and forth and pray that I survive the Christmas pageant. Please, stay, enjoy your mother."

"Ms. Anderson, Beth—"

"Yes?"

"Before you go, I have a present for you."

She stood stunned. "That's not necessary."

"Humor me. My husband made and distributed gifts for a living. Some of it has unfortunately rubbed off."

"Please, Beth," Nicholas whispered. The gift spoke of attrition.

Reluctantly she accepted the small package, but as her hands clasped around it, she looked at Nicholas with all the hurt and betrayal she felt visible in her eyes. This then, whatever it was, would be all she would have to remember him. Beth would have rather opened it in the privacy of her room, or never opened it at all, for an unwrapped present held almost limitless potential, where one that was opened, could never be more than it was. She didn't want a token to remember him. She figured a broken heart would be enough of a memento. She tore the paper, unwrapped a smiling Santa. What shook her, really shocked her, was its resemblance to the carved Santa she already had, the one that Santa himself had given her. Yet this one was different, in subtle, but significant ways. The features on this one were of a much younger man. And he looked exactly like Nicholas. Her throat filled, and she had to swallow before she could speak. "Thank you. It's lovely."

"Handmade by elves. A lot of the gifts in the hidden recesses of my shop are made by elves."

"I'll treasure it always." She would rather use it for fireplace kindling.

"Beth, you're not alone in your love of Santa Claus," Lorraine said, but when she spoke, she looked at her son. "Loving Santa is a good thing."

Nicholas walked Beth upstairs to the door, waited while Beth slid into her winter wear, the new Santa never leaving her hands. "Does your mother have an MBA?" Beth asked.

"Why?"

"She looks like she does."

"Yeah, actually, she does. How did you know?"

"Nicholas, it's thirty minutes shy of seven, it's twenty below zero outside if you consider wind-chill, who knows how far she had to drive to find us this morning and her clothing is impeccable, her nails two inches long and gleaming, and there isn't even any snow on her shoes. What else would she be besides an MBA?"

"She is rather daunting, isn't she?"

"Yes. Is she always like that?"

"I've never known her any other way." Still, what he wanted was a woman who looked bedraggled as she escaped from a twelve hour day dealing with eight year olds and Christmas preparations, a woman who iced sugar cookies with the precision of Michaelango painting the Sistine Chapel, who kissed him so profoundly he could even forgive her for having a naked Santa shower curtain, for he hoped the image got her thinking along the same lines that he was plotting. Getting naked had never quite seemed so appealing.

"She's like the tooth-fairy," Beth continued, "Helen Gurley Brown and an army drill sergeant all rolled into one."

That about summed his mother up, that, and the fact that she'd been married to a rather single-minded Santa Claus for over thirty years.

With Beth out the door, Nicholas met his mother coming up the stairs. "I've got to be going," she said. "Places to go, things to buy, and all that."

"I am sorry Marlett bothered you."

"No problem. It's nice to be needed for something. Your father never did, you know. He was so damned self-sufficient. If he could have reproduced himself, he never would have had anything to do with me."

He hoped his mother didn't notice how sharply her comment stung him. "You don't believe that, do you?" For there were memories of picnics and small tucked away antique shops where they scouted bargains, and hours cuddled up together while it rained during which they played cards until they were giddy with laughter. Times when Christmas didn't intrude into their lives.

"No, I don't believe it. Your father was a good man and I miss him desperately."

Nicholas pondered again what he should tell Marlett, and if he could live without Christmas for long periods of time as his mother forced his father to do, or if he should just give it up altogether, for after that kiss this morning, he wasn't giving Beth up for anything.

After his mother left, he spent the greater part of the day wrapping presents. Although the old woman spent all her time sitting in her rocker, there wasn't much she missed. Catherine knew exactly what was hidden where, and to whom it was to go. The old Victorian house was a beehive of hiding places and Nicholas unearthed presents by the thousands.

According to Marlett there wasn't much need for Santa to make stops along this section of Pennsylvania and now he had a fairly good idea why. Without reindeer, without elves, one sprite third grade teacher created happiness for hundreds.

"Did Beth buy all this?" he asked, more for Catherine's input than for an answer. He finished yet another roll of tape, and empty wrapping paper tubes lined the floor with bits of snipped ribbon, wadded shards of price tags.

"She shops the year round. Just about January first she's out shopping, making lists, checking them twice."

"That's my job."

"You don't have any exclusive on Christmas, let me tell you."

"I never wanted to. But at least I have help."

He set hands on hips, looked around the kitchen that was doing a fairly impressive imitation of his packaging room at the North Pole. Very few of the presents were expensive, not one had been bought at an exclusive shop or toted a designer label, yet each one was precisely and exactly the right thing. He pulled another present off the stack, this one a family tree, done in crewel and embroidery, listing all of Joseph and Catherine Vicchioni's children, grandchildren, great-grandchildren and the dates of their birth. Hastily he attempted to shove it under the stack.

"You might as well go ahead and wrap it. I've already seen it. It's what Beth did as she sat by my bedside this summer while I fought pneumonia." The old woman chuckled, started by the rocker swaying back and forth. "Trouble is, I don't think she left enough room. The family's still growing."

He found Beth's name, caressed the handiwork through the

non-glare glass. Through some form of poor planning or insecurity her name butted up against the edge of the matting, leaving no room for the names of her future children. Should she marry him, it was an oversight they'd have to rectify.

The phone interrupted his thoughts of filling the family tree with more names. Nicholas left the kitchen, answered it in the dining room. He was back a few minutes later, tears of laughter riding down his cheeks.

"What happened?" Catherine asked.

"That was Rachael on the phone. I've just been fired. It seems I wasn't exactly what she was looking for in a Santa."

The old woman rolled her eyes. "That girl could never read the writing on the wall, that's a fact. Did she say anything else?"

"Just that she had a surprise for Beth tonight at the pageant."

"Probably is going to blow up some stink bombs, but that's neither here nor there. We'll find out soon enough. So, did she say what she was looking for in a Santa?"

"No. Not that it matters. I did what I had to do. I've touched children. If I haven't quite made a difference in their lives, at least they've made a difference in mine."

"What are you talking about? Santa always makes a difference."

"How could he—I? I can't even convince Rachael, and she believed once. The legend is strong enough. Beth by herself is strong enough. I think it would be better if I just left."

"So you think you know her heart better than she knows it herself? You're a good man, Nicholas patron saint of Christmas, but you're tearing that woman to pieces."

"I'm far more selfish than my father was. I want her with me, in my arms and in my bed, not traipsing around the globe."

"Is that what you think Beth wants?"

"No. She deserves to have her schoolchildren and her PTA work, and not to be an appendage to me, even if I do need her."

"What are you talking about?"

He tightened his eyes, remembered the look of dejection his father wore, the look of apology from his mother. Their separations had been painful, inevitable, and far too frequent.

"I'm afraid that in loving her, I'll only make her unhappy."

CHAPTER 13

"Beth?"

She shielded her eyes from the stage lights and looked into the darkened auditorium. A figure moved, firm and decisive, strong and sure. Within her chest, her heart leapt. Without seeing his face, she knew who it was, simply from the answering response deep within her body. "Nicholas, you startled me. What are you doing here?"

"Looking for you. Are you busy?"

"Not really. Everything's set. If the pageant is going to be a disaster there's nothing I can do about it now."

He climbed onto the stage, walked toward her, toward the Santa's workshop she had worked so hard to perfect. Around them, poinsettias bloomed in glorious profusion and an artificial Christmas tree stood court over a mound of wrapped boxes. With his senses, he knew the boxes were empty, stage props only.

With his senses, he knew his next words would hurt her.

"I'm leaving. I wanted to say goodbye."

"What?" The words were expected, still her voice cracked, her knees buckled.

He stood his ground, hands deeply embedded in his pockets, his eyes studying his boots, destroying her entire world without looking at her at all. "Please don't lecture me. Your grandmother's already given it her best shot."

"But the pageant—" Which was foolish, for the pageant meant nothing to him, only to her, and her foolish dreams of the night before, that if her pageant were good enough she could make him stay, as she'd never been able to make her mother stay.

"Your grandmother made me swear a blood oath that I would stay for that. She said I—especially considering who I am—couldn't miss it, so I'll be there tonight. But I'm leaving right after. I suspect you'll be too busy taking curtain calls then, and I didn't want to have to say goodbye in front of a couple hundred people."

Then he held her, which surprised her, for she hadn't seen

him move, and he had been a good ten feet from her the second before. The emptied auditorium had been cold, but leaning against Nicholas, Beth felt warm again. Her cheek rested against his shoulder, her arms wrapped around his back, and she felt warm all the way through. She concentrated on the heat permeating through her, for if she thought of anything else, she would be lost. She didn't moan, didn't move, just stood there, molded against his firm body, accepting silently that if this were all he was able to give her, than this would be all she would take. She was a fine one for living alone on memories.

It was more than a hug, it was an embrace, and her analysis was only confirmed when Nicholas began to kiss her. He started at her forehead, her ears, the length of her neck and that which had been warm started boiling. The auditorium was empty, it wouldn't start filling for another three hours, but Beth doubted if her response would have been much different had the entire community been on hand to witness her humiliation. She supposed she should be grateful for small favors, that if he were leaving, at least he was doing this—farewell—privately.

She didn't resist, didn't understand how this man could say goodbye and kiss her with the same breath. His hands caressed the back of her neck, through the light, fluffy curls, and his lips found their way home as his mouth settled against hers. A kiss of passion. A kiss of love.

A kiss of farewell.

But she was strong. Beth had learned that, over the years, defending a myth no one else believed in. Her hands, which had been wrapped around his back, moved forward, pushed against him, giving her some breathing room, a chance to recollect her sanity. She pulled in a deep breath, found herself completely without oxygen, as if she had been underwater for far too long, as if by his very magnetic personality, all the oxygen clung to him, leaving none for her at all.

His face was shadowed, the expression unreadable. She looked at him hard while she struggled to breathe, trying to identify remorse, or masculine superiority or even that impish gleam which had been present when he had whispered, *How about if Santa tells you what he wants? One kiss, Beth. Just one kiss.* But she found nothing.

Cold permeated her bones as he moved back, but she had indignation and resolve and that would be enough. "Go. With my blessing. I wish you happiness. It's been fun."

His eyes were dark, fathomless and then they twinkled although where they picked up the extra light, she had no idea. "It's been a lot of things Beth, but what it hasn't been is fun."

She was about to protest this final slashing indignity to her self-esteem when he continued. "It's been passionate, and warm and involved, but what we had was far too intense for fun."

Beth swayed, saw black dots, thought she might pass out. Nicholas' arms were around her once again. "Although I have to go Beth, and I do have to go, I promise you I'll be back."

Her eyes were dry. She had cried foolishly over her mother, and now, when tears mattered they wouldn't come. "I don't want or need your promises."

"I won't argue that with you now. There are too many other far more important things we need to discuss. I wasn't going to tell you, I thought this one thing I could spare you—"

Blood rushed in her ears and she could feel his pulse beneath her fingertips. "Nicholas, please, I can't take any more."

"I have a confession I have to make." He let her go, slumped on the stage, rocking his legs back and forth over the edge. She sat beside him, knowing suddenly the tables had turned. A moment before, he had been strong, holding her up, now it was time for her to return the favor.

"Nicholas, whatever it is—"

"Beth, I'm Santa Claus."

Her first impulse was to laugh. There were so many other things she was expecting. That he had a horrendous, incurable disease. That he was married. That he had decided to take Rachael up on her idea of playing house.

"Santa Claus," she said, saying the words abruptly and sharply, tinged with seasonal disbelief. It might have been easier to deal with if he had decided to cohabit with Rachael. At least that was something she had experience with.

"Don't deny it, Beth. You know it's true."

"And do you?" she asked with heightened intuition, "Do you know it's true?" She meant to scorn, not hurt, but her barb hit its mark. He shuddered, tightening his eyes in fresh, visible agony.

"I've doubted it so many, many times. I don't want to be Santa Claus. I'd rather be Nicholas St. Noel, loving you. Beth," he held his hands out and they shook. There was a haunted look to his eyes, and the twinkle had long since vanished. "Beth," he started again after clearing his throat, his fingers knotting with each other. "There is no one else. Certainly a bad Santa Claus is better than no Santa Claus at all?"

"A bad Santa Claus?" she asked. "What does that mean, Nicholas?" She was having no trouble dealing with her own disbelief, or rather she was having less trouble accepting it than he seemed to be having. "Do you put on a red costume and—"

The possibilities frightened her. It was entirely possible that Nicholas was some monstrous maniac who entered homes in the name of Christmas and did what? What would make a Santa bad? Stealing presents? Or something far worse, involving children and innocence and trust and depravity?

No. No matter what, she could never believe he was capable of any degree of sickness. He could wound her at Christmas, but she very much doubted he could hurt anyone else.

"Nicholas—"

"I've got to go, Beth. If I get the chance, I'll speak to you after your pageant. And Beth, one more thing before I go—"

"What?" she didn't think she could survive another shock.

"I love you. I never meant to hurt you, but by the same token, I couldn't help but fall in love with you. I'm fairly certain I've been in love with you for nineteen years."

She got to her knees, then to her feet, awkwardly, like an old woman. With a broken heart, it was very difficult to move.

"Go away, Nicholas. Believe me, whatever else it is that you tried to accomplish, you have hurt me. And I'm not going to let you sit there and thrust the knife in again and again. Just get out of my life for good this time because if this is what your love is like, I don't want any part of it."

Superimposed over his image, for just a second, stood Santa Claus. The real Santa. But it was gone before she could wonder if George Lucas was experimenting with holograms.

"There's really nothing more that I can say."

That, at least, was a relief. He'd said enough. Images cascaded around her, as she walked the empty stage. Her heart warred with her mind and she no longer knew what she believed in. Telling her he was Santa Claus was a fairly cruel joke, something Rachael would have been capable of. Beth had always believed in Santa Claus. And she had wanted to believe in Nicholas. Now, alone, she had neither. He had destroyed the one thing in her world which had consistently given her pleasure.

Beth had no idea how much time passed from when Nicholas left until the secretary in the main office buzzed her on the intercom announcing she had a telephone call. She only knew that he had felt like Christmas. That he had made her wish for the things Santa Claus could not pull from his magic sack.   Beth expected the call was from her grandmother, warning her, belatedly, of Nicholas' betrayal. It might have been one of her student's parents, worried about a costume or a cold or checking if there were room for another dozen relatives to squeeze into the auditorium because no one would miss her pageant. If she were scared, if she had premonitions of a developing disaster, it only involved her pageant and the selfish feelings that she wasn't capable of pulling off the play, and not something far worse than even the loss of a dream.

Her youngest sister's voice quivered over the phone so badly over tears that Beth could barely make out the words. "Beth, I'm so sorry to bother you on your big night. I'm so sorry. I know how busy you are, how many thousand things you do at the last minute."

"Susan, what is it?"

"Beth, you know I would never bother you if there were anyone else."

"Susan, please, what's the matter?"

"I'm starting to miscarry the baby."

In the brightly lit office, Beth crumpled. "Oh, no. Please, no."

"Jim is driving me to the hospital. The doctor will be waiting. Will you watch Jamie for us?"

"You know I will."

"We'll probably miss the pageant." *And more* came the unspoken thought. *We'll lose so much more.* "Beth, you've got to promise not to tell anyone about this. If I lose the baby, I don't want Gram hurt, and I don't want Mom to know. Will you promise?"

She swiped her eyes, crying freely. "You need their support, Sue. They care about you. They will help you."

"No, this close to Christmas, I don't want anyone to know."

She swallowed and the words came hard. "I promise."

"And Beth, there's one other thing."

"What?" She didn't think she could survive another shock.

"Remember when I told you that this baby was an accident, something we didn't plan?"

"Yes."

There was a pause over the line, a long pause, then Susan started her confession. "It wasn't that much of an accident. I, um, wanted another baby, even though I knew he'd probably have a heart like Jamie's. I deliberately got careless. Jim knew. He didn't stop me. He wants more children."

"I know." Tears crested, rolled down her cheeks, far too many to control with the back of her wrist.

"We could have a perfect baby, couldn't we?"

They could. But the odds were not good. Genetics was often far more powerful than even the best intentioned wishes.

"Does that make me bad, Beth? Wanting a baby this desperately? Bringing a baby into this world, knowing it will probably die at birth?"

Make her bad, when only seconds ago Beth thought that the worst thing that could possibly happen would be that her Christmas pageant would be less than perfect?

"No, not bad, because you'll love it, no matter what its heart is like."

"I knew you'd understand. I've got to go. Jim's already got the car warming. Please, don't tell anyone. Especially if I lose this baby."

"I won't. My prayers are with you."

She dropped the receiver. It didn't quite catch the cradle, dangled, hanging low, like her spirits.

Bad. Oh, yes. How many definitions could one word have?

***

Before the final notes of '*Silent Night*' faded, the audience rose to its feet, and the applause went on as if it would never end. Parents and neighbors would stop, wipe an eye or two, and remember some touching facet of the pageant, and the applause would freshen. The rosy-cheeked children bowed. Beth, to one side, holding a single pink rose, still directed them, and they watched her. Finally she gave them the nod they needed and they split their polished ranks and headed toward waiting arms.

And, Christmas, as if it had been a secret, was shared again. Everyone within the crowded auditorium felt her vision of peace and happiness and devotion. Beth smiled, the crowd parting for her, yet as she got closer Nicholas realized that the smile was forced, that she looked brittle, about to shatter.

His eyes met hers, locked, unspoken communication passed between them, descriptive, sensual. *I'm glad I stayed. It was marvelous.*

Did you like it? she asked.

Very much, he answered. *It touched me. You were marvelous.* He'd always been a stickler for community level Christmas pageants, scrubbed children, music made magic. Joy radiated through each scene, laughter, and traditional family values bubbled. It wasn't religious. There were parts of it that weren't necessarily Christmas. But it spoke of giving and sharing and bonds that time could not break.

There hadn't been a dry eye in the place. Nicholas might have embarrassed himself if Catherine hadn't warned him to bring a handkerchief. He'd followed the old woman's wishes, not because he suspected he'd cry, but because he didn't want to start an argument. It was a good thing he had. Beth had a gift. He would tell her, Nicholas decided, the first minute he got a chance. The lady was incredible.

Flustered and caught a bit off balance by the communication between them, Nicholas watched as Beth denied what had happened. She bent down, picked up Jamie, held her face against his silky blond curls. Not defiance, avoidance, but Nicholas could hardly blame her for that. She whispered something to the child, and he brightened, but didn't speak. They both looked exhausted past endurance.

When she looked up, she scanned the crowd, finally coming to rest on Nicholas and her smile had faded.

Don't you understand why I have to do this? he asked her, but she had closed the communication, and wouldn't respond to his magic. Then before he could rephrase the thought into words, she shouted "You're here!" and still holding Jamie, she wrapped her arms around her sister.

"Is everything—"

Jim lifted his son from Beth's arms. Susan shrugged, tried to smile, tried to nod, said through fresh tears, "For now," which added no comfort to the tears they shared.

"He was marvelous," Nicholas said to the parents, and they fed on his words since they had so little else.

Susan hugged the child while Jim wrapped his arms around both of them. "We're so sorry we had to impose on you."

"It wasn't a problem. He kept me calm." When life was crazy, when the problems mounted, she had hugged her nephew and had found the strength to go on. And once, before the curtain rose, when the hushed expectation had finally reached all the children and they stood quiet, waiting, Jamie had whispered to her, "Do you think Santa will be here this year?" and Beth had answered, "I'm sure he will," and for the first time she believed what Nicholas had told her during his confession, even if it had been a short-term belief.

"He was the best one up there," Catherine agreed.

Whereas in pregnancy, many women glow, with Susan, the new life within her was having the opposite effect. Her eyes were dark, swollen, spoke of something more profound than fresh tears. Her face was sallow, her cheekbones far too prominent. Her hand, when she reached out to touch the boy, trembled. Still, she smiled when she looked at her firstborn, and the love there couldn't be denied.

Beth hugged her sister and her tears which she had managed to keep under tight guard during the pageant, sprang forth. "Is there anything I can do?"

"No. Whatever will happen, will happen." They were strong, hardworking people who believed in fate almost as much as they believed in the doctor and anything written in the Holy Bible. "I've got to rest."

"Take care of yourself," Beth whispered.

Susan tightened her grasp on her sister's love, and her answer was for Beth's ears alone, and only with Santa's preternatural hearing could Nicholas have detected the next words. "The doctor hasn't said anything encouraging. He doesn't even think—" but then she broke off, from the sentence, from the embrace, to wipe her eyes and set distance between them.

"Shh," Beth comforted. "We'll pray for a miracle."

"We've got to get him home." Jim offered his own congratulations on the success of the pageant, then with a quiet desperation which matched Susan's, took his wife and son and disappeared through the crowd.

Beth watched them go, the naked emotions of shock and desperation and sorrow visible on her face.

Without her shield, she turned to face him. "I suppose you'll be leaving now too," she said. She hadn't had time to think about him, not really. What with one thing and another, she had closed her mind to the fact that he was leaving her.

"Beth—" Nicholas reached out, touched her lightly on her heated cheek.

Warmth filled her, and strength and vitality, as if she swallowed an elixir filled with red blood cells and vitamins and life. She further analyzed the feeling, recognizing it was wrapped in Christmas somehow, in miracles, in the touch that she had no doubt belonged to Nicholas alone.

She wasn't ready for his comfort, for his insight or his lies about Santa Claus. Too much was too crazy in her life. After Christmas, maybe. After this was all over, there would be time to grieve for the relationship. At the moment, she only wanted to wallow in exhaustion, misery, in the fears she had for her sister, and the let-down of having her production finally over.

"Did you enjoy the Christmas pageant, Gram?"

The old woman looked spry in a red Christmas dress, her cheeks as rosy as any Christmas elf's. "You surpass yourself every year, my dear. Nothing is more precious than watching children sing carols."

Nicholas was too close. Why didn't he just go? Couldn't he see she was about ready to scream?

"You'll have to clean up," Nicholas said, hoping the redness of his eyes wasn't too visible, but knowing that if it were it was no mark of shame. "Tell me what to do. I'll help."

"There's nothing. The pageant is mine and the kids. The advertisement, the refreshments and the clean-up fall to the other teachers."

"Can I get you a cookie?" The line for the store-bought sugar cookies was about a three dozen deep, and the punch, a watered down mixture of canned fruit juices and lime sherbet, didn't look that impressive, but he'd do whatever she wanted. That afternoon he couldn't wait to leave. Now, torn, he wanted to stay.

Beth shook her head. "No. I'll get something at home."

She held her hand out, handshake style. "Well, Mr. St. Noel, it's been fun."

He didn't call her on it this time as he had just that afternoon. Instead Nicholas wrapped his arms around her, feeling the fragileness of her bones. The only thing holding her up now was adrenaline. With the pageant over, that rush would fade. "I'll be back after Christmas."

He struggled from her side, intent only on escape but it wasn't to be. Twenty people stopped her. Thirty. A hundred. Each, holding a third-grader, or a sixth grader, or holding kids of their own, for she had been teaching in this small town, in this ancient schoolhouse for a long time and before that she had been a student here and her friends were legion. Everyone knew her talent and they had come back year after year and had never left disappointed. She had touched their lives. Taught them multiplication and elementary geology, spelling and state history. She organized fund raisers and volunteers, offered fresh coffee and a shoulder to cry on, gave of her talents and herself. And every year Beth brought Christmas into their hearts as a fresh, vibrant entity. And each accolade her friends offered her, the closer to the ground Nicholas felt. He was doing the right thing in leaving her, for she had a life here and didn't need him at all.

She wasn't one to seek applause, but many here knew where it was due. Beth accepted their lauds with grace and modesty, passing all credit to the eight-year-old talent, to the band borrowed from the high school, to the principal who allowed her time for practice, and even to Nicholas who'd helped her with the scenery. Still the people crowded, no one willing to leave until they had touched her, thanked her personally for giving them back the true meaning of Christmas.

She knew them all, generations of them, and had a kind word to say to each. And tissues were brought out again. Cameras flashed. Each mother wanted a picture of Beth with her child. Each adult who knew her way-back-when wanted something of her, little realizing she'd already given all she could, that there wasn't much more.

"Rachael wasn't here this year," Beth said when she could get a word in edgewise. There was a small trace of relief in the words.

"But she sent a present," the old woman grumbled. "I suspect we'll find it soon enough."

"It's too late to ruin the pageant, so how bad can it be?"

Catherine's wry look said clearly that any degree of disaster was possible.

Slowly they wormed through the overflowing auditorium, now emptying. Older students, fifth graders perhaps, were cleaning napkins and paper cups and confetti, directed by teachers with red rimmed eyes. The Santa's workshop from the final scene was torn down. Beth heard the paper rip and she cringed, and there might have been a tear in her eye that she didn't allow anyone to see, but which Nicholas inferred. Come January when the sixth grade started Shakespeare, there would be no trace of glitter or Rudolph or miracles.

"I'm glad that's over." She spoke only a moment too soon.

"Well, well, well, Beth, another unqualified success."

She shuddered and a potent type of ugly pain traveled through her. Whoever this man was, he was no friend.

"Michael."

Her acknowledgement was clipped, curt. Nicholas looked over at him, a balding man with a beer gut that looked about third trimester pregnancy. From his impressive height he probably played football or basketball in high school, from his overbearing aura he was undoubtedly a bully. He might have been handsome once, now he only looked malicious.

"Rachael said she'd send a present and here you are."

"Honeybuns, I've been Rachael's present for a lotta years."

"Yes," Beth said, more exhausted than rude. "I'm sure of that."

"We were just leaving." Nicholas thrust himself between Beth and the interloper and remembered Michael as the tormentor from the bus stop, the year he first met Beth. His father embodied "kind" and his mother taught him politeness, but he'd lived on his own for a few years and knew that to keep the image intact sometimes he had to cut his losses and run. If he had to, he'd drag Beth straight through solid wall.

"Leaving? And miss the opportunity for me to tell you how especially moved I was by the drama?"

Nicholas, feeling snide, decided there was only one kind of movement this idiot was capable of, and even then he doubted the guy could accomplish that without help.

"I'm glad you enjoyed it." Beth sounded about as glad as she would be if she'd just discovered termites in her Christmas tree. "My companion and I were just leaving."

"Ho, ho, ho!" And the expression didn't sound anything like

Santa. "A companion? My, my. Little Beth, don't tell me you've actually found yourself a lover?"

Nicholas had enough of this. His escape had clearly turned into a rescue mission. "We're leaving."

"No, stay a minute, what's your hurry? Beth, introduce me to your, now what was that quaint little word you used? Companion? Oh, I'm sure you two are just as companionable as possible, aren't you?"

"Nicholas, this is Michael Jardino. Michael, Nicholas St. Noel. Michael is Rachael's ex-husband."

"Oh, you sly little thing. Why don't you tell your companion that before Rachael and I were a number, you and I were engaged?"

"We were never engaged."

"Don't you remember the time in third grade when you let me kiss you and you told me you'd marry me and give me your cookies forever?"

Beth blanched to the roots of her soul. "Nicholas, I didn't—"

"I know what you meant, Beth," he said kindly.

"Then, right after college, we had this thing going. Almost tied the knot, we did."

Beth steeled herself for the blow. As often as it came, she was never prepared.

Michael guffawed. "I tell you, we were all set to start a little love nest, but then I had this dream. In it, I suspected Beth, my own dear, sweet wife, was dead. I couldn't be sure. The sex was the same, but the dishes were starting to pile up in the sink." He howled with laughter. A real knee slapper. Nicholas thought of something else he would have preferred to slap.

"Thank you very much for sharing that," Beth said.

Without a comment, but with every muscle in his body tensed for a physical confrontation, Nicholas brought his shoulder against the heavy outer door, fighting gale force wind to get it to open.

"Of all the insufferable, idiotic, rude, ignorant bas—"

"Now, Nicholas," Catherine said, interrupting his tirade, "there's no need to bring his parentage into this. I've lived in this town a long time and his parents were married."

"Well maybe they did one thing right."

The weather had turned nasty in true December form. During the school day the cold front had blown in, frigid and wet and ugly. The roads were all but impassable. Beth shivered, covered with her coat and her hat and scarf and Nicholas wrapped his arm around her, supporting her with his love as he led her to the car.

"I thought you were leaving."

"I was." What he couldn't do was leave her alone after that. Ten minutes more. He'd see her home, see her safe, then he'd leave. Nicholas unlocked the car doors, and wouldn't let her drive, for he knew of her exhaustion more than she did. Then he turned the heater up full blast, and another miracle, this time it deigned to provide warmth, even when most of it would be needed for the windshield. Holding the steering wheel with white knuckles, he watched the pain materialize in her face.

"Beth—"

"Please, I don't want to talk about him."

The parking lot was all but emptied, except for the last stragglers cleaning up the mess. "He's scum, Beth."

"He was really much nicer after college, before Rachael got her talons into him."

"He's always been scum."

She sighed, defeated. "I know."

"There's never been a Santa that ever did a malicious thing, although I understand there have been several times one or another of them has been tempted, but I promise you, if the reindeer and I ever come against him some deserted Christmas night he's going to be hurting."

She struggled against a giggle, fighting down the image.

"What I don't understand is how he could consider you unfeeling—if that was what that hideous excuse for a joke was supposed to represent."

"Nicholas, be realistic. Frigid was the word he used to me."

"I've kissed you Beth. I've held you in my arms. You are the warmest, most passionate woman I've ever met. Beth, you sizzle."

"Nicholas, please. Maybe you don't know me—"

"I know creeps like him. By belittling you, he builds himself up. What a sorry way to live."

"Nicholas, I'm not," she stopped, not having the words to finish.

"Beth, listen to me. We're going to be lovers. And when I join with you, when you explode, you'll never doubt yourself again. You'll never let that worm have power over you."

"I'm not ready." For anything. And she didn't believe he'd be back.

"I'm trying not to rush you. The only way we won't become lovers is if you say no. Believe me, I want you."

Nicholas leaned over brushed his lips against hers, then tasting honey, he kissed her again, just a little bit deeper, a tiny bit more insistent. Beth answered his kiss, opening her mouth, allowing his invasion. He groaned, merged his tongue with hers feeding the flames that sparked between them. His head swirled and his body reeled and he could only think of kissing her, and wanting her and needing her.

He broke the kiss only after remembering they were in a public parking lot and that it was the tail end of December and the blizzard around them hadn't quite finished spewing its fury.

"Warm enough?" he asked, when he had control of himself enough to speak.

"Yes." And she wasn't frigid. Not by a long shot.

Nicholas pulled the car into gear, drove up to the door, exited long enough to help Catherine, who had been waiting in the lobby, into the back seat.

"We were waiting for the car to warm," he said without mendacity.

"Yes, I can see that," Catherine answered from the back seat, looking at the dreamy, dazed expression on Beth's face, the heightened color to her cheeks, the swollen fullness of her lips. "Nothing I like better than a good, warm car."

Freed from chains of her own forging, Beth felt almost giddy. "I can't believe it's over. I'm always so afraid it's going to be a disaster. You should have seen the little monsters at rehearsal this afternoon. Honestly, I was hoping this storm would be worse than predicted and that we'd have to cancel for this year."

She was babbling and she knew it, trapped in her emotional roller coaster. Tomorrow a form of depression would hit, and she'd have to try very hard to disguise it. But Christmas would be here, and she'd be ready for the holiday. Somehow, she'd find the time to get everything done. She was free now for the holiday break. School wouldn't resume until after the New Year. Not that that was anything to look forward to. Nicholas would be gone and her life would be empty. And she wouldn't even have her illusions of Santa any more to keep her company. He had even ruined that for her.

CHAPTER 14

Nicholas led Beth and her grandmother downstairs, back to the warmth of the coal stove, which although banked for the evening, was still allowing heat to barrel out. Beth had shivered in the car, her teeth rattling along with the grunting of the car engine and she had looked as fragile as Jamie had. Once while driving, he reached for her hand, hoping to wrap her chilled fingers in the warmth he'd absorbed during her pageant, but she pulled her hands away, and alone she froze, bereft of all that could comfort her.

Nicholas could feel the chill of his fears and indecision creeping back into his bones. The emptiness he had felt had vanished in the love of the third graders and the teacher who exemplified Christmas.

Feeling superfluous, Nicholas cradled Beth, filled her full of beef barley soup he'd made and thick crusted black bread that he'd bought. Beth took about three bites as if she were famished, then pushed the bowl away from herself. "I'm not hungry."

"Nerves, from the show," Catherine said. Nicholas had recently converted her from coffee to his special brand of hot chocolate and she gingerly sipped at the brew. "We've got a few minutes. Are you set to open the presents?"

Beth sighed in exhaustion. "Tonight? I don't think I have the energy."

"Come, you will sleep better when you see."

Nicholas shadowed the women as they trailed up the stairs. He lit the Christmas tree for them as they slumped into living room chairs. He was ready for more magic. Beth's special magic.

"Show me what's in your bag," the old woman insisted. Then she explained for her houseguest. "It's another one of our Christmas traditions that Beth does not open the presents given to her by her students during the school day. She saves them to open after the pageant."

Yes, that was exactly like Beth, who savored the quiet, introspective times of Christmas, even if they were so very few and far between.

Nicholas sat beside Beth on the couch, trying to tease her, trying to rekindle the spark of exuberance he had noticed in her in the store grabbing his microscope, or by an undecorated tree whistling about a missing pair of front teeth, or decorating her Santa's workshop in chalk dust and love. "You surprise me."

"Oh?" She didn't have the strength to raise an eyebrow and he missed its erratic motion.

"I didn't think you were the type of person who would open a Christmas present early."

She leaned deeper into the couch, rubbing her hands against closed eyes. "I'm not. I've been known to stretch the adhesive strength of the tape a time or two, but my presents always wait until Christmas morning to be opened."

"Yet you're going to sit here, in front of us, and open what, thirty presents?"

"These are gifts from my children." Her voice cracked. He wondered if she felt she would never have children of her own, that these children which she borrowed for the school year would be the only children she would give her love to. How like Beth. My children, not my students. And he knew, with his Santa honed powers that if he were to give her a present, the kind of present that Marlett talked about, which changed lives not for a day or a month, but forever, that all she wanted, needed, was a child of her own to grow under her heart, to nurse from her breasts, to give meaning to every minute for the rest of her life.

"Let's get down to the serious business of opening the presents," Catherine said, rubbing her knotted, arthritic fingers lightly against Beth's knee.

"Let's wait," Nicholas insisted. She was too tired, too stressed for anything else, even happiness.

Beth opened her eyes, bloodshot from her exhaustion. "No. This is a special time for me when I think about my students. Christmas morning here is a madhouse with the great grandchildren stealing the show. Tonight, basking in their glow, I want to open these."

She reached into the bag, and he understood the power of miracles for she seemed to draw strength. Beth opened the first present. Candy. Every year the presents yielded candy, small decorative bars of bath soap or homemade items the children had crafted which she cherished for years. This year was no different. She'd given them all gifts and pencils and erasers during the class party they'd held that afternoon. And more than that, she gave them her heart during the year.

Nicholas picked up a small, poorly wrapped present. "What's that one? You've saved it for last."

"It's from Vinnie Scalano, I had him in the pageant last year as well." Beth should have suspected she was making a mistake when he volunteered to be the turkey in the Peace On Earth segment. Oh, he'd worn his tailfeathers all right, but he held a placard, "This year, try ham!" a sentiment he'd undoubtedly picked up from any one of a thousand mail-order catalogues.

"That one is a devil," Catherine continued, but the word was pronounced "dibble" and was not, necessarily, a criticism.

Nicholas had kept an eye on Vinnie himself. When the boy suspected none of his classmates were watching, he was enthralled with the drama, and his singing, although louder than most, was sincere.

"You hated Vinnie Scalano," her grandmother said with a growl.

"I never hated him. You're right in that he did give me plenty of aggravation, but he was and is a good kid."

"Do you think it's a spit ball or something disgusting like that?"

Beth caressed the present as if it were more precious than gold. "No. I think it's probably something really nice."

Catherine humphed. "I'll bet Santa has him on the naughty list."

"Why don't we ask Santa himself?" Snide sarcasm was hardly her forte but what other avenue had he left her?

"I'd like to hear your conclusions," he said gently, his words as soothing as the taste of hot chocolate on a cold December morning.

Beth smiled, suddenly, inexplicably, in her element. She could out-Santa Santa. After all, she knew more about the man than he did himself. Nicholas said nothing, waiting to hear Beth's answer, knowing whatever she said, she wouldn't disappoint him. Here was a woman with integrity greater than the cold of the North Pole, a woman who understood it wasn't a price tag that made a gift, but the love that was imbedded within.

"I don't think Santa would jump to any conclusions about him. Vinnie is stubborn and argumentative and I can't deny that he finds it difficult to stay in his seat, yet he has more than his fair share of honest intelligence. I'd love a whole class like him."

"You'd kill them all in a week."

"Gram, when will you learn that the quiet ones who sit in the back and vegetate are the ones I'm not reaching? Sure Vinnie gives me trouble, but he questions and he learns. He's rough on the edges, but I'm willing to bet Santa has him on the nice list."

Nicholas smiled internally. There were problems in that family, but they were coping and he suspected the worst was over. Vinnie was another of Beth's conquests. And he doubted Santa would have to make a stop there this year. Neighbors, organized by one Beth Anderson had formed a Santa-watch funded by donations and a summer pancake breakfast and bake sale. The Scalano children would be receiving new shoes and boots and toys, maybe not as many as their neighbors, but enough to make it a Christmas to remember.

The paper tore. She unwrapped the present, found a Santa, carved from soap, the artwork both juvenile and creative. "See, what did I tell you? A good kid." Beth would add it to her Santa collection, the dozens of Santas she had over every square inch of her bedroom, and spilling over every inch of the house.

Catherine set aside her cup and slowly creaked to her feet. "I'm heading off to bed. It's been a long night."

"But Gram, it's not yet nine o'clock."

"The family's arriving tomorrow by the thousands, and there's things that I can better do in the morning. Your play was marvelous. I wouldn't have missed it for the world."

The statement left Beth feeling sick. She knew what her grandmother meant, and while she had been trying to ignore it, the thought couldn't be put off much longer. That fall, with her grandmother so ill, there had been fear she wouldn't live to see another Christmas. In bed, pneumonia draining life from her, Catherine had whispered, "All I want is to live long enough to see another one of your pageants."

"You will, Gram," Beth had promised her. "You'll get better and you'll be there in the front row. And I'll make it the best pageant ever."

And then the words that had stabbed her like a friend's betrayal, "Then I'll be glad to die. I'd be happy if I could just slip away in my sleep."

Beth swiped at the tears ringing her eyes, watched her grandmother hobble toward the front bedroom. "Gram, sleep well."

Nicholas picked up the hot chocolate cups and carried them down to the kitchen. He had plans for this evening. If he left now, he could be back with Marlett in a couple of hours. The old elf must be having apoplexy about now. He would oversee the final loading of the sleigh. He would talk to the reindeer, see if they were ready for their flight. He would curse himself for a fool for leaving the woman he loved when nothing between them was resolved.   He sensed the change in Beth's mood immediately. Silently he turned off lights, found a radio station playing fifty continuous hours of Christmas favorites, this one, unfortunately, Karen Carpenter's song about two lovers apart at Christmas.

Beth followed him, her hands clumped into fists, tears cruising from her eyes. Perhaps he shouldn't be taking things for granted, for the woman who faced him now was not the woman he left a moment before.

"Don't think I don't know what you're doing," she accused.

"What?"

"I've been wise to you from the beginning, and I want you to go now."

"Beth, we need to talk." His voice was smooth and relaxing,

fuzzy like the velvet used in his suit. It was the tone he used with small children frightened of a boisterous man in a red costume. "There's nothing for you to fear."

His head felt foggy, but the rest of him felt alive, tingling, and very probably on fire. Left with her in his arms for very more minutes he would easily become a believer in spontaneous combustion. Lust...desire...love, when you met the right woman it all boiled down to the same thing, didn't it?

He meant to take it slow, or as slowly as he could, knowing he had a timetable. He couldn't stay away from the North Pole much longer. He had responsibilities as Santa Claus that he couldn't ignore no matter how many impersonators were out there doing good work in his name. There were certain things he had to do himself, although at the moment, nothing felt quite so right as holding Beth in his arms.

She was getting angry. Tension radiated from her in waves, thick enough that Nicholas had no difficulty discerning them, even without the powers he had at his command. It had been the last thing in the world he wanted, to hurt her in any way, or he muttered to himself with a pragmatism that Santa Claus was known for, he hadn't meant to hurt her over this. The love they had building between them should be the easy part.

He reached out a gentle hand to sooth her, but she snapped him away with a flash of her fingers, the warning clear. Stay away. He could do many things, but he doubted that was one of them. "Do you want to talk?" Nicholas asked.

"I sure as hell don't want to—" the words dropped off, and her face flushed with embarrassment. The emotion was stronger than the anger that had infused her moments before. "I don't want to be used," she spat out, her green eyes flashing. There was high color on her cheeks, twin blotches of red that made her look vibrant.

"I wasn't going to use you."

"You think not? I may be innocent, but believe me, I am far from naive. Our relationship nineteen years ago doesn't give you the right to possess me now. I was grateful to you then...."

"Beth, it's not your gratitude I want."

"I like you. I like the way you sing when you work. I like the way you laugh and the way your eyes twinkle when you look at me but I don't understand the feelings soaring through me. I have a life I've made myself. A life I'm proud of. I may have made some wrong choices over the years, but they are my choices. I won't let you embarrass me in front of my relatives and I will not compromise my principles for an hour or two of gratification."

Perhaps he should have left an hour ago, but his heart was here and his love was too strong to fight. Marlett would have to cope without him. He didn't see how she'd left him any choice. "I love you. I want to share your life, have you share mine."

"And you've come to this marvelous conclusion after knowing me only three or four days after a nineteen year absence?"

"I knew the minute I looked in your eyes. Don't try to deny it, for I knew you felt something as well. There's a spark within both of us that recognizes that."

"Do you write poetry? I've never heard bull put quite so liltingly."

He didn't know how to react. His world had twisted unexpectedly in a direction he couldn't fathom. "Do you deny the attraction you feel?"

"Yes. Yes, I do."

"Then you're only lying to yourself."

"My parents fought. I don't need a man to define my life."

"You were never meant to live alone. I want you."

"I wish I could believe that, but it all boils down to motivation. Why would you want me when I am certainly no prize?"

"Do you believe that? How badly have you been hurt in the past that that is how you see yourself?"

"You only want to use me."

"Do I? Am I lying when I take you in my arms? I know what's causing this reaction, Beth. Believe me, I know. Your grandmother is ill and yes, she is dying. You have a nephew who will never see adulthood, and you see me as another responsibility but don't you see? Haven't you realized what I'm doing? I here to support you. To give you my love."

"And if I give you my heart, what does that mean? You've already made it very clear that you can't stay for Christmas."

"You'll see me, I promise you that, because it was never my intention to go alone. I'm asking you to marry me."

"You're going to leave me."

The anger drained from her, leaving her shaking and hollow. It was all the invitation Nicholas needed, for all he had to do was open his arms, and she filled them, burying her face in the hard muscled flesh of his shoulder, wrapping her arms around his back. It was sweet torture, and his body reacted quickly.

You're going to leave me, she had accused, terrified that she would give her heart and he would abuse it. And oddly enough, it was exactly what he feared, that she would leave him. "What you are offering is a gift, Beth. Love is the most precious gift one person could give another."

"I'm so afraid." A tiny spot of wetness burned through his shirt.

"I'm afraid too. But not about my love for you, or the life we can have together."

"You said you'd leave."

"I have to, for Christmas. I've made other commitments I can't ignore, but except for Christmas, my time is my own, and all that I have is yours. Marry me, Beth. If you answer me, we can be gone tonight."

The wet spot on his shirt grew larger. She raised her head, rubbed at it, searing her love into his heart.

"I can't. There's so much I have to do. Don't ask me now."

"I need an answer soon."

"I understand." And to show she did, Beth parted her lips. For just a second he hesitated, not quite believing his luck in finding this one woman out of the billions he'd had to choose from. He murmured a short, silent prayer of gratitude, offering thanks to Beth, to her grandmother, even to Marlett for shoving him out the door, when it was much easier to pretend that nothing was wrong.

They had been standing by the coal stove the moment before but when he came to his senses, he had no idea how many minutes later, he was seated on the couch, with Beth resting on his lap, her arms around his neck, her teeth nibbling his ear. He no longer smelled the scent of her perfume, but an earthy, warm fragrance of arousal.

She stopped kissing him and pulled back the length of her arms, fingers still entwined behind his neck. "I'd like you to make love with me."

He groaned. While his body screamed immediate agreement, his mind had other plans. Nicholas shifted uncomfortably, rubbing her soft body against the hard, aching part of him. "I had thought we'd wait until we married."

"No. I need to know if what I feel for you is real or if it is just frustration." He must have blanched, for she continued. "I know what the words mean. There's been more than a time or two when I desired to be held by a man, regardless of whether there was a chance for love or not."

"There's nothing wrong with your feelings. They're perfectly natural."

"Then will you do it? Will you make love with me?"

"Are you certain? Are you very, very certain?"

She took a deep breath, let it out slowly. "Yes, I am. And if you never come back—"

"Beth, I promise, I'll be back."

"And if you never come back, I don't want to be left without memories. I'm losing too much. I want you to love me now."

"I want you so much I'm ready to crumble if you don't want me, but I don't want to rush you. What is happening between us should develop slowly. It should build until we are both to the point where we can't live another minute without the other."

"I'm there already, Nicholas."

"I am too, my love. But I need you to consider all the consequences. After I make love to you this evening, *if* I make love to you this evening, our entire relationship will change. You need to tell me it's what you want."

"Nicholas, I don't want to think. I only want you to love me."

"I don't want any regrets. I can't believe I'm saying this. I want you so badly I ache, and here I am, trying to talk you out of this."

Her smile this time was honest, and if her eyes sparkled with innocence, at least there was awareness as well. "You aren't going to succeed, you know. All my life I've done the safe thing, the expected thing, and all my life I've never made any major blunders, but you want to know something, I've never loved either. When my heart swells in the springtime it's only because I know there's only two more months of school, and when I cry at sentimental movies it's because I realize I've never loved that deeply. I've never touched another person's life the way I want to touch yours. I don't care who you are, or what you're after. This, tonight, is a gift I'm giving myself and I'm going to enjoy every single second of it."

With a gentle, trembling finger he touched her eyes. There was moisture there, but it didn't have to be tears. It could be happiness. While she watched, he brought the dampened fingertip to his lips and kissed it gently.

Beth smiled, lowered her lashes, suddenly feeling embarrassed. She had never been this brazen before. She had never done any of this before. She hoped he would sense that on some level, for she didn't have the courage to spell it out for him. She was used to dealing with third graders, not opening herself up emotionally and physically to a man she didn't know, who, she was still certain, was only using her.

"I really don't know how to start."

"That's all right. I do. Now bundle up."

She giggled, unexpectedly. "I thought the main idea was to take off all my clothes."

"It is. But I've decided not to rush this. I want to make it special for you, and I want this relationship to be more than a quick tumble on the sheets whenever I get the urge. Miss Anderson, would you like to go for a moonlit walk with me?"

"Mr. St. Noel, I'd be delighted to." Her laugh, and her obvious degree of flattery prevented her statement from becoming too stilted.

Feeling considerably less self-conscious than she had the few minutes before, Elizabeth slipped her shoes off and tugged on her boots. She nodded her silent thanks as Nicholas held her coat for her, then waited, feeling pampered as he fastened the zipper and secured the last button under her chin. He kissed her lightly on the nose and gave her a knowing wink that had her blushing down to her curled toes.

"While you're snug in that winter coat I want you to think of how warm you're going to be later this evening after I remove it."

Elizabeth shivered in anticipation but said nothing.

Nicholas put his own rugged outer coat on, and held the heavy door open for her. The cold hit her hard, freezing the inside of her nose, stinging the small portion of her cheeks that were open to the air. The storm which had been raging like a banshee when her program let out had passed, leaving a fresh three to five inches of new thick snow and the snow plows hadn't had time to find on the street in front of Beth's house.

Like so many Pennsylvania winter nights the sky was crystal clear and visibility was limitless. Nicholas wrapped his arm around her back and gently tugged her until they walked hip to hip.

"Warm enough?"

"Delightful."

"Wrap your arm around me, and stick your hand in my pocket. I want to feel you against every inch of me."

Beth followed his commands. "How did you know one of my favorite things was taking a quiet, midnight walk?"

"I didn't know," he answered honestly, "but we were rushing things a bit in there, and I didn't want you to feel pressured."

The streets were deserted. An occasional house still had lamps burning, indicating that the entire world hadn't gone to sleep yet, but most of the bright Christmas lights were still on, increasing her impression that they were indeed walking in a fantasy world.

On the way out, Beth pointed to several decorated houses, the ones she liked, the ones she thought overdone. Apparently over the past few years the neighborhood had gone through some kind of light-wars with entire blocks banding together, trying to better than the next street down. It was, she told him, only a symptom of what was wrong with Christmas these days. Nicholas found it quite amusing, this neophyte lecturing *him* on what this particular holiday should be like. Besides, she had a naked Santa Claus on her shower curtain, and she had the nerve to call flashing lights and chiming musical bells gaudy?

"What's this in your pocket?" she asked.

"Huh? There shouldn't be anything."

"No, there I've got it." She tugged out an object, and held it up under a street lamp. "Candy canes?"

"Believe it or not, I'm addicted to the things," he answered as if embarrassed. "Do you like peppermint?"

"I love the taste of traditional candy canes. I've tried those designer ones, the grape, cherry, chocolate mint and the rest, but I grew up on red and white peppermint candy canes. I don't think it could be Christmas for me without them."

He laughed, feeling young. "I feel the same way."

"I don't like the way Christmas has changed, heading off in too many different directions. I like a traditional Christmas."

"I'm very involved with Christmas, and my heart will always be with a traditional Christmas and all the values associated with it, but I think as the generations change, Christmas needs to change as well. Not the underlying meaning, not the togetherness, the neighborliness and the spirit of giving, but if the world wants to celebrate Christmas with pistachio candy canes, let them."

"I suppose you're right." Beth studied the wrapped candy cane in her hand, then facing him, went to deposit it back in his pocket.

"No." He stopped her with firm pressure on her hands. "Open it. I want to kiss you with the taste of peppermint on your lips."

She pealed the clear cellophane wrapping paper back from the straight end. She slipped the candy cane in her mouth, licking it with a sensuality that was new to her. Nicholas caught his breath. Then he leaned over and softly let his lips make contact with hers.

He nibbled gentle teasing kisses against her warm, responsive lips, and when she opened her mouth to sigh his tongue slipped inside her mouth, feeding, feasting, with a hunger which touched both of them to the depths of their being. Beth responded to the magic, answering his kissing with a matching fire of her own.

He must have removed his gloves for it was the warm flesh of his palm that cupped her chilled cheek. "You are so beautiful," he said.

"I feel beautiful when I'm with you. Like a teenager, I'm discovering these things for the first time."

"Thank you for waiting for me. Thank you for having the courage, even though you had no idea I'd ever come for you, to wait."

"Nicholas, can we go back now? I'm getting...cold."

He stared at the stars shining bright with promise above him and nodded. "Yes, it is time to get back." Then, because he was hungry for the taste of her, he kissed her again, deeply.

"Do you like winter sleigh rides?"

"Yes, I do."

"I have a sleigh. I'd love for us to go riding through the tundra together. It is only one of so many things from my life that I'd like to share with you."

"It will be something I'll look forward to."

That, and long winter nights wrapped in his arms, holding him close.

CHAPTER 15

Silently Nicholas and Beth walked through the snow drifts to her grandmother's house. Neither wore mittens, instead they merged fingers, sharing more than warmth. Just the simple intimacy of that gesture, the trust it implied, the pleasure it promised, was enough for now. He tightened his fingers, Beth echoed it in unspoken communication.

She had fallen, accidentally she insisted, into a deep pile of pristine snow. Nicholas might have believed her had she not wiggled her arms and her legs and made a snow angel. Yes, the elves would have no trouble at all falling in love with her.

"Get up before you freeze to the spot," he ordered, but she just laughed and her happiness was contagious. He couldn't quite remember when he felt so frivolous himself.

Beth held a hand out, and Nicholas tugged, pulling firmly, quickly, so as not to ruin the impression her slender body left in the thick snow. Nicholas had brushed snow off her collar, had promised her a lingering runny nose, but the adrenaline which had abandoned her after her pageant had returned, and with that perky grin of hers, Beth assured him that she was protected by the spirit of Christmas present. He suspected that was true.

Nicholas settled her under his shoulder, securing her tightly against his side by the arm wrapped around her. Their hips rubbed as they moved. Unconsciously they picked up their pace.

And there was a song that occurred to her as they walked in their winter wonderland. *'I'll have a blue Christmas without you.'* It was, undoubtedly why she had been so depressed at the beginning of the holiday season. She was missing him and she hadn't even known that he existed.

It was a night for contrasts. They were cold, but soon they would forge a joint warmth. She was frightened, but she knew he would be kind. She was innocent, but that innocence would not be destroyed. It would be altered by his loving, but would still remain an essential part of her character.

Beth followed, taking two steps to his one, and Nicholas slowed, realized that in his enthusiasm, his eagerness, he was dragging her behind him.

He licked his lips. He could still discern the taste of peppermint and Beth and his hunger grew. It had been a too long since the last time he kissed her, almost two full minutes. He bent to kiss her again.

"Let's go inside." It was too cold for what he had in mind standing on the snow shrouded sidewalk, in full view of anyone who cared to roll up their window shades.

"I'm going to write to Santa, tell him how grateful I am for you," but then she blanched, for she remembered what he had said and how sometimes she believed it.

He tweaked her nose, playfully, teasing. "And I've always known that Christmas wishes come true."

Nicholas opened the door, bit back a foolish impulse to carry her over the threshold. She must have read his mind for she laughed, and the sound was more beautiful than carols. They stamped snow off their boots on the broad porch, once inside they bent, tugging, removing the heavy footwear, a prelude to removing the rest of their clothing.

The living room was deserted. From the front bedroom came Catherine's deep rhythmic breathing just this side of a snore. If Beth were to be believed, ten thousand relatives would start descending on the house in just a few hours. They would not have this much privacy again until they reached his workshop far in the north.

It was dark. A dim trace of light worked its way up the stairs from the kitchen, a nightlight which was kept burning twenty-four hours a day. For safety's sake, he had unplugged the tree before they left.

Beth stepped out of her boots, stood stocking footed and stared at him, mouth agape, eyes wide. Passion was still there, as was the traces of fear he'd witnessed earlier. If it killed him, he would go slowly with her.

Her hands fumbled awkwardly against the buttons. Her brain had turned to cookie dough, undeniably sweet, but lumpy and unformed. She found it impossible to access the synapses necessary to remove the rest of her clothing. Nothing worked, except her eyes and parts of her which trembled. She wanted to do this, more than she ever wanted presents under the tree. She wasn't going to change her mind and she still couldn't move.

He arched toward her, each step closer, another choreographed move in her seduction. She waited. Love and promise had made anything else impossible. His lips were full, swollen from her kisses. Funny, she'd never thought a man's lips could be swollen from kisses. Her senses heightened. His eyes had ceased twinkling long before. Now they burned, hot, feverish, and dark like the night around them.

"Let me," his hands captured the buttons of her parka. "I want to unwrap you like a Christmas present I've been waiting all year for. I want to cherish and anticipate and savor."

"Nicholas..." Her voice was soft, like a sigh.

"Believe me when I tell you there is no rush. We will have decades to celebrate the love we initiate this evening."

He liberated the outer buttons, pulled the tongue of her zipper down, the clasps making a sound which was loud in the silence of the deserted night. The grandmother clock softly chimed the hour, then twelve firm steady bongs beat through the night like the thumping sound of her heart.

"Frightened?" he asked as he turned his back to her to hang up her parka in the closet just inside the front door.

She felt very vulnerable, and was embarrassed that she must have looked that way as well, for he had no trouble discerning her emotions.

"A little. Not of you. Of myself. I don't know how to act."

With tenderness born of love he wrapped her in his arms then, a spontaneous hug, meant only to reassure. "I don't want you to act. I want you to respond."

"You'll have to show me what to do."

Nicholas bowed formally, as if in the presence of royalty. "It would be my honor."

A strange man, she thought, and a strange time to bring up

the word honor, when there was nothing between them, not even promises.

"Do I...what do you want me to do?"

"Relax. Should I get you a glass of eggnog?"

"Yes." It would steady her nerves, but more than that, she wanted him to disappear, even if it were only for a moment, so she would have time to come to a better understanding of her own emotions. She couldn't breathe while he looked at her like that.

A dimple tightened in his chin. "There is still time to back out. I'll do nothing to hurt you."

"I know that." And she did. Those were more than words, more than a line handed down. "I want this. I want you."

She was like Christmas ribbon, curled, shredded, very lovely and it occurred to him rather belatedly that he didn't want a decoration in his life. He needed a lover, a companion, the half of his soul that had been missing for far too long.

"I've disappointed you. You're upset that I'm inexperienced."

"No. Never think that. It is one of the greatest gifts you could give me." And he would change her as an skilled man could change a virgin woman, but the rest of her, her goodness and light, he wanted to keep exactly the same.

Beth smiled, timid and slightly sad. "You know, I've never felt like an adult. Every single time I spoke with a parent at teacher conferences I felt like a fraud. They had something I never had. Even if their marriage, or their relationship failed, they had found someone willing to give them children."

"Be honest with yourself, Beth. If it were just sex, you could have had that almost any time you wanted. You've been propositioned. There was that time in college—"

She didn't ask how he knew. Some things were so private even her grandmother didn't suspect. "All right, I had opportunity. But I was always too scared to take it."

Scared? She put the wrong name to it. "No. It was never right. Sex without love is just groping. You know that, even if the vast majority of people in the world don't."

"I've been desperate." She felt shame in her confession. Her relationship with Michael, if relationship was the right word for it, had been based in large part on desperation. There were so few single, unattached men in her small town who weren't first cousins, and she had wanted a man with ties to her past. Beth had bought into the Hollywood fantasy of being swept off her feet, had forced herself into a temporary blindness to his faults, feigned a response to his kisses thinking she would grow to love him. Marriage, she decided, would make her feel like she belonged. She would become an adult, a woman and have a home, with the single phrase "I do." Yet Michael had mocked her Santa Clauses and her innocence.

He had been only interested in the parts of her life when she was horizontal. It never would have occurred to Michael to take a midnight walk in fresh snow, to consider her feelings for peppermint candy canes or that if she said yes to intimacy, that it didn't mean she was ready to have her clothes torn off her and be attacked. She had been delighted when Rachael won him, had been sincere with well-wishes at their wedding, even if Rachael hadn't believed her and Michael had suspected she still carried a torch. Michael, under Rachael's tutorage, had grown much worse, although the same might be said for Rachael. They had fed on each other's worst characteristics.

As if he read her thoughts and didn't want her thinking of another man, Nicholas kissed her, long, passionate, and again, like his handshake by the undecorated tree, clearly a prelude.

"Wait, I'll be right back." With a bound he was down the stairs.

Nicholas returned with two long stemmed crystal champagne goblets and she had no idea where he found them. This was an old fashioned household. They were more likely to drink their evening milk from former jelly glasses than stemware, but she was flattered with his attention. Nicholas brought the cup to her, and she parted her lips and took the smallest of sips. The thick, creamy liquid coated her tongue with the sensations of Christmas and above all else, the overwhelming feeling of rightness.

"Did you drug it? It tastes so marvelous."

"No, there's nothing here but eggnog and love. It's an old

family recipe I don't share with many."

"I see." The man kept a private cache of eggnog. But, considering the taste, the sensations it evoked, she heartily approved.

With little more than a look, a gentle touch at the small of her back, Nicholas led her to the couch and sat her down. Because of her trust, she followed his unspoken suggestions docilely, her eyes wide. She rested her head on the lace doily at the top of the high backed couch, her heart beating too rapidly to relax.

"Are you cold?"

"Not with you."

"I could light a fire if you need one."

"Maybe later. Not tonight." Already her senses hummed on overload. Cold was one of the furthest things from her mind.

With sure, deft movements he went to the record player where he chose Christmas music, instrumental, but a loved record she had listened to for almost two decades. The opening tract was '*O Holy Night*'. Somewhere in the back of her mind Elizabeth had the feeling that it was sacrilegious to prepare to make love to the most beautiful, pious Christmas hymn written, but another part of her, a part closer to the surface of her consciousness, cheered. It was exactly right.

The music swirled, almost subliminally, and while she shut her eyes she let the music take her back, over all the years of her childhood, through all her youthful dreams of a home and family. As the song progressed, she felt her dreams mature. But they hadn't changed. They were exactly the same as they had been when she was ten.

"I used to write to Santa Claus," she said. She had no idea where that confession had come from.

"I know." His voice was low and filled with passion. His loins ached with the desperation of filling her. He had never been so fully aroused.

"He never answered my letters or gave me the gifts I wanted."

"I think you'll be surprised just how thoroughly Santa has answered the desires of your heart."

"Tell me."

"I'd rather show you." Pressure built throughout his body making it impossible for him to think. At this moment, he only wanted Beth to want him. Adding Santa Claus, especially a Santa he wasn't sure he believed in, would only confuse matters.

Nicholas knelt in front of her and with precise concentration removed her thick woolen socks. He massaged her toes, sending shivers of awareness coursing through her body. He laid a kiss on the arch of her ankle and she purred. The record player switched to 'O *Little Town of Bethlehem*'.

When he was satisfied Beth had lost her frightened, in-the-crosshairs look, Nicholas moved up to sit beside her, kissing her as deeply as he had under the street lamp.

Nicholas ran his fingers through her fine hair. Her scalp tingled and she felt an increased awareness of him in her breasts, between her legs, even though he had only touched her feet, her lips, her hair.

He muttered, words that sounded like Christmas carols, or prayers, and she wasn't able to determine exactly what he was saying except that it made her feel more like a woman than she ever deemed possible.

"You have such lovely skin." It was velvet soft and driving him insane. She'd lost most of the freckles she'd inherited from her red haired father, but there were still traces of them visible on the bridge of her nose. It pleased him that she did nothing to hide them.

With boldness that she wouldn't have recognized in herself, Beth reached down to the hem of her turtleneck and pulled the cotton sweater over her head. She wanted him to see, to react, but one of the things she was most afraid of was that when he got a glimpse of her body that he wouldn't want her any more, and the suspense was killing her.

Courage—or foolhardiness—abandoned her right then. She held the wadded garment against her chest, her eyes wide like saucers, her mouth open on a broken cry.

He didn't laugh or grapple. He understood. "You have nothing to be ashamed of. Your body is exquisite." With nothing more dangerous than the tip of one finger, Nicholas traced the naked, exposed flesh of her shoulders and upper arm. She forgot to be afraid.

"I want to feel your breasts. Do you mind?"

She shook her head. She was ready, so incredibly ready for his touch. "Please," she answered. "I need..."

"I do too," he said. Nicholas dropped a moist kiss on the soft part of her neck, under her ear. Beth knew he could feel the increased pulse at her throat. He held his hands out, palm up, nothing more than that. He was asking for her trust, indicating he would not take. All that was hers she would have to share. With courage, and a renewed commitment to her own femininity, Beth held out the shirt, removing it in painful increments from across her breasts.

Nicholas accepted the turtleneck, set it aside without righting it, without taking his eyes from hers. Then he lowered his lids and she knew he looked for the first time at her bra covered breasts.

"In the entire world there is no more beautiful woman than you."

Elizabeth didn't see how that was possible. Still, tonight, and for as long as she could, she would adsorb his praises, and keep it wrapped around her heart.

He put his palms flat on the expanse of her breasts. She moaned and felt the motion as if she had been naked. Slowly he circled the turgid nipples, massaging, torturing them both with the pleasure it released. Her breasts had never been large, and the bra she wore was tiny, delicate, sheer. He could see the darkness surrounding the nipples and his mouth went dry.

He licked his lips, then lowered his head, sucked a nipple through the material, the resulting increase in pressure at his groin painful. She was sweeter than any treat left on a plate Christmas Eve. He hungered for her, for the completion they would reach together, for the times they would share over the years. With equal enthusiasm he attacked her other breast with the gentleness of his lips.

She moaned, and his kisses continued, traveling up her neck, her chin, kissing every inch of her, her eyelids, her cheeks, the salty tears that shouldn't be there.

"There's nothing to be afraid of." But he said it needlessly. She had stopped being afraid sometime before. The tears, if that's what they were, came from happiness.

"I want to feel you. And because this is new to you, I'm going to let you feel me." She nodded. It was more than she hoped for.

"Unbutton my shirt," he said with a voice grown husky.

Elizabeth bit her bottom lip and opened her eyes. It was almost impossible to move, for he hadn't released her breasts from the sensual assault he waged upon them, even when he was kissing her earlobes, for his hands had moved in to massage.

She was about to refuse, she *wanted* to refuse, because her body was no longer under her own control and because she was afraid to show her inexperience, but she didn't. Around Nicholas she could be bold. She reached out and released the first button.

His look said he was proud of her, but he uttered no words. There were about sixteen dozen more buttons to go.

"No," he said with a chuckle. "Only five." Again he had read her mind, no invasion of privacy, but a sharing which made what they were about the experience more intimate.

He wore a red and green plaid flannel shirt, soft from countless washings. She rubbed her fingers up the sleeve to his shoulder, reveling in the tensile sensation. She attacked another button. He wore an undershirt. She could see it now that enough of the shirt had been opened. It gave her courage. She could work her way through those endless buttons, remove his shirt, and still not have to face the bare expanse of his chest. One step at a time. One small step.

He kneaded her breasts. The pressure within built. She would have to move faster. With that thought in mind, and with an increasing desperation that the sun would rise and she still wouldn't have seen any more of him than his clothing, she finished her assignment, the last button ceding gracefully under her confident fingers.

"You did it. I knew you could." Nicholas removed the shirt, tossing it toward the reclining chair beside the couch. Then, before she could protest, he pulled the undershirt off as well. She had very little experience with staring at a grown man's chest. At the movies it was too impersonal and she had never spent much time drooling at public swimming pools. She had seen her uncles, her cousins, and even her brother on occasion, but they were family, and never would their physique have the effect Nicholas's did for her. Even this morning, by the bathroom he hadn't quite seemed this potent.

She noted a fine tracing of dark chest hair, just the right amount, she decided, and his chest was broadly muscled. He removed his hands from her breasts long enough to reach for her wrists. Without telling her what he intended to do, he placed her fingers over his small, tightly nubbed male nipples. She gasped and would have pulled back, but he wouldn't let her. Shock waves rocked through her, which she felt all the way to the moistening part between her legs.

He kissed her before she could protest, an open mouthed kiss which now felt so right it had become a part of her. She teased the nubs of his breasts with curiosity, satisfaction and rampant desire. It was only fair that she should attack him with the same degree of finesse.

She was still too deeply involved in the kiss, and with her own investigation to realize that he had shifted his hands, that he had found the front closing snap of her bra. Before she could decide whether or not she should protest, she noticed it resting on top of his undershirt.

His kisses intensified, as if making up for the lost time. He met her eyes. He looked at her with deep, intense passion.

"Am I moving too fast?"

"No."

"Any time I do anything you don't like, all you have to do is tell me and I will stop."

"I know. I don't think you could do anything I wouldn't like tonight."

"Good."

Elizabeth lowered her eyes, timid again, afraid to let him see the love she held for him shining directly through her eyes from the deepest part of her heart. She watched his chest expand as he breathed, deep, even breaths she felt along the sensitive skin of her cheeks, and felt too along the tingling pads of her fingertips.

"I want you to kiss me," and while she licked her lips in anticipation of his request, he halted her, by raising her chin and forcing her to look at him again. "I want you to kiss me on my nipples," he finished.

"I don't know if I can."

"I will show you how it's done."

Nicholas lovingly cupped her left breast with both hands. He brought his lips around her pebbled-hard nipple. Elizabeth moaned, lifting her hips off the couch as the awareness rippled through her.

"I promise you, if you do that to me, my reaction will be exactly like yours. It will feel that good to me."

She rubbed her thumb over the tight nub of his male flesh, then slowly she lowered her lips. Her tongue reached out timidly and swiped at him.

"That's right, Beth. Just like that."

His words gave her the courage she needed. As he had, she bent her head and suckled on his nipple, bringing a moan of sexual satisfaction to him.

"If you knew, if you only knew how good that feels," he whispered.

"I do."

"My turn. I'm going to remove my pants and my shorts," he told her. "Will that be moving too quickly for you?"

Elizabeth shook her head no. Nicholas stood and unfastened his belt buckle and unsnapped his jeans. She heard more than saw the zipper release. And minute later he was sitting down beside her, removing his socks, then he stood again, and removed his pants and his briefs in one smooth movement. Completely naked, he stood in front of her, waiting.

She had been watching her feet again, but she looked up, ignoring a specific part of his anatomy, concentrating on his face.

There was only love there and tenderness. No condemnation. No anger or animal lust. His chest was broad, the muscles sharply defined. No fat whatsoever, although he had told her more than once that he was so addicted to Christmas cookies that he ate them year round. His waist was slim, his hips beautifully proportioned. She found no flaw, even when she realized that she was looking at that most intimate part of him.

She felt color flood her cheeks, but she did not look away. His male member was large, heavy, engorged, standing outright in invitation. "Now you can see what you do to me."

He held his hands out, and with trust she reached up, putting her hands in his. Nicholas pulled her to her feet. "Lean against me. I want you to get used to the feel of me first."

"Yes." That way she wouldn't have to look. Except that as her body molded against his, as she felt the steamy heat of him, Beth realized that touching was worse. Much worse.

She quivered in sexual response and instinctively moved back, trapped by the couch, penned in by the aggressive size of his arousal. But her body knew what she needed even as her mind sought retreat. She stood her ground, let the tip caress her through her pants. He touched her nowhere else. Her lips still tingled, her nipples throbbed, and there was an unfamiliar rocking to his hips so that she rubbed against him, slowly, gently, inexorably.

"Put your arms around me. We'll go at your pace."

"I'm ready. There's no need to be so nice."

"I have to be nice. What we're doing tonight is setting the foundation for our sexual relationship that could last the remainder of our lives. Don't you realize that?"

"No. I only want to think about now."

Elizabeth put her hands on his hips, lightly, keeping a distance between them that a Pennsylvania coal car could fit through. She was naked above the waist, and as she stood, she realized she was cold without his warmth. She leaned against him, her breasts making contact with the soft yet scraggly hair of his chest. His hands rested warmly on her shoulder blades. He made no move to pull her closer.

She rocked, ever so slightly to the sound of Christmas music she hadn't heard in a long time. Bare foot to bare foot, hips swaying, she moved closer, a half-step, hoping he wouldn't notice. His erection stood out between them, hard and firm. She felt it through the material of her pants, against the naked skin above her navel. Decisively she moved closer, until it was trapped between them.

"See, that wasn't so bad, was it?" He kissed the top of her head.

An explosive happiness built. "It was perfect."

"Are you ready to touch me?"

"Yes."

Nicholas backed up enough so that there was room between them. He waited, not saying anything, until she looked down. Her mouth dropped open. She tried to swallow, to find moisture from under her tongue. It was impossible to speak, harder to think.

"Wrap your hand around me and stroke it, back and forth."

"Will it feel good?"

"Better than you could imagine."

It was hot and firm, and above all else, welcoming. She did as he told her, her hands finding purchase against his swollen flesh, and felt an answering response deep within her own body.

"My love, that's right. It feels so good. You know just how to touch me. How to reach me."

His words soothed her. She had been afraid she was holding him too tightly, too roughly. Her hand continued to stroke.

"I want to return the favor."

"Yes." Breathless, the pace increased. She could no longer afford to be hesitant about anything. She was very close to an explosion herself.

Elizabeth released him, put her hands upon his shoulders in support for her knees had grown weak and she doubted she had the strength to stand up under her own power any longer. It was a slender, decorative belt, but he had it unfastened before she could breathe in. He unhooked the top clasp, and released her zipper.

She was hypersensitive, very aware of his every movement, her body calling out to his, calling out for completion.

Instead of removing her pants directly, he slid his hands within her clothing, in between her twirling stomach and her panties.

When his long index finger reached the nest of hair between her legs that no man had ever touched, she thought she would shatter into a million pieces right there.

"It gets better," he whispered into her ear, finding a nub just above her feminine opening and caressing it, teasing it, torturing it.

Elizabeth forgot that she couldn't stand, forgot that she should be shy and reserved. She reached for his shaft and in a desperate attempt to give to him the pleasure he was giving her, rocked him, with force and with love and with an increasing type of desperation.

He lifted her into his arms like a child or a lover, and she wrapped her arms tightly around his neck and met his kiss with all the passion which boiled within her. He carried her smoothly from the living room, into the middle bedroom, his bedroom. She had expected he would take her to her own, but she was glad he hadn't. That was her room since she had been a child. This would be her room when she became his lover.

The bedspread must have been pulled back already for he laid her gently down upon the soft flannel sheets. Before she could respond with her acknowledgement he had her pants off, and then, in a second trip, her panties.   Like all women from time immortal, she lay naked on his pallet, waiting, her arms raised, her legs spread, and her soft, woman's part of her moist and willing.

"Do you want to stop here?"

"How can you ask me that?"

"In another minute we're going to become lovers. If you want me to stop, you'll have to tell me now."

"Nicholas, we've always been lovers. We just didn't know it until today."

Her answer pleased him, for he smiled, showing bright, even white teeth, and he knelt down beside her, kissing her fully on the lips. "That's right, my love."

He positioned himself over her, and while her first impression was that she should shut her eyes and act maidenly, she kept them wide opened, fascinated with the look of intense concentration on his features, with the love she read in all his tender movements.

She felt his shaft trying to gain entrance to that woman's part of her, a gentle probing that shook her to the core of her being.

"You will have to guide him inside you," Nicholas said, poised over her, his weight resting on the palms of his hands and his knees. "Position him where he needs to go."

Yes, that would be part of her education, part of her seduction, to do this last, significant action herself. She wrapped a hand around him, and poised him on the cusp of her femininity.

"It will hurt for a minute. That's part of it, while I break through the last of your body's defenses. I will feel big and full within you, but your body will wrap itself around me so that there will only be pleasure for us both."

"Yes, I know that."

In unconscious response her hips gyrated, already parroting his movements. Elizabeth shut her eyes, held her breath, and lifted her hips in one dynamic thrust which ended her hated virginity forever.

Tenderly he kissed her closed eye lids, first her left, then her right. He repeated the movement to her eyebrows, keeping his hips completely still.

"Did that hurt?"

Silently she shook her head no.

"Are you all right?"

She nodded yes. Her eyes still tightly closed, but a trace of sparkling tears crested at the far edges of her eyes.

"Then why are you crying?"

"I think because I never thought I'd have this." Then, to show him she was telling the truth, she dropped her hips deeper into the mattress, increasing the distance between them by a slight, but significant increment, then she pulled his body back down into hers.

And they rocked, their bodies matching each other perfectly, until she felt the stars exploding all around her. They set a pace they could not keep, for they kept getting faster, then faster still, all the while pressures building up to explosive levels, forces she couldn't—wouldn't—control, ready to burst.

Nicholas felt the tremors of her body, recognized her climax as he gave into the desires of his own.

He thrust one last time, much deeper than ever before, and he grunted and she felt his seed flush. Spent, he lay on top of her until his breath regulated, then he removed himself from her body, and lay on his back, pulling her tight against him.

"I want to give you a child."

"Yes," he whispered, his hand caressing her soft, flat stomach. "Children are the most important part of my life and I've always wanted one of my own, but for now don't think of it. This is a night for us. Tell me you're happy."

"Nicholas, I've very, very happy."

"And you have made me happy. I love you completely and without reservations. Do you understand that?"

"Yes. I love you the same way."

"Good. Now I'm going to collect our clothing for your grandmother wakes up early in the morning and it wouldn't do for her to find out about the change in our relationship that way."

"No," she agreed.

"I'll be right back."

Her heart ached as he slipped out of bed as if half of her soul had been ripped out. Elizabeth pulled herself up on her elbows and looked around her. Sometime, and she had no idea when, he had lighted half a dozen fat Christmas candles and the room was redolent with the familiar aroma of bayberry which never before had smelled so erotic.

He was back, still stark naked, holding two glasses of eggnog. "I thought you would need something to replenish your strength," Nicholas said, handing her the glass.

"And am I going to need it?"

His chuckle warmed her as his loving had done. "You better believe it, my love. The night is still young."

CHAPTER 16

Nicholas couldn't stop the shudders that traveled through him, although it might have been easier, he might have had more control, if he couldn't still feel the powerful spasms sweeping through her. The release had been total for both of them, a simultaneous explosion, as if they were making up for years of depravation with this second intimate encounter.

The candle flames flickered, then grew tall and straight and very bright. The yellow light brought out the highlights of her hair, and let him witness the glow to her eyes which spoke of happiness.

As a child her eyes had sparkled with excitement, belief, innocence. As a woman he had witnessed glimmers of anger and family pride, and more times than he wished it, the dull patina of exhaustion. Now there was fulfillment, completion, and a depth of love which might have frightened him, had it not exactly matched the emotion deep within his own chest.

She lay on her back, while he stretched over her, his weight on an elbow. Candle glow, or passion, her smooth, responsive skin had a red flush, from her cheeks to the valley between her breasts.

"Don't look at me. You make me feel so very...."

So very. That was precisely how he felt.

With damp and quivering fingertips, Beth reached out touched his eyelids until they closed. Nicholas took that to be an invitation to explore her by tactile means, hands and lips and tongue. He rasped day-old stubble against her responsive skin, reveling in the images flirting against his retinas. He experienced a desperation to touch her again, as if he couldn't get enough. He wanted her. Heavens above how he wanted her.

Throughout her life Beth had been a woman who understood the value of giving. He was pleased he had been able to give her something of himself in return which was not born of legend.

"Merry Christmas." Her words were throaty, warm, sincere.

He thought about her statement for a heartbeat or two, decided there was nothing sacrilegious about it.

"Merry Christmas," he answered back. Mistletoe hung in glorious profusion at the North Pole, but he doubted he and Beth would need it as an excuse or an invitation, by the same token, he doubted it would go to waste. He was an opportunist. He would make due, or, more specifically, take advantage. He kissed her again feeding flames burning hotter than he could control.

He had to leave. Although he tweaked time, and could do basically what he wanted with the reindeer, he had to leave very soon. He contracted some of his muscles, checking, basically, to see if any of them were ready to answer to voluntary commands. They were lethargic and replete, but beyond that, functioning.

Nicholas removed his hands from her hair, set them, palms to the sheet, on either side of her shoulders.

"Don't leave." Internally, where they were still joined, Beth tightened her clasp on him, and her legs wrapped around him like manacles. It occurred to her that she still knew so very little about this man who once as a boy had been nice to her. He could have a woman in every small town, lovers from coast to coast or for that matter around the globe for he had a very cosmopolitan air about him. She might be one of many, nobody special. The intimacy kept her safe a little while longer and even if he were volunteering no pieces of his past, at least he wasn't flaunting it in her face, either.

Still, for all that she didn't know about him, there was one thing that she had learned about herself in the past few hours. Her capacity to love had increased dynamically. She'd been raised in love, every minute of her life. Love surrounded her, not necessarily from her parents, but from her grandmother, from her aunts and nieces, even from her school children who offered a kind of wide-eyed adoration but even in a life filled to overflowing with love, this was something new. Something wonderful. Something unexpected.

And although the love-making had been a delicious part of her discovery, it was just that, only a part. The love she was referring to existed deep within her heart, had nothing to do with her loins. She had always suspected she'd been missing something, but reality far exceeded her expectations.

The skin along his chin was scratchy where his beard was

coming in, dark like his hair, regardless of where he had found the long, flowing white one, this was short, stubby, scratched her lips. Beth could cherish all the different feelings of him, the unique sensations he evoked within her. The softness of his cheeks, the calluses on his fingers, the ticklish nature of his chest hair against her naked breasts, the long, smooth lines of his back that had arched and strained and drove her out of her mind.

Nicholas shifted, or rather tried to. "I must be too heavy for you," he muttered for although she had started out on top, he had found some way keeping them joined, to lay atop her to finish what they had started. Her arms, wrapped around his neck, held him firmly, as did her teeth at an earlobe.

"Don't go." Don't go now. Don't go ever. Let me keep my illusion of warmth and intimacy and honesty.

"I'm not going away, only far enough to let you breathe."

Sensually she arched her neck into the pillow. Her toes were still curled. Casually, although there was nothing idle about the motion at all, she slid her foot up and down his calf. New sensations. He was like a drug to her. "I don't need to breathe."

"Sweet marzipan." He called her by the nickname her grandmother had given her, for it seemed to fit. Everything about her seemed to fit.

"Are you happy?"

Her answer was very important to him. He knew he had pleased her, but Beth wouldn't necessarily associate sexual gratification with happiness.

"I am very, very happy. I'm glowing. I wish—"

"What, angel? What do you wish?"

"Nothing, it's foolish."

"I want to know." His look of deep sincerity rocked her.

"I wish you could stay for Christmas. I just want more time with you." She didn't want to beg and she didn't want to tie him, but then, she didn't want to have to be strong either.

"Marzipan, did you think I would just leave you, without a second glance?"

She understood Santa Claus. He came, but he never stayed.

And if you were one of the lucky ones who saw him, then you had memories, and perhaps a present or two, and the ridicule of your friends, but never any more than that.

"Do you have to go right now?"

He did. His body hummed with an inexorable pull which he was finding hard to ignore. Nicholas knew he should leave her, but to go now, would be the cruelest injustice.

"No, I'll stay."

After all, denying Santa Claus was second nature to him. He'd been doing it almost all his life. The love was new. This he needed to cherish, for a little while longer. "A few minutes."

Satisfied, she settled her head against his chest, sharing an intimacy as potent as their explosive joining by just laying beside him.

The phone woke them as they drifted into sleep, nestled against each other like long time lovers.

With the first shrill, invasive ring, Beth's eyes grew wide, shocked. She let it ring a second time before she thrust herself away from him and abandoned the tousled bed.

She searched his room. "Where is my robe?"

"Calm down." He handed her his, then she raced to answer the phone now somewhere on the fifth or sixth ring. Nicholas pulled on his clothing, his briefs and his pants, his socks, his shirt. For she knew when the phone rang at two o'clock in the morning that it was never good news, and he knew precisely how horrible this bad news was.

"Beth." Jim, crackling with pain. "Beth, I'm so sorry to wake you."

"That's all right. I wasn't asleep. I was working on a Christmas present." For herself. The most beautiful, spectacular gift she could imagine. "Is it the baby?"

Jim continued, trying hard not to break down, to say the inevitable words he had never wanted to say. "Jamie had trouble breathing at bedtime. We rushed him to the hospital where his frail young heart gave out."

He had died half an hour before. Not the baby at all. Jamie.

Her treasure.

"I'm sorry...Yes, I know...I loved him, we all did...He'll be happier now...We'll be right there...I love you...."

Beth hadn't turned on any lights, and the combination of the darkness, her sobs, and the ecstasy they had reached only an hour before shattered his soul. He flicked on the tree lights as well as a small, dim lamp, not wanting to invade her privacy, but needing all the same to see her.

The receiver clicked against the cradle, but she didn't raise her head. Beth huddled on the worn patterned carpeting, shoulder shuddering, tears flowing unchecked down her cheeks, her eyes already puffy and bloodshot.

"No. Don't. Touch. Me." She made it four, separate, distinct words. "I'm too fragile right now, Nicholas." But he read her heart and he wrapped his arms around her, in love, in desire, in the passion that wasn't sexual but which offered the support of understanding, the only comfort he had.

"What happened?"

It took her a long minute to get the words out, her grief having priority, robbing her of the ability to speak. She felt tiny and frail against him. "Jamie died."

His heart constricted, squeezed painfully in a too tight chest. Santa embodied happiness. It only made tragedy that much harder to bear. "He was special. We'll all miss him."

"It's just that he was my favorite of all of them, because he was so sick, because he tried so hard, always going to school and doing everything the other kids could, even when his body betrayed him."

After the pageant she had been frail but at least she had adrenaline holding her up, now she didn't even have that. She felt boneless, as if all the supports had been stolen from her life, as if one tiny boy had put the strength in her limbs.

"His heart wasn't defective," she whispered against Nicholas, "not when it came to the important things like love."

He knew that. Children of death often loved harder, deeper, more intensely, knowing instinctively that they had to use up an entire lifetime's worth in only a few short years.

"I'll take you to be with your family."

Beth pulled away from him, breathed deeply, gained control again, although it was a spun-glass control, apt to shatter at any second. "I have to tell my grandmother."

From somewhere deep within Nicholas heard the call, Marlett needing him, Christmas pressuring him, filling him, surrounding him. For how long, traveling with his mother had he been deaf to it, and the years he spent with his father and since his father's death when he denied it? Now it filled him, made him complete.

Made him Santa Claus.

It all came together, snapping tightly like Leggos or Lincoln Logs. The death of a child steeped in love, the love of a woman simmered in passion, honest tears shed at a community pageant, gingerbread cookies warm from the oven and a manger set cherished for decades. He was Santa Claus, replete.

All around him, Christmas was coming. It seemed to drag on for most of the year, the pace increasing until it was far too fast to stop. Now it was inexorable. He was part of it, caught in the undertow. It was his destiny, what he had been born for, to bring Christmas to those who otherwise would only find it another day in a series of hopeless, despair-filled years.

"Not now, Marlett," he whispered, seeking only a temporary reprieve. There was something he had to finish here first. One miracle for Beth. And hopefully, one for himself.

Nicholas waited, hands in his pockets while she ran to the bathroom and was sick. He heard water running in the sink, and seconds after she was out, holding a towel to her mouth, her eyes wide like black clumps of coal. But this was no snowman he watched, although her complexion had bleached and she was white enough. No, his Beth was warm and loving, and time was moving far too fast for him to mention that.

He didn't go in with her while she woke her grandmother, for with Catherine, Beth had no shields and her soul was naked. He would grant her the dignity of grieving in peace.

His hearing was quite acute and he could hear every word she said, even when to escape he went outside, started the motor of her cantankerous car, scraped the windows, threatened the defroster. The motor skipped, burped, chugged, but it kept running. He thought only of her sorrow and the loss of a child he had come to love.

Stamping snow from his boots Nicholas stepped inside the foyer, remembering a frail young boy, his eyes lit up like light bulbs, singing his heart out with every ounce of enthusiasm he could manage for the Christmas pageant which didn't belong to Beth, for it belonged to the entire community. Jamie's voice had been high, true, clear, and he had been a focal point for many of the audience who knew he fought a mortal illness.

Jamie, who because the veil was so thin had recognized him. *He's the one true Santa Claus, not an imposter like all the rest.* Yes, Jamie, I am the one true Santa Claus, and your wish will be granted. If it is at all within my power, I will see that Beth is happy for all the rest of her life. Now fly, tiny spirit and find your rest.

"Grandma's not coming." Beth had slipped out of the front bedroom, silent like a wraith, twisted and shattered, and vulnerable. "She's not feeling well."

Nicholas held her coat for her, directed her arms into the sleeves, straightened the collar, fastened the zipper. Her bottom lip quivered. How he wished it quivered as it had an hour before, in response to his kisses and his loving.

"She wants to see you."

He bowed, formally, accepting a responsibility he had tried to deny but which now had become as intrinsic as breathing. "I'll only be a moment. Wait."

It was unlikely that she would leave without him, not when her spirit had been shattered, but she was used to being strong, being the only one who coped and doing it all, not matter what. He wanted, needed, to be there, when she offered her condolences to the family, when she offered to help. For now that was all he could give her.

She migrated outside, needing to feel something besides grief, even if it were only cold. The sky was dark, the brilliant stars hidden by clouds which had arrived after their moonlit walk. She cried, and she prayed, and then, she heard the unmistakable sound of jingle bells.

"Santa?" she whispered into the frozen night. Beth hadn't expected, after all Nicholas had told her, that she could feel hope quite this strongly.

"No, not Santa." The bells sounded closer, clearer, magical. The voice was not Nicholas', but gruffer, lower, and oddly enough, more musical.

"Who's there?" She was too grief stricken to be frightened, but she was also, remarkably, disappointed. And, considering the circumstances, the disappointment didn't sit well at all. Beth couldn't see. Her eyes were misted with frozen tears, but surely she could make out his shape, for he sounded close enough to touch.

"Only a friend who cannot stay. I need you to do something for me."

Jingle bells, and perhaps the sight of booties, the tips curled, looking black against the pristine snow. "No. Not tonight. Please." Not anything else.

"You have to ask him why he's so scared."

A round barrel shaped body. A beard long and luxurious. A short person, barely reaching to her chest, there and not there. Grief so real she was having hallucinations.

"Who? Why who's so scared?"

"Santa Claus. Santa Claus shouldn't be scared."

Then she heard the front door opening, saw the shaft of light as it escaped the living room, created a wedge of brightness against the night. Her illusion, and her childhood fantasies, were gone. There was no Santa Claus. Only struggling to make ends meet, loving for a little while, and then pain. Oh, yes. The pain was real. In this life, only pain was real.

She opened the car door, sat inside, her breath patterning against the windshield, more substantial than anything which had happened to her in the past few hours. Jamie was dead and she was losing her mind.

Nicholas settled in the driver's seat, adjusted the defroster, put the car into drive along the deserted street. He smelled of peppermint, and she closed her eyes, tried very hard not to think about candy canes.

"What did my grandmother say to you?"

He needed time before he could answer, time for her belief to return. And what better time than now? Tonight it would start. Families sitting down to dinner, children trying to be good for a few more hours, already checking their flaccid stocking to see if perhaps Santa came early, just this once. Mothers and fathers preparing to drag out boxes from closets, from car trunks and garages, dreading the anticipation of a long night filled with instructions from a bicycle or a doll house or a VCR that needed assembly. Christmas Eve life would develop all around him. Little hands leaving cookies for Santa, carrots for the reindeer, still believing. And all the bedtime stories would have mice wearing stocking caps or trees that weren't picked from busy lots or presents that somehow got diverted. It would be a night of miracles, and he would be responsible for only the tiniest fraction of them. Right now he needed another miracle.

Her tears had frozen, but maybe she was just holding them in readiness for he knew she would need them again. Her teeth chattered. The sun set hours before, and when it arose again, it would be Christmas Eve, the day of joy, but for Beth, it would provide only the warmth of family unity. The temperature hovered a good seven degrees below freezing. In his bed she had been warm.

He took a deep breath, let it out slowly. "She wanted to make a wish to Santa Claus."

"My grandmother doesn't make Christmas wishes," but then she added snidely for she was hurt and he didn't blame her, "or does she buy into your lies?"

"She did this year." He wasn't sure which half of her question he answered.

"And what does she want left under the tree?"

It was not bitterness he heard in her voice, nor was it anger although considering the circumstances, Nicholas could well understand both. "She asked me to take care of you." Please let her think he meant now, facing the death of a child far too young to die.

"I'll be fine."

But he wouldn't answer for he knew Beth wouldn't be fine, not at the hospital where she would be allowed five minutes with the body, not when they returned home and he had to leave.

Her cantankerous curmudgeon car skidded on the frozen streets. It was an old vehicle, well past its prime, but he knew why she didn't have a better one. Her minimal teacher's salary went into Christmas presents, to the relatives, to those who had nothing. She took so very little for herself.

He pulled the car into the nearly deserted visitor's lot. Turned off the engine, waited for what he knew was coming. "Nicholas, I'd like to make my wish to Santa Claus too. In his name, will you listen?"

He sniffled, fought the need to wipe his eyes. "Yes, Beth."

Every year her wish to Santa was for someone else. He knew this year would be no different, even as he wished, just this once she could be selfish, ask for something for herself.

"Susan is pregnant again. Did you know that?"

"Yes." It was in her eyes, in the way she moved, in the way her hands trembled. And he knew from the pageant the whispered words he had half understood.

"She is afraid. That she might lose the baby. That it won't be healthy."

"I know."

"The heart condition Jamie has—had—is congenital. They want more children. A hundred more children, although they had their hands full will Jamie. They were always afraid of bringing a new baby into the world."

He knew that too, but did not speak. He let her continue.

"All I want is for this one to be born healthy with a heart that will beat for years and years without problems." She'd been staring out into the hollow night, now she turned to him, looking at him with a desperation that had his heart breaking. "Nicholas, do you think Santa can manage that?"

"I'll do my best." It would take a miracle and he suspected he had about used up his allotment of miracles for this year. The baby, right now only eight weeks past conception, had a tiny hole in his heart, large enough to kill him within a week after birth, even with emergency surgery and all the best doctors in the state. But he was Santa, and his wishes were never selfish, at least they hadn't been, until this year.

"Susan has lost so much already, after having coped with more than any mother should have to. I don't want her to lose this child as well." The stress of her grief alone would be enough to miscarry this child. If he were to save the baby, it would have to be done soon. Not tomorrow, not after Christmas, not when his own strength, his own commitment, had recovered.

It would be easier if she had asked for a fishing rod for her uncle or toys for a particular family with parents out of work for those he could manage. But if she had, she wouldn't be the Beth he loved, always expecting a miracle from Santa.

A healthy baby.

It was a tall order.

His powers were not unlimited. He wanted every ounce of the miracles left him to go to Beth. Should she decide to be his wife she would need them. There wasn't any extra magic for saving sick babies. And he was frightened. The fear paralyzing him, making it hard to think, to move.

"I feel so responsible."

He thought she only gave, but it didn't surprise him that there were things she took. Stray guilt. Responsibility for tragedy which could not have been altered.

"Don't blame yourself, Beth. You could not have prevented it. No one will blame you for what happened." She wasn't talking about the fetus, but of a boy who had sang with the light of angels in his eyes.

"He needed a heart transplant. Did you know that?"

"Yes."

"And we couldn't even hope that he would get one. That was the worst part of it. Because, for Jamie to get a heart, another child would have to die, suddenly, horribly, in an accident, and not one of us could wish that on any mother."

"Beth, I love you."

But she folded her frozen hands in her lap, and dejectedly shook her head. "Nicholas, that doesn't make anything better. It makes everything worse."

CHAPTER 17

A seven foot artificial tree towered in the hospital lobby, decorated in silver and gold bows, with tiny pinpoint lights that blinked on and off. Decorations insidiously found their way into every corner, from the elevator to the intensive care nurses' desk. Smiling Santas with bulging packs, stars and gingerbread men and snowmen and gifts with ribbons.

"I don't much feel like Christmas," Beth said, but then she caught sight of her sister and her brother in law, and there was no more talk of Christmas, only of death taking an eight-year-old boy and what he would miss, proms and driving and dating and children of his own. There would be presents under that tree that wouldn't be opened this year and a gaping wound that would throb with a vengeance every time the season returned.

With her family, Beth hugged and cried, offered prayers and words of encouragement, words of sorrow. Merry Christmas, she had told him as they lay entwined together. How happy she had been then.

All the local relatives had arrived, in twos or threes or fours, aunts, uncles, cousins, for this was a tight knit family, and they would share in the sadness as they did when they had something happier to celebrate, a wedding or a birth.

She went in alone to see Jamie, a final farewell. Nicholas waited outside the door, granting her a time to come to terms with her religious beliefs that let her cry when a child died, and yet know that death was not the end, that there was another life beyond this one.

Minutes later when Nicholas saw Susan rising, he followed her, whispering a silent invocation to keep everyone in their places, giving him the privacy he needed. The fear renewed, but he fought it. He could handle this. He could be Santa and demand a miracle. He could fight his own inner nature.

In her grief, Susan Steelgrave was a beautiful woman, not physically, for her eyes were swollen and most of her hair had

escaped from the band which should have held it back, her
complexion was too pale and her hands shook, but beautiful in
strength, in dignity, in a young mother's love.

"Mrs. Steelgrave?"

She stopped, turned. Her eyes were red, her lips swollen. It
was the worst pain in the world, a mother losing a child.

"Mr. St. Noel." She reached out, touched his hand, offering
her strength, her dignity. "How kind of you to come to help support
Beth." Her strength of character shone around her, glowed with a
spirit tattered but not yet broken.

He felt inadequate, wished for his father or his grandfather,
felt again the awkwardness of slipping into a position he wasn't
ready for. How very much harder this was than sneaking in through
closed doors and leaving presents.

"I am very sorry for your loss."

"He was a very special young man," she said, fighting fresh
waves of sorrow.

"He was."

Then grief made her blurt out what she otherwise would
never have mentioned so bluntly, what she had been conditioned to
disbelieve. "Jamie said you were Santa Claus." Then she tried to
shift away, was forcing her thoughts into words of denial,
conditioned words, but there is no Santa Claus, and there are no
miracles. But she didn't speak, except for the tears which crested her
eyes and which were far more expressive than words would ever be.

Nicholas reached out, returned her earlier gesture, touched
her sleeve, gently, with compassion. He absorbed some of her pain,
traces of it, enough so that she could take one breath after another.
Enough so that she could cope.

"There is no need to be ashamed. Because he was so close to
death, he saw things most people can't."

Crystal tears freshened her smile, in remembrance that wasn't
forced. "He was always special that way. I believe—"

He wouldn't let her finish, would give her the dignity of not
allowing her to beg. "Would you let me give you a Christmas
present?"

"From Beth?"

"From the family, and especially, belatedly, from your son. May I?"

She blinked rapidly, swiped at her cheeks with the back of her hand. Her lips trembled. This wasn't a time when she wanted a present, no thing could ever replace what she lost. But in memory of her son, and because, like her sister, she did believe, she nodded, slowly, and her eyes showed their first trace of hope. "Yes, yes of course."

Nicholas pulled a deep breath into his lungs, held it until it burned deep within, then let it out slowly. Fears flooded him, that he wouldn't be good enough, that he didn't have what it took, but he straightened his back and his resolve. If nothing else, he would try.

He gently placed his hands against her flat stomach, waited until he felt life, the throbbing beat of a heart, the solid awareness of another presence, then he started his prayer. Not all of Santa's powers came from Santa. Some of it came from a power much greater than him, and had more to do with the Christmas season than a sleigh riding aberration ever would. It didn't take long, only a minute or two before he finished.

As soon as Nicholas removed his hands, Susan placed hers over the exact same spot. Her cheeks were dry, and when she raised her eyes, they were clear and dry. "Will he be all right? This little one?"

"Now, yes."

"Thank you. Is it a boy? I'd like to name it Jamie, but then we could use Jamie for a daughter just as easily."

Slowly Nicholas shook his head. "Every child needs his own identity. Let this one have a fresh start, without having to live up to any expectations."

"Yes, all right. And thank you. I...we've been so scared since we found out."

"This one will be healthy. As will the next one."

"Another baby after this one? I'll have another baby?"

"Yes." And one after that. And one after that. If they wanted. If they were able to get past the fears of what happened tonight.

"I'm so very grateful to you." Impulsively Susan reached up and kissed his cheek. When she stepped back she brought her fingers to her eyes, fighting vertigo.

"Excuse me, did I bump into you? I...um...must not have been watching where I was going."

"Please, do not apologize." He slipped into a stilted formality, where after all, he felt more comfortable. "I would like to offer my sympathy on the death of your son."

"Thank you. I think I'll go into the chapel and sit for a few minutes. Again, if I bumped into you, I'm sorry."

He let her go. She wouldn't remember their conversation although this pregnancy would go smoothly. For the next eight months she would glow with an inner confidence and when family would ask her if she were afraid she would smile and say with a surety, this one will be perfect. And it would be, as a present from Beth. As would the next child, a gift from St. Nick himself.

He closed his eyes and completed a prayer of thanksgiving and when he opened them, Beth stood before him, surrounded by grieving family, each, perhaps hoping that an ugly mistake had been made, that the boy wasn't really dead after all.

"We won't be leaving for a little while. Susan and Jim want to wait until the mortuary comes to pick up Jamie. You can go if you want. I can get a ride home with someone. There's not much of the night left, but you can go. I know you want to go."

"I will stay and take you home."

"Someone should get some food ready, put on a pot of coffee. Everyone will congregate at Gram's."

"There's food enough ready. I will wait for you."

He watched all her hard won composure shatter. "Hold me, Nicholas. Just hold me. I don't want to think any more."

He readily complied, offering his shoulder for her to cry on and the strength of his arms to support her. He hadn't felt like an outsider over the past three hours, instead he felt like a member of the family. And he thought of Jamie's last wish while he held the boy on his lap so he could listen to all the things Santa could bring. But Jamie's list didn't have fire trucks or Nintendo games. "I only want

Aunt Beth to be happy," he said. "Could you do that for me? She believes in you. She always has."

He nodded, his throat too thick for words.

"And can you make her happy?"

"I can try," but it wouldn't be his decision, it would be hers.

When the worst of the tears passed into broken sobs, Beth came to her senses and found herself sitting on a green waiting room couch. She held a tissue in her hands but apparently it was for holding only, for she rubbed her eyes with her palm. She swallowed, then swallowed again. These were tears she could not shed. "I don't want to think about him. Could you please for the next few minutes talk to me about something else so I can get my tears under control?"

He sought something happy. With Santa Claus, there was often happiness. "I'd like you to see where I live. I know you would like it there. It's magical. Everywhere you look, any day of the year, miracles are happening. It's a place of joy and peace and love. There's a lot of singing. In the morning to welcome a new day, in the afternoon while we work, in the evening to praise or offer thanks. There are children, not many, but a few, and they've never known hunger or want or violence. They grow up in freedom, running wild across the tundra. And everyone works. No one is idle, for even the very old are productive, even if it is only to show us by example what a good life they've led."

"It sounds like heaven. I want to go."

"I would love to take you. If you agree to be my wife, we could be there for Christmas day."

There it was, the pull which would sever her from her family and make his marriage a disaster.

"No. I want to stay here for Christmas."

He'd been rubbing her back, and the soothing motions must have helped for her breathing wasn't as broken, and the tears, although they had not stopped, had slowed. And he held her tighter, then tighter still, as if the human strength of his arms would be enough to keep her with him.

From the nurses' station music was playing, yet it sounded like angels, clear and vibrant like Jamie's voice had been. Even as

Santa Claus he didn't often hear angels. He hoped it was another miracle, an indication that he hadn't been left alone.

"What are you afraid of, Nicholas?"

The question surprised her. She hadn't meant to ask it, and once the words were spoken, it took her a while to remember where the question had come from. When he didn't answer immediately, she realized she had changed it significantly. Ask <u>Santa</u> what he is afraid of. The idea seemed ludicrous. Santa was kind and good and perfect. What could he be afraid of?

He shivered, and the look in his eyes grew haunted. Nicholas had not been this naked when she lay underneath him.

"I not afraid of anything."

He had been strong, yet he had also seemed haunted. His confession, Beth, I am Santa Claus, had been rolled in pride, but beyond that, it had been flattened by some discomfort that she hadn't understood.

"Yes, I think you are. I think you're afraid of something that you shouldn't be afraid of."

Nicholas looked away, took a deep breath, tried to compose himself as the fears returned. He hadn't been afraid while he preformed his miracle for Susan, for he knew he could make her forget. And he had understood Jamie's mortality, and when the boy inferred the truth it hadn't mattered. Telling Beth he was Santa Claus had been a mistake, but she already knew. That disaster had occurred nineteen years before.

He had hoped that the fears would disappear with experience. Yet the fears still gnawed at his gut making him sick, and it was far easier to face a grieving family as a neighbor than it was to return to Marlett as Santa.

She felt no triumph as she watched the confusion of memories shift across his features. Some fears were private. And oddly enough, some fears were comforting, an excuse when things didn't go right. She wasn't qualified to deal with his fears. Her expertise was third graders and Christmas and family, not closely guarded paranoia. Beth held her hand out, about to retract the question, but he shook his head, started confessing.

"My father was Santa for a lot of years. I never met my grandfather so to me my father was Santa."

Beth nodded again, this time acutely disappointed. There came a time when every child understood that his father "was" Santa. She had, for some reason, expected more than this.

"He'd let me go on his ride every year."

Ride, she thought. She often brought accomplices with her when she would drop off her clandestine presents.

"Normally we'd go in together, or I'd wait with the sleigh, handing him packages, rearranging the load. But I asked him if I could make the delivery to your house alone. It was my first time."

She shook her head. Somehow this had stopped making sense. "You were actually in my house?"

"And you caught me. I thought I'd turn to salt right on the spot. Believe me, I didn't go in alone again until my father had died and it was my responsibility."

"Nicholas, what are you talking about?"

"You don't remember?"

"I do, but I'd like to hear your version."

"You were a spunky ten year old child who recognized me. "Hello, Santa," you said. "I'll always believe in you." And you have always believed in me. When I didn't have the courage to believe in myself, you believed in me."

"Nicholas, back up a step. This is coming too fast. You're mixing too many different images."

He smiled, took her hand, knew, at least on one level, she believed. "I am Santa Claus."

She didn't look at him, or rather, she didn't raise her head to meet his eyes. Instead she picked up his hand, studied it, as if the truth were there. "Santa Claus. This is absurd. I don't believe."

He heard her stop, let her falter. She did believe. It would only take a little convincing.

He pumped a deep breath into his lungs, felt his chest expand, felt his own identity solidify. "I am Santa Claus." The acknowledgement was as much for his benefit as for her. Over the years he had come to a kind of understanding with his mother, but he had never straightened his spine, met her eyes, defiantly stated, "I am Santa Claus."

She chewed a knuckle, his, not hers, and washed his fingertips with fresh tears. *Then why, Santa?* he expected. He decided to make it easy for her.

"You met me when I was a boy. My father was Santa Claus, and my grandfather. We are a family steeped in tradition. Sons follow in their father's footsteps. My child will do it after me."

"A new Santa Claus every generation?" She hadn't quite expected that.

"Yes."

"So, do you deliver presents to every good little boy and girl?"

"I was wondering when that one was going to come up. It's usually the first."

"I've had other things on my mind. I've been distracted."

Nicholas' lips twisted upward. He'd been rather distracted himself.

"Do you really deliver presents?"

"Yes, I really deliver presents. Over the centuries, that much hasn't changed."

"To every child in the world?"

"No. I wish I could. I really do. But I can't. It's a physical impossibility. More than that, it's not really necessary that I get to every child. It just doesn't work that way."

"Oh?" She acted surprised. No, more than that, she acted superior as if she'd known all along that he couldn't possibly be Santa Claus and he'd only just now painted himself into a corner. "And how exactly does it work?"

He rubbed his hands across his eyebrows, then massaged his tired eyes with his fingertips. "When the family first got involved with this, they had such high hopes of reaching every child, of celebrating youth and Christmas by a special gift to every person under the age of say, thirteen. There was never a hard and fast cutoff date. Too many young adults were worthy, or I suppose, more appropriately, needy. But the reindeer didn't move that fast, and even dealing with the different time zones, and with what little bits of magic we have at our disposal, it was too much. We've had to trim our gift list. I can only reach about two hundred thousand children each Christmas night, and even at that I only leave toys less than half the time."

"And what do you leave, candy canes?" Her words were dull, held none of the emotions usually elicited by a confession of that kind. It wasn't after all, an easy thing for him to admit. He had expected incredulity or denial or anger, but most of her stronger emotions had been washed away by tears, destroyed by loss. The only emotion she gave him was resignation and that hurt, even more than her tears had.

"I've been known to." He didn't react to the hostility in her tone. He was far too involved now to take offense.

"I leave hope. I drop off medicine, or food or that one secret gift of the heart that will make a Christmas memorable. A train ticket to bring a loved one home, a memento from a cherished grandparent long thought lost, a token that will bring a family back together and mend a rift between generations or siblings or friends. It's not much, and it's never enough, but it's the best I can do. People do the rest. People are meant to do the rest."

"What do you mean by that?"

"Just that Santa Claus, on the whole, isn't supposed to solve all the world's problems, neither are the angels for that matter. I am to stand more as a symbol than anything else."

She looked down the stark hospital corridor, to the room where the nurses would not be taking vitals every fifteen minutes, at least not until the room had been sanitized and some other critically ill child was rushed in.

"This isn't making much sense. I don't suppose you could elaborate, even slightly?"

"There are some rather complicated answers to that, but I'll give you the easy one. Take world peace for example. There is a power that has the ability to force Peace on Earth."

"Then why doesn't He do it?"

"Because forcing was Satan's plan. People have dominion,

and they have to learn to live together by themselves. You teach. You must know what I'm talking about. It's so much easier to tie a child's shoe laces than it is to try and teach him over and over the right way to do it, but he has to learn to be independent, to take care of his own world."

"There's a vast difference between tying shoelaces and world peace."

"Not really. The scale is different, but the principle is exactly the same."

"But people are dying."

"Indeed they are. And there are far worse things than death. People, on the whole, have all the powers of the angels. They only have to learn to tap into those powers—like compassion—and they never will if forced no matter how benevolently."

"And they never will if left alone."

"True. That is why there is a fine line I walk at Christmas and through the year. It makes people feel good to sacrifice their own talents and resources to make someone else happy. Every time a father scrimps to make his son a gift, every time a nation signs a peace treaty or avoids a war altogether, then they are growing. Person or nation or planet, there is no difference. What matters is that they have to do it by themselves."

"And what is the role of Santa Claus in all this?"

"I teach them how to tie their own shoe laces, and then leave them alone so they can practice and struggle until they can do it all by themselves. Sometimes I give them crayons so they can color their rainbows and make their world more beautiful, but most of all I give them hope that there is a more powerful being and that life itself is worth not only living, but cherishing."

"Then why are you afraid?" It was, after all, the original question.

This time he didn't hesitate. "I'm afraid to get caught."

That didn't make sense, and then it did when she remembered how disconcerted he had looked when she raced from the bathroom that morning holding handfuls of shredded beard. He had been afraid.

Her eyebrows lowered, as her incredulity rose. "Afraid of what?"

"Beth, please."

"No, you've asked me to share your life. If there is something to be afraid of, I need to know now."

"It's nothing like that."

"Like what?"

"You don't have to worry. There are no monsters at the North Pole, no demons trying to destroy Christmas. Only me."

She reached out, touched him. His hands were ice cold, trembled slightly. She wouldn't have suspected that this night she'd be able to offer comfort. "You're afraid of the legend?"

"Of having people find out. They shouldn't. It's a secret. A deep secret."

Oddly, she almost smiled, almost felt life trickling back into her. She'd always known that she knew more about Santa Claus than Santa Claus himself. Didn't she tell her students that? The pain was still there, real and visceral, but so was something spunky, deep inside that made her feel smug. "You've got it wrong."

"No. True believers should be true believers based on faith, not on sightings. The legend couldn't continue if fifty thousand people knew for a fact that Santa does exist. I'm afraid to get caught."

Puzzle pieces were starting to fall into place. She'd thought she had the picture all put together, but now she realized she'd underestimated the complexity. It wasn't simple, flat image, visions of sugarplums, but three dimensions, length, width and height and it looked like a man.

"The first time you were caught, was by me?"

"Yes."

"And you haven't been caught since?"

He shook his head. It wasn't an accomplishment, it was a shame. "My father and I fought. He thought I should go in with him more, develop experience as Santa that I would need. I don't mind leaving presents. That's what Santa does. But I didn't want anyone to see me."

"I know your father has been caught. I suspect that all the Santas have, at one time or another."

He shrugged, looked away. "I ruined your life."

"No, never."

"Your mother left you because she couldn't deal with your fanciful nature. The kids teased you. You've always had to defend yourself. Beth, you told me before you could get your job teaching third grade you had to explain to the principal that you saw the real Santa. You shouldn't have had to live that way. It's my doing. My curse. You should have been free from it."

Her hands now were warm, as was her heart. She would marry this man in an instant, but first she needed to help him to heal himself. "Nicholas, sometimes the greatest gift Santa can leave is the gift of showing himself."

"No, Beth."

"Yes. Seeing Santa made me strong. My mother didn't leave because I saw you, she left me because she had troubled dealing with a divorce, with too many kids and a confusion that she had to be Supermom all the time. Because I had to defend my belief in Santa, I learned to defend myself. I learned not to be ashamed of my own beliefs, not to criticize other beliefs different from mine. Seeing Santa made me special. I knew it was a miracle not many other people are given. I was unique. My self-esteem developed over seeing Santa."

"A myth, Beth."

"How can you, of all men, say that?"

"My mother denied it."

"I can't believe that. Your mother only wanted you to be more fully developed, to understand more of the world and the people in it, which you wouldn't have gotten stuck in some northern workshop. She wanted you to have the joy of Christmas, and a life beyond that. Even for Santa Claus, there is nothing wrong with celebrating Valentine's Day."

"Christmas is too important."

"Nicholas, last year I had a boy in my class who could draw. I'm not talking stick figures, I'm talking Michaelango quality definition of muscle and emotion and beauty. Other teachers recognized his talent, and his parents are putting him in private art lessons. He's going to be famous one day, he's that good. And you know what? I still taught him to multiply. I still made him do his spelling words and his state capitals. Because although drawing was more than what he would do, it was intrinsically what he was, he also needed the other skills to survive. You don't deny kids who ice skate with Olympic quality technique, or kids who could play piano concertos at Carnegie Hall, a grade school education. You find a way to fit it all in."

He was digesting that, knowing that Beth had more to say when subtly, quietly, unobtrusively, two strangers walked in, rolling a stretcher between them. A high pitched cry shattered the stillness, only one, broken off before it could be completed.

"Oh, Nicholas, I love you so."

Her statement would have made him feel better, had she looked at him, not at a sheet-draped stretcher leaving, slowly, painfully, then at the family, clustered in the doorway.

They left soon after that, piling into a cold car, for an empty ride home. Her words made sense, but correcting the problem wouldn't be easy. He was still, very much, afraid, although now, he was afraid that he had lost her too.

"You need your family."

"I do."

"I need a wife who will be there for me. I can't live divided in half. I tried that for a long time. Christmas is my life. If you marry me, you can have Santa Claus and make a difference on a global scale. There is work. I can promise you'll never be bored. And every day you will have my love."

"I can't."

Her answer shocked him, caught him off guard. If she loved him, she would come, although hadn't he learned at a very early age that it wasn't that simple?

Nicholas tried to hide his disappointment, tried to be diplomatic, forgiving, understanding. He did have magic, but it didn't always provide him with what he needed, especially patience.

For all his self-avowed self-control, patience at this moment wasn't high on his list of virtues.

"You don't have to make your decision tonight. I'll be back, Christmas day, when it's still dark."

She shook her head, twirling curls in glorious profusion. "I suppose you'll be the first one who comes down the chimney."

"Something like that."

"I wish...no, I'll think about it. I'll have my answer for you Christmas morning."

"Beth, I'm not the only one who's afraid here. You're afraid, aren't you?"

"Afraid? Of Santa Claus?"

"Believe me, it's not so unique a concept as all that. Look at all the tiny children who scream when they see a fat bearded old man. You're afraid of giving your heart, of loving."

"Maybe I am."

"I'll never let you down."

"I don't know that. I believe in Santa Claus, Nicholas, in all he stands for on so many levels, but I'm an adult now and I have been for some time. Do you even listen to yourself, Nicholas? Santa Claus? Elves? It's a delightful fantasy, and maybe while I was waiting for them to take Jamie away it was exactly what I needed to dull the pain. I believe in Santa, I do, but I'm still not sure I believe in you."

Her hand was on the door latch. He tried to speak as she was getting away.

Beth turned back to him, offered a smile lacking in sincerity, one filled with dismissal. "You painted me a picture and with your loving you made me feel more alive than I ever have been in my whole life, but that doesn't mean you aren't some con-man out for something. Since Jamie's birth every spare dime has gone to medical bills. And my money is long gone before I ever see it. My grandmother hasn't got a cent to her name."

"Don't discount your riches. In love and unity what you have is more precious than all the money on the planet."

"Still sticking to the pretense, aren't you? Have you been to my room, seen my Santa collection? I have Santas, replicas and originals from St. Nicholas and Black Peter and everything in between. Believe me, buster, there isn't one who looks like you." Except perhaps, the one his mother had given her. Or had that been illusion too?

"What did you expect, that when you found Santa he would be the image you've got on your shower curtain? Chubby and jolly and a caricature of a man? Tell me, how many real, live men have you ever met that look like that?"

"I'm not talking about the shower curtain. If you are Santa, why are you doing this? Why can't you just grant my Christmas wish and be done with it? Why do you have to be here, fouling everything up?"

"This year I answered the wish of your heart. I know what you wanted. It's what I want too. Don't you think I love you? Don't you think I want you for as many years as we can steal from eternity? That's true love, Beth, and it's nothing to be ashamed of."

"Nicholas, go away. Leave me to my dreams of Santa. Leave me to my fantasies where no one gets hurt and once a year at least, dreams come true. I'll always love you, and I'll always be grateful for the tenderness you've shown me. No legend could do that. But my dreams are safe Nicholas."

"You could have Christmas every day."

"I don't want Christmas every day. I want to dream and anticipate and when you go I want to cry, but I do want you to go."

"I'll be back for you Beth. Tonight. I guarantee it. Then it will be your decision. You can come with me or you can stay. There will be no second chance."

She opened the car door, hit broadside with a gale of northern wind which almost knocked her off her feet. Her scarf took flight. Beth didn't even stop to watch it soar.

"I won't go with you, Nicholas. I'm happier with my illusions."

Nicholas got out of the car, too, slamming his door with a resounding thud. "Tonight, Beth, I'll be back."

And laying a finger aside of his nose, he turned and walked

away.

"I don't want you, Nicholas," but she knew as she choked out those words that she had lied, and because of the lie had made a grievous mistake.

CHAPTER 18

They were a somber family, unsmiling and in shock. The tree was lit, as were some indistinct lamps, and the nightlight downstairs, but they sat in the near dark, silently, mourning. In hands that shook, Beth held the small box Nicholas had given her before he left. "This actually isn't your present, it's mine," he said. "I want you to have this. You'll understand when you open it."

Inside, resting on black velvet lay a diamond engagement ring, small but perfect. She'd tried it on, just to dream, before she took it off, returned it to the box.

The grandmother clock ticked, bonged every hour, sounds that oddly were not disruptive to the silence, but instead complementing it. The number of tissues in the box had decreased significantly, but now their eyes were dry. Snores came from the bedrooms, family members stacked like cordwood, in beds, sleeping bags, cots. Only the four women waited up, as if each knew something significant was about to happen.

"What have you got, Beth?" Rachael asked. Beth had been twirling that box between her fingers for almost twenty solid hours.

"A present from Nicholas."

"May I see?" she asked.

Her legs untrustworthy, Beth tossed the jeweler's box. Rachael opened it, whistled low. "He asked you to marry him?"

Beth nodded, grabbed a tissue, strangled it. Her eyes watered, but the tears didn't spill. Rachael took the gift to Marta, Beth's mother, then to Catherine. "Are you going to go with him, girl?" Marta asked.

"Maybe." She had thought that love would be easy, like her belief in Santa Claus, but now, even that was suspect.

"Will he treat you well?" Marta again. "It's a small stone." She puckered her lips as if the worth of the marriage could be determined by the size of the diamond.

"Maybe." She had discovered why Nicholas was afraid, but that indistinct stranger with the musical voice should have asked why she was afraid.

"Then he'll be back?"

"Maybe," Beth answered, but Catherine's "Yes," drowned her out. "I said things to him," Beth said, struggling now. "Things he couldn't possibly be happy with."

"You only told him the truth," Catherine said, "and both of you needed to hear it."

Beth swallowed, knew instinctively truth was nothing to be afraid of. Over the long night, she had faced her fears.

When the doorbell rang, the four women looked at each other. "Who could that be?"

"Santa," Beth whispered as she answered it. Her back strengthened, her breathing grew even. It was her heart thumping which made her think she might not survive the next ten minutes. Nicholas stood on the doorstep, dressed in the traditional Santa suit. After all, she'd been expecting him. He said he'd come. She hugged him, long and hard and deep, and knew at that exact second, what her answer would be. How could anything else matter more than this?

He kissed her, infusing her with love and Christmas and hope for all Christmas' to come. "How come you didn't come down the chimney?"

His smile reminded her of a boy she met once long ago at a bus stop. "I didn't want to startle you."

She believed in him with all her soul, beyond logic and intellect and reason. He didn't exist, yet he had parked reindeer in the middle of the street and he waited. "Mom, Rachael, Gram, there's something I want you to see," she said.

The three stood, looked at him, then past him. She expected protests, denials, that they would rush out into the snow, need to touch the sleigh before they would believe, but each of the three nodded silently.

"I thought they were supposed to be miniature reindeer."

He laughed, that traditional Santa sound. "Yeah, well, 'full-sized' didn't quite work into the rhyme scheme."

"Mom, Gram, Rachael—"

"Are you going to invite the man in?" Marta asked. "It's getting quite chilly in here."

Her mouth dropped open. All these years she had been protecting them from her Santa belief, and they believed far easier than she had? Still, on the front porch, Nicholas waited, as if he expected her to believe in him.

"Santa." It seemed rather too late to make it a question.

Through miles of fluffy white beard, Nicholas smiled, glowed. Then, without her permission, he stepped past her, into the living room and shut the door behind him. He looked at the three women individually, then turned and locked his gaze on Beth. "You were right. Sometimes the greatest gift I can give is to show myself."

"I love you." Her voice held incredulity, but her heart was another matter. It sang with acknowledgement, and commitment. If love could be weighed on a scale like parcels at the post office, then she knew the emotion within her would far outweigh all the gaily wrapped gifts towering within his sleigh. Perhaps it would be heavier than all the packages any Santa had ever delivered.

She wouldn't have blamed him if his voice held censure, but it was gentle, and as full of love as her own heart. This was Nicholas from her Christmas party, but far more than that, this was Santa, real and visceral and her heart jumped and felicity swelled through her like a rush of spiked Christmas punch.

She moved toward him a step, two, before she became paralyzed, and oddly enough frightened. He had accused her before of being afraid of Santa Claus, although hadn't he qualified his statement, said she was afraid not so much of the legend, but the flesh and blood man. Afraid of giving her heart.

Beth stood shivering. There never had been anything ordinary about him. Not a few days ago when she faced him for the first time by that perfect Christmas tree, not during all the hours he had replaced enchantment in her heart, definitely not while she studied the perfection of his body as they prepared to make love, but his man was extraordinary. Everything about him was larger than life. Even without the suit, the reindeer, he was more charismatic, more potent than she could handle. Not a mortal man, a magical man, a piece of fiction since the beginnings of the first Christmas.

"Nicholas?"

"It's your decision, Beth. You can stay or you can come with me. I've got to move. This is Santa's big scene. You know how the song goes." From a bulging sack he unloaded wrapped presents he placed carefully under the tree, and two or three small things into the stockings. Then he straightened, faced not her but Rachael. Beth grew suddenly, unbelievably terrified, but he only held out his hand, and Rachael dropped into it a small gray jeweler's box. He opened it, removed the ring, got down on one knee. The fear vanished, but now Beth was mortally embarrassed.

"Will you get up?"

"Not until he gets an answer," Catherine, always pragmatic.

"I love you, Nicholas." She might never get tired of saying that. She held her hand out. He slipped the ring onto her finger. When she had tried it on, initially it had felt cold, now from his hands, it radiated warmth. And she knew this ring would never leave her finger again.

He stood, touched her with nothing but his gaze. "I love you, Beth. I want you to come to the North Pole and be my wife."

She heard Christmas carols, '*Angels we have heard on High*', perhaps, or '*O Come all ye Faithful*', the traditional Christmas songs. Midnight services would be getting out. But this magic was internal.

"You'll be able to come back home when you want, especially for the funeral, and I'll make sure you're here every year to work on your Christmas pageant. I do need help, but more than that, I love you."

She nodded, sensing he had more to say. "I'll do whatever it takes to make you happy," he told her, "even if you find you can't live with Christmas year round."

"Can't live with Christmas?"

"We'll buy Easter baskets. Valentine candy. Halloween costumes. We'll take vacations anywhere in the world you want. I love you. What I am is defined by the love I feel for you. I'll change."

She tentatively reached out. The pile on the costume was thick, soft. "I don't want you to change. I love Christmas. I love you. I'll never want anything else."

The lead reindeer trumpeted, the others followed suit. In a minute every neighbor would have the shades pulled up, would be in for the shock of their lives.

Nicholas bent, kissed Catherine's onionskin cheek. "Your present is under the tree." Then he moved to Beth's mother. "Mrs. Anderson, I've left you a gift there as well."

"I never," she said. But she did now.

"And Rachael." Nicholas dug into his pocket, handed her a small gift. "Open it later."

"I will. I promise." The tree was bright with steady light, green, yellow, blue, red, all of them reflecting in his eyes. On the worn carpet the presents were stacked, five or six deep. Already those he had placed there were merged within the bounty already present. They might never knew which ones were from him, except all three, five really, knew they would.

Christmas night silence surrounded them, still and pervasive, but then, this was the night of solemnity. Beth met her mother's gaze, held it for a long moment, hoping that just this once her mother wouldn't ruin it by some derogatory comment. But the look was different. It was softer, more yielding. There was almost compassion in it. Almost forgiveness.

Beth wove her way through the presents, around the cheer that could be bought at a store, until she knelt by her grandmother's feet, to re-experience that kinship that had to come from within.

She grasped her grandmother's gnarled, frail, cold hands, kissed the top of one knuckle, stunned when one fat, burning tear splatted on her grandmother's wrist. She hadn't thought she was crying, until she gazed up, met the over-bright look from the old woman.

"I'm getting married, Gram," she said.

"Go, child," Catherine said. "Go and be happy." She broke the embrace, cupped Beth's chin with fingers suddenly warmed, kissed her on the top of her forehead as she had so many thousand times before. "He needs you and you need him." It was a blessing and a benediction.

"You'll see me again, I promise."

"I know, but you concentrate on that man of yours. There's rarely been a man born so full of miracles as that one."

She kissed her grandmother's forehead, swiped her eyes, stood to face her mother.

"I only wanted what was best for you," Marta Anderson said.

"I know that."

"I only wanted you to grow up."

She didn't want to cry. This was too important to view through shifting emotions. Beth bit her trembling lip. She straightened her spine and her resolve. "Sometimes to grow up you have to accept Santa is a myth and acknowledge that for good to be done, it has to be done by yourself." The tears were flowing freer now, but they matched the sparkle she witnessed in her mother's eyes. "Sometimes, in order to grow up, you have to know that he's real, that the goodness and the dedication and the selflessness need a little help, that people, by themselves, can't do it all."

"That's what miracles are for," Marta Anderson said, suddenly, surprisingly becoming a true believer, "to help us see that there is a little bit of magic within each of us."

Beth smiled, and her lips trembled. "A little bit of Christmas, which shouldn't be limited to the last week of December."

"Here, take this, although I doubt you'll need it." She shoved something into her daughter's hands, kissed Beth with far less condemnation than she'd managed in years.

"Rachael?"

"Go. I'll watch over Gram."

Without bothering to wipe the tears now blinding her, Beth ran out of the house, with joyous abandon jumped into the sleigh, stared at the presents, at the reindeer, at Santa himself. "You know I've always wanted to do this."

He laughed, a full, throaty, ho ho ho. "Good, because I can't do it on my own."

"Wait! Nicholas, you've got to wait."

Beth ran back into the house, hunted around the presents under the tree, came back with a fairly large one in pretty paper. She was back in the sleigh in under two minutes.

Nicholas hiked an eyebrow. He knew what was in the box. He had that much magic.

"Could you find someone to give this to? It's the microscope. Jamie isn't going to need it."

Her eyes misted, for the pain of a life cut short remained fresh, but already it was mutating into joy for a life lived. Nicholas picked up the reins, clicked his tongue lightly as he twitched the leather harnesses. The sleigh picked up speed, almost instantly was airborne.

"Yes. I know where it should go. If you'd listened to me at the store that morning..."

The sleigh dropped down an instant later. "Vinnie's house? This is going to Vinnie?"

"You won't believe this, but the boy has all the makings of a research doctor. We give this to him and in twenty years, I promise you Beth, he'll be responsible for more than a few miracles himself."

"I'm glad. I always suspected he'd be on the 'nice' list. You do good things here Santa," she said when he bounced back into the sleigh.

"Don't discount your own contribution. I haven't been to this house before, Beth. There hasn't been a need."

"But they're desperate. The dad's out of work..."

"They're not desperate. Not when the community bands together and makes sure that there's always plenty of gifts under the donated tree. You may not know this, but you've been Santa's helper for a good long time."

A completion radiated through him, one he would cherish for the rest of his life. But as the sleigh lifted it was her firm voice not his which called out--

"On Dasher, On Dancer, On Prancer...."

Riding beside Santa, having the wind in her face and the spirit of Christmas in her heart was everything Beth expected, and far more. She laughed out loud, a laugh that carried across oceans and continents, representative of the happiness which cascaded within her.

"Here, put this on." Nicholas handed her a heavy red coat, similar to his own. Before that, she hadn't realized that she had been getting cold. It fit perfectly, with just enough room to allow her to move. Warmth permeated her being once again.

"I hadn't expected it to be this bumpy." The sleigh rocked, she bounced against him, found she liked the position, snuggled tighter.

"Air currents," he explained. She didn't quite believe him. Beth doubted anything quite as commonplace as air currents could affect the magic of Santa Claus.

Plastic crinkled in her hands, the present her mother had handed her, which she still hadn't looked at. She was still, clearly, in a state of shock. He did something with the reins that she didn't quite catch and the sleigh started losing altitude. "We've got to make a couple quick stops here," he said, his face although intense with concentration, radiant. The sleigh stopped.

"Where are we?"

"Northern Mexico."

"Already?"

"The guys don't waste any time. You want to come in?"

"Not this time." She grinned at him. "I wouldn't want to get caught." He took some packages. They weren't gaily wrapped, which surprised her for there were presents that she could see which were. Was he pulling favorites, giving the pretty presents to those who had money? Then, as she snuggled deeper into her thick coat, she decided not. He needed to leave presents which would blend in, which would add joy, not questions and distractions.

He was back before she expected him, and the sleigh was airborne once again.

"You will marry me, won't you?"

"A Christmas day proposal. What I always wanted."

"Answer the question, Beth."

"Of course, Nicholas."

"We'll go back to your home, have the official ceremony there. There are some relatives of mine that will come, my mother, I'm sure.

"And Marlett has a special service, another marriage you could call it although it's a commitment. It's not really necessary if you don't want, but it's sacred, a dedication for the family, devoting us to doing good, that kind of thing."

"I'd be honored."

"And we'll have to have a child."

"One?"

The laughter bubbled up again at her question. "At least one. You don't mind, do you? I never got around to asking. There's so much I assumed."

"I'd love to have your baby, Nicholas, to be the mother and grandmother of Santa Clauses."

"And wife. I need you more than I can say, Beth."

"I always wanted to be like you, you know."

"I know."

The sleigh stopped again. He vanished in a twinkling, arms loaded, reappeared equally as rapidly, hands empty. Her heart swelled. She carried on the conversational trail as if he'd never left.

"Nicholas, I'll never leave you. Never." She snuggled under his arm. "Our love will help bring peace to the world."

Airborne again, she really felt she was flying. She finally had time to look down, determine what the present her mother had handed her was. She started laughing.

"What's so funny, Marzipan?"

"This. From my mother." She held out the plastic wrapped mistletoe, the sprig that he had bought, that he had removed from his pocket at that breakfast so long ago. They hadn't once used it. It had been rather superfluous to the sparks which ignited whenever they were anywhere near each other.

Nicholas groaned and Beth kissed him, then because she liked the taste, the feeling, she kissed him again. One handed, he pulled her away. "You'll have to stop that. We've still a long night ahead of us."

She would never be jealous of the time he devoted to Christmas, but her body pulsed, throbbed, ached. She didn't mean to be either rude nor bold, but her hand searched, found him already hard, his arousal taunting her with promises of pleasure.

The sleigh dipped, an unscheduled dive as he inadvertently pulled on the leather. The reindeer were confused. He moaned again, whistled, told the team to carry on as he let this laughing woman play as if she'd discovered a new toy.

He was probably the first Santa that ever made the majority of his trip in that condition. It gave impetuous as he made short work of the presents stacked in his sleigh. Certainly in the two years he'd been Santa, he'd never been this efficient.

"You know, I'm going to get you for that." She had him in the palm of her hands. The thought gave her rich, vibrant power. She laughed again, the sound loud enough to wake the sleeping inhabitants of whatever backwater town or village this was. He disappeared, his step, she thought, looking a bit strained. She'd have to remember to thank her mother for the impromptu present, even if traditionally under mistletoe it should have been his lips she kissed.

He never again lost control, of himself or of his reindeer, although his Christmas journey took hours and she was relentless in her quest for discovery. He did growl occasionally, and moan far more often than that. She doubted very many Santa Clauses growled, and when she told Nicholas of her observation he clearly looked like he would prefer to strangle her. After that she kept most of her comments to herself, even if her hands were busy, even if every time he stopped he had to readjust his clothing. She wasn't cold again.

The sleigh was eventually emptied. It was far too soon for Beth's tastes.

"Let's do this again sometime."

He slapped toward, not at, her hands, chuckled, that merry ho, ho, ho, resonating around the stars. "I think I'll never recover."

"Yet, Christmas came, didn't it?"

"Yes, sweet Beth. Christmas came."

She was cheeky and she was obnoxious, and she had him, literally right where she wanted him. "And you'll let me ride with you again?"

Nicholas groaned again, rolled his eyes heavenward, but that twinkle was back. "You can count on it. Are you ready for the North Pole?"

She licked her lips, considered options. "In a minute."

"Why, what have you got in mind?" He didn't like the tone of her voice, even as he seconded it. He was in no condition to meet Marlett and the rest of those miserable, prying elves.

His beard was tousled, windblown. She wished it held traces of soot, but it was as pristine as ever. "The back of the sleigh is empty. There's plenty of room. Could you find a spot, a secret spot where no one would find us?"

Nicholas didn't need a second invitation. He whistled at the reindeer and the sleigh veered sharply to her left.

It landed only seconds later in a deserted, snow decked field. The moon hung low, but still bright enough that she could see trees off in the distance, rolling hills, further on, mountains. She jumped from the sleigh before he could grab for her, ran through the six inch snow, kicking up her heels and laughing with total joyous abandonment. She held her arms out, twirled in circles until she was dizzy, until the earth itself tilted on its axis. She had no idea where they were, North America, Europe, the Soviet lands, China, she could narrow it down no further than the northern hemisphere, not that it mattered. This was their secret spot.

He let her dance, hungry for her, but knowing she needed this almost primal rite to come to terms with her happiness in loving Santa Claus. Then, when she was ready, he chased her, and she ran, and she screamed and their footsteps twisted along the field, intertwined, united. He could have caught her at any time, for she was laughing too hard to perfect her escape, but she was prey and it was the chase that mattered. They had the rest of their lives for the capture.

Eventually he wrapped an arm around her middle, pulled her to him, manacled her body to his, with his arms and his lips. She screamed and kicked, in the fun of total sexual abandonment, and he carried her to the sleigh where he didn't have the control to strip off all her clothing, only her pants and her panties which he lowered as he settled his own throbbing body between her raised knees. She was ready for him, moist and welcoming and tight as her body accepted this physical manifestation of their love.

She quivered, and tremors deep within started almost immediately. He brought her to one climax after another, barely letting her catch her breath before they reached another peak and then another. It might have been the magic of Christmas, but he suspected it was love that had him believing that no couple had ever found the degree of pleasure and satisfaction that they did, that night in the secluded glen. He held her tightly, pulled himself deeper, and deeper still. The explosion, when it struck him, hit hard. He spilled seed, and love and joy and the magic of Christmas.

Sweat dampened her forehead when he came to his senses long enough to pull back on his elbows and look at her. "Are you all right?"

She smiled, completely satisfied, even if the laughter within her had been banked. "Never better." Beth combed the beard. It felt funny kissing it, kissing his lips all around it, although she decided she could get used to it without much trouble. "Have we conceived your son tonight?" she asked. It wouldn't bother her if she were pregnant when they officially married.

"I hope so." he answered. He tried to pull away, to remove himself from the body which had given him so much pleasure, but her legs still had some strength left in them, and she locked her ankles around his thighs in a tight embrace.

"Beth, haven't you had enough?"

"Never."

Apparently, he hadn't either, for his body grew hard again, although he would have suspected that was impossible, considering the magnitude of his release. But the passion burned again, and this time they were able to love slowly, more passionately, even if there was nothing sedate about the act itself. Because he was Santa Claus, because he had the power, he had little difficulty seeing her with her stomach swelling, giving birth to his children. It was a good feeling, knowing every single day he would love her more.

He eventually let her dress, although he was an honest man, and knew the truth was that she allowed him to dress. The mistletoe, when they finally found it on the seat beside his reins, was crushed. Beth held the limp package in her hands and he thought she might cry. "There's plenty of that where we're going."

She was too weak, too satisfied, to argue. "Really, will you let me go again on your sleigh ride?"

He clicked his tongue. The reindeer flew, anxious now to be home in their own familiar stalls. "Yes. But I'm going to make certain you have no mistletoe with you, even if I have to search you."

"Strip search?" She looked altogether too eager.

It wasn't much longer before the sleigh approached the North Pole. She saw about ten buildings nestled together under a sky brilliant with a million stars. "It's smaller than I thought."

"We are dedicated to Christmas, but we don't have to put up with tourists. There's no hotels. Everything here is for the elves and me."

"And for the world."

The runners hit the hard packed snow and eventually the large sleigh stopped. Nicholas jumped out. "I'll be just a minute." He spoke to the reindeer, one at a time, praised them for their dedication, their good work, patted their sweating hides. There were elves all around them, short, troll-looking characters with curly-toed boots and floppy hats with jingle bells, who waited while Nicholas preformed this absolution.

"The elves will take care of them now," he said, reaching out his hand, helping her to exit from the coach. Her knees were watery. She didn't have much endurance left.

A short, rather pompous being approached them. He looked more like a dragon for she was certain he was breathing steam from his nose.

"Where have you been?" he demanded, stamping a booted, belled foot. "You should have been back hours ago. I've been worried to death that something happened, that you'd been picked up by Interpol for violating airspace, that the woman broke your heart."

Beth didn't let him finish. "You must be Marlett," she said, then she bent down, for he was short, and kissed him on his bulbous nose.

"Was there trouble?"

Santa Claus veed his bushy eyebrows. "Trouble?"

"Nicholas, you're three hours late. I know how much time it takes to deliver those presents."

"Marlett, there wasn't any trouble. I'd like to introduce you to my wife-to-be."

"I've heard an awful lot about you, Marlett," Beth said. The laughter was back. It radiated from the walls, the ceiling, from the elves themselves. She would have no trouble finding happiness here. And she would thank him, privately, when she got the chance, and tell him that Nicholas wasn't afraid of anything anymore.

Nicholas introduced her one at a time to all the elves, and she knew she'd never keep their names straight, at least not for a while, but it didn't matter. They were united here. Forever.

Marlett, preening, tugging on the beard which was the source of his pride, took them on a tour of the buildings. The bunkhouses, the workrooms, and finally, to the Big House, where Nicholas, and all the Santas before him had lived. Nicholas kept his comments to himself, but every time he came to another sparkling room, he raised an eyebrow, and Marlett shrugged his shoulders, and Beth was obvious to it all.

"One day, Santa," Beth said, "you'll have to tell me the rest of the story about how the elves got trapped."

"You'd do better to ask me," Marlett answered, fluffing out his beard. "I'm sure my version would be more accurate than anything you'd get from him."

"Different," Callie responded with a humph, "not necessarily more accurate."

Beth bent down again, kissed Marlett on the nose. "I do have a lot to thank you for."

Marlett blushed, bells tinkled as he shuffled his feet. Nicholas laughed, lifted Beth into his arms, for his heart was full and he had to do something. "You'll have time for Marlett later. Right now, I'd like to show you a bit more of the house."

He was warm and he was real. Christmas had come. She laughed, that bubbling laughter that he would never get enough of.

"Come, it's time I showed you my bedroom."

"But she hasn't seen the rest of the compound," Marlett sputtered. "We spent all this time cleaning—" A female elf, one whose name Beth couldn't remember, clasped a hand over Marlett's face.

"I'll see it later," she called, wrapping her hands around Nicholas' shoulders, anticipating again the renewal of their love.

And then together, for everything they would do for the rest of their lives they would do together, they vanished into the bedroom.

"I suppose this means she accepted the ring," Callie said.

"It does indeed," Marlett answered, proud, and feeling personally responsible for everything that happened. "Although I forgot to ask him about that microscope." He took a step forward, toward the bedroom.

Callie pulled him back. "It doesn't matter now, does it?"

Marlett stroked his beard. "I suppose I can wait, find out in the morning."

"And leave them to celebrate Christmas in their own fashion."

"Aye. They do seem to have some celebrating to do."

It was Callie, who laying a finger aside of her nose said, "Merry Christmas to all, and to all a good night."

EPILOGUE

CHRISTMAS EVE:

Under a bright moon and the dancing, shifting colors of the Northern Lights, the sleigh stood ready, packed to overflowing with presents. From the front, and heard even over the elves celebrating in the workshop, the reindeer jingled bells as they stomped, anxious to get moving. This was, after all, their big scene too.

Marlett moved up, rubbed his work-worn fingers over Comet's soft nose. She was not the lead reindeer, but the one who seemed to have the pulse of the rest of the team. When Comet settled, the others did too.

Marlett shifted back keeping his eyes locked on the presents. He knew that something as insignificant as an unkind thought could have the entire mess tumbling down and then where would they be? Having to repack the entire sled, that's what, and he wasn't about to do that, not with Christmas already here. Rubbing his fingers through his beard, he looked over at Callie, but his wife stood beside Mrs. Santa, bouncing joyously on her little booties, and had no time for him at all. Nicholas' bride had certainly captured the hearts of each and every elf.

Santa and his Beth stood wrapped in an embrace, his nose rubbing hers, her arms around him, with that massive belly between them. Marlett hated to break it up, but really, this was Christmas, wasn't it?

"If you don't leave now, you'll never catch up," Marlett insisted, tugging on the traditional red suit. Nicholas ignored him. It had been a year of ignoring him, with didn't really matter, since Beth hung on Marlett's every word.

Santa inched back, giving him enough room to point a finger. "You will not, and I repeat, will not have that baby before I get home."

She smiled, rubbed her extended stomach, knew the contractions were getting worse, more frequent. "I can't promise anything."

"Really, there's only one night a year that I'm busy. Whoever planned that every Santa would be born on Christmas should be boiled in oil with a stake of holly through his chest."

She was about to call him Scrooge, but knew this past year she had had Christmas every single day, and between the two of them there had only been joy. "Go, do your deliveries. The world needs you, Santa. I'll be fine here."

He kissed her deeply. "I'll hurry. Next year you can come with me. And I promise, next year we'll get to your pageant."

"I told you the pageant wasn't important."

"It's important to me. We'll go. I promise."

"I'll look forward to it. Now you have to go. The sooner you leave, the sooner you'll be back."

He took three steps toward the sleigh, having Marlett breathe a sigh of relief, before he turned back and started kissing her again. "I mean it. I want to be here when the baby is born."

"Santa," she had taken to calling him Santa. Marlett doubted Beth had even once called her husband by his given name. "Go now. Christmas needs you."

"You need me."

"I'm going to party," she said, forcing a smile to her lips, but when she saw his eyes tightening, Beth realized she might have pushed the lie a bit too far. "Party, from the comfort and security of my bed. I promise, I'm going to get off my feet the minute you leave. It's because you're still here that I'm not resting."

It was exactly the right thing to say. Nicholas bounded into the sleigh, causing the presents to teeter for an instant, before they settled. Instead of his traditional "Merry Christmas!" as he flew away, he bellowed, "Don't have that baby until I get back!"

"Well, that was a good day's work," Marlett said as he approached his wife. "I swear there isn't room for so much as a prayer to be added. Now we are going to party!"

"No," Callie said, taking Mrs. Santa's hand, and walking not toward the workshop where the festivities were already underway, but toward Santa's private rooms.

The bedroom, which had been comfortable when Beth

arrived a year ago had been transformed into a Christmas scene, with holly and brightly lit red, blue, green and gold lights. Candles burned, scenting the air with bayberry and in a decorative bowl ten-thousand candy canes which both she and Santa ate year round. Beth swore there was magic in them. Callie tugged off Beth's heavy coat then rooted through the dresser. Seconds later, she helped Beth get into comfortable pajamas. As Beth slid between the sheets, the elf hopped from foot to foot. "You could have told him."

"Told him?"

"That you're in labor."

Beth shook her head as she breathed through another increasingly painful contraction. "And make this night miserable? Then he never would have left."

"Everything's ready. In case you're wondering, I've delivered every Santa since the beginning."

"Then I'm in good hands." Beth sucked in a huge lungful of air as another contraction hit and her water broke.

The weather over most of the globe had been horrendous. Really, what was it about Christmas night that so often blizzards moved in? Nicholas flew high, above the storms whenever he could, dropping down only to drop off a present or two. Marta, Rachael and Catherine were awake, so he showed himself, handed off his gifts, and muttered "She's having the baby tonight," before walking through the closed door back to his sleigh. He dropped presents off at Vinnie's house, only because Beth insisted. The father had found work, and life in that family was again good. This time it was a chemistry set. The microscope was on the dining room table, and showed signs of continual use, with neatly labeled slides showing salt crystals and pond water and blood smears. Standing in the Scalano home, he knew Vinnie was not the only child in that family facing a career in scientific research.

He left presents for Susan and Jim and their new daughter Nevaeh, who had been born with a perfect heart. They slept soundly, although four-month-olds rarely sleep through the night. He peeked in on the infant, because Beth was certain to ask.

All in all, Santa made his deliveries in record time that year.

Finally, the back was empty. "Come on guys, we've got to get back," and the reindeer, feeding off his energy, headed for home.

He came in hot, handed the reins to the first elf he saw, and ran through the door and into his house. Nicholas was moving so quickly he did not realize he had traveled through the closed door.

Beth lay on the bed, speaking softly to a blanket wrapped bundle in her arms. Callie was asleep in the rocker by the fireplace, and Marlett was hopping from foot to foot, looking anxious.

"Don't blame me," he insisted, tugging on Nicholas' sleeve. "I had nothing to do with it."

"You had the baby."

Beth smiled, and a radiant glow lit the room. "I'm sorry. I know you wanted to be here."

He sat on the bed before he collapsed, his knees suddenly useless. "It's not your fault. Every Santa is born on Christmas. I don't know why."

"Something to do with tradition, no doubt."

"Speaking of tradition, I don't suppose I can convince you to name him something other than Nicholas. George or Simon or Adrian, anything but Nicholas."

Beth grinned, looked radiant. "I have absolutely no intention of naming her Nicholas."

"There's a lot of great names out there."

"I've chosen one. Maybe you'd better calm down before I tell you. You need something to eat, and maybe you should get out of that suit first."

"I'm fine!" he roared, shaking the rafters, but the infant slept peacefully on.

"Ok, then. I've decided to call her Ginny."

"Ginny?"

"It's pretty, don't you think?"

Nicholas dropped boneless to the bed. "It's a girl?"

"A perfect little baby girl."

And Nicholas realized what she had been saying when he walked in the door.

"Yes, Virginia, there is a Santa Claus."

The End
Virginia St. Noel's story continues in the novel "Yes, Virginia."

www.ingramcontent.com/pod-product-compliance
Lightning Source LLC
Chambersburg PA
CBHW022148170626
46807CB00005B/2128